MW01125942

THE

FRONTIERS SAGA

PART 2: ROGUE CASTES

EPISODE 11

A ROCK AND A HARD PLACE

RYK BROWN

The Frontiers Saga Part 2: Rogue Castes
Episode #11: A Rock and a Hard Place
Copyright © 2019 by Ryk Brown All rights reserved.

No part of this book may be reproduced, scanned, or distributed in any printed or electronic form without permission. Please do not participate in or encourage piracy of copyrighted materials in violation of the author's rights. Thank you for respecting the hard work of this author.

This is a work of fiction. Names, characters, places, and incidents either are the product of the author's imagination or are used fictitiously, and any resemblance to locales, events, business establishments, or actual persons—living or dead—is entirely coincidental.

CHAPTER ONE

The cavernous hall was filled with the voices of countless caste leaders as they argued incessantly over the fate of their empire. The past few months had been difficult, and tempers within the halls of the Jung leadership were nearly as high as those of the public at large.

A gavel struck the metal plate on Kor-Dom Borrol's podium several times as he tried in vain to quiet the raucous debates threatening to escalate out of control at any moment. "Silence!" he demanded as he continued to pound away. "SILENCE!"

Although the level of discourse diminished greatly, the room was still far from quiet. Kor-Dom Borrol knew it would have to suffice. Pressing matters were to be decided. "The time has come!" he demanded. "The people of the empire demand action!"

"The Tonba-Hon-Venar must be invoked!" Dom Zorakh bellowed from the gallery.

"You are out of order!" Dom Jung-Torret objected from the leadership table.

"Tonba-Hon-Venar!" several others shouted in support of Lord Zorakh.

"We cannot stand against the Terran jump ships!" Dom Dais argued. "They will pick our fleet apart, disappearing before we can retaliate."

"Your confidence in our forces is truly inspiring," Dom Immoritt quipped, obviously annoyed by the isolationist's remarks.

"I speak the truth!" Dom Dais insisted.

"The only *truth* you present is your own ignorance of our fleet's abilities," Dom Immoritt retorted.

"Can you defeat the Terran fleet?" Kor-Dom Borrol challenged.

"It is possible," Dom Immoritt insisted. "We have four times their number."

"But our battle platforms have all been destroyed!" Dom Jung-Torret reminded them, siding with Dom Dais.

"Not *all,*" Dom Immoritt replied, a wry smile on his face.

"Explain yourself, Dom Immoritt," Kor-Dom Borrol instructed.

"We have kept three platforms in hiding," Dom Immoritt explained. "Since the destruction of Zhu-Anok."

"Why have you not told us of this sooner?" Kor-Dom Borrol demanded to know.

"Fleet operations are the purview of Jung-Mogan caste," Dom Jung-Mogan reminded Kor-Dom Borrol in a most indignant manner. "We are neither required nor compelled to report on the movement of every ship to any other caste...not even the Borrol caste," he added with a menacing gaze.

"The platforms were on the outer rim when Zhu-Anok was destroyed," Dom Kirton explained, jumping in to defuse the confrontation between Dom Jung-Mogan and Kor-Dom Borrol. "They were moved toward Sol a few months later, as soon as word reached them. Their route was circuitous, as one might expect, but all three ships are currently only a few months from striking distance of Sol."

"You're saying we have battle platforms *inside* Alliance space?" Kor-Dom Borrol questioned.

"I assure you, they are still well outside the Sol Alliance boundaries."

"Three battle platforms are not enough!" Dom Dais argued.

"Again, you demonstrate your ignorance," Dom Jung-Mogan seethed. "We still have more than eighty warships, twenty of which are battleships. The Sol Alliance has a single capital ship, a few hundred gunships, and a handful of destroyers."

"I ask you again, Dom Jung-Mogan," Kor-Dom Borrol repeated, appearing impatient, "can you defeat the Sol Alliance?"

Dom Jung-Mogan looked at the faces of the leadership council. "There will be losses...many losses. If we attack, they will target our worlds. Millions will die, perhaps billions. It will make the Day of Blood look like a spring festival. However, their jump weapons are useless if they do not know where their targets are located. We must be constantly on the move. We must be unpredictable. By doing so, we force them to face us head-to-head, to fight it out."

"But their jump drives..."

"I am tired of your fear of the Terran jump drive," Dom Jung-Mogan said as he waved his hand dismissively. "With but a few modifications, we can do the same with our FTL drive. The only difference is the range and, in battle, that advantage withers."

"But they have the *Aurora*," Dom Dais pointed out.

"I often wonder just how you rose to the head of your caste," Dom Jung-Mogan said, eying the leader of the Dais caste with disfavor.

"Your insults fall on deaf ears," Dom Dais replied, looking away from his adversary.

"This bickering must come to an end," Kor-Dom Borrol insisted. "The people are crying out for vengeance." He looked at Dom Jung-Mogan once again. "Can you defeat them?"

"Call for the Tonba-Hon-Venar, and our forces will bring the Sol Alliance to their knees," Dom Jung-Mogan promised confidently.

"We vote now!" another Dom demanded. Within seconds, his sentiment was echoed by nearly everyone in the great hall.

"Very well," Kor-Dom Borrol agreed, banging his gavel on the metal plate, on the corner of his podium. "Let the vote begin!" He turned to Dom Jung-Mogan. "Dom Jung-Mogan, for the Tonba-Hon-Venar, how say you?"

Dom Jung-Mogan rose to his feet, his cape spilling down behind him. He pulled at his uniform jacket as he took a breath. "The Jung-Mogan caste calls for the Tonba-Hon-Venar!"

Cheers rang out as the first vote in favor of war was cast. Kor-Dom Borrol, again, slammed the head of his gavel down hard, trying to gain control of the room. There were still twenty-six more castes to be polled.

* * *

Captain Madrid paced the width of the Manamu's bridge as she waited for her crew to be ready for their first test jump. They had spent the last two weeks in refit, during which dozens of technicians, most of them from Rakuen, crawled about her ship, much to the chagrin of her chief engineer.

"We should have full charge in all banks in ninety seconds," her first officer reported.

"What about bank thirteen?" the captain wondered.

"They managed to settle it down," Vemados

assured her. "It hasn't fluctuated more than one percent in the last ten minutes."

"Any explanation as to what was causing the problem?" she wondered.

"Yes, but not one that I understood," Vemados admitted.

"The first jump is only one hundred light years," Ewan, her chief engineer, reminded her, "so we don't even *need* all sixteen energy banks."

"*Only* one hundred light years," Garland moaned from the Manamu's helm. "Has anyone here done the math? A one-hundredth-of-a-degree variance off our course would result in a..."

"We've done the math, thanks," Captain Madrid interrupted her nervous pilot.

"I can assure you that there is nothing to fear," Mister Esari insisted. "The gen-four emitters have individual fail-safes. If any two adjacent emitters develop problems in the final moments prior to the jump event, they send out a signal that causes the entire system to abort before the release of energy."

"And this, too, is a new feature that has yet to be tested," the pilot commented.

"We have conducted numerous computer simulations on the system," Mister Esari assured him.

"Then, why are we even testing it?" Garland asked.

"All new systems must eventually be validated by actual testing," Mister Esari insisted.

"Why not test them with a drone?"

"Enough, Garland," Captain Madrid chided.

"The system requires considerably more energy than any drone could generate," Mister Esari explained. "The Manamu has large enough bays to accommodate the additional energy storage banks and the mini-ZPEDS to charge them."

"He knows," Sheba told Mister Esari. "He's just being difficult."

"Banks are fully charged," Vemados announced.

"All systems show ready for the first jump," Ewan reported from the engineering station.

Captain Madrid looked at Mister Esari. "One hundred light years?"

"That is correct, Captain."

"Eesh," Garland said, only half to himself.

"In order to complete the validation testing as expeditiously as possible, it is necessary to conduct three tests, each at the maximum range of the energy transfer threshold for one, two, and three sets of energy banks," Mister Esari began.

"Please, don't," Garland interrupted. "Let's just get it over with."

"He's a 'pull the bandage off quickly' kind of guy," Captain Madrid explained.

"I see," Mister Esari replied, turning back to his console. "Whenever you are ready."

"How's our jump line, Tobi?" the captain inquired.

"Clear out to max sensor range," her sensor officer replied.

"Mister Kreuz, if you please," the captain invited.

"If I *please*, then we don't jump," Garland muttered as he entered one hundred light years as the jump distance. He paused a moment, waiting for the jump navigation computers to finish their calculations. When the ready indicator flashed, he reluctantly announced, "One hundred light years, plotted and ready, Captain."

"Very well," Sheba replied. She took a deep breath and added, "Execute the jump."

Garland also took a deep breath, placed his finger on the jump button, closed his eyes, and executed the jump.

The Manamu's small bridge flashed with blue-white light. For a brief moment, Sheba allowed herself to ponder all the ways the jump could go terribly wrong. Space was vast and relatively empty, but it wasn't *completely* empty. Stars, planets, asteroids big and small...any one of which, when collided with, could destroy them, shields or no shields. Surprisingly, it wasn't the larger objects that worried her. Such objects had known orbits, and their positions could be calculated by her ship's jump navigation computers with incredible accuracy. It was the smaller objects, the ones too large to be stopped by their shields but too small to be detected, tracked, or their position predicted. Those were the ones that nagged at her every time her ship jumped.

Over the years, she had learned to ignore the risk. After all, there was little she could do about it. That risk had been there long before; the invention of the jump drive had only magnified it. Besides, if they did collide with something, they would never know it. Death would be instantaneous.

At least...she hoped.

The flash subsided, and they were still there.

"Position?" Sheba asked.

"Nav-com is recalculating our position," Garland replied, still anticipating disaster.

"It will take a few moments," Mister Esari warned. "Your jump nav-com was not expecting such a drastic change in position after a single jump."

"Position verified," Garland interrupted, a hint of pride in his tone. "We are currently twenty-seven light years from the Porus system." He turned to his captain, a look of disbelief on his face. "Precisely one hundred light years from the Rogen system."

"You just conducted the longest controlled jump in history, Mister Kreuz," Captain Madrid congratulated, also smiling.

* * *

"The installation of mark three plasma cannons on the Glendanon has been completed," Cameron reported to the senior staff gathered in the Aurora's command briefing room. "She now has a total of four mark three turrets, as well as point-defenses, and a pair of jump missile launchers."

"What about the Weatherly?" Nathan asked from the head of the conference table.

"Both of the Weatherly's jump missile launchers will be operational in a few days."

"Excellent," Nathan replied. He looked to Vladimir next. "How is our jump drive upgrade going, Commander?"

"We have completed the upgrade of the power transfer trunks and are now working on the individual runs to each emitter," Vladimir reported from the opposite end of the conference table.

"Aren't you getting a little ahead of yourself?" Cameron wondered.

"I was instructed to proceed with..."

"It was my idea," Nathan interrupted, taking Cameron's focus off their chief engineer.

He was successful; Cameron's building ire was evident by the look she flashed him.

"For expediency's sake," Nathan added, seemingly unconcerned with his first officer's anger.

"Wouldn't it be wiser to wait until all testing has been completed?" Cameron suggested.

"The Manamu successfully jumped to a distance of

three hundred light years during her first validation flight," Abby reported. "The power-handling requirements given to Commander Kamenetskiy were based on the emitter's maximum power-handling capabilities and provided plenty of buffer. The majority of the work will be in reprogramming the Aurora's jump navigation and control systems to deal with the increased range and its greater power requirements."

"Even if the new emitters are capable of jumping twice the distance anticipated, the new power distribution system will be able to handle the load," Vladimir promised. "As ordered, we have made it quite robust, as well as building in considerable redundancy."

"How long until the long-range jump system is operational?" Nathan inquired.

"That depends on how quickly we get the new emitters," Vladimir replied.

"Validation testing should conclude tomorrow," Abby explained. "We will start mass production in a few days, and we should have enough emitters for your first array two days later."

"Then, two weeks; perhaps, three," Vladimir surmised. "Assuming validation testing does not reveal any problems," he added, taking the opportunity to jab at Abby.

"It will not," Abby insisted, unaffected by his remark.

"Very well," Nathan said. "Moving on, then. Jump missiles?"

"Mass production has begun in two plants on Rakuen and one on Neramese," Cameron reported. "A second plant on Neramese will become operational in a few days. The first missiles won't begin rolling off the assembly lines for nearly a week, but once they do, we expect the four facilities to produce one missile per day, each, for a total of four missiles per day."

"That will take some time to reach satisfactory levels," Nathan said, concerned.

"Two more plants are under construction on each world," Cameron added, "So within a couple weeks, the production rate will double."

"What about the surface-based jump missile launchers?" Nathan asked.

"By utilizing the same design as the Orochi and beefing up the hydraulics to operate in a gravity environment, we were able to speed up production," Deliza announced with pride. "More than twenty of them have already been assembled and are being installed on both Rakuen *and* Neramese."

"In equal numbers, I assume," Nathan said.

"Of course," Deliza assured him. "They should be ready by the time new jump missiles start rolling out of the factories."

"Good work," Nathan congratulated.

"Thank you, sir."

"Speaking of the Orochi," Cameron interjected, "the sixth ship is launching today, and the seventh a few days from now. We should have all of them operational within a few weeks."

"Then, it sounds like the Rogen system's ability to defend itself is coming along nicely," General Telles opined. "If the Aurora is able to transit between the Pentaurus cluster and the Rogen system at will, and without delay, then we will be free to press the attack and turn the tide of this conflict."

"Let's hope," Nathan agreed. He looked at the faces around the table. "Anything else to report?"

he asked, noticing a distressed expression on Lieutenant Commander Shinoda's face. "Lieutenant Commander?"

Lieutenant Commander Shinoda sighed. "There is some unsettling intelligence."

"Let's hear it," Nathan urged.

"Operatives on Takara report that General Hesson, Lord Dusahn's senior military advisor, has been absent for six days, now. The timing of his absence coincides with our attack on Rama."

"Maybe he was taken ill, or something?" Cameron suggested.

"He has been spotted at restaurants, parks, even shopping," Lieutenant Commander Shinoda added. "He appears to be healthy."

"A vacation?" Vladimir suggested.

"In the middle of a war?" Nathan retorted. "Unlikely."

"We have another theory," Jessica insisted.

"It also seems that one of General Hesson's subordinates, a younger officer by the name of Tolkan, has been meeting with Lord Dusahn in General Hesson's absence."

"You think Lord Dusahn has changed advisors?" Nathan surmised.

"Either temporarily or permanently," Jessica replied.

Nathan studied both the lieutenant commander and Jessica for a moment, neither of whom looked comfortable. "There's something else," he realized.

"We have received a message from Lord Mahtize," General Telles announced.

"We?" Nathan wondered.

"The message came to me, through one of my

operatives on Takara. One who has been tasked with being Lord Mahtize's handler."

"How do you manage to get messages out of a Dusahn-held system?" Nathan wondered.

"It is not as difficult as one might think," General Telles assured him. "Bounce it off a few comm-sats, and make sure it is in the air when one of our recon drones makes a pass."

"And it's secure?"

"Very."

"What was the message?" Nathan wondered.

"It seems that General Hesson wishes to meet with you, Captain," General Telles replied.

The news caught Nathan by surprise, causing him to recoil slightly. "Really." After thinking for a moment, he added, "Did he say why?"

"No," General Telles replied. "Only that he wishes to meet. He *has* offered a neutral location, one away from Takara..."

"Yet still inside Dusahn space," Nathan assumed.

"Traveling at *all* would raise suspicion," the general replied, "let *alone* traveling *outside* the Dusahn Empire."

"Let him take the risk," Jessica insisted. "*He's* the one making the request."

"Merely *making* the request is a risk," Nathan said. He looked to General Telles. "Assessment?"

"Intelligence suggests several possible scenarios," General Telles replied, "the most likely of which is that General Hesson has fallen out of favor with Lord Dusahn."

"Wouldn't *Lord Dusahn* just kill him in that case?" Jessica said.

"The Dusahn are an honor-driven culture," Lieutenant Commander Shinoda added. "They also have a significantly longer life span than most humans—the reasons for which we have yet to establish. It is entirely possible that the general's life has been spared as a reward for his long history of service."

"General Hesson is significantly older than Lord Dusahn," General Telles said, adding to the lieutenant commander's assessment. "It is possible that he served the previous leader, as well. It is also possible, assuming he *did* fall from favor, that his life was spared for fear of discontent among those Dusahn officers loyal to the general."

"It could also be a ruse," Cameron suggested.

"I'm with her," Jessica agreed.

"To lead us into a trap?" Nathan concluded.

"What else?" Cameron replied. "They're not having much success attacking us directly."

"Tell that to my engineers and repair teams," Vladimir snorted.

"Deception *is* one of the oldest and most effective weapons in one's arsenal," General Telles stated. "It has been used throughout history, often with great effectiveness."

"And with great failure," Nathan added.

General Telles nodded in agreement.

Nathan took in a deep breath, letting it out slowly. "Deception or not, we *should* meet with him."

"I'm not so sure about that," Cameron objected.

"If the general is in earnest, he may be offering us an advantage," General Telles said.

"And if a hundred Zen-Anor crash the party?" Jessica wondered.

"Anything is possible," General Telles admitted. "However, such a move would make little sense."

"The Dusahn are not afraid of *me*," Nathan

insisted. "They're afraid of the Aurora...especially an Aurora powered by ZPEDs."

"Then, why didn't they guard them more carefully?" Abby wondered.

"Underestimation of our daring?"

"*Desperation* might be a better word," Cameron said.

"If you are to meet with General Hesson, it would be best to do so on Takara," General Telles insisted. "That way, if he *is* acting without knowledge of his empire, he is less likely to raise their suspicions."

"You can't do it, Nathan," Cameron insisted. "It's too risky."

"Meeting with the general or meeting with him on Takara?" Nathan asked her.

"Take your pick."

"Again, I'm with Cam," Jessica agreed.

"The Dusahn aren't going to try to capture me during the meeting with General Hesson. If this is a ruse, the target *is* the Aurora," Nathan insisted. "I'm certain of it."

"Certain enough to meet one-on-one with their top general...*on* Takara?" Jessica asked.

"Yes," Nathan replied confidently. "But who said I'm going alone?" he added with a grin.

* * *

Kareef could feel his pulse racing as he struggled to avoid the deadly streams of energy streaking past him from behind. The Ahka raider had managed to slip behind him without warning and refused to let him out of his crosshairs until...

"*You must shake your attacker, and get behind him,*" Commander Prechitt urged over Kareef's helmet comms. "*You cannot evade him forever. Your shields will not hold that long.*"

"I know! I know!" Kareef exclaimed as he pushed his Sugali fighter into a spiraling dive toward the surface of Casbon. "*Bashwan*!" he cursed as energy streams walked across his aft shields, shaking his tiny cockpit violently. "I need assistance! Anybody!"

"*In space, your fellow pilots may be too far away to help you,*" Commander Prechitt reminded him. "*Remember your relativity training.*"

"*Bashwa-coysfanay*!"

"*Language, Mister Shamoon,*" Commander Prechitt scolded. "*A good fighter pilot is always in control of his emotions.*"

"I am obviously *not* a good fighter pilot!" Kareef retorted as another energy bolt rocked his ship.

The barrage from behind suddenly stopped. Kareef glanced at his tactical display and found that the Ahka raider had disengaged and jumped away. "Ha-ha!" he exclaimed triumphantly. "I shook him!"

"*No,*" the commander replied, "*he left because he knows you're already dead. Gravity made the kill for him.*"

Kareef looked at his speed and rate of descent indicators, as well as his altitude indicator. A cold chill traveled down his spine as he glanced forward just in time to see the surface of his homeworld taking his life.

Everything went black.

Three seconds later, his canopy slid open, and the cool morning air of Casbon rushed into his cockpit, a welcome sensation after twenty minutes of nervous perspiration.

Kareef looked over at Commander Prechitt and Talisha, both of whom were walking toward him. He then glanced at the Sugali Nighthawk next to him, spotting Lieutenant Commander Cardi, her long, auburn hair spilling out as she removed her helmet.

The lieutenant commander smiled at Kareef. “Fish in a barrel,” she said with a laugh as she climbed up out of her fighter.

“I do not like her,” Kareef stated to Talisha and Commander Prechitt as they approached.

“You should be thanking her,” Talisha replied. “She just taught you a valuable lesson.”

“Which is?”

“Flying is always first,” Talisha replied.

“If you aren’t flying, you’re not fighting,” Commander Prechitt added, “and if you’re not fighting, they’re not dying.” The commander walked up to the bottom of Kareef’s boarding ladder, looking up at him. “The Gunyoki have a saying, ‘Fly, fight, win.’” He looked at Talisha. “Pretty much sums it all up, doesn’t it?”

“I believe it does,” Talisha agreed.

Kareef looked over at the lieutenant commander, now sitting at the top of her own boarding ladder, a satisfied grin on her face. “What are you smiling about? You are proud to have beaten such an easy target?”

“Don’t take it so hard, Shamoon,” Lieutenant Commander Cardi insisted. “We’ve all been there.”

“Again,” the commander ordered.

“I have to teach a ground school class in twenty minutes,” the lieutenant commander warned. “I know he isn’t going to last that long, but I would like to grab a bite beforehand.”

“Very well,” the commander replied. “Kareef, start from liftoff, and I’ll meet you at the simulated engagement area.”

“You are to be flying with me?”

"No, I'll be trying to kill you," the commander told him. "Now, go."

Kareef muttered another expletive in Casbonese as his cockpit closed around him.

"Maybe he's had enough for one day?" Talisha suggested to the commander.

"I know that you probably have daily training limits in civilian flight training, Talisha," Commander Prechitt replied, "but the enemy doesn't care if you're tired. In fact, he prefers it. It is better that our pilots become accustomed to exhaustion and fear. Facing it is how they build courage."

"Fear also causes hesitation," Talisha pointed out.

"Kareef and all the others must learn to *master* their own fears," the commander explained. "Only then will they have the courage needed to defend their world."

"Let's hope they have it in them."

"Let's hope," the commander agreed, turning to climb into the other Nighthawk.

* * *

Josh sat at the Aurora's helm, both arms crossed and a determined look on his face as he listened to the technician explain his ideas. When the technician stopped talking, Josh glanced to the left at Loki. "Are you getting any of this?"

"Yes."

"Good, because I'm not."

"What is it you aren't getting?" the technician asked Josh.

"Primarily, why you think I need all that crap," Josh replied, pointing to all of the data displayed on the clear panel before him.

"Because that's all the information about the ship's flight systems. You *are* the pilot, right?"

"Ah-ha!" Josh exclaimed. "Then, you *do* know what the person who sits in this seat does. Now we're getting somewhere."

A confused look came across the technician's face. He turned to Loki for help.

"Don't look at me," Loki said, throwing his hands up. "I don't understand half of what goes on in his head."

"Dude, let me put it to you as simply as possible," Josh began. "I'm the pilot. I fly the ship. I don't care about the status of every little thruster or power transfer relay, or all the other doohickeys that make this thing fly. Attitude, speed, velocity, rate of closure or separation, range to this, that, or the other thing...*that's the kind of stuff* I need to know. All this other garbage just distracts me."

"But..." Again, the technician looked to Loki. "How are you supposed to know if something is wrong? How are you supposed to know what the ship *can* or *cannot do* at any given moment?"

Josh did not reply, only pointing to Loki.

"That would be my job," Loki said, raising his hand.

"But you're the navigator," the technician insisted.

"That's old school," Josh told him. "The Aurora doesn't need a navigator. The jump-nav com does all of that for us."

"By that logic, she doesn't need a pilot, either," the technician argued.

"Wrong," Josh snapped.

"Oh, don't go there," Loki warned the technician.

"We come head-to-head with a Dusahn battleship, and you'll quickly realize this ship *needs* a pilot,"

Josh insisted. "And one who isn't distracted with all this crap!" he added, pointing to the display in front of him.

"So, all you want is flight dynamics data?" the technician asked in disbelief.

"Finally!" Josh groaned.

"Do you know how long I worked on this?"

"You figured it would be a good idea to rework the pilot's displays without first consulting with, say, the pilot?" Josh laughed. "I think I've found where you made your first error, fella."

The technician simply stared at Josh.

"What?" Josh asked. "It shouldn't be too hard to fix. Just delete all that other crap and leave me the flight dynamics data. Hell, I'll even arrange it properly for you."

The technician shook his head as he walked away.

"You're going to fix it, right?" Josh called after him. He turned to Loki again. "He *is* going to fix this, right?" he asked Loki, pointing to the display in front of him.

"You could have handled that a little better, Josh," Loki suggested.

"You saw it, Lok," Josh replied. "It was a mess."

"Yes, it was."

"He's going to fix it, right?"

"I heard you the first time."

"But you didn't answer me," Josh pushed.

"I'm sure he'll fix it, Josh," Loki replied. "Just give him time."

"No problem," Josh agreed. "This ship's not going anywhere soon."

"Thankfully," Loki said.

"I need to fly something," Josh decided, rising from his seat to leave. "We haven't flown in a week."

"Where are you going?" Loki asked.

"I'm going to find Cameron to see if there are any shuttle runs we can take," Josh replied as he headed for the exit. "You coming?"

"But we have the next watch," Loki reminded him.

"That's not for two more hours," Josh replied. "A shuttle run will take half that. Maybe we can get a run to Rakuen to pick up some seafood."

Loki groaned as he rose to follow. "We just ate an hour ago."

"Well, I'm hungry already," Josh insisted as he headed out the exit.

"Where the hell do you put it?" Loki wondered as he followed.

* * *

More than anything else, Sanctuary was a marketplace. Over a dozen massive caverns were carved out of the rocky asteroid, which served as the facility's main core. Each of them was meticulously detailed, making those within feel as if they were walking on the surface of a planet in an open-air marketplace. Blue skies stretched overhead, disappearing behind the various structures lining each cavern's perimeter. Those skies faded into starry nights, in keeping with Sanctuary's day-night cycles.

Unlike real open-air markets, Sanctuary's were always a comfortable twenty-two degrees. It never rained, and the breezes were always just enough to keep those who trolled the hundreds of merchant booths comfortable, while not creating problems. Even on those days when the markets were overcrowded, the temperature remained the same.

Being that it was Sanctuary, it was not uncommon to see more than a few nefarious-looking types mixed into the crowds. For this reason, Marcus preferred to keep his face unshaven and his dress similar to those less desirable guests. More than once, he had witnessed the pockets of the well dressed being picked, or other undue attention being paid to them, by con artists from all corners of the quadrant.

Yes, even Sanctuary, with all its security forces and technology, had its criminal element, most of whom could be found in the tech markets that Marcus favored. He had tried the other markets: culinary, grocery, clothing, and accessories. He had even made the mistake of visiting the jewelry markets with Neli; one that he would not repeat any time soon.

The tech markets were where Marcus felt most at home. He would sleep there if he could. There was nothing *wrong* with his accommodations, but they were quite sterile and bland. The markets were full of color and activity, and littered with all manner of gadgets, the likes of which most people couldn't even imagine. Marcus used this as an excuse for his daily visits—to search for tech that might be of use to the Aurora and the Karuzari Alliance. He adored Miri's kids and enjoyed their company, but his daily forays into the seedy tech market domes were what kept him sane. It also gave him a chance to ingest something *other* than the overly healthy crap that Neli was constantly forcing him to eat.

Marcus had developed a sort of game during his visits to the tech markets on Sanctuary. He would select a patron, sometimes a group of patrons, and then follow them around the markets. Their interests often told him much about the subjects. Mercenaries seeking unique weapons and technologies that might give them an advantage over their adversaries, physicians who were looking for new and better imaging and treatment tools for the worlds they represented, fabricators and manufacturers seeking to improve their processes and increase their profits, researchers and scientists looking for better tools through which to further their understanding of the universe; all of them forever searching.

Marcus often wondered how fruitful their searches truly were. In his weeks of visiting the tech markets, he had seen a few faces more than once. Some left with new acquisitions; whereas, others departed empty-handed.

On this day, Marcus had chosen to follow an odd-looking fellow with a shaved head and poorly fitting clothing, which did not seem to suit his personality. Even more oddly, the man didn't seem to favor any particular line of tech. He methodically worked his way down each row, up and back, making sure to take a visual inventory of every item on display in every vendor's booth. So perfect and efficient was his method that Marcus wondered if the man, himself, wasn't some kind of robot, or cyborg, being guided by algorithms.

Marcus had been in the market this day for twice as long as his average visit. He had received more than one text message on his comm-unit from Neli, wondering how much longer he would be. He continued to make excuses, unable to complete his visit until he discerned the odd fellow's purpose.

He had followed the man through three of Sanctuary's four tech market bays and was halfway through the last cavern when the odd-looking fellow suddenly turned around to face Marcus.

"Are you an evaluator?" the odd-looking man asked Marcus directly.

"A what?"

"An evaluator."

"I don't even know what that is," Marcus replied gruffly.

"You've been following me for some time. Either you are secretly evaluating my performance for my employer or you intend to rob me. If the latter, I should warn you that I carry no credits, nor anything else of value, and that I am well able to defend myself."

"I ain't a thug lookin' to rob you," Marcus grumbled. "If I was, I would've done it already."

"Perhaps you are also a scout?" the man surmised, one eyebrow raised.

"I guess you could say that," Marcus admitted.

"Who is your employer?"

"I can't say," Marcus replied. "Low profile, and all that."

"Of course."

"And you?" Marcus asked.

"I work for SilTek," the odd-looking fellow stated proudly.

"Never heard of them."

The man cast a cockeyed look at Marcus, unsure of whether to believe him.

"Sorry," Marcus added, noticing the odd-looking man's disbelief. "Should I have?"

"SilTek is the largest tech company in the Poron quadrant."

"Never heard of the Poron quadrant, either."

"You don't leave this station much, do you?" the man laughed.

"I'm not from here," Marcus told him. "I'm just visiting."

"How long have you been here?" the man wondered.

"A few weeks, I think. On assignment, you might say."

"Then, perhaps, we can help one another. I am newly assigned to this post. My employer has only recently been welcomed into this facility. I would appreciate any insight you might be able to give me into the culture and protocols of these markets."

"You might start by getting the right clothing," Marcus said, fighting back a laugh. "And don't walk with your hands locked behind your back. It makes you look like an easy target for a punch n' pick."

"A punch and pick?"

Marcus rolled his eyes and sighed. "Buy me lunch, and I'll help you out."

"Deal," the odd-looking fellow agreed. "Lead the way."

* * *

"What's the word?" Nathan asked as he entered the Aurora's intelligence shack.

"We received a confirmation message," Lieutenant Commander Shinoda replied.

"Hesson has agreed to meet on Takara, at a place and time of our choosing," Jessica reported.

"Any ideas?" Nathan wondered.

"There is a lake a few kilometers east of Answari," General Telles said. "Its western shores are dotted with resorts. Egress and ingress should be easy, and the water is warm year-round, due to volcanic activity at its deepest point. It is quite common for residents of Answari to spend time there and should not raise any suspicions if the general does so, as well."

Nathan looked at the map on the view screen. "Is it big enough?"

"I'd prefer a larger target, to be honest," Jessica

admitted, "but the jump sub *should* be able to get us in safely."

"Why don't we jump into the same place you guys did last time?" Nathan wondered.

"It was a considerable distance from Answari," General Telles explained. "It would be safer if your escape was nearby and quick, just in case things don't go as expected."

"Nice way of putting it," Nathan commented. "When?"

"The sooner the better," Jessica insisted. "Don't give him any time to prepare."

"I would suggest that you meet him first thing in the morning," General Telles said.

"Theirs or ours?"

"Theirs," the general replied. "We can time the return message so he has just enough time to reach the rendezvous point, further restricting his preparation time."

"Are you sure you want to do this?" Cameron asked, looking to Nathan.

"*Want* or *need*?" Nathan replied. "When do we leave, then?"

"Now," Jessica said.

"Very well," Nathan sighed.

"Keep him out of trouble," Cameron told Jessica.

"Always."

"Shouldn't you be telling *me* to keep *her* out of trouble?" Nathan asked Cameron.

"That was coming next," Cameron replied. "Good luck."

* * *

"This place makes the best haiga sandwiches on the entire station," Marcus bragged as they took their seats on the patio.

"I'm not familiar with 'haiga'," the odd-looking man admitted. "What exactly is it?"

"You don't want to know."

The man looked troubled. "Maybe I should look at the menu, first."

"Trust me," Marcus insisted.

"I don't even know your name."

"Marcus Taggart."

"Gunwant Vout," the man replied, offering his hand.

"Gunwant?" Marcus replied, shaking the man's hand.

"My friends call me Gunwy. I assume your friends call you Marki?"

"Not if they wanna live," Marcus grumbled.

"Marcus it is, then," Gunwy agreed, picking up the menu.

"I'm telling you, you're gonna love haiga," Marcus said, taking the menu away from Gunwy. "I've yet to meet a man who didn't."

"As a general rule, I prefer to know what I'm eating. I'm funny that way."

"If I tell you what it is, you won't want to try it, and you'll be missing out on a real treat; one that you can't find anywhere else in the galaxy, as far as I know."

"It is a tempting offer, but..."

"I tell you what," Marcus said, "if you agree to try the haiga, I'll tell you what it is after your first bite. I'll even order you a backup, in case you don't like it."

"Do I get to keep the backup order, even if I eat the haiga?" Gunwy asked.

"A slick negotiator, huh?" Marcus chuckled. "You gotta deal, Gunwy." Marcus rotated the order pad on the table toward him and tapped the screen several times. "I'm kinda surprised that you haven't heard of haiga yet."

"I've only been on station for a few days. I've been eating the food I brought with me until I become accustomed to local cuisine."

"Sensitive gut?"

"A bit."

"Then, you might want to drink a lot of water with the haiga."

"Oh, my."

"You'll be fine," Marcus assured him. "Where you stayin'?"

"SilTek maintains a suite on level eight."

"Pricey. SilTek must be doin' pretty good."

"It's the largest corporation in the Poron quadrant."

"Where exactly *is* the Poron quadrant?" Marcus asked.

"Technically, we're *in* the Poron quadrant," Gunwy explained. "Albeit, on the outer fringe."

"I thought this was the Parre sector."

"Probably just a different name for the same area. It happens a lot. The SilTek system is just over seven hundred light years from here."

"I thought SilTek was a *company*, not a system."

"It is both. The star's original name was Kromov Four Eight Seven, after the astronomer who first charted the system. SilTek was formed on Kromov Three, which was then called Ellenson. When SilTek took over control of the system from Ellenson's failed government, they renamed the system."

"So, SilTek, the *company*, is located on *Ellenson* in the SilTek *system*."

"Yes," Gunwy replied. "Except that Ellenson

was later renamed Chaym, to honor Ian Chaym, the former CEO of SilTek who masterminded the takeover that saved Ellenson from its own corrupt leaders."

"I think I've got it," Marcus said unconvincingly. "What does SilTek do, other than run the system?"

"Primarily, SilTek is a technology company. When the system was first colonized, a virus native to the planet wiped out three quarters of the population. Two young women, Silvia Wilkie and Tekka Lin, successfully resurrected several of the colony's original, long-defunct labor bots and set them to perform tasks that helped save the colony. They later reprogrammed the artificial intelligence algorithms of the labor bots so they could learn and make decisions on their own, within certain guidelines and restrictions. They managed to fabricate additional labor bots over the years, which helped the fledgling colony grow and thrive again. From those humble beginnings, the company grew."

"So SilTek is basically a robotics company," Marcus surmised.

"Robotics, software, AI, transportation, weapons... anything that can be automated."

"Weapons, you say?" Marcus said, trying to hide his curiosity from the man.

"Yes, but they are a *very* small part of SilTek's business. They only make defensive systems. *AI* is SilTek's biggest market. Now that the jump drive has opened up the galaxy to us, we hope to spread our AI division to neighboring quadrants, perhaps even across the galaxy."

"Lofty ambitions," Marcus decided.

A disheveled-looking, young man in a dirty, white apron arrived carrying three plastic plates of food and two bottles of water, all of which he unceremoniously plopped down on the table in front of them. “Two haiga and pera.”

Gunwy examined his food with suspicion, lifting the bun to peer at the meat patty below. “Some kind of animal, I’m guessing.”

Marcus just smiled as he picked up his own haiga sandwich and took a hearty bite. “Dig in,” he said with a full mouth.

Gunwy replaced the bun top and picked up the sandwich with both hands, mimicking Marcus’s style. He sniffed the sandwich, paused for a moment, and then took a modest bite, his face slightly contorted with apprehension. He chewed for a few seconds, trying not to taste what was in his mouth. As his saliva began to mix with the food, his taste buds were hit with a flavor he could not describe. “Wow,” was the only word that came to him at the moment. He swallowed his first bite, eagerly taking a second.

“Uh-huh,” Marcus said, pleased with himself. “I told ya.”

“This is amazing,” Gunwy exclaimed after swallowing his second bite. “So many flavors and textures, all melding together, and the meat... I can’t even begin to classify it. Maybe poultry mixed with some type of red meat, perhaps?”

“Not even close,” Marcus chuckled.

“What then?”

“Ground beetles. Big problem on the lower levels.”

Gunwy suddenly stopped chewing, a wad of food still in his mouth.

“I don’t rightly know which ones, but they grind them up and mix them with some other fillers and binders and such, add spices, and then make patties out of it, and fry it up nice. It's the bun that makes it, though. That, and the dressing."

Gunwy forced himself to swallow and then placed his half-eaten sandwich back on his plate. "I'm afraid to ask what's in the pera sandwich."

"Water snake meat," Marcus replied. "Tastes like chicken. Imported from Dygon, I hear."

"Maybe later," Gunwy decided, pushing both plates away from him.

"Should I have them wrapped to go?" Marcus wondered.

"Yes, that would be fine."

"Suit yourself."

Gunwy took a long drink of water. "So, you never told me *what* you are scouting for."

"Neither did you," Marcus pointed out.

"I'm assigned here to scout for technologies that SilTek can incorporate into its own lines."

"I thought SilTek was mostly into AIs," Marcus commented between bites.

"It is their primary focus, but as I said, we make many things. SilTek has grown exponentially over the last three years, thanks to the introduction of the jump drive. So many markets are opening up to us, we have to be ready to jump on opportunities as they present themselves."

"I don't get it," Marcus admitted. "If someone has tech for sale here, then someone is already making it somewhere else, right?"

"Yes, but more often than not, their method of production is inefficient, their scale of operation is too small, and their access to markets are limited. We often buy out their interests, make modest improvements, and then release it to much broader markets. Economies of scale, and all that."

"Well, this place is crawling with tech. I'm kinda keeping an eye out for useful tech, as well."

"For your employer," Gunwy surmised. "The one who shall remain nameless."

"Yup."

"What type of tech are you keeping an eye out for?"

"Power generation, computer systems, medical technology, propulsion systems, a bit of everything, really." Marcus looked around briefly and then leaned closer. "But mostly for weapons."

"Personal weapons?" Gunwy asked under his breath.

"Naw," Marcus replied dismissively. "We got lots of them. Bigger stuff, mostly. Ship-to-ship, ordnance... that kind of thing."

"Are you fighting a war?"

"I'm not really at liberty to say." Marcus looked at Gunwy for a moment. "Unless, of course, you might know of something like that."

"SilTek doesn't make any offensive weapons, but as I said, we do make defensive systems."

"What *kind* of defensive systems?" Marcus wondered.

"Everything from shuttle defenses up to planetary defenses," Gunwy explained. "We even upgraded the detection and targeting systems for this station's defenses. That's how we got our transponders."

Marcus smiled. "We're going to be spending more time together, you and I."

"That would be fine with me," Gunwy replied. "However, I will bring my own food next time, if you don't mind."

* * *

"Four of our Reapers are out on recon, one crew

is helping to train the Orochi pilots, and one crew is out with the flu," Cameron explained as they left the intelligence shack.

Nathan spied Josh and Loki coming around the corner, carrying sandwiches. "What are they doing?"

"They have helm duty in a couple hours," Cameron replied.

"Extend the current helm crew a few more hours," Nathan suggested.

"They're already working twelve-hour shifts," Cameron warned.

"The Aurora is stuck in orbit. Let them take a nap in the break room, or something."

"Round trip to Takara is going to be six hours," Jessica reminded Nathan.

"They can take a *long* nap, then." Nathan turned toward Josh and Loki. "Hayes! Sheehan! With me!" he instructed, turning to head down the ramp.

"Uh, we were gonna ask Captain Taylor for a flight assignment," Josh replied.

"You just got one," Cameron told Josh, pointing toward Nathan and Jessica as they disappeared down the ramp. "If you hurry."

"Hot damn!" Josh declared, quickening his pace. "Adventures!"

CHAPTER TWO

"We are now in Dusahn-controlled space," Loki announced. "Four more jumps to the insertion point." Loki looked over at Josh, who was smiling.

"Pretty cool, huh?" Josh commented.

"Remind me to run away the next time you cheer for 'adventures'," Loki moaned.

"Come on, Lok, it's not like it's our first time going into enemy space, and you've got to admit, it beats the hell out of chauffeuring the princess from one business meeting to another."

"I much preferred being a corporate pilot," Loki insisted. "Good ship, good hours, good pay...and I was home with the family every night."

"Sounds boring as hell to me."

"Did I mention that no one was shooting at me?" Loki added.

"Like I said, boring as hell."

"I suppose hauling cargo and passengers in the Seiiki was so much better?"

"At least we had a few skirmishes here and there," Josh replied. "Hey, did I tell you about the time we had to break the Seiiki out of the Inklen spaceport?"

"Three times," Loki groaned.

"What about the bar fight we got into on Kaladossa?"

"When you got your ass kicked by a teenage girl?"

"That teenage girl was fucking huge," Josh defended. "She even knocked Marcus down." He laughed to himself. "Good times."

"Three jumps to insertion point," Loki reported.

Josh sighed. "The Seiiki was a good ship."

"That she was," Loki agreed.

"You guys ready back there?" Josh called through the hatchway to their Reaper's payload bay.

"We're ready," Nathan replied. He looked at Jessica. "Are you sure we're dressed appropriately?" he asked, looking at her revealing swimsuit, as well as his own.

"We're jumping into a warm-weather, warm-water resort," Jessica told him as she climbed up onto the jump sub. "This is what most people will be wearing. We want to blend in, remember?"

"It just seems wrong," Nathan stated, watching her drop down through the jump sub's hatch. He climbed up onto the sub and dropped down through the hatch, himself, taking the seat behind her. "Jumping into enemy territory, half-naked, with no weapons."

"Not like you haven't seen me naked before," Jessica joked as she checked the jump sub's systems.

Nathan reached up and pulled the hatch closed. "That's one of my memories that's still a little fuzzy," he admitted. "Plus, it was a long time ago."

Jessica placed her comm-set on her head. "We're good to go," she reported.

"*Twenty seconds to final insertion,*" Loki replied.

Nathan buckled himself in, tightening his restraints in preparation. "Sometimes I wonder why I do these things," he admitted.

"When all this is over, and we're retired and wasting away our days in rockers on our front porches, you should write a book about your experiences."

Nathan chuckled. "No one would believe it."

"*Jumping in three......two......one...*"

Within the confines of the jump sub, there was no indication of their transition into the outskirts of the Takaran system.

"*Jump complete,*" Loki reported.

"Ready for release," Jessica announced.

"*Release in five.*"

Jessica checked her displays one last time as Loki counted down.

"*Release.*"

There was a faint click as the clamps, holding the jump sub tightly against the fitted opening in the underside of the Reaper's payload bay, released their hold.

"*Translating up and away,*" Josh reported.

A few seconds later, they felt the pressure of their bottoms against the seats lessening as the Reaper, which had carried them to their insertion point, placed them on the proper course and speed, and drifted up and away; the Reaper's artificial gravity losing its hold on the tiny vessel.

"Thirty seconds to jump point," Jessica announced.

"*Comms blackout,*" Loki replied. "*Good luck.*"

"See you tomorrow," Jessica replied confidently. Another glance at her displays told her all was well. "All systems are green. Auto-jump sequencer is running. Jumping in twenty."

"How hard will we hit the water?" Nathan wondered.

"Low-speed jump," Jessica replied. "Shallow target. You'll barely even feel it."

Nathan braced himself, just in case.

"Three......two......one......jumping..."

There was a loud thump that shook the jump sub so hard it felt as if it would break apart. Nathan was thrown forward against his restraints. Just as suddenly, he felt gravity return to his body. There was the sound of rushing water flowing over the exterior of their hull, which faded quickly. He could feel the resistance of the sub traveling through the water as it plunged into the warm depths of the lake.

"*That's* what you call *barely feeling it*?"

"Don't be a wuss," Jessica laughed.

"Now what?"

"Now I drive this thing along the lake bottom until we're close enough to shore to swim in without looking suspicious."

* * *

Admiral Galiardi stood at the window of his office, staring out at the Sol Alliance Command Center below.

"You must leave this place at some point," Commander Denton told him. "The people of Earth need to *see* that you are in command; in control of *all* the core worlds."

"I am needed here," the admiral stated with conviction.

"The Jung are not going to attack Earth," the commander insisted. "Even if they do, our forces will immediately follow your standing orders and respond with maximum force. There is nothing that your presence would change in the first few minutes of battle."

"And what am I to do on Earth?" the admiral asked, turning to look at the commander.

"Lead the people."

"I can lead the people from here."

"Yes, you can," Commander Denton admitted, "but the people's support will wane with each passing day. They need to see a strong leader in the place they expect him to be: in front of the houses, in front of the cabinets, in front of the cameras. You must *appear* to be the leader that Dayton Scott was *not*. There is not a soul on Earth, nor on any of the core worlds, who does not want us to stand strong against the Jung."

"Oh, but there is, believe me."

"The last of those foolish enough to speak out against us have been rounded up. The voices of opposition are nearly silent. Soon, the court of public opinion will swing your way. When it does, you must be in the public eye to receive that support. At that moment, you will be able to declare war against the Jung Empire, and none of the senators will risk opposing you. The vote will be unanimous."

"I do not intend to ask permission to wage war upon those who wish to destroy us," Admiral Galiardi stated as he returned to his desk.

"But that is the law."

"We are under martial law," the admiral reminded him, "which means *I* decide when we go to war...no one else." Admiral Galiardi took his seat, appearing more resolute than before. "I will stay here. The Earth will run itself, and the cabinet heads can report to me via vid-comms. My primary responsibility is the defense of the core worlds. I shall not ignore that concern for the sake of propaganda. That is precisely what was wrong with our government."

"But..."

"Once the Jung are defeated, I will take my place in Winnipeg...not before," the admiral insisted. "The people will understand."

* * *

Nathan and Jessica slowly broke the surface of

Lake Aranda, just under the far end of the pier where no one would notice them.

Jessica looked around. The sun was still relatively low in the sky, and the usual beach crowds had not yet developed. There were no boats nearby, and the lifeguards were just opening up their observation towers. Thus far, their arrival had gone like clockwork.

Satisfied that their appearance from the lake's depths had gone unnoticed, Jessica swam toward the nearby shore. Staying to one side of the pier, Nathan followed behind. To anyone on the pier, they appeared to be a young couple finishing a morning swim.

Two minutes later, they walked out of the water, moving directly to a pair of beach chairs under a large shade about ten meters up from the waterline. As expected, they found appropriate beach attire and footwear waiting for them.

Jessica picked up one of the towels and dried herself off, donning a beach wrap afterward. She then picked up the small beach bag next to the chair and pulled the wallet out to check its contents. "Not bad," she said under her breath as she inspected the Takaran ID card in the wallet. "Even a comm-unit."

Nathan also examined the contents of his wallet. "I had no idea we had operatives on Takara," he admitted. "Especially ones with such capabilities."

"Well, you *have* been a little distracted lately."

"Someone's coming," Nathan said, noticing a man in a resort staff uniform coming toward them with a tray balanced on his left hand.

Jessica took her seat as if resting after her swim.

"I thought you might be in need of liquid refreshment after your long swim," the man commented politely as he neared. "Mineral water, ma'am?" he added, kneeling down next to Jessica and holding out the tray.

"Thank you," Jessica replied as she took one of the two bottles. "Honey?" she said, looking at Nathan. "You thirsty?"

"A bit," Nathan replied, reaching for his own bottle.

"My name is Taavi," the man added. "I am one of four waiters working this beach today. If you need anything, please... *Telles.*"

"I'm a little hungry," Jessica said. "Is there anything open nearby?"

"There is a small café just on the other side of the pier," Taavi replied. "It opened at sunrise, but I would not wait, since it will become quite busy within the hour. Beautiful views of the lake... *if* you get a corner booth. Very secluded, as well."

"Thank you, Taavi," Nathan replied, putting a credit on the man's tray.

"That is unnecessary," Taavi assured him. "It is all included in your stay."

"I believe in showing appreciation for good service," Nathan insisted.

"Thank you, sir," Taavi replied. "Enjoy your morning," he added as he backed away and turned to depart.

"Wouldn't that be nice," Nathan murmured under his breath.

"What?" Jessica wondered as she pulled on her sandals.

"To actually *stay* here for a few days."

"I'd be bored out of my skull," Jessica disagreed. She rose from her seat. "Let's get this over with, shall we?"

"Ladies first," Nathan replied, gesturing for her to lead the way.

* * *

Aiden Walsh sat in the pilot's seat of his Orochi jump missile frigate, staring out into space, as usual.

"Bored?" Ali called from behind him.

"I feel like a cargo pilot," he sighed. "This thing is so automated, a monkey could fly it."

"You miss Kenji?"

"More than I thought I would," Aiden admitted.

"I miss him, too," Ali agreed. "Ash and Dags, too."

"I *don't* miss Ashwini," Aiden insisted. "That woman scared me."

"Ash is a pussycat," Ali told him, taking a seat at the systems station. "She just acted mean so you wouldn't make too many demands of her."

"I'm pretty sure that wasn't acting," Aiden declared as he checked his flight displays.

"You get to talk to Kenji lately?"

"With all the jumping around we do? Not hardly. The most I get is a bounce-back relay saying, 'Things are great, how are you?' I haven't talked to him or Charnelle in over two weeks, now. I'm just not used to that. I think I'm going through withdrawals."

"You've still got me and Ledge," Ali reminded him. After a sigh, she added, "I miss our ship, as well."

"She was a nice, little ship."

"There's so much room on this thing, I can't get used to it," Ali said.

"Enjoy it while you can," Aiden told her. "After the second phase of refits, we'll have a full crew of fourteen."

"That still leaves four empty cabins."

"Those will probably be turned into storage bays,"

Aiden replied. "Word is, Orochis are going to be on patrol around the clock for some time."

"Then, the long hours aren't going to end any time soon," Ali realized, failing to hide her disappointment.

"I'm afraid not. All the bickering between Rakuen and Neramese is seriously slowing down the selection process. Orochi Seven just launched, and Eight should be ready in a day or two. Both are being crewed by Corinari, for now, but if those politicians don't get their act together soon, we're going to have Orochis sitting in the water, waiting for crews."

"Could be worse," Ali decided. "At least these patrols are nice and quiet. I'm getting a lot of reading in. You'd be amazed how much literature there is in our database. Stuff from all over the Rogen sector. Plus, they've added everything from the Pentaurus and Sol sectors, as well. Even the stuff from the Data Ark...the stuff from before the fall of the core. More material than you could read in a thousand lifetimes."

"I may have to take up reading, then," Aiden said, laughing. "Lord knows there's nothing else to do around here."

* * *

Jessica stood at the railing along the walkway, gazing at the lake. Casual, lingering glances to her right and left allowed her to scan the area for threats while still appearing to be just another Takaran enjoying her stay at Lake Aranda Resort. Once satisfied, she looked toward Nathan, who was still standing on the pier feeding the squawking birds that were everywhere. A subtle smile was his cue to join her.

As he approached, Jessica turned around and leaned against the rail, pretending to look at a visitor's guide while she scanned the small café recommended to them by Taavi.

"Hungry?" Nathan asked as he joined her.

"A bit," she replied, playing her part.

"What does the guide say about this place?"

Jessica glanced in either direction again, speaking in hushed tones. "Only a few customers. Two public exits, plus a private one in the back. Two waiters, both too scrawny to be ops. The cook is good-sized, but I'm betting he's just a cook. If it's a trap, we go through the kitchen, out the back, quick right, and then through the back door of the curio shop on the left. Up the stairs to the apartment above, onto the roof, and then run along the roof back toward the pier. Jump off onto the awning at the end of the building, then down the pier, into the water, and swim to the jump sub."

Nathan looked shocked.

"What?"

"You figured all that out in five minutes?"

"The cook has a thing for one of the waiters," she shrugged. "Keeps coming out of the kitchen to chat with him. I can see the curio shop's back door between the buildings to the right. The girl in the apartment above works there. I saw her come down."

"And none of the passersby were suspicious?"

"None were threatening, no repeats, no lingerers. No one standing around in the distance."

"Is he inside?" Nathan wondered.

"Not that I can tell," Jessica replied, "but if he's in the booth that Taavi suggested, we wouldn't be able to see him."

"What's the abort word?"

"If I say something gives me gas, we leave."

"What if there is something on the menu that *does* give you gas?" Nathan joked.

"Nothing gives me gas," Jessica replied, dragging him by the hand toward the café.

"Good to know," Nathan replied.

Jessica smiled, trying to appear carefree and happy, like one might expect to look on vacation. They entered the café, stepping up to the reception stand, where they were greeted almost immediately.

"Two?" the young waiter asked.

"We're supposed to meet someone," Jessica replied. "An older gentleman."

"I believe he was expecting one," the waiter replied.

"I decided to bring her along at the last minute," Nathan told him.

"More like I *made* him," Jessica laughed.

"Of course," the waiter replied. "This way, please."

Jessica visually scanned the young man for any signs of a weapon as he turned, spotted none, and then followed him into the café.

The room was small, with fewer than a dozen tables. The decor was unremarkable, but clean, and the aroma from the kitchen was not unpleasant. As expected, the place was not yet busy, but she could see they were preparing for the morning breakfast rush by the large tray of condiments the other waiter was using to stock the tables.

"Would you like anything to drink?" the waiter asked them as he stopped next to the corner booth and gestured toward it.

"Two waters to start," Jessica replied.

Jessica stepped around the corner of the booth and looked. There sat an elderly, but fit-looking, man with distinguished, gray hair, and a look of confidence on his face. He was dressed in casual attire, although a bit more coiffed compared to most of the patrons.

"Mind if we join you, General?" Jessica asked.

The man stood with grace and precision, unsurprised by her presence. "Please, I am retired. The reference to rank is not necessary." He looked at Nathan, a content smile creeping onto his face. "I am pleased you could make it," he commented, sitting back down.

"Kind of a difficult invitation to pass up," Nathan replied as he took his seat and scooted over to make room for Jessica, whom he knew wanted to sit on the outside edge of the booth.

"I must say, you look a bit younger than I expected."

"I get that a lot," Nathan replied, picking up a menu.

"I took the liberty of ordering for us," the general announced. "I assumed you would not want this to take any longer than necessary. I hope you do not mind."

"Depends on what you ordered," Jessica said.

"Dollag and quaba eggs, ala Harra," the general replied. "They say this place prepares it in quite a unique way."

"Steak and eggs works for me," Nathan replied.

"You must be the infamous Jessica Nash," the general said. "It is an honor. You are probably the most formidable female I have ever met, my third wife not included."

"Gee, thanks."

"I would ask how you are able to come and go from a Dusahn-held world so easily," the general said, "but I doubt you would tell me."

"Smarter than he looks," Jessica mumbled.

"Behave," Nathan scolded. "So, what did you want to discuss, General?"

"Our futures."

"*Our* futures," Nathan noted.

"Correct," the general replied. "I believe we can help one another."

"Aren't our goals in opposition?" Nathan wondered.

"You might be surprised."

"Try me."

"I want peace for the Dusahn," the general stated plainly, getting directly to business.

"A warrior caste that wants peace," Jessica said, trying not to laugh.

Nathan flashed her a sidelong glance of disapproval as he spoke. "Forgive me if I find that difficult to believe. You see, nothing the Dusahn have done since they arrived would indicate such a goal."

"I speak the truth," the general insisted.

"You speak for *Lord* Dusahn?" Nathan asked.

"I speak as the oldest living member of the caste," the general replied. "I speak as one who knows the hearts and minds of those who serve under our lord... most of whom do not share his thirst for conquest and expansion." The general leaned back in his seat as the waiter arrived with three plates.

"I took the liberty of adding a third order of the same," the waiter said. "If you require something different..."

"This will be fine," the general replied. As soon as he left, he continued. "The Dusahn were once the noblest of all the warrior castes. Our leaders were part of the twelve founding castes of the Jung

Empire, all of them founded by the sons of Kristoff Jung, himself."

"Wait, it's pronounced *Young*?" Jessica wondered.

"A common mistake. It does not translate well into English."

"And all this time I thought the Jung Empire was founded by some oriental dude," she chuckled.

"It was founded by Kristoff Jung, the captain of the ship that brought the first colonists to Nor-Patri, just before the bio-digital plague swept through the core worlds. The plague had already killed the advance team on Nor-Patri. They could not return to the core, and they could not survive without support from those same worlds. So, Kristoff Jung took it upon himself to coerce nearby settlements to share their resources with everyone within reach of his lone ship, the Estebbe. But his noble efforts were eventually corrupted by the sons of his twelve wives. Within a few generations, the coerced became the conquered, and the Jung Empire was born."

"You had us come all the way here for a lesson on Jung history?" Jessica wondered, sounding a bit annoyed.

"It is necessary to set the context for my sentiments," General Hesson assured her.

"Ignore her," Nathan insisted. "She's not a morning person."

"I'm sure you will see the parallels soon enough," the general assured them. "You see, for centuries, the sons of Kristoff Jung twisted their father's survivalist logic to meet their own desires for power and glory. It wasn't until the original twelve castes subdivided, and grew in numbers, that the disputes between philosophies began. The Dusahn were cast out, not because they disagreed with the growing desire for peace among the new castes, but because they failed to honor the decision to stop the expansion of the empire."

"It was my understanding that the Dusahn led a revolt," Nathan told the general.

"History depends on who is telling it," General Hesson replied. "The Dusahn were ordered to relinquish their military assets; namely, their ships. Their captains were given the option of swearing allegiance to the new leaders of the empire, the isolationist castes, or to give up their commands... something they would never do. The new leaders *knew* this. They *knew* the Dusahn would not hand over their ships. *They* started their own civil war, as a way to convince the population that the old expansionist ways of the empire were detrimental to their very future."

"Your leaders could have just taken the oath and avoided the bloodshed," Nathan suggested.

"Agreed, but the structure of the Dusahn caste at the time simply would not allow it. You're talking about a caste that had been conquering other worlds on behalf of the empire for more than five hundred years."

"From what I've seen, the Dusahn are no different now," Nathan observed.

"You only see what we show you," the general replied. "There is far more going on behind the curtain. Ours is a caste in turmoil. It has been such for the last four generations, going all the way back to when I was but a lad. Our caste has wandered the stars for centuries, searching for a place to call home. But our leaders were not satisfied with just a 'home'. They wanted to build a *new* empire, one that would someday return to defeat the Jung Empire, making it their own, as they feel they should have done in the beginning, all those centuries ago. But, with each passing generation, the unrest grows. These men have not grown up with the tales of glory in battle. They lust not for such things. The Dusahn have had to mix with the races they have conquered in order to maintain their numbers. This has turned generations of men, who should have been fierce warriors, into husbands and fathers who want to be home with their families each night. They no longer seek glorious deaths in battle but, instead, want to *survive* for the *sake* of their families. This is the reason we have been forced to automate much of our operations. It is also the reason for the Zen-Anor."

"As a student of history, this is all very fascinating," Nathan said. "However, I am here on a world whose leader wishes to see my ship and my people destroyed, and my body swinging from a noose in his courtyard. Unless you have something to offer, this meeting is over."

"You cannot defeat the Dusahn by simply destroying our fleet." General Hesson proclaimed. "Even if you could, Lord Dusahn would simply execute the populations of every world he controls, until you surrender."

"Then, why hasn't he done so?" Jessica wondered.

"Because he needs to defeat you in battle," the general explained. "His ego demands it."

"His ego," Nathan said.

"He was not the heir apparent to the Dusahn lordship," the general explained. "That was to go to his oldest brother. He was actually fourth in line."

"Then, how did he end up as lord?" Nathan asked.

"He spent more than a decade training in the ways of the Chankarti."

"Chankarti?" Jessica asked.

"The highest form of personal combat."

"Hand-to-hand?"

"Yes, and with hand weapons such as knives and swords, as well," the general told her. "His dedication to the art was so intense that he surpassed the skills of his masters. He then proceeded to challenge each of his brothers to combat, killing them all until he became lord of the caste."

"He killed his own brothers?" Jessica said in disbelief.

Nathan said nothing.

"I realize it is difficult to understand," General Hesson admitted. "If you understood our ways, it would make more sense to you, I am certain."

"Don't be," Jessica retorted.

"You want me to fight him, don't you?" Nathan surmised.

"What?" Jessica snapped.

"If you defeat our ships...even if you kill him in the process, there will be survivors who would seek revenge. Not all of us have softened over the years. Killing the leader of the caste in personal combat will make *you* the lord of the caste, at which point you can disband it, and allow us all to live out our lives in peace."

"That's insane," Jessica spouted.

"And it still won't guarantee that some pissed off Dusahn—say, a Zen-Anor—won't come looking for me later," Nathan added.

"The same would be true if you simply destroyed our fleet and drove us from the Pentaurus sector," General Hesson insisted. "At least, this way, the majority of the Dusahn would not be gunning for you."

"This has got to be the worst offer I've ever heard," Jessica declared, scowling at the old man. "We should just lob a handful of jump missiles into Lord Dusahn's palace while he's taking a dump and be done with them all."

"And have tens of thousands of Dusahn troops, not to mention their ships, looking for vengeance?" Nathan added. He looked at General Hesson, "Suppose I decided to challenge him to personal combat. Why wouldn't he just kill me the moment I arrived?"

"No one would follow him if he broke the Dusahn code," the general explained.

"The same code that allows you to kill your own brothers, in order to seize power," Jessica commented.

"However, there is one complication," the general warned.

"This is bullshit," she told Nathan. "This is some elaborate trap."

Nathan was not listening to her, but rather he was recalling all the moments in history where similar events had changed the course of civilizations, for better or worse. "Which is?" Nathan asked.

"You are not Jung. Therefore, you cannot fight him for the lordship."

"Then, why even bring it up?" Nathan asked.

"*I* can challenge him and invoke the right of *Can-chor-ti-rye.* The right to choose a champion to fight on my behalf."

"That makes even less sense," Jessica laughed.

"Few of us have reached the age and position that gives us the right of *Can-chor-ti-rye,*" General Hesson explained. "Our leaders usually find a way to be rid of us before we reach that point."

"Why didn't Lord Dusahn get rid of you?"

"Out of respect for his father, who had placed considerable trust in me. Also, I was one of the only generals who stayed with him after he'd fought and killed his brothers to seize the lordship."

"This is just a scam," Jessica said. "He gets *you* to kill Lord Dusahn in personal combat and then takes control of the Dusahn Empire, himself. You do the dirty work, and he reaps the reward."

"Not if we defeat the Dusahn fleet first," Nathan said.

"He'd still be in charge."

"Of what?" Nathan said. "Ten thousand troops on the surface of Takara?"

"All of whom would be happy to become citizens of Takara and serve to protect whatever government takes over, once I disband our caste."

"You would do that?" Nathan wondered.

"It is the only way to end the centuries of pointless suffering—not only of my *own* people, but of all those we have, and have yet, to conquer."

"And if I do *not* agree to this plan?" Nathan asked.

"Lord Dusahn is obsessed with you and the Aurora. He will continue to send ships to destroy you and all those who support you. Rakuen has only survived because of its abundance of water and marine life. If he loses a few more ships, he will begin targeting Neramese, which has little to offer them in way of resources. Millions will die. Eventually, he will target Rakuen, as well, and millions more will die."

"I *can* defeat your ships," Nathan stated confidently. "Every one of them."

"Doubtful," the general insisted, "but again, just defeating them will not provide you with the peace you seek; not for yourself or for the entire quadrant, which is precisely what I am offering you, young Captain."

"How do we know we can trust you?" Jessica asked.

"The Rogen system will be attacked again, in less than a day, in fact."

"*That's* the best you can do?" Jessica replied. "Hell, he could be sacrificing a couple of broken-down ships just to convince us," she told Nathan.

"I beg you to consider my words," General Hesson urged. "If not for yourself, for all those whose lives you might save." The general's expression suddenly became more serious. "But you must act quickly," he added. The general then picked up his napkin and wiped his mouth, rising from the table. "Thank you for dining with me, Captain Scott. It was an honor to meet you both."

They watched a moment as the general departed. Jessica scanned the room and the outside furiously, certain the Zen-Anor were about to descend upon them. "We should go," she whispered.

The waiter arrived a moment later, placing the bill on the table.

Nathan smiled, a small laugh coming from him as he picked up the bill. "The old fart just stuck us with the check."

* * *

"You called?" Tariq stated as he, Tham, and Alayna entered Vol's office deep within the Gunyoki platform orbiting the Rogen star. "Did we get another mission?"

"I thought we were supposed to be on a break," Tham complained as he plopped down in one of the chairs along the wall.

"Yeah," Alayna agreed. "Between patrols and missions, we've been logging a lot of hours in the cockpit. Whatever it is, let the new guys take it for once."

"I'm afraid I can't do that," Vol insisted.

"Look, I know most of them aren't that good," Tariq admitted as he also took a seat. "Only a handful of them have ever made it to the finals, but they've got to learn sometime, right?"

"Especially if it's another recon run," Tham added. "Those are a breeze. Even a *rashi* can handle a cold-coast."

"This assignment requires the best we have," Vol stated plainly. "Unfortunately, you three are the only ones who are remotely qualified."

"Great," Alayna grumbled, taking a seat to join them in their shared misery. "Sounds dangerous."

"*Different* would be a better word," Vol corrected. "Especially for a bunch of life-long pilots."

"Now, you're making me worry," Tariq admitted. "What's the assignment?"

"Wing commanders," Vol replied. "We've got more than one hundred jump-enabled Gunyoki now. It's time we broke them up into different squadrons."

"You're putting us behind desks?" Tariq objected. "You can't do that!"

"We're the most experienced pilots you have," Tham added.

"I'm not putting you behind desks," Vol insisted. "Am I not still flying missions, myself?"

"What, then?" Alayna asked.

"You will each be put in charge of twenty-five Gunyoki. It will be your responsibility to get them combat ready and to keep them that way. You will also lead them into battle if called upon to defend the Rogen system or to support the Karuzari Alliance in the battle against the Dusahn."

"Still sounds more like desk work than flying," Tariq complained.

"I'm not going to lie to you," Vol said. "There is some administrative work involved. But you will be given administrative assistants, and you will each be allowed to select subordinates to whom you may delegate some of your responsibilities."

"Now, we're talking," Tham exclaimed. "I'm in."

"I suppose I am, as well," Tariq added.

Vol looked at Alayna.

"I get to tell twenty-five people what to do?" Alayna asked.

"More like thirty, including administrative staff," Vol replied.

Alayna smiled. "Yes, I'd like that."

"Don't let it go to your head, Alayna," Vol warned.

"I'll try," Alayna promised, "but it's going to be difficult."

"Why us?" Tham wondered.

"I think he means, 'Why him?'" Tariq joked.

"There's at least a dozen pilots who would be better candidates," Tham continued. "Damus Inada would make a great squad leader. So would Dosne Hamsa."

"Agreed," Vol said, "but none of them have as much battle experience as the three of you. We have been together on every mission, and you three were the first to stand by me when I chose to honor Master Koku and support Captain Scott. You three also stood with me against our own brethren. There is no one I trust more."

"I have known you for more than thirty years,"

Tariq said. "You know I will always stand with you, Vol."

"The same goes for us," Tham said, speaking for Alayna, as well.

"Don't you need four squadron leaders?" Alayna wondered.

"I will command one of them, myself," Vol explained.

"Aren't you going to have your hands full coordinating the entire Gunyoki wing?" Tariq wondered.

"That day will come soon enough," Vol admitted. "If I can lead multiple squadron leaders, I must first know what the job entails. Nothing teaches one better than experience."

"That's going to be a lot of work," Alayna warned.

"Yet another reason I have chosen you as wing commanders," Vol replied. "I can trust each of you to do the job with little oversight by myself."

"That's a big leap of faith, Vol," Tham said. "None of us has ever served in such a role, not even you... at least, not until recently."

"Which is why I would like us to meet every morning...to share our experiences and learn from one another. Together, we will define the role of a Gunyoki wing commander."

"So, *before* first watch?" Alayna wondered.

"She's not a morning person."

"Perhaps in the evenings, then, over dinner," Vol suggested.

"That sounds much better," Alayna agreed.

"Then, it is agreed," Vol declared. "The four of us are now the wing commanders for the first Gunyoki combat ichis."

* * *

"I can't believe how little faith you have in him," Josh exclaimed as he checked the Reaper's flight displays. "Especially after all we've been through together."

"It's not a matter of faith," Loki insisted. "It's just simple math."

"But it's *Nathan* you're talking about!"

"And if *anyone* could find a way to defeat twenty some-odd jump-capable Dusahn warships, it *is* Nathan."

"He has defeated way more than twenty Jung ships," Josh reminded him.

"When he had the only jump drive around, yes," Loki agreed as he adjusted their sensors, "but things are different this time. The *only* advantage we have, now, is a greater single-jump range. I'm sorry, but that's not enough to beat twenty ships. Especially when half of them have more than three times the Aurora's firepower."

"It's not about the firepower," Josh argued, "it's about the man wielding the gun."

"That only goes so far," Loki replied. "I just think that, in *this* case, it's not enough."

"Then, why the hell are you even here?" Josh asked, becoming infuriated with his friend's fatalistic attitude.

"Because Nathan and the Karuzari are the *only* chance we have," Loki replied. "Even if it's a *slim* chance, it's a chance. What kind of man would I be if I wasn't here, with you, with Nathan, with Jessica? We have history, and every one of you would be by *my* side if *I* needed *you*."

"Now, you're at least making *some* sense," Josh decided.

The sensor display beeped.

"New contact," Loki reported, his eyes focused on the sensor display.

"Another Takaran comm-drone?"

"If it is, it jumped in precisely at the jump sub's return point."

Josh suddenly straightened up in his seat. "Is it them?"

"I can't tell yet," Loki replied. "They're still too far away, and we can't go active."

"Or the Dusahn will spot us, I know," Josh replied. "Not my first cold-coast, remember?"

"Laser flash," Loki suddenly reported. "That's the signal. It's them."

Josh immediately started firing up the Reaper's flight systems. "Start the clock."

"Clock is started," Loki assured him as he activated the ship's recovery systems. "We've got one minute until the Dusahn are all over us."

"Or less," Josh commented as he double-checked the contact's course. "Moving into recovery position," he added as he took hold of the Reaper's flight control stick and throttles.

The Reaper's engine pods rotated into position and fired up, sending the ship into a tight turn to the right as it accelerated forward.

"Speed?" Josh asked.

"Two seven," Loki replied. "Fifty closure."

"Two seven? Jesus, I can run faster than that."

"It's a submarine, Josh," Loki reminded. "Forty closure."

"Lining up."

"Thirty seconds on the recovery clock," Loki warned. "You need to move quicker."

"No problem." Josh fired his thrusters, increasing their rate of closure on the approaching jump sub.

"Don't ram them, Josh."

"Oh, ye of little faith," Josh responded as he fired his braking thruster at full power at the last second.

"Fifty meters, ten closure," Loki reported. "Shit, new contacts. Two octos; active sensors."

Josh flipped on his comms. "Hang on, guys. It's a hot extract."

"Thirty meters," Loki reported. "Octos are painting us."

"Be ready to jump," Josh told him.

"I was ready hours ago," Loki replied. "Twenty. Octos are launching missiles!"

Josh added a little more thrust to increase their rate of closure.

"That's too fast," Loki warned.

"So, they get jostled a bit," Josh replied. "Better that than getting taken out by Dusahn missiles."

There was a thud that shook the Reaper as the grappler made contact with the jump sub.

"Got 'em!" Josh declared.

"Ten seconds to missile impact!"

"Pull them in, and let's get the fuck out of here!"

"Locking the jump sub in place!" Loki replied.

"Come on!"

"Locked! Clear to jump!"

Josh didn't wait for Loki to finish his statement, pushing the jump button the moment the word 'locked' came out of his friend's mouth. "Taking evasive," Josh announced, twisting the Reaper into a tight turn and then jumping again.

"Pressurizing the bay," Loki announced. "You guys okay in there?" he called over his comm-set.

"*What the hell is going on?*" Jessica demanded.

"Hang on!" Josh warned as he rolled the ship in the opposite direction.

"We were detected," Loki explained over comms as he climbed out of his seat and headed aft. "We've got two octos on our ass," he added as he passed between the engine bulkheads and pressed the door override. The door slid open, and a rush of air washed over him from behind as the pressure between the cockpit and the jump-sub bay equalized.

Two flashes of blue-white light revealed a pair of Dusahn octo fighters jumping in only a few seconds after the Reaper. Missile turrets on both ships suddenly dropped open, pivoting toward their target, and launched a pair of tiny missiles each.

"*Shit! They're still with us!*" Josh yelled from the cockpit. "*Incoming missiles!*" he added as he jumped, yet again.

The hatch on the top of the jump sub popped open, and Nathan quickly climbed out. "Did they see us?"

"I don't know," Loki replied. "Maybe. They were pretty far out when they first painted us."

"Maybe?" Jessica barked as she followed Nathan out of the jump sub.

The Reaper rolled to the right and spun, causing all three of them to lose their balance, reaching for anything to steady themselves.

"*What the hell are you doing?*" Loki asked over comm-sets.

"Fighting back!" Josh replied as he spun the

Reaper around. Two flashes of light appeared as he brought the Reaper around, and Josh immediately opened fire as he brought his throttles up to full power. Both octos flew past them on either side, unprepared for the sudden increase in their rate of closure.

Josh twisted his flight control stick slightly, altering his course just a bit before jumping again.

"We've got to lose them," Loki declared as he jumped back into the copilot's seat.

"No shit," Josh replied. The sensors beeped again. "They're still with us."

"How the hell do they do that?" Jessica wondered.

"Just jump us directly back to the Rogen system," Nathan ordered. "Rapid-fire jumps so they never get a chance to get missiles on us."

"What?" Jessica said, shocked.

"If the general was telling the truth, they won't follow us all the way back, for fear of putting all our forces in the system on alert, which would spoil their next attack," Nathan explained.

"What next attack?" Loki wondered as his fingers danced across the weapons console.

"Long story," Jessica told him.

"I'm dropping spoofs and mines behind us after each jump," Loki announced. "That should shake them."

"Whatever works," Nathan agreed. "Just get us back home."

CHAPTER THREE

"I'm sensing that you believe the general is in earnest," General Telles surmised, staring at Nathan from across the conference table.

"I can't know for certain," Nathan admitted. "There's just something about it that rings true to me."

"It could be an elaborate plan just to get you into the combat arena with Lord Dusahn," General Telles pointed out.

"To what end?"

"If the general is telling the truth about his leader's obsession with you and the Aurora, it would be understandable that he might want to kill you himself, personally, in front of all the castes. Doing so would cement his position as leader of the new Dusahn Empire. With you and, presumably, the Aurora eliminated, nothing would stand in his way. The Dusahn would finally have their interstellar empire, and with the resources and technology available to them in the Pentaurus sector, they would soon become a threat to all of humanity."

"Which is why I'm tempted to take him up on his offer," Nathan said.

"You're not fighting him," Jessica stated plainly.

"Why not?" Nathan wondered.

"Seriously?"

"Seriously."

"Because he'll kill you," Jessica replied.

"How do you know?"

"This guy has been training his entire life, and you haven't. *That's* how I know."

"But I'm the new and improved version of myself," Nathan said, half joking.

"What did Josh call you?" Cameron wondered, trying to remember.

"Conathan," Nathan replied. He turned back to Jessica. "I'm not suggesting that I fight the guy tomorrow. We have to defeat their entire fleet, first, and *that's* going to take time...probably months."

"He has been training for *years*, Nathan," Jessica reminded him.

"I'm a fast learner, and you can train me."

"I can kick ass with the best of them," Jessica boasted, "but I'm not the one who should train you, not for something like this."

"Then, who?" Nathan wondered.

"I will train you," General Telles said.

Everyone in the room looked at the general.

"Not me, personally," the general added. "The Ghatazhak will train you."

"It would probably help if we knew something about this *Chankarti* stuff that Lord Dusahn is trained in."

"It would be reasonable to assume that the Zen-Anor have had similar training," General Telles said. "We have ample footage of them in action."

"You're seriously going to do this?" Cameron asked, dumbfounded.

"I'm not saying I am, but I'm not ruling it out, either," Nathan replied. "However, I think it would be prudent to prepare myself for that eventuality, just in case."

"I suspect, after we slap you around a bit in training, you'll realize what a dumb idea it is," Jessica chuckled.

"I'm still your CO, remember?" Nathan said.

"Not in the training ring, you're not," Jessica replied.

"*Captain, Comms,*" Naralena called over the intercom. "*Urgent call from Commander Kaguchi.*"

"Put him through," Nathan ordered.

"*Aye, sir. One moment.*" A few seconds later, she added, "*Go ahead, sir.*"

"Commander Kaguchi, this is Captain Scott."

"*Captain,*" the commander began, "*one of our patrols detected two Dusahn frigates tucked in behind Venshi Seven.*"

"How long have they been there?" Nathan wondered as Cameron pulled up the Rogen system chart on the main view screen.

"*The last time that area was scanned was two and a half hours ago, at which time it was clear,*" the commander replied.

"The seventh moon of Venshi has a short orbital cycle," Cameron said. "Its next orbit will bring it in line with Rakuen in approximately ten minutes."

"Why take the risk of hiding in the system?" Jessica wondered. "They could have just launched jump missiles from outside the system."

"The closer they are, the better their target tracks," Nathan reminded her.

"Jump missiles need a few seconds to reacquire their target after coming out of the jump," Cameron said. "The further out you are, the longer the missiles need to reacquire. It is only a second or two, but those two seconds can mean the difference between a hit and a miss."

"Why only two frigates?" Nathan wondered.

"Force recon?" Jessica suggested.

"Which means it's likely there are more attacks to come," Cameron surmised.

"It would also cast some doubt on General Hesson," General Telles commented.

"*Pardon, Captain,*" Vol interrupted, "*do you have orders for us?*"

Nathan studied the plots on the view screen a moment. "Have the Gunyoki attack the frigates at precisely two minutes prior to their reaching their missile launch point, but instruct them *not* to destroy the targets."

"*You want us to allow them to escape?*" the commander wondered.

"I want you to let them launch their missiles," Nathan corrected.

"We're going to have less than three seconds to intercept the incoming missiles," Jessica warned.

"If we already know their launch point and when they are coming, it shouldn't be a problem," Cameron insisted. "Close, but not impossible."

"Why not just kill them now?" Jessica asked. "One Orochi could take them both out."

"We're already dangerously low on jump missiles," Nathan explained.

"*My Gunyoki are fully capable of destroying both targets,*" Commander Kaguchi insisted.

"The more capable of defending ourselves we appear, the sooner the Dusahn will send more powerful ships," Nathan surmised. "We can defend against jump missiles, but if the Dusahn park a battleship in front of us, forcing us to duke it out, we'll lose. We need to appear more vulnerable than we are."

"*Understood, Captain,*" Commander Kaguchi replied. "*We will do our best to appear to be 'vulnerable'.*"

"Not an easy task for the Gunyoki, I'm sure," Nathan commented respectfully as he ended the call.

"Are you sure about this?" Jessica asked as they all rose from the conference table.

"Am I supposed to be?"

* * *

"Miss Avakian," Nathan called as he led Cameron, Jessica, and General Telles onto the Aurora's bridge. "Contact the Glendanon and the Weatherly, and tell them to prepare to defend against incoming jump missile attacks from Venshi Seven, but instruct them not to change position or engage those missiles without direct orders."

"Aye, sir," Naralena replied.

"You're really going to play this game," Jessica said as she took her position at the tactical console.

"All of war is a game," Nathan said as he continued to the command chair.

"I could use another pair of hands, here," Jessica admitted.

"Will these do?" Cameron asked, stepping up next to Jessica with her hands held up.

"Nicely," Jessica said, moving to her right to make room. "You take port, I'll take starboard."

"Has it occurred to anyone that there could be another explanation for the Dusahn only sending two frigates?" General Telles asked. "Not to mention allowing them to be spotted prior to the attack?"

"It has," Nathan said. "The question is, if they *are* decoys, where will the main attack come from?"

"The opposite direction?" Josh suggested.

"Too obvious," Cameron said. "I'd attack from forty-five degrees off axis of the decoy attack, from well outside the patrol perimeter, and time the attack to occur only seconds after the decoy missiles come out of their terminal jump."

"So, we'd have to reassign point-defenses that were *already* assigned, causing a delay, which would allow at least *some* of the missiles from either wave to reach us."

"Perhaps you should task the Glendanon and the Weatherly to intercept any missiles *not* coming from Venshi Seven," General Telles suggested.

"Good idea," Nathan agreed. "Naralena, tell the Weatherly to handle any inbounds coming from zero to one seven nine on both axes, based on a direct line between the Aurora and Venshi Seven. Tell the Glendanon to take one eight zero to three five nine. We'll take anything coming down the center."

"Do you wish to modify the original restrictions on engagement?" Naralena asked.

"The restriction only applies to inbounds coming down the center. We'll ask for help if we need it."

"Aye, sir."

"Which way do you want us to face?" Josh wondered.

"Directly toward Venshi Seven," Nathan replied, "but don't come about until I give the word."

"You got it...sir," Josh replied.

"One minute until the targets behind Venshi Seven will have a clear line of fire on our position," Kaylah announced from the sensor station.

"Gunyoki Command reports they have dispatched two squadrons. One to the far side of Venshi, the other to the opposite side of Rakuen from us."

"Apparently, Commander Kaguchi has similar suspicions," General Telles said.

Venshi Seven filled the windows of Vol Kaguchi's Gunyoki fighter as he came out of the jump. A quick glance at his tactical display showed that the other twenty-four fighters had jumped in behind him. "How's it look?" he asked his weapons officer.

"This side of Venshi Seven is clear," Isa assured him. "If they are on the other side, we cannot see them; which means *they* cannot see *us*."

"I am adjusting course to skim the surface of Venshi Seven. When the targets launch, we will be able to jump in to their starboard beam, turn, and attack them directly." Vol activated his nav-link. "Transmitting course to all Gunyoki."

"Holy crap," Chief Mando gasped as he read the message on the view screen.

Aiden turned his head, concerned. "What is it?"

"Flash traffic. A Dusahn attack is about to occur."

"From where?" Aiden wondered.

"It doesn't say."

"How do they know?"

"It doesn't say."

"Did we get any targeting orders?" Aiden asked.

"No, they just want us to go to general quarters and await orders."

"We're just supposed to sit here and do nothing?" Aiden turned back around to face his console. "I can't wait until they install more guns on these things. Flying a missile frigate sucks."

"New contacts!" Kaylah reported from the Aurora's sensor station. "Missiles! Eight inbound!"

"I've got them," Jessica announced. "Ten seconds to impact. Engaging starboard point-defenses."

"Direction?"

"Directly from Venshi Seven," Kaylah replied.

"Two down," Jessica said.

"Helm, turn toward the inbounds," Nathan ordered.

"Four down."

"Bringing in port-defenses," Cameron reported as the ship turned its nose toward the remaining inbound missiles.

"Six down," Jessica reported, her tone intensifying as the last two missiles closed on them.

"New contacts," Kaylah interrupted.

"Seven down," Jessica continued.

"Twelve gunships!"

"Brace for impact!" Cameron called over the ship-wide intercom.

"Eight down!" Jessica declared triumphantly.

"Gunships are vectoring toward the Glendanon," Kaylah added. "They are engaging."

Nathan's eyes danced across the displays surrounding him—the ones floating on the spherical main view screen, the see-through displays on the front of both helm stations, the ones on the overhead to his left and right—each of them relaying vital information about the battle.

"Gunyoki Command reports the frigates jumped away immediately after launching the first wave of missiles," Naralena reported. "They are pursuing."

"More contacts!" Kaylah warned. "Eight more! Eight seconds out!"

"Eight missiles headed toward the Aurora!" Bonnie reported from the Weatherly's weapons and sensors station. "Engaging!"

Captain Hunt glanced at his tactical display, noting that the missiles were in their assigned engagement area.

"Twelve gunships are attacking the Glendanon," Denny reported. "They are defending."

"Two down," Bonnie reported. "Octos! Six of them! Just jumped in off our starboard side! They're targeting us!"

"Target the octos with main guns, and keep the point-defenses on the missiles," Captain Hunt ordered.

"Four down!"

"Main guns can't track fast enough to keep up with those octos, Chris," his XO warned.

"Six down!"

"That's all we've got, Denny,"

"Two got through!" Bonnie warned.

"Aurora! Two slipped through!" Captain Hunt called over comms.

"Brace for impact!" Cameron warned again.

Two explosions rocked the Aurora, threatening to knock her crew off their feet.

"Two impacts!" Jessica reported, clinging tight to the edges of her console. "Starboard ventral side! Shields are down to twenty percent but holding!"

"Eight more missiles!" Kaylah warned. "Two five seven, twenty up, ten seconds out!"

"They're in the Glendanon's engagement zone," Nathan stated.

"The Glendanon's trying to hold off those gunships," Cameron reminded him. "I'm locking onto them."

"New missile contacts!"

"Jesus!" Nathan exclaimed.

"Eight more!" Kaylah continued. "Coming over the horizon from aft of us. Eleven seconds out!"

"Where the hell are they all coming from?" Josh wondered as he swung the Aurora's nose into the missiles coming in from their port side.

"There's got to be more than two frigates out there," Nathan decided.

"These guys are jumping like crazy," Vol said from the front seat of Shenza One. "How are they managing to launch and reload so quickly?"

"The targets have four missile launchers each," Isa explained from the back seat. "Twice as many as usual. I believe they are alternating between launchers."

"They're trying to make each ship appear to be a pair, by firing eight missiles each time," Vol realized.

"Two frigates jumping around, firing eight missiles at a time with only ten to twenty seconds between launches... That's got to be difficult to defend against," Isa said.

"Another wave of missiles," Denny warned from the Weatherly's sensor station.

"That's twelve in our engagement area," Bonnie exclaimed.

Captain Hunt sensed the uncertainty in his

weapons officer's voice. "Michael, move us between the Aurora and the inbound missiles."

"Four down!" Bonnie reported.

"Jack, divert all available power to our starboard shields," Captain Hunt continued.

"If we take more than two or three hits, our shields aren't going to hold," his engineer warned.

"Better us than them," Captain Hunt said to himself.

"Six down!"

"Four seconds to impact!" the XO warned.

"Eight down!"

"In position," the helmsman reported.

"Nine down!" Bonnie updated.

"Brace for impact," Captain Hunt ordered.

"Ten down! Eleven..."

Suddenly, the Weatherly rocked violently as the twelfth missile impacted their shields.

"Shields are holding!" the engineer reported as the shaking subsided. "They're down to eleven percent, but they're holding!"

"We can't take another hit on those shields," the XO warned.

"We'll put our best shields toward any incoming missiles," Captain Hunt decided.

"Uh, that may not be enough," the XO said, his eyes widening as he spotted the new contact on his sensor screen.

"The gunships are too fast for our main cannons, and our point-defenses are unable to penetrate their shields. Especially if we must continue defending the

Aurora," the Glendanon's XO reported. "Our shields won't hold forever."

"We stay on station," Captain Gullen stated firmly. "We *protect* the Aurora."

"New contact!" Kaylah reported from the Aurora's sensor station. "Dusahn heavy cruiser!"

"So much for the force recon theory," Jessica muttered as she assigned the heavy cruiser as the primary target for the Aurora's plasma cannon turrets.

"The cruiser is targeting the Weatherly," Cameron reported. "She's having to roll to keep her best shields toward it."

"That's not going to work for long," Nathan said. "Josh, put our nose on that cruiser, and translate upward so we can hit them with our torpedoes."

"Translation thrusters are still a bit weak," Josh warned.

"Just make it happen," Nathan ordered.

"I can slave in the docking thrusters," Loki announced. "That should help a little."

"Comms, relay through Gunyoki Command. The Glendanon needs some help against those gunships."

"Aye, sir," Naralena acknowledged.

"Surely they can hold their own against a bunch of gunships," Josh snickered.

"They can, but we need their guns to help defend against missiles *and* that cruiser," Nathan said.

"Gunyoki Command reports a squadron will join the Glendanon in thirty seconds," Naralena announced.

"Sori Leader to Sori Squadron," Tariq called over comms from the cockpit of his Gunyoki fighter. "We are to engage the gunships attacking the Glendanon. Maintain a five-kilometer perimeter. Do not pursue the enemy outside that perimeter. Our job is to free up the Glendanon's guns so she can defend the Aurora."

"*Let's go get them, boss,*" one of his pilots exclaimed.

"Easy, Salis," Tariq urged. "Excitement reduces focus. Remember your teachings."

"*Oh, please, not that old Gunyoki bunka.*"

"Insulting your squadron leader on your first day is not a strategy for success," Tariq replied.

"Gunyoki Command reports that Tekka Squadron has split up, and both elements are engaging the missile frigates," Naralena reported from the Aurora's comm-station.

"That would explain why the missile barrages have stopped," Cameron commented.

"Not quite," Jessica corrected. "There's still a few coming in, and every one of them is targeting us."

"Apparently, the general wasn't lying about Lord Dusahn's obsession with destroying us," Nathan said.

"Captain, that cruiser is trying to get *around* the Weatherly," Kaylah warned.

"And toward us, no doubt," Nathan added.

The ship rocked as new incoming weapons fire impacted their shields.

"The cruiser has shifted its focus to us," Jessica confirmed.

"Be sure to extend the same courtesy to them," Nathan suggested.

"I'm trying," Jessica replied, "but the Weatherly keeps blocking our firing line. I'm only able to get short spurts off."

"Request permission to get jittery," Josh asked.

"Get jittery?" Nathan wondered.

"We may not be able to jump...or break orbit, or do much more than spin around, but we can at least shift back and forth to make us more difficult to hit."

"By all means, then," Nathan replied, "get jittery."

"Gettin' jittery, sir," Josh confirmed, smiling.

"I'm not sure you can make a ship this size 'get jittery'," Loki commented. "The most you can do is translate around in an unpredictable fashion."

"Okay, so we get 'slow-motion jittery'," Josh replied.

The ship shook violently as another round of weapons fire struck their forward shields.

"We *are* firing back, right?" Nathan wondered.

"Yes, sir," Jessica assured him.

"That's not jittery enough, Josh," Nathan decided.

"Forward shields are down twenty percent," Cameron warned.

"Where the hell are Strikers One and Two?" Nathan wondered as the ship continued to shake with incoming weapons impacts. "They should have returned by now."

"We can't take this kind of pounding for much longer," Cameron warned.

"I don't plan to," Nathan replied. "Comms, flash traffic for Orochi Command."

"Flash traffic," Chief Mando announced. "From Orochi Command." The chief looked at Aiden. "Launch orders."

"Finally," Aiden exclaimed. "What are we shooting at?"

Chief Mando handed the data pad with the launch orders to Ali.

Aiden looked her. "Well, what are we shooting at?"

Ali swallowed hard. "The Aurora."

"Message from the Aurora," the Weatherly's XO reported. "They want us to climb to a higher orbit but continue targeting the cruiser."

"How much higher?" Captain Hunt wondered as his ship shook from the incoming weapons fire.

"Twenty kilometers," Denny replied.

"Are you sure about that?" Captain Hunt wondered. "That will allow the cruiser to slip past us."

"That's what the message says, Captain," the XO assured him. "They say not to make it look too obvious, though," he added, sounding a bit confused.

"You heard him," Captain Hunt told his helmsman. "Take us to higher orbit, but make it look like we're just trying to keep our strongest shields toward them."

"You are ordered to descend to a lower orbit and try to get *under* the cruiser, but remain slightly ahead of her," Naralena stated over comms.

"*That will leave us with very little maneuvering*

room and dangerously close to the upper atmosphere," Captain Gullen argued.

"Captain Scott's orders, sir," Naralena replied. "Aurora, out." The ship shook again, causing her to grab the edge of her console to steady herself. "The Weatherly and the Glendanon have been notified, and Orochi Command has confirmed the relay of launch orders."

"Forward shields down to forty percent," Jessica warned, glancing at the shields display in the center of the tactical console.

Nathan glanced at the time display on the lower, right edge of the main view screen as the ship shook from incoming weapons fire. "Helm, be ready to translate hard upward on my command."

"Aye, sir," Josh replied. "You want me to stop being jittery?"

"Negative," Nathan replied. "Just be ready. I'll tell you to stop being jittery just before I give the order to translate upward."

"Understood," Josh acknowledged.

"The cruiser is descending below the Weatherly and accelerating to pass her," Kaylah reported.

"They're about to get an unfettered line of fire on us," Cameron warned.

"One they won't want to lose once they get it," Nathan commented as he tapped the comm-controls on the arm of his command chair. "Engineering, Captain."

"*Go ahead,*" Vladimir replied.

"On my mark, I need you to vent plasma from the forward plasma torpedo generator manifolds."

"*Which ones?*" Vladimir wondered. "*There are four of them.*"

"All of them," Nathan replied, "but not until I give the word."

"*Understood.*"

"Incoming weapons fire will ignite that plasma, Captain," Cameron warned.

"I'm counting on it," Nathan replied.

"If the ignited plasma reaches the vents, it *could* ignite the plasma *within* the ship," she added.

"I'll only vent for a second or two," Nathan assured her.

"If that was supposed to put my mind at ease, it hasn't," Cameron stated.

"Aiden, from this distance, if we're so much as a millimeter off..."

"I know, I know," Aiden said, cutting Ali off mid-sentence.

"Won't the planet's gravity alter their trajectory?" Chief Mando asked.

"A little," Aiden admitted as he double-checked his Orochi's flight displays. "But they will only be there for four seconds before they hit...*something.*"

"I don't suppose someone else wants to push the button," Ali said as she armed the missile launch system. "Turret seven is active," she added. "Four missiles—loaded, locked, and ready for launch."

"Twenty seconds to release point," Aiden warned.

Ali flipped back the launch button cover, causing the button to glow. "Launch rails are hot."

"This seems like a really bad idea," Ledge groaned.

"I'm sure Captain Scott knows what he's doing," Aiden assured him.

"Let's hope so," Ali said as she watched the clock

count down the last few seconds. When it reached zero, she pushed the launch button hard, holding it down firmly until all four missile indicators on the number seven missile launcher flashed three times and then went dark. "All missiles away," she announced, her eyes shifting to the active missile status display. "Missiles are making final course adjustments." A second later, all four clusters of data on the screen stopped moving and changed to a single word: jumped. "All missiles have jumped."

The Aurora shook violently; the constant bombardment rattling her to the core.

"Forward shields are at twenty percent!" Cameron warned.

"Keep pounding them!" Nathan ordered.

"I'm pretty sure we're feeling it more than they are!" Jessica declared as she continued to fire plasma torpedoes at the enemy cruiser.

"The only thing worse than running away is running ass-first," Josh grumbled.

"Just be ready, Josh." Nathan glanced at the time display. "Cease firing on all forward tubes," he added. "Engineering, Captain. Vent now! Tactical, drop all aft and ventral shields!"

"What?" Cameron replied.

"Do it!"

"Dropping aft and ventral shields," Cameron acknowledged.

"Contacts to stern!" Kaylah reported urgently. "Four missiles! Ours!"

"Now, Josh!" Nathan ordered, rising to his feet. "Jess! Fire all tubes!"

"Translating up!" Josh acknowledged as he pushed the translation toggle forward as hard as he could.

"Resuming fire!" Jessica replied.

The Aurora quickly rose in relation to her flight path, just as the outbound plasma torpedoes ignited the plasma floating outside the tubes. The cloud of plasma flashed a brilliant orange, fading out only a second later, just as four missiles passed under the Aurora, barely missing the underside of the ship.

The missiles slammed into the forward shields of the pursuing heavy cruiser, causing them to flash brightly. Sparks exploded all about the cruiser's bow as her forward shield emitters were overloaded by the incredible amounts of energy dumped into them by the missile detonations.

"Four direct hits!" Jessica reported.

"The cruiser's forward shields are down!" Kaylah reported with glee.

"Pound them!" Nathan ordered.

"Firing all weapons!" Jessica replied.

"Target is turning," Kaylah reported. "They're charging up their jump arrays."

"Keep firing..."

The main view screen filled with blue-white light. When it faded a second later, the cruiser was gone.

"Target is gone," Jessica reported.

"Scan the area," Nathan ordered. "He may have just jumped out of range. If so, he'll send another wave of jump missiles our way first."

"Scanning," Kaylah acknowledged.

"Captain, Gunyoki Command is reporting that the frigates have jumped away. Jump power signatures indicate they were jumping out of the system."

"The jump signature of the cruiser was high, as well," Kaylah added.

"Maybe it was a force recon, after all," Cameron suggested.

"Either that, or the Dusahn aren't fighting to the death any longer," Jessica added.

"Don't bet on it," Nathan said. "Stay at general quarters. Comms, order the Weatherly and the Glendanon to resume protective positions again, and tell Gunyoki Command to scour the area, random search patterns, to a distance of two light years."

"Aye, sir," Naralena acknowledged.

Nathan turned to Cameron. "Divert all available energy to the shields. I want them all back at full strength, in case they come back."

"Yes, sir."

"Comms, new orders for Orochi Command. Dispatch four ships to Takara—full missile spread; military targets only. Launch and return."

"Aye, sir."

"Maybe we should wait a while," Cameron suggested. "Long enough to be sure."

"Sure about what?" Nathan wondered. "That we were attacked again? I'm pretty sure we were. No, the Dusahn need to know that every action has consequences. No attack can be left unanswered. If they think they have the upper hand, they will send more ships; *bigger* ships."

* * *

"Where are we going?" Marcus wondered as he followed Gunwy down the passageway.

"To *my* favorite dining establishment," Gunwy replied.

"I didn't know there were any restaurants in this section."

"There are dining establishments all over this station," Gunwy explained. "Have you ever taken the time to examine the plans for the entire station?"

"Can't say that I have," Marcus admitted.

"You should. They are really quite fascinating. Did you know that this station was built by mining the interior of the asteroid and then building it outward using those mined resources? The end result was a station more than twice the size of the original asteroid."

"I'm pretty sure it's even bigger than that," Marcus insisted.

"Indeed," Gunwy agreed, "but that came much later, *after* they began trading with nearby systems."

"Clever people."

"Necessity often forces one to become more clever than usual, as was the case for my people long ago." Gunwy stopped at an unmarked door. "We are here."

"You might want to study those plans a bit more," Marcus suggested. "That's a storage closet."

"Sometimes, discovery requires that one opens a door that appears to be not worth opening."

"You always talk this way?"

"It pleases me."

"It's damned annoying," Marcus grumbled as he opened the door and entered. To his surprise, Gunwy was right. Instead of the expected closet, there was a modest but tastefully decorated foyer, complete with overstuffed chairs and a vid-screen displaying the Sanctuary news feed.

Within moments of entering, a man in

monochromatic attire appeared from the interior doorway.

"Two?" the man asked.

"Yes," Gunwy replied.

"Follow me, please."

Marcus followed Gunwy and the man down a long corridor lined with evenly spaced doors on either side. Halfway down the corridor, the man turned to his left, opened a door, and then stepped aside. "Gentlemen."

Gunwy entered first, turning to his right, then to his left, navigating the short screen that obscured any view of the interior of the room from the corridor.

Inside was a single table that sat low to the floor, surrounded by luxurious cushions. The room was adorned with rich tapestries that hung from the ceiling, hiding the metal walls. Lilting music played from hidden speakers, and there was a pleasant aroma, reminiscent of the spice garden Neli had once tried to cultivate in their cabin on the Seiiki.

"I'm feeling a bit underdressed," Marcus admitted.

"This place may cater to a select clientele; however, I am not aware of any dress code."

"How did you find this place?"

"SilTek created this establishment in order to feed its technicians during the upgrade of Sanctuary's targeting systems. Needless to say, its menu is predominantly Tekan."

"Tekan?"

"That's how we refer to ourselves, as Tekans," Gunwy replied. "Eventually, some of the locals learned of it, and their clientele quickly expanded beyond the Tekans on station. When the project was completed, this establishment was left behind, fully functional, at the behest of several prominent Sanctuarians. Lucky for me, right?"

"Then, you're not the *only* Tekan on Sanctuary," Marcus surmised.

"Oh, I am the only one."

"What about the cooks?"

"The preparation of the food is completely automated," Gunwy bragged. "In fact, ninety percent of the operation is automated."

"Was that guy who brought us in a..."

"No, he was a Sanctuarian. There are no androids in this facility."

"SilTek makes *androids*?"

"Yes, but only in limited forms. We do not create sentient artificial beings."

"Why not?"

"Most people find such creations off-putting, at the very least. Some find them outright offensive. SilTek has always sought to strike a balance between the benefits and the side effects of androids that are *too* realistic."

"So, your androids still look like robots?"

"Most, but not all. There are some custom-made models that are so lifelike it is difficult to tell them apart from humans, without a detailed examination."

"Seems to me it would be great to have a bunch of androids to do all the grunt work," Marcus said.

"Human beings need a purpose," Gunwy explained. "Even if that purpose is, what you call 'grunt work'. If an android housekeeper enables its owner to spend more time doing that which brings him, or her, their feeling of purpose, then that is a good thing. If it takes their purpose away, it is bad."

"Too much of a good thing, I suppose," Marcus commented. "What are we going to eat? I'm starving."

"This time, *I* will order for both of us," Gunwy insisted, picking up the order pad from the table and sitting down on one of the large cushions. "Is there anything I should avoid?"

"Whattaya mean?" Marcus asked, plopping down, himself.

"Any food allergies? Any gastric system sensitivities?"

"My *gastric systems* are about as sensitive as a rock," Marcus bragged. "I can eat just about anything, especially if it's meat."

"I'll keep that in mind."

Marcus leaned back, pulling some additional cushions in around him. "I could get used to this. Is this place expensive?"

"Very."

"SilTek must pay you well."

"I expect you can afford it, based on your lodging."

"My employer pays for that."

"Surely you receive generous compensation for such an important assignment," Gunwy said.

"Uh, actually, I don't receive *any* compensation. I guess you could say I'm a volunteer."

"Do you work for a charity of some kind?" Gunwy asked, puzzled.

"More like a *cause*," Marcus corrected.

"I hope it is an honorable one."

"I guess that depends on which side of the line you stand."

Gunwy examined Marcus a moment.

"What?"

"I have a confession."

"You're not gonna hit on me, are you? Cuz I've got a mate already."

Gunwy laughed. "No offense, but you're not my type."

"That's a relief."

"I have made inquiries about you," Gunwy explained. "More as a matter of business than anything else. It is standard procedure when establishing a business relationship."

"What did you find out?"

"That you work for the Karuzari Alliance. In what capacity, I could not determine, but you are more than a technology scout, of that I am sure. You have often been spotted in the company of two youths: an adolescent male and a female child. *Relatives*, I hope."

"Something like that," Marcus replied. "I'm sort of a babysitter. My mate, Neli, and I are keeping an eye on my employer's niece and nephew, while their mother is undergoing treatment."

"With Doctor Symyri, I hope. He is the best in the quadrant."

"Yes."

"I trust the treatment is going well?"

"It's a long process."

"I also learned that you have a contingent of highly trained mercenaries as your personal guards."

"*You* ask a *lot* of questions, don't you?"

"Sanctuary attracts a wide variety of individuals, many of whom are of ill repute."

"I'll let that slide, seeing as how you're payin'," Marcus commented.

"I meant no disrespect, I assure you."

"Don't worry about it."

"Would you like to know my conclusions?"

"Your conclusions about what?"

"About whom your employer is."

"Why not."

"I believe your employer is Nathan Scott, captain of the Aurora and leader of the Karuzari Alliance, and the war you are fighting is against the Dusahn Empire."

Marcus offered no reaction.

Gunwy smiled. "I have no intention of revealing your secret to anyone, I swear to you."

"My connection to the Karuzari Alliance is remote, at best," Marcus insisted. "I have never met Captain Scott. *My* employer is Connor Tuplo, captain of the Seiiki, a small cargo ship that smuggles information and people out of Dusahn-controlled space to the Karuzari Alliance."

"Then, why the mercenaries?"

"Captain Tuplo has made a few enemies in his day. He cares about his sister, and her children, very much."

"But eight men," Gunwy said. "That cannot be cheap."

"Actually, they were provided by the Alliance, free of charge, as were the accommodations."

"Your *Captain Tuplo* must do a lot for the Alliance."

"We have been involved in a few key missions, yes, but nothing too crazy. It was more a matter of timing. We were there for them when they needed us most. They have not forgotten that."

"Interesting," Gunwy observed. "Odd that you are so willing to share this information when, earlier, you refused."

"Better to tell the truth than let you believe I have direct connections to the leader of the Karuzari Alliance," Marcus explained. "Especially, since you're buyin'."

* * *

More than forty blue-white flashes of light appeared in high orbit over Takara. A split second later, every ship in orbit had swung their point-defenses around and opened fire on the incoming missiles. The few that made it through the onslaught impacted the shields of those ships. However, little to no damage was caused.

Elsewhere in the Takaran system, another group of forty some-odd missiles appeared behind flashes of light and was immediately met with similar defensive fire. Again, most missiles were torn apart, and the few that made it through found the Dusahn shields difficult to penetrate, if not impossible.

By the time the third wave had arrived, every ship in the system was on full alert, and not a single missile had made it past the Dusahn defenses.

In the end, the Dusahn lost only three gunships and suffered damage to several frigates. However, the message had been clear. *Attack us, and we will strike back.*

* * *

The leader of the Jung-Mogan caste knew upon entering his residence quarters, in the Hall of Leadership on Nor-Patri, that he was not alone. "I would be well within my rights if I killed you where you sit," he said as he removed his jacket and hung it in the corner of the darkened entry foyer.

"Five hundred year-old coran is meant to be shared," a man replied from the darkness.

"I should have known it was you," Dom Jung-Mogan stated as he removed his gun belt and hung it next to his jacket. "Politicians have their own, unique aroma. Much like the doral...you know, that little rodent whose only defense is to release a terrible smell and then run away."

"I did not come to exchange insults, Penta."

"I wasn't aware we were on a first-name basis, Kor-Dom Borrol."

"We will be after a few shots of this gut-rot," Kor-Dom Borrol said, offering a glass to Dom Jung-Mogan.

"Lights half," Dom Jung-Mogan said. The lights slowly came to life, stopping at half-intensity, providing enough illumination to see his unexpected guest and accept his offering. He tossed the contents down in a single gulp, wincing as the intoxicant grabbed hold of the back of his throat. He reached down to the arm of the chair behind him to steady himself, taking his seat slowly as he wrestled with the effects of the beverage. "I should have sat, first," he admitted. "I am not a young man."

"None of us are," Kor-Dom Borrol agreed. "I suspect recent events have only served to accelerate the aging process," he added, pouring another round.

"If you are trying to get me drunk and convince me to vote against the Tonba-Hon-Venar, you will need more than a single bottle. I may be old, but I can still drink any member of the Borrol caste under the table."

"Of this, I have no doubt," Kor-Dom Borrol agreed, handing another glass to Dom Jung-Mogan. "While I am hoping the coran will make you more pliable, I do not seek to change your mind. I only hope to get an honest opinion from you, free from the influence of the council or the reporters."

"Then, this conversation is off the record, Mogi?" Dom Jung-Mogan surmised as he took another drink, this time sipping it instead of tossing it back, whole.

Kor-Dom Borrol smiled. "I have not been called that in some time." He looked at the leader of the

Jung-Mogan caste. "There are not many whom I would allow to use that name."

"I meant no disrespect," Dom Jung-Mogan stated as he took another sip.

"The hell you didn't," Kor-Dom Borrol replied.

Dom Jung-Borrol set his glass down on the side table, looking at his guest. "What is it you wish to know, Kor-Dom?"

"The truth, nothing less."

"Truth is often subjective."

"The *truth* as you see it will suffice."

"Very well," Dom Jung-Mogan replied.

"Can you defeat the Sol Alliance?"

"Of course, I can," Dom Jung-Mogan replied confidently, "but what you *should* be asking is, can I defeat them without destroying the empire?"

"I thought I was."

Dom Jung-Mogan leaned back in his chair, taking another sip of the coran. "The cost will be high, perhaps too high...for those who do not have the stomach for such."

"I should tell you that the public voted in favor of the Tonba-Hon-Venar," Kor-Dom Borrol said.

"Of this, I am aware."

"It was not an overwhelming majority, but it was enough that I have not the right to veto, *unless...*"

"Unless the leader of the warrior castes tells you the enemy cannot be defeated." Dom Jung-Mogan laughed, tossing back the last of his drink. "You expect a Jung-Mogan to make such a claim? Even if it were true, my subordinates would line up to challenge me for leadership, were I to make such a statement."

"The ships you spoke of, the ones that are hidden, where are they?"

"If I told you, they would no longer be hidden."

"Can they reach Earth soon enough to prevent the destruction of Nor-Patri?"

"That depends more upon the Sol Alliance than it does on the position of our ships," Dom Jung-Mogan stated. "We have no way of knowing the *true* reason for their attack. A believed intrusion on our part, or a lie meant to justify their attack in the eyes of their citizens...this we cannot know." Dom Jung-Mogan leaned forward again, his expression becoming more serious. "This much I can promise you, Kor-Dom Borrol: should the Sol Alliance destroy Nor-Patri, the Earth and her core worlds will cease to exist."

"Then, you are confident that your fleet can defeat them, despite their jump drives," Kor-Dom Borrol surmised.

"We will isolate each world, destroying them one by one, until all that remains is the Earth, itself. Then, as they beg for mercy, we will glass their entire world so that, decades into the future, the Jung can remake the birthplace of humanity...*correctly.*"

Kor-Dom Borrol closed his eyes a moment, imagining the destruction the people of Nor-Patri would suffer. "Then, our world is finished."

"The Tonba-Hon-Venar is not about saving a *world*, Kor-Dom Borrol, it is about saving an *empire.* That is the difference between a politician and a warrior. *You* fight to preserve what *you* have. *We* fight to preserve what *everyone* has."

* * *

"My contacts within Dusahn command have informed me that the latest attack against the Aurora did not succeed," Lieutenant Vulan reported.

General Hesson appeared unsurprised by the news. "And Lord Dusahn's response?"

"General Docca did not leave Lord Dusahn's office, *alive.*"

Again, the general did not appear surprised. "How did the Karuzari defeat our forces?"

"They drew our cruiser in close. Captain Fenta believed that he was about to achieve victory and did not foresee the trap he was approaching. The Aurora vented plasma and ignited it as they translated upward. The explosion disrupted Fenta's sensors, and he did not see the incoming jump missiles. His forward shields were obliterated, and he was forced to jump away to save his ship."

This time, General Hesson *did* look surprised. "He disobeyed orders?"

"His orders were *not* to lose his ship," the lieutenant replied.

"He was *not* to fight to the death?"

"He was not," the lieutenant confirmed. "It seems that Lord Dusahn's concerns have shifted to the preservation of his remaining ships, at least until the Orswellans can complete the Jar-Oray and the Jar-Yella."

"How long until they are ready for launch?" the general wondered.

"Both ships will be able to depart the Orswellan shipyards in three months. They have been ordered to proceed directly here and will perform their operational validation testing in transit."

"Our lord is wasting no time," General Hesson noted. "He fears failure."

"He becomes increasingly agitated," the lieutenant said. "He has called for the destruction of Rakuen more than once. Were it not for his advisors, Rakuen would have been the target of the last attack, and not the Aurora. But, as his agitation grows, his advisors become hesitant to speak their minds for fear of execution."

General Hesson said nothing, contemplating the situation.

"You met with him?" Lieutenant Vulan asked in hushed tones.

"I did," the general replied in a similar tone.

The lieutenant was in disbelief. "How did he get onto Takara?"

"They did not say," the general replied.

"They?"

"He was accompanied by a female, Jessica Nash."

"The executioner of Caius?" the lieutenant realized, almost gasping.

"Indeed."

"What was she like?" the lieutenant wondered. "Is it true that she is as large as any man?"

"She was of normal size and appeared as feminine as any woman I have known. Quite attractive, actually."

"Incredible," the lieutenant said, shaking his head. "Did he accept your offer?"

"He did not say," the general replied. "The female was against the idea, to be certain."

"Maybe he knows," the lieutenant decided.

"He would be foolish not to be suspicious," the general said. "However, it would be impossible for him to ascertain the full extent of my plan."

"I hope you are correct," the lieutenant said. "If you are to challenge Lord Dusahn, it will need to happen soon, *before* the Jar-Oray and the Jar-Yella arrive. Otherwise, it will be too late." The young lieutenant noted the look of concern in the general's eyes. "You *did* tell him about the Jar-Oray and the Jar-Yella."

"I did not."

"General..."

"*Timing* is everything, Lieutenant."

* * *

"All I'm saying is that you should *not* have used so many missiles in the attack," Cameron insisted, "not while we are unable to adequately defend ourselves."

"The Dusahn have to know that we will strike back, and with force," Nathan replied. "Otherwise, they will keep attacking until they destroy us."

"They'll keep attacking us anyway," Cameron argued, "regardless of whether or not we strike back."

"You'd prefer we *don't* retaliate," Nathan questioned, "just to save a few jump missiles?"

"What if they attack Rakuen or Neramese next?" Cameron challenged.

"Then, we'll defend *them* in the same way, and we'll retaliate for any attack on any Alliance ships or member worlds. *That's* what an alliance is about."

"You have to think long term, Nathan. You could have simply targeted a few ships, using a fraction of the missiles, and achieved the same effect."

"If we retaliate with limited force, the Dusahn will realize our resources are minimal, and they will come at us with everything they've got. Or, have you forgotten how this ship was so badly damaged to begin with?" Nathan told her. "That is exactly why we have imposed such severe restrictions on incoming and outgoing traffic in this system, to prevent the Dusahn from gaining *any* intelligence on our capabilities. If we strike with *far* less force than they did, they will surmise why."

"If they continue these attacks with *any* regularity, our missile production will not be able to match our need."

"Then, we will build more plants," Nathan replied.

"You're assuming the Rakuen and Neramesean economies can support so many plants," Cameron pointed out.

"They'll have to if they want to survive."

"And what about once the Aurora has been repaired?" Cameron challenged. "How will we be able to leave this system and take the attack *to* the Dusahn, ourselves, if Rakuen and Neramese do not have enough missiles to defend themselves?"

Nathan leaned back in his chair, taking a moment to calm himself. He knew his executive officer was just playing devil's advocate to ensure he was considering all possible angles, but it was no less irritating. "Attacking with less force and conserving our jump missiles *guarantees* a negative; whereas, not doing so only *risks* one. *If* the Dusahn attack with enough force and regularity to warrant the conservation of our jump missiles, then I will consider doing so."

"Nathan..."

He held up his hand, indicating that he wasn't finished. "However, I am willing to listen to reasonable compromises, to be considered if warranted. Work up a baseline estimate of the number of jump missiles we must always have in inventory to defend against an attack *no* bigger than the last one, and I'll try to make sure we don't go below that number."

"And if they attack with *more* force than last time?" Cameron wondered.

"Then, I will consider increasing that number."

Cameron held her tongue a moment. "It's a hell of a risk, Nathan."

"It's a war, Cameron. Risk is unavoidable."

CHAPTER FOUR

Lieutenant Rezhik entered the dining area of their suite on Sanctuary, taking a seat a few chairs down from Marcus. "Nelyana tells me you wish to speak with me."

"Not a matter of want, really," Marcus said. "No offense."

"What can I do for you, Mister Taggart?" the Ghatazhak lieutenant asked.

"I met a guy at the tech markets a few days ago. Had lunch with him...twice, actually. By the second meeting, he seemed to know quite a bit about me."

"Like what?"

"Like that I was here with Neli and the kids, and that I had eight security guards."

"Easily deduced with observation," the lieutenant concluded.

"He also knew that I worked for Nathan."

"Indeed."

"Well, he *suspected*, actually," Marcus admitted. "I convinced him that I worked for Connor Tuplo, captain of the Seiiki," he added, proud of his clever deception. "I told him we had run a few key missions for the Karuzari, but that was all."

"That was good thinking on your part," the lieutenant congratulated.

"I told him it was Connor's sister who was getting treatment, and that I was watching his sister's kids."

"Did he know we are Ghatazhak?"

"He thought you were mercs, so I let him keep on believing that."

"Who is this man?"

"Gunwant Vout," Marcus replied. "Goes by the

nickname 'Gunwy'. Says he works for some big corporation called SilTek. Claims he is stationed here to scout the tech markets for potential technologies to develop and bring to their own markets."

"Do you believe him?"

"For the most part," Marcus replied, "but I thought I should tell you, in case you wanted to check him out for yourself."

"Indeed, I would," the lieutenant stated. "How long has he been stationed here?"

"Not long. He said SilTek gained clearance to come here by upgrading Sanctuary's targeting systems for free. That's pretty much why I agreed to meet with him a second time. I thought this SilTek company might have some tech we could use against the Dusahn."

"Are you scheduled to meet with this man again?"

"Not at the moment," Marcus replied.

"Good," the lieutenant said. "Give me a few days to look into the matter. I am especially curious as to how he learned so much about us, particularly our connection to the Karuzari."

"The only people outside of our group who know are Doctor Symyri and a few of his staff, and the head of station security, right?"

"That is what I was led to believe," Lieutenant Rezhik confirmed, "and that is where I intend to start."

* * *

Kellen Lee nervously paced the length of the small, portable control shack, anxiously awaiting word from the lead installation tech. Today was the day they were to complete the installation of Rakuen's first surface-based jump missile launcher, but it was so much more. By the time the project was complete, he would have installed over one hundred launchers all over his world.

The pressure to stay on schedule, if not ahead of it, was great. Although Neramese's first missile launcher would be operational a mere two days later, it was important for Rakuen's national pride that they always stay one step ahead of Neramese in their ability to defend themselves against all aggressors, be they from outside the Rogen system or from within.

Since day one, the first installation had been plagued with problems. Due to their strategic significance, it was decided that the sites needed to be a safe distance from any inhabited areas. With Rakuen's general lack of landmass, that meant floating launch platforms. To make matters even more complicated, although tethered to the planet's relatively shallow ocean floor, the platforms needed the ability to be relocated from time to time. This added additional complexity to an already high-pressure, highly public project.

"*Shack, Launcher,*" Kellen's portable comm-unit squawked.

"Please, tell me something good," Kellen replied.

"*I think we solved the problem.*"

"You *think*? I need better than that, Cori. I can't have that thing blowing up with everyone on Rakuen watching."

"*We fixed it, Kell,*" Cori assured him. "*You can start the test.*"

"Tenna," Kellen called to his launch controller, "how does it look?"

"Everything's green, Kellen."

Kellen took a deep breath, then pressed a button on his comm-unit. "Command, Site One, online."

"Copy that, Site One. Go active."

"You heard him," Kellen told his launch controller.

"Going active," the controller replied. "All hands, clear the launcher," the controller called over the loudspeakers outside.

"Captain, Rakuen Defense Command reports Site One is active and ready for the test," Naralena reported from the Aurora's comm-station.

"Very well," Nathan responded from his command chair at the center of the bridge. "Relay the launch signal to the drone."

"Aye, sir," Naralena acknowledged. "Launching comm-drone."

"Comm-drone is away," Kaylah confirmed from the sensor station. "Comm-drone has jumped."

"Cross your fingers, everyone," Nathan said, his eyes glued to the tactical display on the main view screen.

On the outer edge of the Rogen system, an odd-looking ship waited patiently. The old, interplanetary, light cargo freighter had been decommissioned long ago but had been pressed back into service, fitted with a single-use jump drive, and had her flight systems upgraded to be fully automated. All to perform one last mission.

A small flash of blue-white light appeared nearby, and a few seconds later, the converted ship fired up its engines, turned back toward Rakuen, and accelerated. A minute later, it disappeared behind its own flash of light.

"Flash traffic!" the launch controller at the missile launcher site announced. "We have a launch order!"

"Confirm the launch order," Kellen replied, according to procedure.

"Launch order confirmed," the Rakuen missile officer acknowledged, turning his launch key to the launch enabled position.

"Launch order confirmed," the Neramesean missile officer agreed as he also turned his key.

"Good launch orders," the controller announced. "We have target lock," he added as he flipped the launch button cover open and pressed the button beneath it down firmly.

Outside, at the launch pad twenty meters away, one of the four missiles ignited its engine and leapt off its guide rail a second later. Two seconds after that, it disappeared behind a blue-white flash of light.

"Good launch," the controller inside the control shack announced. "Missile has jumped."

"New contact!" Kaylah reported from the Aurora's sensor station. "Rakuen jump missile. Four seconds to impact."

Nathan watched the tactical display on the main view screen as the icon representing the newly arrived Rakuen jump missile quickly converged on the icon representing the target drone, which had jumped in ten seconds earlier. Precisely four seconds later, the two icons converged and then disappeared.

"Clean intercept," Jessica reported from the tactical station.

"Target drone has been destroyed," Kaylah confirmed.

"Total time?" Nathan inquired.

"Twenty-two seconds from the time the target arrived, to time of intercept," Kaylah replied.

"Plenty of time for a Dusahn battleship to launch enough ordnance to lay waste to an entire city," Jessica commented.

"If they don't agree to automate the people out of the launch confirmation, the entire system is going to be useless," Nathan complained as he rose from his command chair.

"Maybe they'll get faster with practice," Kaylah commented.

"Not eighteen seconds faster," Josh remarked.

"Get me the Rakuen and Neramesean ministers on vid-comm, and pipe it into my ready room," Nathan instructed as he passed by the comm-station.

"Aye, sir," Naralena replied.

"You have the conn, Cam."

"I have the conn," Cameron replied.

Jessica paused a moment, waiting for Nathan to disappear into his ready room. "Someone's about to get a reality slap."

* * *

"I have Defense Minister Toyon and Defense Minister Koro on vid-link for you, sir," Naralena reported over the intercom.

"Put them on my screen," Nathan instructed. A moment later, both men appeared on the main view screen, on the ready room wall over the couch, each minister occupying half of the screen. "Good afternoon, gentlemen. Congratulations on a successful test, Minister Toyon."

"*Thank you, Captain.*"

The Neramesean defense minister did not look as pleased.

"*I look forward to a successful test of your first launcher in two days, Minister Koro,*" Minister Toyon added.

"Despite the successful launch and intercept, there is still the problem of the time to intercept," Nathan added. "As predicted, requiring confirmation of a launch order by both a Rakuen and a Neramesean officer, *at* the launcher, creates a delay that could cost millions of lives during an actual attack."

"*Our analysis of the launch site control shack video shows only a five-second delay,*" Minister Toyon insisted. "*We find that an acceptable number, considering the magnitude of protection that the confirmation process provides both worlds.*"

"It takes a Dusahn battleship less than three seconds to release a single OSCM," Nathan replied.

"*I am unfamiliar with this term,*" Minister Koro admitted.

"Orbit-to-surface cluster missile," Nathan explained. "A powered, self-guided, fire-and-forget weapon that, once through the atmospheric interface, breaks apart into anywhere from twenty to fifty smaller missiles, each with their own separate target. It takes three seconds to release that weapon from one of the battleship's four surface weapons bays. That means, during the four seconds your officers waste confirming that neither one of you is shooting at each other, enough ordnance to take out a million of your people is being launched. Add to that the five seconds it takes for your missiles to clear the launch rails and jump, and the three seconds it takes for the missile to acquire the target after coming out of the jump, adjust its course as needed, and transit the last few kilometers to the intercept point, and you've got enough time for that battleship to ensure the death of millions, and still jump away unscathed. In short, gentlemen, your fear of one another will make your defense systems useless."

"*Captain,*" Minister Toyon interrupted, "*we have had this discussion before, and the result is always the same. The confirmation process, although time-consuming, is necessary, at least for the time being.*"

"The day will soon come that the Aurora must leave the Rogen system, in order to take the fight *to* the Dusahn, instead of waiting for them to come to us," Nathan explained. "If they attack while we are away, and you are still using humans in the confirmation loop, both your worlds will be destroyed."

"*You promised to defend us,*" Minister Koro reminded Nathan.

"Yes, I did, but you make this impossible by continuing to embrace the hatred and mistrust of generations long past."

"*Our people demand such precautions,*" Minister Toyon exclaimed.

"Your people couldn't care less about the decades-old war between your two worlds!" Nathan argued. "They have seen the destruction the Dusahn can bring, and they stand united. It is only their political leaders who seek to keep this mistrust alive, most likely for their own personal power. Now, the two of you occupy *appointed* positions; therefore, you must answer to the elected officials who *appointed* you. So, I will give you a message to deliver to your respective leaders. Remove the humans and automate the jump-missile defense system, or we will consider both your worlds to be in violation of the charter, and the Karuzari will *withdraw* from this alliance, leaving you both defenseless. Then, you will be free to target one another with your missiles and resume your war. Either way, your worlds will come to an end, and I will not be party to it."

Nathan abruptly ended the call, turning off the view screen. "Comms, Captain. If either minister calls back, ignore their hails until further notice."

"*Aye, sir.*"

A moment later, Cameron entered the ready room. "I take it the call didn't go well?"

"Actually, it went exactly as expected," Nathan replied, his frustration obvious.

"What did you say to them?"

"I threatened to withdraw from the charter and leave them defenseless if they didn't automate the entire defense process."

Cameron's eyebrows shot up. "Can you do that? Legally, I mean."

"Hell, yes. Article four, section two, subsection eleven."

"You know, you could just take control over *all* the launchers," Cameron reminded him. "That capability was built in, and that option was also written into the charter."

"I know," Nathan assured her. "But they need to face up to their own prejudices and hatred. They need to overcome it and learn to work together."

"At gunpoint, though?" Cameron wondered.

"Sometimes, that's the only way," Nathan replied.

* * *

Vladimir watched the displays in the power generation control center. He could remember back, years ago, when he was a fresh ensign newly assigned to the Aurora. He had been stationed in this very department, tasked with the monitoring of the ship's four antimatter reactors. He had been quite proud of that tasking, since it was uncommon for an ensign to be given that much responsibility. Antimatter reactors had always been a finicky, dangerous method of generating energy. Unfortunately, at the time, it had been the *only* way to generate enough energy to operate a faster-than-light vessel. That is, until the Aurora had accidentally found its way to the Pentaurus cluster and discovered zero-point energy devices.

At the time, the Takarans had only just introduced the technology, managing to scale it up in order to power their capital ships. Since then, it had been considerably refined, and the old gravitational side effects the ZPEDs caused for the jump drive had long since been overcome.

In fact, the Aurora had been slated to have her antimatter reactors replaced with zero-point energy reactors at her next major overhaul. Had that overhaul not been interrupted by the Dusahn's false-flag attack on the Sol Alliance, and their subsequent decision to defect from the Sol Alliance and join Nathan and the Karuzari in their fight against the Dusahn, they would still be in the midst of that overhaul. So, in a way, their change of plans had led to their shift to zero-point energy a few weeks sooner than expected.

It wasn't soon enough for Vladimir. He had never been comfortable with antimatter reactors. Yes, they produced a great deal of energy and were very efficient, but they required constant monitoring and maintenance, and their delicate containment systems were a constant threat. Any power generation system that required a method to quickly jettison it, to protect the ship from a catastrophic failure, is one that should never be installed in a starship. That's what his professor of antimatter engineering had said to them on their first day of class, and it had remained in the back of Vladimir's mind ever since.

The ZPEDs, on the other hand, were a marvel of engineering technology. Although they, too, were a delicate balance of physics; now that they were somewhat perfected, they were far more robust, reliable, and more importantly, immeasurably safer than antimatter reactors. The only thing antimatter was good for was a warhead; another opinion of his professor's that had stayed with him all these years.

"Primary and secondaries show ready," his lead ZPED tech reported. "Reaction chamber shows ready for start-up."

"Spin the reactor up," Vladimir ordered.

"All safeties are off," the technician replied. "Initiating zero-point reaction sequence."

Vladimir stood there, his eyes glued to the main status view screen, half concerned and half fascinated by the process that was taking place deep within the complex reactor.

"Reaction confirmed," the technician reported.

"Increase reaction level to ten percent," Vladimir instructed.

"Reactor to ten percent," the technician replied as he increased the reactor level.

Vladimir continued watching as the reactor

reached ten percent of its maximum output. "Unbelievable," he said with a giggle. "Any problems?"

"Negative."

"Open the breakers and charge the main power trunks," Vladimir instructed.

"Shall I take our fusion reactors offline?" the other technician asked.

"Negative," Vladimir replied. "Leave them at idle until we are certain they will not be needed."

"Aye, sir," the second technician replied.

"Main power trunks are charged," the ZPED technician announced. "We are now generating enough power to run *all* the ship's systems, *including* main propulsion *and* the jump drive, once it's operational again."

"On only *twenty percent* of maximum output," Vladimir said, astounded. "And with only a *single* reactor." Vladimir giggled again as he touched his comm-set. "Bridge, Cheng," he called over his comm-set.

"*Go ahead, Commander,*" Cameron answered.

"ZPED one is operational. The ship now has full power for *all* systems."

"*Well done, Commander,*" Cameron congratulated. "*Well done.*"

Vladimir patted his lead ZPED technician on the back. "One down, one to go."

* * *

"Where are we going?" Nathan asked Jessica for the third time since they had left the command deck.

"We're going to meet General Telles."

"On G deck? There's nothing down here but cargo bays and machinery."

"Jesus, Nathan, it's your ship, and you don't know

what's in here?" she said, stopping and pointing to a door.

"The sign says raw materials storage," Nathan said.

Jessica shook her head as she opened the door and headed inside.

To Nathan's surprise, the room did not contain raw materials. In fact, it was relatively empty, with only a few benches and lockers along one side, as well as a drinking water dispenser. "What is this?"

"This is where the Ghatazhak train, when aboard," General Telles announced as he entered from a side hatch. "Captain Taylor was kind enough to let us take over the space."

"There's no training gear," Nathan commented.

"It's where we practice hand-to-hand combat," Jessica explained. "I figured, since you were thinking about fighting Lord Dusahn, we should see just how much training you're going to need."

"I said I was only *considering* it," Nathan reminded her.

"In order to make a sound decision, you should first have a proper measure of your own abilities, as well as your opponent's," the general said.

"Fair enough, I suppose. So, who am I going to spar with?" Nathan asked as he took off his uniform jacket.

"Who else," Jessica replied, taking off her jacket, as well.

"You're wearing a Ghatazhak assistive suit."

"What's the matter?" Jessica teased. "You afraid of a little girl?"

"If you're trying to prove to me that I'm not ready to fight Lord Dusahn by kicking my ass, don't bother," Nathan told her. "I'm the first to admit that you can kick my ass any day of the week and twice on Sundays."

"The purpose of this session is to establish your baseline ability, and to determine how quickly you learn and adapt," General Telles explained. "This information will give us half of the data you need to make your decision, if and when the time comes."

"What's the other half?" Nathan wondered as he took off his boots.

"How good Lord Dusahn is," the general replied.

"Of course."

"Don't worry, Skipper, I'll go easy on you," Jessica teased. "Hell, I'll even turn off my super-undies."

Nathan twisted back and forth a few times, loosening up. At the same time, Jessica went through a series of unusual moves. "What are you doing?"

"She is performing the *Kentora*," General Telles explained. "It is a series of moves designed to quickly stretch every muscle in the body prior to training."

"Maybe I should learn that?"

"If we train you, you will," the general replied.

After a few moments, Jessica finished her Kentora, returning to a normal standing position. "Ready to be embarrassed?" she asked with a wry smile on her face.

"You can stop trying to psych me out," Nathan said as he stepped forward and prepared for whatever was about to happen, "I'm already scared of you."

Jessica's smile grew more pronounced. "At least you're not stupid."

"I'm still your commanding officer, remember."

"At least you're not stupid...*sir*."

"Your opponent will start with a basic attack combination, against which you will do your best to defend," General Telles explained. "Do not try to counterattack, as I am only trying to analyze your defensive skills, at the moment."

"Are you ready?" Jessica asked.

"Show me what you've got," he replied, raising his hands and settling into his stance.

Jessica also assumed a fighting stance, although hers appeared somewhat more relaxed and confident than her captain's. She waited only a few seconds, then went through a basic left-right-left combination of punches, all of them targeting his face.

Nathan blocked all three punches with all the skill and efficiency expected of an officer who had just completed basic, personal combat training.

"Well done, Captain," the general congratulated. "You did not give any ground to your opponent."

"It's not the first time that she and I have sparred since my memory was restored," Nathan admitted.

"You're actually a little faster than the last time we sparred," Jessica admitted. "Have you been training without me?"

"Not that I can remember," Nathan replied, feeling good about himself.

"Try another combination," General Telles suggested.

"Anything in particular?" she wondered.

"Surprise us."

"Can do," Jessica replied, taking her combat stance once again.

Nathan, too, prepared himself and was immediately under attack again. This time, Jessica delivered six blows, ending with a spin, which brought her right elbow around in an attempt to catch him in the chin. Nathan, however, instinctively leaned back just enough to avoid her elbow.

"Excellent," General Telles praised. "There may be hope for you, Captain."

"Gee, thanks."

"Your moves are fluid and efficient, and you do not seem to be expending undue energy," the general continued as he stepped forward. "However, I would like you to try something." The general took Nathan's place, facing Jessica. "Repeat that last series of attacks, Lieutenant Commander, but at one quarter speed."

Jessica began the same sequence of attacks, albeit at a much slower pace.

"Instead of actually blocking your opponent's blows," the general explained as he demonstrated, "redirect them just enough so they make no contact with you at all. Any less, and you will be struck; any more, and you are wasting energy. In addition, your opponent will be expending more energy, as their movements will be traveling their full range. It may also increase the time between blows, making them a bit easier to manage." The general dealt with Jessica's elbow in the same fashion as Nathan, but leaned to his left, as well as back. "Did you notice the difference between my last evasive move and yours?"

"You leaned to your left, as well as back," Nathan replied, "which means that you did not have to lean back as far."

"It also adjusted my center of balance, making me better prepared for the next attack," the general added, stepping back to make room for Nathan. "Many think that personal combat is about remaining calm, defending oneself, and waiting for an opportunity to attack. While all that is true, there is more to it. There is analysis, anticipation, and strategy. Personal combat is much like fighting a war. You must gather intelligence on your opponent. This you do by watching how they attack and how they defend. You measure the strength of their blows to determine how many of them you can tolerate. You try to spot patterns, favorite moves, and weaknesses in both offense and defense. It is not about strength, speed, or training. It is about awareness, focus, and control. Control of yourself *and* your opponent."

"Understood," Nathan replied.

"Now, Lieutenant Commander, the same moves at normal speed," the general instructed.

Jessica looked at Nathan. "Ready?"

"Ready," he replied, again assuming position.

Jessica launched her attack again, and Nathan defended as expected, this time redirecting her blows as the general had suggested.

"Very good. You learn quickly," the general praised. "Again, at full speed. Do not hold back."

"Are you sure?" Jessica asked.

"I am," the general assured her.

"Let me have it," Nathan insisted.

"Okay," Jessica shrugged, immediately launching her attack. She quickly delivered all six moves but continued further, sweeping her leg. Nathan managed to hop over her leg, then spun around to his left to avoid the blow he expected to come next, which was her opposite hand coming around as her body continued to rotate.

But it wasn't her hand, it was her opposite knee, and it caught him in the side, hard, knocking the wind from him. A split second later, he felt a sharp blow to the left side of his neck. Before he knew what was happening, he was on his back, his right hand flipped over and held tightly by Jessica's left hand, her foot on his throat, and a grin on her face.

"I thought you were supposed to stick to the same moves," Nathan was barely able to say.

"Sorry," she said, removing her foot from his throat and releasing his hand. "I guess I got carried away."

"Isn't that cheating?" Nathan accused.

Jessica reached out and pulled him up from the floor. "No such thing."

"The first rule of personal combat is that there are no rules," General Telles told him.

"You could have told me that to begin with," Nathan complained, shaking out his hand.

"It seems rather obvious, don't you think?" the general replied, smiling.

"Don't enjoy this too much," Nathan told the general. "You either," he said to Jessica.

"Shall we continue?" the general asked.

"Do I have a choice?" Nathan wondered.

Jessica smiled. "Nope."

* * *

"Good morning, Commander," Nathan greeted as he sat across the table from Vladimir, in the Aurora's mess. Although he usually ate dinner in his private mess, he and Vladimir met for breakfast in the main mess nearly every morning.

"Good morning." Vladimir stopped eating for a moment, examining Nathan's face as he sat. "Who beat *you* up?"

"That obvious?"

"*Da*."

"Jessica."

Vladimir giggled.

"Don't laugh," Nathan said. "She could kick your ass, as well."

"Of this, I have no doubt," Vladimir agreed as he continued eating. "Did you two have a spat?"

"General Telles wanted to see how I handle myself in a fight," Nathan explained.

"I would ask how you did, but..."

"I did all right," Nathan insisted, "but I'm pretty sure Jessica was holding back a bit."

"How do you know?"

"If she wasn't, I'm pretty sure I'd be in medical right now." Nathan scooped up some eggs and began to eat.

"Maneuvering is fully operational again," Vladimir said.

"When did that happen?"

"Early this morning."

"How long have you been up?"

"Five hours," Vladimir replied. "This is my second breakfast."

"You were up at oh-three hundred?"

"There is still a lot of work to do."

"How long until main propulsion is back?" Nathan wondered.

"About a week," Vladimir replied. "You have about twenty percent capability right now, using only the inboard drives."

"What about the second ZPED?"

"Five or six days. The second one is always easier than the first."

"How are things going with the jump arrays?"

"On schedule. You should have long-range jump capability in about ten days."

"Not a moment too soon," Nathan said. "We can't hold the Dusahn off forever. Sooner or later, they're going to send in everything they've got and glass both Rakuen *and* Neramese."

"Surely, they realize we can just go find another ally," Vladimir said.

"Of course, but that takes time, during which the Dusahn will build more ships, making them more difficult to defeat."

"Then, you *are* going to fight him?"

"Not if I don't have to," Nathan said, "but I'm starting to wonder if I even have a choice. If what General Hesson said is true, destroying the Dusahn fleet may *cost* more lives than it *saves*. Do I even have the right to make such a decision; to doom billions?"

"You can't think of it that way," Vladimir insisted. "You have to choose the path that offers the greatest chance of success."

"Or the path resulting in the fewest unnecessary deaths," Nathan argued. "If I fight him and lose, everyone else will still live, and they can continue to fight without me if they choose. If I *don't* fight him, and we lose, it will be after months of war, and most likely two worlds will end up glassed...worlds that I promised to protect."

"What makes you think we'll lose?" Vladimir said, trying to be positive.

"That's the point," Nathan replied. "Even if we *win*, just as many people may die. So, you see, it's not just about which course of action has the highest probability of success."

"*Captain, Intel,*" Jessica called over Nathan's comm-set.

"Go ahead," Nathan replied.

"*We've got a new message from our friend on Takara.*"

"On my way," Nathan replied. "Duty calls," he told Vladimir.

"Are you going to finish that?"

Nathan shook his head. "Help yourself."

* * *

Dom Jung-Mogan strode confidently down the boarding ramp of his personal shuttle, onto the deck of one of the Ton-Mogan's numerous hangar bays.

"Welcome aboard, sir," Admiral Korahk greeted as his commander approached. "It has been too long."

"It has," Dom Jung-Mogan agreed. He paused a moment, taking in the sterilized, processed atmosphere of the massive battle platform as he looked around the bay. "It has always struck me as odd that the very thing we pledge our lives to protect is also the very thing we wish to get away from at the earliest opportunity."

"The natural worlds are for the citizens of the empire," the admiral said. "Men like you and I belong in space."

Dom Jung-Mogan smiled. "Of all my admirals, you understand this best."

The two men headed across the hangar bay toward the nearest exit, both accompanied by their junior officers and personal guards.

"I trust the doms are still in disagreement," the admiral said as they walked.

"It is a perpetual state," Dom Jung-Mogan agreed. "We are fortunate that the people's voice has been so clear."

"Then, the word has been given?"

"It has," Dom Jung-Mogan replied. "A Tonba-Hon-Venar has been declared."

"Are they aware of our positions?" Admiral Korahk wondered.

"I confessed that we have many ships that are hidden, even battle platforms. However, I did *not* reveal their locations."

"Then, they do not know how close we are."

"They do not," Dom Jung-Mogan confirmed. "Our decision to reposition our ships for attack the moment the treaty was signed has finally paid off. The duplicity of the Sol Alliance was never in doubt."

"The scrolls of history will speak favorably of that decision," Admiral Korahk stated. "You will be considered a visionary."

"It takes not a seer to recognize the honorless. The moment Galiardi was reinstated, I knew this day would come."

The two men and their entourage entered the corridor and headed for the elevators.

"How many ships do we have on the border?" Dom Jung-Mogan asked.

"Eighty-seven," the admiral replied. "Twelve of them are allowing themselves to be detected from time to time, to keep the Alliance busy patrolling their borders."

"And how many ships do we have *inside* Alliance space?" Dom Jung-Mogan inquired as they entered the elevator.

"Thirty-four," the admiral replied. "Six frigates, seven cruisers, ten destroyers, eight battleships, and three battle platforms. *All* are within one month's journey of Sol, and *all* are running in full stealth."

"Excellent."

"I am surprised the Sol Alliance is still unaware of our ability to conceal our vessels from their sensors."

"They still believe their jump drives to be the ultimate advantage," Dom Jung-Mogan said. "Their dependence on that fact will be their final undoing."

"Your orders, sir?" the admiral asked as the elevator doors opened again.

"Increase the number of ships on the border

and increase the frequency of their detection. Like wild animals circling a cage looking for a way in, we must keep the Alliance's attention focused on the border, while we slowly move our forces into strike positions."

"Why not just turn off our sensor cloaks and charge forth?" the admiral suggested. "We have enough ships to overpower the Alliance."

"I want a *decisive* victory," Dom Jung-Mogan insisted. "Nor-Patri will undoubtedly suffer the brunt of the Alliance's retaliation. Knowledge that Earth has been completely destroyed, and that the Alliance fleet has been eradicated, will ease their suffering."

"What of the core worlds?" Admiral Korahk wondered.

"Each will be given a choice. Pledge their loyalty to the empire, once again, or be destroyed. Without the protection of the Alliance, they will have little choice."

"And if they refuse?"

"We will wipe their worlds clean and repopulate them with the refugees from Nor-Patri. The empire will once again become the dominant force in the galaxy, and Kristoff Jung's dream of peace through forced unification will finally be achievable."

"I am honored to be part of this turning point in the history of the Jung Empire," the admiral stated proudly.

"It has been a long and arduous journey, my friend," Dom Jung-Mogan said, "but the dream so many of us have fought and died for all these centuries is finally within our reach."

* * *

"General," Nathan greeted as he entered the intelligence shack on the Aurora's command deck.

"I trust you are not suffering too much from yesterday's session," the general asked.

"A little sore, but I'll survive. Jessica called you?"

"I was already here, analyzing some recon data."

"I see." Nathan turned to Jessica. "What have you got?"

"A message from General Hesson relayed through Lord Mahtize and then through one of our operatives."

"I never asked how you are getting messages to and from Takara," Nathan realized.

"It is a convoluted process involving messages relayed through anywhere from three to seven worlds, the last of which is usually outside, or on the fringe of, Dusahn-controlled space," the General explained.

"And we never use the same routing twice," Jessica added.

"That must require a fair number of planets and relay accounts," Nathan said. "How did you manage to set them all up?"

"They were created long ago, before the Dusahn invaded the Pentaurus cluster," the general explained.

"The Ghatazhak used them to communicate with whomever they needed, without revealing their location," Jessica explained. "We simply reactivated them."

"The first few required a physical presence *on* Takara, which I handled during my short stay," General Telles added. "After that, we were able to reactivate the others remotely."

"Clever," Nathan said. "So, what did the general have to say?"

"The Dusahn are going to attack again," Jessica replied.

"When?"

"In four days, but the message was sent yesterday, so three."

"Don't suppose he gave a number and type?"

"No. He also said he was only about eighty percent certain that the attack *would* occur."

"Odd."

"Maybe he is just trying to be honest," General Telles suggested.

Jessica gave him a cross look and then looked back at Nathan. "There's more. He sent a video."

"About the attack?"

"Not exactly." Jessica started the video.

Nathan stared at the view screen showing one man fighting three others in some sort of combat practice facility. The man, who appeared a good ten, or so, years older than the others, deftly handled all three attackers, turning each of their attacks into opportunities to strike, which he did. The fight lasted less than a minute, after which all three men were either bleeding, unconscious, or both.

"I suppose *that's* Lord Dusahn," Nathan commented.

"It is," General Telles confirmed.

Nathan looked at the general, then at Jessica. "I'm going to need a lot of training, aren't I?"

* * *

Vladimir entered the Aurora's flight simulator room, sandwich in hand. "Why am I here?" he grumbled as he stepped up behind Josh and Loki, who were sitting at the simulated helm.

"I wanted to show you something," Josh replied.

"In the simulator?" Vladimir balked. "I have a lot of work to do. The only reason I agreed to stop by is because it's on my way back from the galley."

"Five minutes is all we need," Josh begged. "Five minutes to show you how we could make the Aurora the most feared ship in all the Pentaurus sector."

"She already is," Vladimir boasted.

"Then, why is she sitting in orbit, all busted up and barely able to defend herself?" Josh challenged.

"Three minutes."

"I'll take it," Josh agreed. He turned around and started the simulation. "Six targets, one on each plane. Normally, we would put forward tubes on the target off our bow, stern tubes on the target aft, and plasma cannon turrets on all the others. Problem is the plasma cannon turrets aren't powerful enough to take down the shields on anything bigger than a gunship."

"The broadside cannons," Vladimir said.

"Which are great and pack a hell of a wallop, but the target needs to be in their field of fire, which is somewhat limited, especially at close range. To use the broadsides, we have to adjust the ship's attitude, which takes the forward and aft tubes off their targets. So, you haven't gained anything."

"You fire the torpedoes and then adjust your attitude to bring the broadside cannons into firing position," Vladimir stated as if it were obvious.

"Problem with *that* is the Aurora doesn't move fast enough."

"She moves quite well for a ship her size," Vladimir defended.

"True, but she could move a lot faster."

"I can't make our attitude thrusters any more powerful," Vladimir warned. "Not without a complete overhaul of every thruster, which would require a real spaceport and could take weeks."

"The attitude thrusters are more than powerful

enough," Loki said, joining in. "It's the reaction time from control input to thruster reaction."

"Allow me to demonstrate," Josh said, turning back to the helm station. "For the purposes of this demonstration, we've put the firing trigger for both the torpedoes and the broadsides on my flight control stick." Josh pushed his flight control stick slightly forward and to the right, causing the image of the enemy ship on the main view screen before them to shift up and left. The targeting reticle appeared around the ship on the view screen and flashed red. "Firing forward tubes," Josh announced as he squeezed and held the trigger.

Four triplet groups of plasma torpedoes streaked forward from under their nose. Before the red-orange balls of simulated plasma struck the target, Josh was already twisting his control stick to the right and angling it slightly to the left. He flipped a switch on his flight control stick, assigning his trigger to the starboard broadside cannons, and then squeezed it again. "Firing broadsides."

"Aft tubes next," Loki suggested.

Another flip of the weapons selector switch with an adjustment of their attitude, and Josh was firing the aft torpedo tubes.

"See, it moves quickly enough, once it responds, but the lag time means I have to counterthrust well before I reach the alignment I'm looking for," Josh explained.

"To make matters worse, each axis requires a different amount of lead-in when firing counterthrust to stop the motion," Loki added.

"Because there are a different number of thrusters for each axis of motion," Vladimir realized.

"Precisely," Loki replied. "The Falcon's attitude

thrusters had a similar problem, but not so much that Josh couldn't compensate for it."

"The Aurora isn't a fighter," Vladimir pointed out.

"That doesn't mean she can't dance like one," Josh insisted.

"Dance?"

"You know...pitch, roll, yaw, and translate... *dance*."

"Can you compensate for the Aurora's thruster response imbalance?" Vladimir wondered.

"To some degree, yes," Josh replied, "but only because I'm so damn good. But what about when I'm not the one flying her?"

"What do you suggest?"

"Watch this," Josh said, turning back to his console. He reset the simulation and, again, began attacking the targets, only this time with much more speed. First, he fired the forward torpedo tubes, then aft. He yawed the ship around to starboard, adjusting the pitch as they quickly came around and fired, first his port and then starboard broadside cannons. Finally, he snap-rolled the ship ninety degrees and readjusted his pitch, firing at the target above them, which was now on their port side. One last pitch and roll adjustment, and his starboard broadside cannons were on the target that was originally below them, and was now on their starboard aft quarter, in perfect firing position for the starboard broadside cannons. It all happened so quickly, Vladimir almost felt dizzy.

Josh turned back around, smiling. "Ten seconds, six targets, all of them heavily engaged."

"How long does it take now?" Vladimir wondered.

"More like thirty," Loki replied. "However, much

of that is because the helm doesn't have fire control for the static weapons, which it should."

"How long did it take the first time you demonstrated it?" Vladimir asked.

"Sixteen seconds," Loki replied.

"But we only engaged three of six targets," Josh added.

"How were you able to maneuver so much more quickly?" Vladimir asked.

"*And* more accurately," Josh pointed out.

"We asked Aurora for help," Loki admitted, somewhat sheepishly.

"You what?" Vladimir said, shocked. "Without clearing it with me, first?"

"It's not like we were plugging her into the *actual* helm," Josh defended.

"*I apologize if you feel I overstepped my access privileges, Commander,*" Aurora said over the room speakers. "*But I saw no conflict with my current restrictions.*"

"What did you do?" Vladimir demanded to know.

"*I analyzed the maneuvering patterns Joshua was attempting to execute, as well as the data on all targets, combined with the capabilities of the ship's attitude thrusters and weapons. I then used this data to anticipate Joshua's moves in order to time the counterthrusts more accurately. Once the algorithms were successfully written and tuned, I was also able to increase the amount of initial thrust, resulting in a snappier movement of the ship, making it fly more like a Sugali fighter than a large warship.*"

"You can do that?" Vladimir asked in disbelief.

"*The algorithms already exist in the Sugali fighters,*" Aurora replied. "*I simply altered them to fit the Aurora's needs.*"

"It took her like a minute or two, at the most," Josh said.

"*Eighty-seven point four seconds, to be more precise,*" Aurora corrected.

"Will this actually work on the *real* Aurora?" Vladimir inquired.

"*The simulation is based on the Aurora's real-world performance data and is continuously adjusted based on past battles and modifications. Since the simulation accurately reflects the Aurora's capabilities, there is no reason to believe it would not work on the real Aurora.*"

"We could fly the Aurora like we flew the Falcon," Loki declared.

"Better," Josh added.

"Cameron is not going to like the idea of taking the control of our most powerful weapons out of the tactical officer's hands and putting them into, well... *yours*," Vladimir warned.

"But we could fly *and fight* like a fighter," Josh insisted.

"All we're asking is that you present the idea to the captain," Loki said.

"I can do that," Vladimir agreed.

"Yes!" Josh exclaimed with excitement.

"But," Vladimir continued, interrupting Josh's outburst, "do not tell anyone that you used Aurora this way without clearing it with me first."

"Deal," Josh replied without hesitation.

"And don't do it again," Vladimir added.

"We won't," Loki promised.

"*Neither will I,*" Aurora added, the slightest hint of sarcasm in her artificial voice.

Vladimir glanced at the overhead speakers, then

at Josh and Loki. Shaking his head, he took another bite of his sandwich and headed for the exit.

"Do you think the captain will go for it?" Loki wondered.

"Are you kidding?" Josh replied. "The responsiveness of the Sugali fighter was the one thing he wouldn't shut up about after flying it." Josh smiled. "It's a great idea, Lok."

"Thank you."

"And we're going to get to shoot!" Josh added with enthusiasm.

* * *

"Since when did you start eating meat?" Nathan asked, noticing Cameron's plate as the server placed it in front of her.

"It's not meat," Cameron said, "it's a plant called *ori*. It grows in big pods on the ocean floor on Rakuen. They slice them up into cutlets, marinate them, and then fry them."

"Can I try a bite?" Nathan asked.

"You're not turning into a vegetarian, are you?" she teased, cutting a small piece for him.

"Not much chance of that," Nathan replied as he reached over, stabbed the piece with his fork, and brought it to his nose. "Smells good," he said, before popping it in his mouth. "Wow. Are you sure that's not meat? It sure tastes like it."

"I'm certain," Cameron assured him.

"I'm confused. If you like the taste of meat, then why not just eat it?"

"It's not about the taste. It's about not killing a living creature for sustenance," Cameron explained.

"But isn't a plant a living creature?"

"I guess that depends on your point of view,"

Cameron admitted. "But one has to draw a line somewhere."

"Is that stuff rare on Rakuen?" Nathan asked as he cut into his own meal.

"My understanding is that it grows in great abundance. It is one of their primary sources of protein."

"How did you find out about it?" Nathan wondered.

"Deliza gave some to the cook to prepare for me," Cameron explained. "I've been getting bored with the selection lately."

"How is Deliza coming along with the long-range jump emitters?"

"They have produced enough for both of our arrays, and Abby has started validation testing. Installation of the first array should start in a couple days."

"Too bad," Nathan said. "We could use them for the Dusahn's next attack."

"Well, we've added more than thirty jump missiles to our inventory, and both Rakuen and Neramese have two launchers operational. By the way, I heard both worlds finally came around and took the people out of the confirmation loop," Cameron congratulated.

"Not exactly," Nathan said. "They just took out the ones at the launchers and replaced them with ones at the command level. A Rakuen officer and a Neramesean officer confirm the threat, and each arms their world's missile launchers. It's still going to cost them lives, but it's a step in the right direction."

"Have you considered giving each world self-destruct authority over the other's missiles?" Cameron suggested.

"Telles did," Nathan said, "but they were afraid

that one side would self-destruct the other side's missiles during a Dusahn attack, allowing that world to be destroyed."

"I have never seen two worlds in the same system distrust one another so much," Cameron commented, shaking her head.

"Funny thing is, it's not the *people* who distrust one another; it's their *leaders*. Most of them were young men during the Water War. I suspect it's going to take a few more generations for both worlds to figure it out."

"Or a few more attacks by the Dusahn," Cameron said.

"Speaking of attacks, are you still wound up over Josh and Loki's suggestion?"

"I'm not *wound up* about it," Cameron argued. "I'm just not crazy about giving Josh the trigger to so much firepower."

"I've flown with him for five years, Cam. I trust him with my life."

"And with everyone else's?"

"It's not like he can pull the trigger any time he wants," Nathan pointed out. "Tactical *still* has to arm the tubes and pass fire control to the helm, and it *will* increase the speed at which we can bring fixed weapons onto targets during multi-ship engagements."

"I know, that's why I signed off on it," Cameron replied, "but that doesn't mean I *like* it."

"You would think you'd have a little more faith in the guy, after all he's done for us."

"He's just a wild card, Nathan, and I don't like unpredictable people."

"Like me."

"Actually, you're fairly predictable," Cameron

insisted. "You always do exactly what you think is right, regardless of how risky it may be."

"I'll try harder to surprise you in the future," Nathan promised.

"For example, Lord Dusahn," Cameron pointed out. "I have no doubt you'll fight him."

"Hey, even *I* haven't made up my mind about that," Nathan insisted.

"You'll fight him."

"Have you *seen* the video of him in action?"

"I have," she replied. "He's good, but not better than any Ghatazhak."

"I don't know," Nathan argued. "Even *Telles* was impressed."

"Yet, you've been training every day for the last three days."

"Just in case."

"Uh-huh."

"Have I ever told you how annoying you can be?" Nathan said.

"Numerous times," Cameron replied, smiling, "and I take great pride in it."

"I figured as much," Nathan said, smiling as he continued eating his dinner.

CHAPTER FIVE

Vladimir's eyes were fixed on the view screen above his console in the main engineering compartment. It was littered with more than a dozen camera views from the four crawlers installing the first long-range jump emitter array on the hull of the Aurora.

"*Are you sure these things will fit in the original sockets?*" one of the technicians questioned over comms. "*They look bigger.*"

"The base is the same size," Vladimir assured him. "Only the emitters, themselves, are bigger. They will fit."

"*The ship's going to look like it has an acne problem,*" another technician joked.

"As long as they allow us to jump a few hundred light years at a time, I don't care what we look like," Vladimir insisted.

"*I've got mine in,*" a technician announced. "*It's definitely bigger, but it fits.*"

"You doubted me?"

"*Of course not, Chief,*" someone joked.

"*We're probably going to have problems with a few of them,*" a technician warned. "*Mostly around the heat exchangers. There's not a whole lot of room around there.*"

"We can pull a few ribs off the heat exchangers if we need to," Vladimir said.

Vladimir noticed crawler three was not moving. "Crenna, why aren't you moving?"

"*This thing is acting up again,*" he complained.

"I thought you fixed it?" Vladimir questioned.

"*I thought I did, too!*" Crenna defended. "*It's like I*

keep losing the connection between my controls and the crawler's motion systems."

"Do you need to abort?"

"*Negative,*" Crenna replied. "*As long as tapping the housing keeps working, I can continue. Besides, I'm almost at the installation site.*"

"Very well," Vladimir agreed, "but if you have *any* problems with the manipulators, you're aborting and heading for maintenance airlock seven."

"*Understood,*" Crenna agreed.

"We should have waited another day or two, just to be sure," Vladimir's assistant said.

"The attack is already two days late," Vladimir reminded him. "We're already two days behind. For all we know, there *is* no attack coming, and the Dusahn are just trying to slow us down."

"That's crazy, Chief."

"That's what I said when Lieutenant Commander Nash suggested it."

* * *

"Banzi Sector Control, Konay One, point one four one, two inbound, returning from patrol," Isanu called over comms from Konay One's back seat.

"*Konay One, Banzi Control, welcome home. Jump to point two five one and contact Gunyoki Approach.*"

"Jump to two five one and contact approach, for Konay One," Isanu acknowledged.

"*I'll be so glad to get out of this cockpit,*" the pilot of Konay Two exclaimed. "*Eight hours is more than my butt can handle.*"

"I just want a shower," Alayna added. "You got a plot, Isanu?"

"Plotted and loaded," her systems officer replied.

"*When are the others going to start taking patrols?*" Ronny asked from Konay Two.

"A couple more days, and these long patrols will be a thing of the past," Alayna assured him. "Let's jump home, shall we?"

"*Lead the way,*" Ronny agreed.

* * *

"Sorry I'm late, sir," Loki apologized as he passed Cameron in the command chair. "It took a little longer to get the algorithms loaded than we thought."

"I trust everything is in order," Cameron said.

"Validation should be complete in a few minutes," he replied as he stepped up to his station. "Sorry," he told the ensign manning his station.

"No problem," the ensign responded as he vacated his chair.

"As soon as the validation is complete, Josh and I will put the ship through a few basic attitude maneuvers to ensure everything is working."

"Where's Josh?" Cameron wondered.

"He'll be here in a few minutes. He needed to stop by his quarters to change. We've been working on the algorithm since last night."

"I hope your wife isn't angry," Cameron said.

"No more so than usual," Loki replied, "but thank you for asking."

"How is she taking to life on Rakuen?" Cameron asked, rising from the command chair to stretch her legs.

"She loves Rakuen," Loki replied. "She's not one for being closed up inside an artificial environment for long periods."

"I hope her accent isn't causing her too many problems," Cameron said. "I was talking to Doran Montrose the other day, and he was telling me that no one on Rakuen can understand anything his wife says."

"Missus Montrose is originally from the Keller province, on the eastern side of Corinair's main continent. Their accents are very heavy," Loki explained.

"They talk like they have rocks in their mouths," Josh said as he walked onto the bridge. "Sorry I'm late, sir, but I really needed a fresh pair of..."

"I don't need to know, Mister Hayes," Cameron interrupted. "Just take your station and verify those algorithms are working. I want to be damned sure they aren't going to cause us any problems."

"Yes, sir."

"Mister Sheehan, you have the conn," Cameron said.

Loki looked surprised. "Where's the captain?"

"He's in the intel shack with Jessica and General Telles," she replied.

"What if the Dusahn show up?"

"If the Dusahn ever *do* show up, sound general quarters; the captain will be here in short order," she snapped.

"Yes, sir," Loki replied.

Josh kept his eyes on his console, waiting for Cameron to leave the bridge before speaking. "What's eating her?"

"Three days of standing ready for another attack, I suppose," Loki replied.

"It's hard for her," Kaylah said, overhearing their conversation. "Understaffed, with the ship undergoing major emergency repairs, the upgrades, and keeping the crew ready for an impending attack... In her heart, it's still *her* ship and *her* crew. She worries about both."

"It's not like we're not all in the same boat," Josh said.

"We're not," Kaylah insisted. "She still second-guesses her decision to bring her ship and her crew here, putting them in harm's way. Every member of the crew who dies, she sees as her fault."

"That's crazy," Josh said.

"That's being in command," Kaylah told him.

"That's why I don't ever want to *be* in command," Josh replied. "Too much responsibility."

Kaylah just shook her head.

* * *

"Two new contacts," the sensor officer at Rogen Defense Command announced. "Point two five one."

"Probably Konay One and Two coming back from patrol," the officer of the watch surmised. "Two five one is the entry point for the Banzi One approach to the Gunyoki platform."

"Isn't approach control supposed to notify us when they clear traffic to jump into the middle of the system?" a junior officer wondered.

"Probably trainees," the officer of the watch replied. "They forgot to warn us of the last two returning patrols, as well."

"Should we write them up?" the junior officer wondered.

"No need to give them formal writs," the officer of the watch said. "I'll contact the senior approach controller and gently remind her to keep a closer eye on her trainees."

"I'm sure she'll love that."

"Oh, I'll hear about it later, trust me," the officer of the watch commented as he headed toward the back of the room to make the call.

The junior officer looked confused.

"The senior approach controller for the Gunyoki platform is his wife," the sensor officer explained.

The sensor display beeped, demanding the sensor officer's attention. "Two new contacts," the sensor officer reported. His eyes suddenly widened as the system identified the contacts. "Alert one! Alert one! Two hostiles! One one five, elevation two seven! Two hundred thousand kilometers and closing fast!"

"Target IDs?" the officer of the watch barked from the back of the room.

"Dusahn frigates headed for Rakuen orbit!" the sensor officer replied.

"Action officers!" the officer of the watch ordered. "Confirm the targets!"

Two officers, one from Rakuen and one from Neramese, stepped up to the sensor officer's station, looking over his shoulder.

"Rakuen confirms the targets as hostile," the Rakuen officer announced.

"Neramese confirms the targets as hostile," the Neramesean officer confirmed.

"Weapons officer!" the officer of the watch barked. "Activate Rakuen's planetary defenses!"

"Targets are jumping!" the sensor officer reported.

"Reacquire!"

Engineer Crenna adjusted his crawler's manipulator arm controls as he struggled to get the new emitter into its socket. "Come on, you little bastard, get in the hole!"

A blue-white flash of light filled his tiny cockpit, causing him to flinch as he instinctively brought his left hand up to cover his eyes. His right hand jerked at the same time, causing the manipulator arm to push the emitter forward, forcing it into the socket that had refused to accept it for the last few minutes. "What the hell?"

With the flash now gone, he opened his eyes again and saw that the emitter was in position. His smile did not last long.

"*Jesus!*" one of the other crawler operators exclaimed. "*Two Dusahn frigates just jumped in, right on top of us!*"

"You don't think that seat carries responsibility?" Loki asked Josh.

"It's not the same," Josh insisted. "It's flying. They tell me what to do, and I do it. Hell, I don't even..."

"New contacts!" Kaylah interrupted. "Two Dusahn frigates! Two clicks astern! One up!"

"Sound general quarters!" Loki barked as he jumped up from his station and dashed aft to get to the tactical console.

"General quarters, general quarters," Naralena called over the ship's loudspeakers as the bridge trim lighting changed to red, and the klaxons sounded. "All hands to battle stations!"

"What are you doing?" Josh asked, turning to watch Loki.

"I'm making sure the shields come up!"

"Don't they come up automatically the moment general quarters is called?" Josh asked.

"You want to rely on that?" Loki snapped back as he examined the tactical console.

"Flash traffic!" Naralena announced. "Rogen Defense Command has gone to alert and has activated the planetary defense grid."

"Shields are up, thank God," Loki said.

"What grid?" Josh laughed. "They've got like four launchers, right?"

"*Konay One, Command,*" the controller called over comms. "*Flash traffic. Intercept two Dusahn frigates at one one five, elevation two one, four hundred kilometers. Weapons free.*"

"Oh, shit," Isanu exclaimed. "That's the Aurora's position."

"Command, Konay One and Two vectoring for intercept," Alayna replied over comms. "Weapons free." She quickly adjusted her flight controls, changing course toward Rakuen. "Ronny, I'll jump in high and attract their point-defenses. You go low and attack their weapons compartments so they can't attack Rakuen."

"*Got it,*" the pilot of Konay Two replied.

"We don't have the fuel for this," Isanu warned from the back seat.

"We only have to hang for a few minutes, until help arrives," Alayna replied. "I'm jumping in to attack."

The trim lighting that constantly displayed the ship's current condition ran throughout the Aurora, even in the engineering department where Vladimir was monitoring his four crawler operators while they installed the first of the long-range jump emitters. The sudden change of that lighting to red, and the sound of the alert klaxons, came as no surprise since they had occurred only a few seconds after one of his crawler operators had reported the presence of the Dusahn frigates overhead.

"If you haven't got them installed, don't bother securing them," Vladimir instructed. "Just get to the nearest maintenance airlock as quick as you can. The energy bleed from weapons impacts against our shields might affect your systems."

"*You don't have to tell me twice, Chief,*" one of the crawler operators assured him.

A single jump flash appeared in the vicinity of the newly arrived Dusahn frigates, above and a few kilometers to their starboard side. The frigates immediately turned their point-defense weapons toward the inbound Gunyoki fighter, opening fire within seconds.

As the frigates defended themselves, their dorsal weapons bay doors slid open, and orbital-to-surface ordnance began to fall from the open bays. The departing weapons powered up and streaked away, turning in different directions as they angled toward the surface of Rakuen.

Another flash appeared, this one below and behind the enemy frigates. The second Gunyoki fighter immediately fired the bulk of its missile pods, sending more than fifty snub missiles slamming into the closest frigate's dorsal shielding.

Unfortunately, it was too little, too late.

"Report!" Nathan barked as he and Jessica walked briskly onto the Aurora's bridge and headed to their stations.

"Two Dusahn frigates jumped in a minute ago," Loki reported.

"Both targets are launching orbit-to-surface ordnance," Kaylah reported from the sensor station.

"Rogen Defense Command has scrambled the Gunyoki and activated planetary defenses," Naralena added.

"Shields are up, point-defenses are active," Jessica reported as she stepped up to her tactical console. "All departments report general quarters."

"XO is in combat," Naralena added. "Chief of the boat is in damage control."

"Target positions?" Nathan inquired as he took his seat in the command chair.

"Close in, aft," Jessica reported. "Bringing all plasma turrets onto the targets."

"Fire at will," Nathan ordered. "Have they..."

The Aurora rocked violently as energy weapons slammed into their aft shields.

"...That answers that question," Nathan surmised.

"Returning fire," Jessica reported.

"Comms, order the Weatherly and the Glendanon to engage the targets," Nathan ordered.

"We've got flash traffic from command," Chief Mando reported from Orochi Three's systems and comm-station. "Rakuen is under attack."

"Any launch orders?" Aiden asked.

"Negative," the chief replied. "They just want us to jump in closer and be ready to snap-launch."

Aiden tapped his intercom button. "Ledge, Ali, get up here! We're on alert!" he called as he began plotting the jump.

The door to Loki's apartment burst open, and Terris Montrose rushed inside. "Lael! Lael!" she hollered frantically.

Lael came out of the back room in a hurry, recognizing her neighbor's voice, as well as the sound of fear in it. "Terris? What is it?"

A flash of light filled the living room. Both women instinctively looked toward the picture windows that faced the shoreline. In the distance, a ball of red-orange light swelled up from the horizon.

"Is that Pellen Isle?" Lael wondered, her eyes wide.

A realization suddenly hit Terris. "Get down!" she shouted, hitting the floor.

Lael instinctively turned around to head back into the bedroom as the picture windows imploded into the room. Shards of broken glass and a wave of high-pressure air swept across the room, knocking her into the door frame. As her eyes went dark, she could feel a thousand tiny pieces of glass tearing through her clothing and skin.

Alarm klaxons sounded throughout the alert crews' ready room on the Gunyoki platform. Twenty-four men and women dropped what they were doing, running for the transfer tubes along the inboard bulkhead. The first few of them to reach the tubes slapped the buttons to open their doors and grabbed the overhead rail, picking up their feet and swinging into the tubes to slide down two decks, to their waiting Gunyoki fighters.

At the other end of the tubes, the flight crews

came sliding out, landing on the padded surface. As each one landed, they scrambled to their feet and headed out across the wide-open compartment. The deck of the compartment was punctuated by perfectly spaced bulges at the front of each open cockpit of a Gunyoki fighter.

The crews ran across the deck, dropping down into their respective fighter cockpits; the second man to enter, activating the canopy controls to seal them in. Once inside, covers slid forward over their canopies, allowing each fighter to drop free of their moorings and head out the launch tunnel.

"*I've lost lateral servos!*" one of Vladimir's crawler operators cried out over comms. "*I have no directional control!*"

"Try to override the computer-assist and steer manually!" Vladimir suggested.

"*Everything is dead!*" another crawler operator reported.

"*Bozhe moi,*" Vladimir exclaimed.

"*Commander?*" Aurora called over the console speakers.

"*Aurora?*"

"*Yes, Commander.*"

"How is it possible?"

"*You gave me access to the engineering intercom system, in order to assist you with repairs. I cannot help but notice the stress in your voice. Can I be of assistance?*"

"My crawler operators are trapped. Their systems are being affected by..."

"*Energy surges from the shields, created by the*

plasma charges when they made contact. I am aware. May I make a suggestion?"

"Please," Vladimir begged, the cries of his four trapped operators echoing in his brain.

"*The maintenance crawlers can be piloted remotely,*" *Aurora* told him.

"But their motion systems are not working," Vladimir replied.

"*Their motion systems are still functional,*" Aurora explained. "*It is only their control systems that are being affected by the electromagnetic field fluctuations. Those fluctuations can be compensated for, but not by human operators. Your reaction times are too slow.*"

"Are you saying that *you* can compensate for the fluctuations and bring them inside?"

"*I believe so, yes,*" Aurora replied.

"Are you sure?"

"*I estimate the probability of success at ninety-two percent; however, the probability declines with each passing second, since the crawlers' shielding provides insufficient protection against such levels of energy. The operators will be dead in five minutes.*"

"But you don't have access to the external comm-systems," Vladimir told her.

"*That is true,*" Aurora replied. "*However,* you *can give me access.*"

"Not without the captain's permission," Vladimir told her.

"*Then, I suggest you speak to him, immediately,*" Aurora urged.

"Jumping into attack position in five seconds," the Weatherly's helmsman announced.

"All weapons are charged and ready," Bonnie reported.

"Three..."

"Weapons free," Captain Hunt instructed.

"Two..."

"Fire as soon as you acquire," the captain continued.

"One..."

"Weapons free, aye," Bonnie acknowledged.

"Jumping."

The Weatherly's bridge flashed blue-white momentarily as the ship transitioned from its position in orbit around the Rogen star to an orbit above Rakuen ten kilometers behind the Dusahn frigates.

"Jump complete."

"Targets acquired," Bonnie reported. "Opening fire."

"We have valid launch orders," the senior officer announced. "Arm the launcher."

The weapons technician swallowed hard, turning the arming key in the control panel deep within the missile launcher's control bunker. "Launcher is armed," he reported. "Control link is established. Defense Command now has control."

The reinforced cover on the floating missile launcher platform quickly slid open, and the launcher popped up. Its rack of four jump missiles tipped downward twenty degrees as the launcher rotated to its assigned firing position. Within a few seconds of the cover's opening, the first of the four missiles launched, followed in rapid succession by the other three. No more than two seconds after each missile left its launch rail, they disappeared behind brilliant blue-white flashes of light as they jumped from low altitude to their intercept tracks in high orbit above the world they protected.

As each missile came out of its jump, its targeting systems acquired the enemy frigates, adjusted course, and fired their boosters, accelerating across the last few kilometers between themselves and their targets.

Four more flashes of light appeared to the enemies' starboard side, revealing yet another group of jump missiles. As they, too, accelerated toward their targets, they were joined by four more jump missiles, only a kilometer behind them.

The Dusahn frigates had almost no time to react, the incoming missiles impacting their shields as they brought their point-defenses around in failed attempts to destroy the inbound weapons.

The second frigate took the brunt of the attack, its aft shields failing within the first two impacts. The next two missiles slammed into the frigate's hull, tearing it open with their warheads.

The first frigate took several impacts, as well, but managed to jump clear before her shields failed. With no targets nearby, the remaining missiles automatically disarmed themselves and adjusted their speed and course to reenter the Rakuen atmosphere. Their warheads now disarmed, they would ride parachutes to the surface to be recovered later.

"You want to what?" Nathan exclaimed to Vladimir over his comm-set.

"Target two is destroyed," Kaylah reported. "Target one has jumped away."

"*It's the only way to save them!*" Vladimir argued.

"Vlad, are you sure about this?"

"*Just give her access to the short-range comms,*" Vladimir insisted. "*That's all she needs!*"

"I can shut her down if she tries to access any other comm-array," Naralena assured the captain.

"Target reacquired," Kaylah announced. "Five kilometers, directly on our path."

"Do it," Nathan told Vladimir. "Jess, make the helm's trigger hot."

"Helm torpedo trigger is hot," Jessica replied with a hint of trepidation.

"Now's your chance, Josh."

Josh glanced at Loki to his left, a wry smile on his face.

Terris opened her eyes slowly, unable to focus. Her head rang with pain. She tried to get to her hands and knees but cut both of her palms on the broken glass scattered about.

"Mom!" her daughter yelled from the corridor.

"In here!" Terris replied, her voice weak.

"Oh, my God!" Nora exclaimed as she entered the battered apartment. "Dunner! She's in here!" she yelled as she rushed to her mother's aid.

Terris felt her daughter's hands on her shoulders, helping her to her feet.

"Your hands," Nora said, noticing the wounds.

"Lael," Terris said, "she was..." That's when she saw Lael's feet in the bedroom doorway.

Dunner rushed in, immediately joining his sister and mother.

"Help her," Terris directed her son.

Another explosion sounded in the distance, rocking the building as Dunner made his way across the destruction to reach Lael.

"We have to get out of here," Nora insisted.

"She's alive!" Dunner yelled, "but she's badly injured!"

"The baby," Terris whispered to her daughter, struggling to maintain consciousness.

Dunner quickly moved past Lael and into the adjoining room, forcing the door to open against the furniture that had fallen in its path. The nursery was in complete disarray, and the crib was on its side with a fallen dresser half-covering it. "Oh, no," Dunner gasped, climbing over the fallen furniture. He quickly pulled the dresser off the fallen crib and yanked on the mattress that was folded back on top of baby Ailsa.

Dunner's eyes widened with fear when he saw the baby's blue face. "No, no, no," he said as his mind raced for an answer. He picked the baby up, held her to his face, and placed his lips around Ailsa's mouth and nose, blowing gently again and again. After a few breaths, the baby coughed several times and then began to cry, her eyes squinted tightly closed as she wailed. "Oh, thank God," Dunner cried.

"*Dunner!*" his sister yelled from the living room.

"She's alive!" Dunner hollered over the infant's wail. "Ailsa's alive!"

The Aurora rocked violently as incoming energy weapons fire slammed into her forward shields.

"I thought frigates only launched missiles!" Josh exclaimed as he adjusted course to aim the Aurora's forward torpedo tubes onto the enemy ship.

"Looks like someone got an upgrade," Nathan commented, holding the arms of his command chair tightly.

"Target is releasing more orbit-to-surface weapons," Kaylah warned.

"Any time, Josh," Nathan urged.

"Eight new contacts," Kaylah added. "Octos directly astern."

"I've got the frigate," Josh declared. "Firing!"

Four groups of three plasma torpedoes streaked out from under the Aurora's nose on the main view screen, headed toward the enemy frigate. Two seconds later, four flashes of red-orange announced their impact with the enemy frigate's shields.

"Target's aft shields are down to ten percent," Kaylah announced.

"Keep firing, Josh!" Nathan barked.

Josh followed orders, this time holding the trigger down to fire repeatedly. As the torpedoes closed on the target, the enemy frigate disappeared behind a blue-white flash of light.

"Target has jumped," Kaylah announced.

"No shit," Josh grumbled.

"Never fire and wait to see what happens," Nathan scolded. "You fire, and you keep firing until you lose acquisition, or the target is destroyed."

"Yes, sir," Josh replied. "Sorry, sir. I should know better."

"Another contact," Kaylah reported. "Dusahn

cruiser off our starboard side. They've launched missiles!"

The brief respite for the Aurora's shields, which began when the Dusahn frigate jumped away, came to an end with the arrival of the Dusahn cruiser. The ship rocked, nearly knocking Nathan and his bridge staff from their seats.

"Shields!" Nathan yelled.

"Starboard shields are holding at forty-five percent!" Jessica replied, shocked. "I guess that ZPED was worth it, after all!"

"*Accessing motion control systems for all four crawlers,*" Aurora announced.

Vladimir watched the screens, feeling helpless as the artificial intelligence remotely accessed the crawlers.

"*Crawler one is moving,*" Aurora confirmed.

"Yes!"

"*Crawlers two and three are also moving. I suggest you send personnel to assist them to maintenance airlocks five, eleven, and fifteen.*"

"What about crawler four?" Vladimir wondered.

"*I plan to send it to the flight apron,*" Aurora replied. "*However, I am having difficulty getting it to move properly.*"

"Jump complete," the Glendanon's helmsman reported.

"Target both ships, and fire at will," Captain Gullen ordered.

"Acquiring," the weapons officer acknowledged. "Damn! The frigate has jumped."

"Find it!" Captain Gullen barked.

"Helm, move alongside the Aurora's starboard side, two-kilometer standoff. Weapons, all weapons on that cruiser, but remain ready to protect the Aurora against incoming missiles."

A dozen new contacts appeared on Alayna's tactical display.

"*Anyone see a Dusahn frigate around here?*" Tariq called over comms.

"Forget the frigate, it just jumped," Isanu replied from behind Alayna.

"Tariq," Alayna called over comms, "you've got eight octo party crashers at two five seven relative."

"*We've got them,*" Tariq replied. "*Head back and recycle, Alayna. We'll take over.*"

"We'll be back before you know it," Alayna promised as she yanked her flight control stick and turned toward the Gunyoki platform, further out in the Rogen system.

"*Feel free to bring friends,*" Tariq told her. "*Dota Squadron, let's see if those octos want to dance!*"

"Swinging around," Josh announced as he twisted the Aurora's flight control stick to the right and pitched back a bit.

The view on the main view screen quickly shifted, everything sliding from right to left in a blur. The sliding motion stopped a second later with a Dusahn heavy cruiser filling the screen.

"Hello!" Josh exclaimed, pressing the firing trigger on his flight control stick.

The ship rocked as incoming weapons fire slammed into their forward shields. Three quick waves of four red-orange plasma torpedoes streaked out from under the Aurora's nose, slamming into the enemy cruiser directly in front of them, causing the target's own shields to flash as they attempted to absorb the energy.

"They're hitting us with everything they've got!" Jessica warned. "Forward shields are down to eighty percent."

"Keep firing, Josh," Nathan reminded him calmly.

"Trust me, I am," Josh assured him as he held the trigger down, sending additional waves of torpedoes toward the cruiser.

Blue-white light suddenly filled the Aurora's bridge. When it was gone, so was the cruiser.

"Pussy!" Josh yelled at the main view screen.

"Jesus, this is frustrating!" Aiden exclaimed from the pilot's seat of Orochi Three.

"We can't engage if the targets are constantly jumping, Aiden," Ali reminded him.

"I know! I know!" Aiden replied. "What I wouldn't give to have our gunship back!"

"Jump complete," Sasha reported from Striker One's copilot seat.

"*Talk about a target-rich environment!*" the sensor officer exclaimed. "*A cruiser, a frigate, and a bunch of octos!*"

"Give me a vector, Kas," Robert said. "Which one is giving the Aurora the most trouble?"

"*That would be the cruiser, sir,*" Kasma replied. "*They're pounding the shit out of her.*"

"That's our target, then," Robert decided. "Gunners, weapons free. Fire at whatever you can, but attacking octos get priority."

"*Bobby, I'll jump past and come back at the cruiser's stern,*" Gil said from Striker Two. "*Their aft shields are down to fifty percent.*"

"I'll give you a five-second head start, then I'll jump in above her, pound her dorsal shields, and then her aft shields as we pass."

"*Make 'em count, Bobby!*"

"Damn, these bastards have tough shields!" Tariq exclaimed as he broke off his attack and jumped away. "Jova, did we even make a dent?"

"About a twenty percent drop in his starboard shields," his weapons officer replied, "but he'll just channel power from unengaged shields to reinforce them every time we attack."

"We need to multi-prong them, so they don't have that option."

"That's impossible," Jova argued. "They don't stay put long enough to get a multi-pronged attack set up."

"I really don't like the way these guys dance," Tariq decided. "No fun at all."

Another wave of missiles appeared behind blue-white flashes between Rakuen and the Dusahn cruiser that was currently bombarding the planet below. Eight jump missiles quickly adjusted their course to intercept the enemy vessel, but they had come out of their jump a few seconds too far from the cruiser, which jumped away at the last second.

"Second wave missed," Kaylah reported from the Aurora's sensor station. "Cruiser has jumped forward two kilometers."

"Just enough to escape the threat but still continue their attack," Nathan surmised. "The Dusahn aren't stupid."

"Just arrogant," Jessica grumbled.

"New contacts!" Kaylah reported urgently. "Eight jump missiles to starboard! Five seconds!"

Nathan punched the all-call button on the intercom panel, on the arm of his command chair. "All hands! Brace for impact!"

"Channeling all available power to star..."

Jessica's words were interrupted by the missiles impacting the ship's starboard shields. The lights on the Aurora's bridge went dim as the ship lurched violently to the left, rolling right at the same time.

Nathan found himself nearly hanging over the right side of his command chair. As he pushed himself upright, the spherical main view screen flickered several times, threatening to go out completely.

"Inertial dampeners are offline!" the systems officer reported.

"Belt up!" Nathan barked, reaching for his own restraints. "How are our starboard shields doing?"

Jessica checked the shields status display, leaning closer to the tactical console as her seat came up out of the deck behind her. "Starboard shields are down to five percent! If they hit us there again, we're done for!" she replied as she took her seat and strapped in.

"Someone, find that damned frigate!" Nathan demanded.

"She's not on my sensors!" Kaylah assured her captain as she tightened her restraints.

"Josh, if they try to hit our starboard shields again..."

"I'll roll us over to protect our starboard side," Josh replied, reading his captain's mind as he continued sending plasma torpedoes toward the cruiser.

The ship rocked even more violently than before as energy weapons fire, from the Dusahn cruiser directly ahead of them, slammed into the Aurora's forward shields, causing them to flash brightly.

"You need to strap in, Josh!" Nathan ordered, noticing his helmsman could barely manage to stay in his seat.

"I can't!" Josh replied frantically. "My finger's on the trigger!"

"I've got it," Loki insisted, unbuckling himself so he could reach across the center console to assist his friend.

The ship rocked again as the cruiser continued its relentless attack. Loki fell to the deck, knocked off balance by the impact. He quickly regained control and stepped over to fasten his helmsman's restraints before returning to his own seat and strapping himself back in.

"Why the hell are they still parked in front of us?" Jessica wondered aloud. "We can't even jump."

"They don't know that," Nathan realized. "Comms," he continued without missing a beat, "order the Glendanon to jump ahead of the cruiser and take position along her orbit, matching her speed. Then, tell the Weatherly to take a similar position just ahead of the Glendanon and slightly above her track."

"Aye, sir," Naralena replied, bracing herself against the violent shaking with her left hand as her right hand input the commands into her communications console.

"Nice idea," Jessica said, "but they can still turn left or right to get a clear jump line."

"Not if I put some of our cargo ships in their way," Nathan replied. "Naralena, contact our cargo ships on the rim, and get them into similar position to the left and right of the cruiser's track. Tell them to direct all available power to their shields and to jump clear before they take any permanent damage."

"That will only buy us a minute, at the most," Jessica insisted.

"Have all ships concentrate their fire on the same shields," Nathan instructed. "Everyone in front of the cruiser targets their forward shields, and everyone else targets their aft shields."

The ship rocked, yet again, and sparks flew from the panel above Kaylah's station, causing her to flinch. "That still won't do it, Captain," she warned. "That cruiser's shields are incredibly powerful. We'll need more firepower."

"That's what I intend to deliver," Nathan replied.

"New action orders from the Aurora," the Glendanon's XO reported. "They want us to position ourselves directly in front of the cruiser, matching her course and speed."

"That's insane," the helmsman exclaimed.

"He obviously wants us to block the cruiser from jumping," Captain Gullen surmised.

"They'll just alter their course and jump past us," the helmsman argued.

"I'm sure Captain Scott has a plan," the captain told him.

"Or they'll just blast their way through us!" the helmsman added.

"Adjust course and speed, and jump in front of the cruiser," Captain Gullen instructed calmly. "XO, make sure all available power is routed to our active shields."

"The Glendanon is in position," Kaylah reported from the Aurora's sensor station as the ship lurched.

"The Weatherly reports they will be in position in thirty seconds," Naralena added.

"Octos are trying to reach our starboard side," Kaylah reported, "but the Gunyoki are keeping them busy!"

"Starboard shields are holding at five percent," Jessica added as the ship rocked with each weapons impact. "Forward shields at seventy percent!"

"Tell the Gunyoki to ignore the octos unless they attack them directly. I want everyone harassing that cruiser," Nathan ordered.

"The Glendanon is taking fire," Kaylah reported. "They're channeling all available power to their shields, but they aren't going to last more than a few minutes."

"Hopefully, that will be enough," Nathan commented.

"Captain, I'm unable to make contact with Rogen Defense Command," Naralena reported. "I'm not even getting a comm-link signal."

"They may have been hit," Jessica suggested, bracing herself for the next weapons impact.

"Then, get me a direct link to the fourth missile launcher," Nathan instructed.

"Captain, we cannot launch without direct orders from Rogen Defense Command," the senior officer of Rakuen's newest missile launcher argued over comms.

"*Rogen Defense Command is not responding to our hails,*" Nathan explained. "*We suspect their comms are down…or worse. We need your missiles to bring down that cruiser before she destroys half your planet! So, make a fucking decision, Lieutenant!*"

"Flash traffic," Chief Mando reported. "Action orders. We're jumping in close for a missile launch!"

"Finally!" Aiden exclaimed. "Spin them up, Ali!"

"Already on it!" she replied.

"It will take us three jumps to get into launch position without being detected," the chief warned, "and we've got less than a minute to do it."

"I can do it," Aiden insisted. "Just give me the jump plots!"

The main lighting on the Aurora suddenly came back to life, albeit at subdued levels.

"New contacts!" Kaylah reported from the sensor station as the ship continued to shake from the incoming weapons fire. "The Quawli and the Manamu!"

"Comms, send the Quawli to the Glendanon's port, and the Manamu to starboard!" Nathan instructed.

"Cruiser's aft shields are down to forty-six percent!" Jessica reported. "We're making progress!"

"Not fast enough," Nathan commented.

"New contacts!" Kaylah reported urgently. "Four missiles to starboard! Five seconds!"

"Josh!" Nathan barked.

"Already on it," Josh replied, pushing his flight control stick to the right, causing the ship to roll to starboard.

With the inertial dampeners not working, the ship's sudden roll was felt by everyone inside. Nathan found himself clutching the arms of his command chair even more tightly than before, his body being pushed to the left as his ship rolled over to bring its dorsal shields between itself and the incoming jump missiles. The ship rocked violently as all four missiles detonated upon impact with the Aurora's topside shields, his poor ship creaking and groaning as its hull and internal structure absorbed the force of the explosions.

"That was too close!" Jessica declared. "That's not going to work more than a few times!"

"Are the Dusahn jump missiles single or multi-jump?" Nathan wondered.

"We've never seen them multi-jump," Kaylah replied, "but that doesn't mean they can't."

"If they *can*, they'll use the multi-jump to send a

killing blow toward where they *expect* our weak side to be," Jessica surmised. "Then, they'll send a decoy shot at our weak side to force us to roll..."

"Causing us to expose our weak side to the kill shot," Nathan said, finishing her sentence. "Josh, keep rolling us around. Left; right; vary it and try not to be predictable."

"You got it!" Josh replied, immediately putting the Aurora into an opposing roll.

"Comms, get me Striker One!" Nathan added.

"*One more shot to our starboard shields, and this war will be over,*" Nathan said over comms.

"We'll find the son of a bitch," Robert promised. "Gil, you receiving the last missile tracks?"

"*I've got 'em,*" Captain Roselle replied from Striker Two. "*Based on the last tracks from the frigate, and the angles of the last two missile attacks, I'm guessing she's somewhere around position three eight five.*"

"That would make sense," Robert agreed as he entered the parameters for their next jump. "I'll jump to position three eight eight and look back. You go to three eight seven and look forward. First one to find them shouts out and attacks."

"*We looking to kill this bastard or just knock them off their attack?*"

"What do you think?" Robert replied as he pressed the jump button on his gunship's flight control stick.

"You can't do this!" the junior missile officer objected. "They'll throw you in prison, or worse!"

"If there's something worse than everyone *dying,*

I don't want to know," the senior officer replied. "Now, insert your damned key, and switch to manual override, NOW!"

The junior officer shook his head as he inserted his key and turned it to the appropriate position. The launcher status display switched from remote active to manual. "Launcher is in manual," the junior officer announced. He looked at the senior officer. "You now have launch control. I hope you're right."

"So do I," the senior officer said as he typed in the targeting data. After a few seconds, he pressed the launch button, repeating, "So do I."

"Fifteen seconds to launch," Chief Mando warned.

"Why the fuck is it always us?" Aiden mumbled to himself as he finished his turn and pressed the jump button.

"Jump complete," Chief Mando announced. "We're on firing station!"

"Ali!" Aiden called.

"I'm on it!" she replied as she typed the final launch instructions into the missile control console.

"Five seconds!" the chief warned.

"Come on!" Aiden urged.

"Four..."

"Not helping!" Ali snapped as she typed in the last few instructions.

"Three..."

She flipped up the arming button's cover and pressed it down.

"Two..."

Ali also flipped the cover off the launch button and pressed it down even harder.

"One..."

She glanced at the display screen showing the status of all of Orochi Three's missile launchers, just as the two launchers she had activated changed from 'ready' to 'missile launch confirmed'. "Missiles away!" she declared triumphantly.

Aiden twisted his flight control stick hard to the left, bringing their nose around, in the direction that the jump missile had left, just in time to see all eight jump flashes.

"Missiles have jumped!" Ali added, sinking back into her seat. After breathing a sigh of relief, she added, "Twelve hours of boredom followed by a few minutes of terror. There has got to be an easier way to make a living."

"The Manamu's shields are failing!" Jessica warned. "They're jumping!"

"Missile launches on the surface!" Kaylah reported. "Four of them!"

"YES!" Nathan exclaimed.

"The cruiser is turning to starboard!" Kaylah added.

"They're looking for a clear jump line!" Jessica said.

"Good bet they've spotted those missiles," Nathan added.

"The Glendanon is yawing!" Kaylah reported. "They're trying to block the cruiser from getting a clear jump line!"

"That's it, Gullen, sell it," Nathan mumbled.

"Cruiser is turning its ventral point-defenses toward the missile tracks," Jessica announced.

"The Glendanon is translating to starboard, as well," Kaylah reported.

Nathan watched the main view screen as the enemy cruiser in front of him jockeyed for a clear jump line, and the Glendanon tried in vain to stop them.

"Rakuen missiles have jumped!" Kaylah added. "They're now ten seconds out!"

"Cruiser has a clear jump line!" Jessica warned. "They're jumping!"

The Aurora's bridge filled with the blue-white flash from the Dusahn cruiser's jump, but instead of fading away a second later, it was replaced by a brilliant white blast of light that immediately turned yellow, then reddish-orange. Only a kilometer or two beyond the Glendanon, a massive explosion had appeared. The burning gases of the explosion used up the free oxygen from within the enemy cruiser in a split second. When the fireball subsided, the broken remnants of the target's hull could be seen scattering in all directions as secondary explosions tore the remaining section apart, as well.

"What the hell happened?" Jessica asked, shocked by the explosion.

Nathan smiled. "Now we know what happens when two objects collide in a jump and one of them has warheads."

* * *

The Reaper jumped in less than fifty meters above the hospital's shuttle pad, its four engine pods screaming at full power. Its landing gear had barely touched the ground when the side door opened and Loki jumped out, making a mad dash toward the entrance. Nathan and Jessica jumped out, as well, also heading for the door, albeit not as quickly.

Loki burst into the hospital emergency entrance, plowing his way through the crowds of people waiting to be treated. Nothing was going to stop him from reaching his family.

"My wife is here!" he declared to the overburdened receptionist.

"So is everyone else's," the lady replied.

"Lael Sheehan is my wife!" Loki said, demanding attention. "She came in with our baby daughter, Ailsa!" he added, almost pleading.

Nathan and Jessica worked their way through the crowd, as well, coming up behind Loki.

"If you'll just be patient..."

Nathan stepped up next to Loki, leaning in over the counter to speak to the receptionist. "I am Nathan Scott, captain of the Aurora, and with this man's help, we just saved your fucking planet. So, I suggest you tell us where we can find his wife and daughter, or I'll blast that door open and find her myself. Then, you'll have a really hard time keeping all these people from swarming your facility."

The woman stared at Nathan for a moment, her mouth agape. "What was the name?" she finally asked.

"Sheehan," Loki replied. "Lael and Ailsa."

The woman studied her screen, frantically searching for the name. "You have to understand, so many people have come in; we don't even have most of their names, yet..."

Both Nathan and Jessica drew their sidearms, flipping the charge buttons as they turned toward the entrance to the treatment area.

The whine of the weapons charging up caught the woman's attention, as well as the nearby guard's.

"I wouldn't," Jessica warned the guard, turning her sidearm to point at him.

Screams erupted in the waiting area. People ducked down, trying to find cover, while others ran for the exit. The guard froze, his hand on his holstered weapon. The confident smile on Jessica's face convinced him to slowly remove it.

The receptionist pressed a button, and the doors to the treatment area swung open. "If they're not in there, then they're either in one of the wards on the two floors above or in surgery on the fourth floor."

"Thank you," Nathan replied, holstering his weapon as he turned and followed Loki through the doors.

Jessica followed, walking backwards, keeping her weapon trained on the security guard. "Don't worry, we'll be good," she told the guard as she, too, holstered her weapon and then turned to follow them through the doors.

The treatment area was a madhouse of semi-organized chaos. The wounded were everywhere, and various medical personnel were trying their best to provide care for everyone. Even family members had been pressed into service, maintaining pressure on bleeding wounds and providing supportive care to their loved ones.

Loki searched frantically for Lael and Ailsa, calling out his wife's name over and over again. After a few minutes, he turned to Nathan, exasperated.

"Excuse me," Nathan said, catching a nurse as she hurried passed by. "We're looking for a young woman and a baby girl."

"You're Na-Tan, aren't you?" the woman replied. "I've seen you on the news."

"Can you help us find them?" Nathan pleaded.

"Names?"

"Sheehan," Nathan replied. "Lael and Ailsa."

The woman moved to a nearby terminal and punched the names into the system. "Ah, here we go. The baby, Ailsa, is stable. She went to pediatrics on the third floor."

"What about the mother, Lael?" Nathan asked.

The woman glanced at the screen again, then back to Nathan, her expression changing. "I'm sorry, she didn't make it. She's downstairs in the morgue."

"Damn," Nathan sighed.

"Captain, I can't find them," Loki said, coming back to join them.

"I found them, Loki," Nathan told him, "Ailsa's in pediatrics, and she's stable."

"Oh, thank God," Loki sighed. "What about Lael?"

Nathan was unsure how to respond. That alone said more than Loki was prepared to hear.

"Oh, God," Loki said, his voice breaking as his eyes welled up. "Oh, God."

Jessica put her arms around Loki and pulled him in close as he began to weep.

CHAPTER SIX

Nathan studied the images on the main view screen in the command briefing room as Lieutenant Commander Shinoda gave his after-action report of the Alliance's latest retaliatory attack against the Dusahn.

"In total, we've expended another sixteen jump missiles, reducing our total reserve back down to forty-two," the lieutenant commander said. "For this expenditure, we destroyed another frigate, four gunships, and inflicted damage on two cruisers."

"Hardly worth the missiles," Cameron observed.

"The retaliatory attacks are not about the results," General Telles reminded her, taking the pressure off of Nathan. "They are about maintaining an appearance of capability. If the Dusahn believe for a moment that our *ability* to retaliate has lessened, they will send *everything* they've got to destroy us; and *destroy us* they will."

"I wasn't arguing against immediate retaliation," Cameron insisted, "I was merely pointing out the costs. Forty-two missiles are not enough to defend Rakuen, let alone the entire system."

"I think we're all aware of how dangerously low we are on jump missiles," Jessica stated.

"Now that the Dusahn know Rakuen *has* surface-based jump missile launchers, it's a safe bet that the next time they attack, those launchers will be the first thing they target."

"RDC started moving them the moment the battle ended," Lieutenant Commander Shinoda assured them.

"Rakuen *and* Neramese must triple their efforts,

and more quickly build both missiles *and* launchers," General Telles said.

"That may not be possible," Nathan replied. "To get them to agree to the missile defense program, it was important for both sides to develop their capabilities at an equal pace. Neramese may be able to triple production, but Rakuen was just hit pretty hard. They may not even be able to maintain current production levels."

"This could be an opportunity," General Telles observed.

"How so?" Nathan wondered, a puzzled look on this face.

"If the Nerameseans *were* to triple production and then *gift* enough missiles to Rakuen to *maintain* the balance of power, it could help build trust between both worlds."

"It might," Cameron agreed. "The problem is, the Dusahn seem to be attacking every six to ten days. That's not enough time to produce more missiles, regardless of how much effort is put into production."

"We have to go on the offensive," Nathan said, seemingly out of nowhere.

Everyone in the room stared at him in disbelief, except for General Telles, whose expression remained unchanged, as usual.

"We have to keep the Dusahn busy defending what they have so they *cannot* attack us as frequently," Nathan explained.

"Preferably, not at all," General Telles added.

"In order to prevent them from attacking this system again, anytime soon, we will have to harass them constantly," Jessica pointed out, "and Cameron's right; we don't have the missiles for that."

"Then, we don't use missiles," Nathan stated.

"We're down to two Strikers," Cameron reminded him. "They're the only ships we have that can reach the Pentaurus cluster quickly *and* have enough firepower to take down anything larger than a frigate. Even *that* is questionable, with only two of them."

"We've got one hundred Gunyoki," Jessica pointed out.

"Yes, we do," Cameron agreed, "but they have very little training in swarm-attack tactics, as of yet. Besides, with so few jump missiles available, the Gunyoki will be needed to defend the Rogen system."

"Cameron's right," Nathan said. "We're not sending the Gunyoki anywhere. In fact, we're not sending *any* of our forces to harass the Dusahn."

"We're not?" Jessica wondered.

"The Dusahn aren't after the Rogen system," Nathan continued. "It's too far away to be of use to them. They're only here because *we're* here. The Dusahn want the Aurora, and that's what we're going to give them."

"Come again?" Cameron said.

"Commander Kamenetskiy, how long until the long-range emitter array is operational?"

"At least a week to get the emitters installed," Vladimir replied. "Then, a few more days of jump testing to get them properly tuned."

"I need that cut in half," Nathan instructed.

"Uh..."

"No *uhs*," Nathan insisted. "Pull all the resources and personnel you need to make it happen."

"I can get the array ready in that time, but the jump testing..."

"Will have to be done on the fly," Nathan said, cutting his chief engineer off mid-sentence.

"I'll have to pull engineers from the second ZPED installation," Vladimir warned.

"Nope, I want that ready in three days, as well," Nathan instructed. "You have permission to fully integrate the Sugali AI into our systems to assist, if necessary."

"Yes, sir," Vladimir replied.

"Captain," Cameron objected, "I'm not sure that's wise."

"I have to agree with Cameron," Jessica said. "This could be part of a Dusahn plan to get the Aurora back in the Pentaurus cluster so that Leta can hand us over."

"It's a gamble we'll have to take," Nathan insisted, "and she's no longer called Leta. On *this* ship, she's called *Aurora*."

* * *

Loki sat in the middle of what was once his family's home on Rakuen. The apartment looked much like he felt inside: torn up, chaotic...destroyed.

He reached down and pushed a large shard of glass aside, picking up a holo-cube that had been buried under it. He activated the cube, and a holographic image of his wife and daughter appeared. He remembered taking the image a few weeks ago, only days after they had settled on Rakuen. He had taken them to the docks to watch the fishing boats unload. Lael had always loved seafood and could never get enough of it. It had been one of the few reasons she had taken so well to life on Rakuen, instead of her native Corinair to which she longed to return.

Lael had been so strong, so determined. For the life of him, Loki never understood how he had managed to attract such a mate. He had never felt worthy of her, and when they had been blessed with a child only a few years into their marriage, he considered himself doubly blessed.

Now...

Loki tried not to think. He longed to be stupid, to be numb to all the horror around him. The only woman he had ever loved, the mother of his daughter, was gone. All of his life, Loki had tried to do the right thing. He followed the rules, did the work, met his responsibilities...and what had it all gotten him?

Pain. More pain than he could possibly imagine.

He tried to remind himself that he was not alone in his suffering. Countless others had suffered at least as much. What right did he have to feel as if fate had been unfair to him?

But the despair would not leave him, despite his best efforts to drive it away.

Loki heard the sound of broken glass crunching underfoot. With a slight turn of his head to the left, he spotted a uniformed pant leg. "It was such a good day," he said, looking back at the holographic image.

Nathan didn't know what to say.

"What can I do for you, Captain?" Loki asked.

"Actually, I came to see if there was anything I could do for you, Loki."

Loki let out a pitiful laugh. "Can you clone her and bring her back to me?"

"If I could, I most certainly would."

"Then, I guess there is nothing anyone can do," Loki said, exasperation in his voice.

"I'm so sorry, Loki," Nathan apologized. "I let you down. You have always been there when I needed you, and now *I* let *you* down."

Loki closed his eyes. He wanted to cry again, but he had no tears left in him. "You don't fight for *me*, Captain. You don't fight for any *one person*. You fight for *all* of us. Even for our enemies' families. You always have. It's why we follow you." After a moment, he turned to look at Nathan. "How do you deal with the loss?" he wondered. "Your mother, your brother, all of them. Does it not tear you up inside?"

"It did," Nathan admitted. "In many ways, it still does."

"How do you carry on?"

Nathan sighed, moving deeper into the room, stepping carefully. "If I were to die—I mean, *permanently*—I would want everyone to carry on and live their lives. I would not want them to grieve over me...at least, not too much. So, I try to do what *they* would want *me* to do. I mean, you really only have two options. You can dwell on your loss, and fall into abject depression, or you can continue on with your life. The former does no one any good and, eventually, destroys you." Nathan took a seat on the couch next to Loki. "However, men like you and I don't *have* a choice."

"How so?" Loki wondered.

"When my family was assassinated, I wanted to give up. I wanted to take the Seiiki and disappear. Let the galaxy solve its own problems. But I couldn't. I had to find a way to save Miri. I had to be strong for her children. I had to be strong for everyone, for all those who had suffered a loss, or will suffer one. What right did I have to give up? *You* have Ailsa. If *you* give up, and let yourself fall into depression and despair, she will never know about her wonderful mother, nor how brave a man her father is. In essence, you will be taking away the two most important people in her life. As hard as it may be, you cannot do that to her." Nathan felt his eyes welling up, his voice breaking. “You can’t,” he added, putting his hand on Loki’s shoulder.

“I won’t,” Loki promised, also getting choked up. After a few moments, he asked, “What do we do next?”

“We finish getting the Aurora ready for action, and then we take the fight *to* the Dusahn. We make them pay for what they have taken from us all.” Nathan patted his shoulder. “We attack in four or five days. I hope you’ll be there with us, but if not, I will understand.”

“Thank you, Captain.”

“You know, you *can* call me Nathan.”

“Yes, sir.”

* * *

Nathan entered the office of the prime minister, escorted by the minister’s personal assistant. Unlike the government offices on Rakuen, the ones on Neramese were simple and unpretentious.

“Captain Scott,” Minister Cornell greeted, coming out from behind his desk. “It is good to see you well,” he added as he grabbed Nathan’s hand with both of his own and shook it vigorously. “We have had so few updates as to the condition of your ship and, in particular, her crew. I, for one, feared the worst.”

“Both came through relatively unscathed,” Nathan replied, “thanks to the new jump-missile defense system.”

“I suspect you and your ship had more to do with our success than you are willing to admit,” the minister insisted. “Please, sit. I will order comfa.”

“Comfa?”

“Similar to what you call *tea*. It helps with mental focus and emotional balance. It is customary for my people to consume it prior to any negotiations.”

"Negotiations?"

"You are an important man, Captain. A busy man, I might add. It is doubtful that you would seek my audience without an agenda."

"Of course," Nathan admitted. "However, I'm not here to negotiate, Minister. I have come to ask a favor. A big one, I'm afraid."

"I see."

"The current level of jump missile production is insufficient," Nathan explained.

"Our fourth factory goes online tomorrow," the minister stated. "By the end of the week, we will be producing four missiles per day just on Neramese."

"The Dusahn are attacking at a rate of once every six to eight days," Nathan explained. "Just enough time to travel here, attack, and return home. Now that they know the Rogen system has developed the means to defend itself, they will be forced to attack more frequently. They will learn how to quickly detect and eliminate the surface-based defenses."

"This is why we allowed the resurrection of the Orochi, is it not?"

"Yes, but currently there are not enough missiles to arm all of the Orochi. To make matters worse, Rakuen has suffered considerable damage and will be unable to increase their missile and launcher production rate. They have become far more vulnerable than before, and that's from *one* attack."

"What is it you ask of me, Captain?" Minister Cornell wondered.

"I'm here to ask you to share your missiles with Rakuen, to maintain an equal balance."

"Captain, this is the first time in decades that Neramese has been equal in defense capability to Rakuen. Now, by a twist of fate, we are actually *ahead* of Rakuen, and you want me to give that up? What kind of leader would I be?"

"One with vision," Nathan replied. "One who understands that the futures of both worlds are too closely intertwined to be ignored." Nathan leaned back in his chair. "Minister, Rakuen has held power over your world under a belief that if Neramese were to gain military might over that of Rakuen, then Neramese would attack once again. Gifting the missiles, to not only provide for the defense of Rakuen but also to *maintain* the balance of power, would demonstrate beyond all doubt that Neramese desires a *partnership* with its neighbor and not to renew a decades-old conflict."

Minister Cornell also leaned back in his chair, contemplating the captain's words. "I doubt that Rakuen would do the same, were our fortunes reversed."

"You may be right," Nathan admitted, "but the lack of moral character in Rakuen's leaders should not dictate your actions."

Minister Cornell sighed. "My military advisors have told me that we cannot defend ourselves from the Dusahn, should they continue to attack at this frequency and, now, you're telling me these attacks will occur more often."

"They will move supply ships closer to this system so their ships can rearm, refuel, and return in half the time. I predict the next attack will come in six days and after that, in three," Nathan explained. "Even if they do not attack Neramese, Rakuen will fall. Can your economy survive *without* Rakuen's?"

"Doubtful," Minister Cornell replied. "Although, it pains me, greatly, to admit this."

"There is a way to prevent these attacks," Nathan added.

"How so?" Minister Cornell wondered.

"The Aurora must go on the offensive. The Rogen system is currently of no strategic value to the Dusahn. They only attack because the *Aurora* is here."

"Then, why do they attack Rakuen?"

"Because Rakuen supports the Aurora."

"So does Neramese," the minister pointed out.

"Yes, but the Aurora was in *orbit* over Rakuen, so they could attack both with fewer ships. Trust me; they will eventually attack Neramese, as well, unless we leave."

"But if the Aurora leaves, we will be defenseless," Minister Cornell argued.

"Not necessarily," Nathan replied. "First, the Aurora will give all of her jump missiles to the Orochi."

"Will that be enough?"

"No, but it will buy us time," Nathan replied.

"Time?" Minister Cornell wondered. "Time for what?"

"Time for the Aurora to return and join in the defense of the Rogen system."

"Return from where?"

"The Pentaurus cluster," Nathan replied. "You see, I intend to take the fight *to* the Dusahn. I intend to harass them so much that they cannot afford to send ships to the Rogen system, for fear of leaving themselves without sufficient defenses."

"But it is a three-day trip for the Aurora, just as it is for the Dusahn," the minister replied.

"Not for long," Nathan explained. He took a deep

breath before continuing. "You can share this with no one, Minister, at least not for now."

"Share what?"

"The Aurora's single-jump range is about to increase...significantly," Nathan stated.

"How significantly?"

"Enough to put Takara within single-jump range," Nathan replied. "Enough to allow us to return in the blink of an eye should the Dusahn attack the Rogen system while we are away."

"But you cannot defeat the Dusahn fleet, not with a single ship," the minister insisted.

"No, I cannot," Nathan admitted. "But I can chip away at their fleet, one ship at a time, keeping them so busy defending what they have, that they dare not venture beyond their defensive perimeter."

Minister Cornell studied Nathan for a moment. "I am not a military man, Captain, but even I know that such a strategy will make for a very long war."

"Perhaps," Nathan admitted. "However, it will allow Neramese and Rakuen the time they need to build impenetrable defenses, as well as time for us to find a way to defeat the Dusahn once and for all."

"I hope you have something in mind, Captain."

"I do," Nathan replied. "I don't like it much, but I do."

* * *

Vladimir straddled the bracing between the wall of the containment cylinder and the ZPED being raised into place. Only a few short weeks ago, the cylinder had served as the outermost shell of the Aurora's number two antimatter reactor. In fact, the reactor, itself, had only been removed a few days ago and taken to a makeshift holding facility on an asteroid, at the outskirts of the Rogen system.

He watched as his engineers raised the ZPED into place and began connecting the isolation braces, which were designed to absorb any vibrations emanating through the ship's structure and prevent them from disturbing the zero-point device's own delicate containment fields.

"*Commander,*" a voice called over Vladimir's comm-set. "*The crawlers are reporting difficulty with the lateral bracing on all of the midship dorsal emitters.*"

"Tell them to skip them," Vladimir instructed over his comm-set.

"*You mean, not install them?*"

"*Da*! That is what I mean!"

"*But, Commander, without the proper bracing, the emitters could shift...*"

"The lateral bracing is a redundancy," Vladimir insisted. "If the emitter *does* shift, its attitude sensors will recognize the change and adjust their field appropriately. We can come back and deal with the lateral bracing later, *after* the jump array is back online."

"*Are you certain?*"

"One moment," Vladimir said, tapping his comm-set. "Aurora, are you monitoring this channel?"

"*Affirmative, Commander. Your solution poses a risk level of point zero one three percent. Unless an emitter receives a direct hit, or the ship experiences a collision, the lateral bracing is unnecessary. In fact, you could safely skip the installation of lateral bracing on all emitters and save approximately thirty hours of labor.*"

"Why didn't you tell me this before?" Vladimir wondered.

"*You did not ask.*"

"*Gospadee,*" Vladimir exclaimed. "I am asking now. Aurora, please identify any shortcuts we could take to get the long-range jump system operational ahead of the captain's deadline."

"*I will analyze and report back momentarily,*" Aurora answered.

"Thank you," Vladimir tapped his comm-set again. "I'm sure," he told his engineer. "In fact, skip the installation of all lateral emitter braces."

"*Yes, sir.*"

"*Commander?*"

"Yes, Aurora," Vladimir replied.

"*I have identified no other shortcuts that would speed up the installation of the long-range jump system without resulting in an unacceptable risk of failure. However, I think I should point out that the zero-point energy device you are currently installing is approximately two point four kilograms heavier than the one you previously installed. I would recommend additional vibration couplings on the lower supports.*"

"Thank you, Aurora," the commander replied. "Computers," he mumbled to himself. "Dortson! Shelky!" Vladimir yelled to the men working seven meters below him. "I want an extra vibration coupling on every one of those lower supports! Understood?"

"*Why?*"

"Because I said so, Ensign!" Vladimir barked.

"*Yes, sir!*"

* * *

Nathan sat patiently in the interrogation room, in the makeshift prison on Neramese. The past two days had been a flurry of activity, both on board the Aurora and across the Rogen system. Nathan had pushed his engineers and repair crews to the brink, and had asked equally as much of the Neramesean prime minister. Now, he would be asking much of another man.

The door opened, and two Neramesean guards stepped inside, followed by Commander Andreola, the Orswellan officer who had been so earnest during his initial interrogation.

The commander walked toward the table, looking at the captain as he stood. "Captain," he greeted, nodding respectfully. "It is a pleasure to see you again."

"The restraints will not be necessary," Nathan instructed the guards.

"Removing them is against operational policy," the senior guard stated.

"It's quite alright, Captain," Commander Andreola insisted. "The restraints are not uncomfortable, and the policy is logical."

"As you wish," Nathan agreed. "You may leave," Nathan told the guards.

"That is also against operational policy."

"No one on this base has sufficient security clearance to hear the questions I am about to ask this man," Nathan explained. "If you remain, I will have to place you in isolation until such time as the topics discussed in this room, over the next few minutes, are no longer sensitive information...which *could* be indefinitely. The choice is yours."

The senior guard looked at the captain, then at the other guard. "Secure the prisoner to the table." The other guard did as instructed, directing the commander to his seat and then attaching his restraints to the table before him.

"We will be outside, should you need us," the senior guard informed Nathan before leaving.

"The room is monitored from outside," the commander warned.

"My security detail has seen to that," Nathan assured him. "I trust they are treating you well."

"As well as can be expected," the commander replied. "It is difficult for the guards. This facility is not properly designed to house enemy prisoners of war; hence, the need for restraints whenever a prisoner is being moved between zones. The fact that I am not terribly liked by the majority of the prisoners here causes additional burdens for the guards, which they tend to resent."

"I apologize for the conditions," Nathan said.

"On the bright side, the food is not bad," the commander replied, smiling.

"I'll take your word for it."

"How can I help you, Captain?"

"You told Lieutenant Siddens that the Dusahn were forcing your people to build ships for them. You also stated that you did not know exactly what types of ships were being assembled at the moment, but that you were fairly certain at least two of them were battleships."

"Based on the size of the hulls the last time I was in the Orswellan system, yes."

"And the rest of the bays?" Nathan wondered. "You have no idea what was being assembled in them?"

"As I said, twelve of the bays are kept open to provide service for existing ships. Of the remaining twenty-six bays, the majority of them have historically been used to create gunships or to convert Orswellan ships for use by the Dusahn, mostly as troop landers and mass bombers."

"Assuming that those two large ships you saw *are* battleships, how long until they are completed?"

"As I told Lieutenant Siddens, I have no way of knowing. However, it generally takes about a year for the Dusahn to complete a large ship, something the size of a heavy cruiser or battleship. The last battleship took nearly a year and a half, but that was one of their heavy battleships, which is a bit larger and more heavily armed."

"And it has been at least half a year since you saw those ships?" Nathan verified.

"Yes. Again, as I informed Lieutenant Siddens, at the time that I observed those ships, their hulls were still under construction, so I expect they were a little less than half complete; a little more, if they were not heavy battleships."

"Then, those two ships could be ready for service," Nathan surmised.

"Yes," the commander replied. "That is the conclusion Lieutenant Siddens came to, as well."

"Yes, I know."

"Perhaps I am not understanding something," the commander said. "Is there a reason you are asking me questions that Lieutenant Siddens has already asked...multiple times, I might add?"

"I am considering an attack on the Orswellan system," Nathan admitted.

"I see." The commander thought for a moment, obviously concerned with the prospect. "The Orswellans are not your enemy, Captain, at least not by choice."

"I understand that," Nathan assured him. "However, your people are building ships for the Dusahn, and that is something I cannot allow to continue."

"Understandable," the commander said.

"The last time we spoke, you said if the Orswellan ships turned *against* the Jar-Razza, the troops on the surface would turn against the Orswellans, possibly committing genocide," Nathan began. "Assuming we are able to destroy the Jar-Razza, and at least disable the other four Orswellan ships, what would the Dusahn troops on the surface do?"

"That is hard to say," the commander admitted. "If our ships were allowed to survive, then the Dusahn commanders on the surface might feel threatened. Even worse, they might suspect collusion, in which case they would most certainly turn against the population."

"But surely the Dusahn lack the manpower to control an entire population using troops on the ground."

"Our entire civilization is unarmed," Commander Andreola told Nathan. "It always has been. Our constabulary was armed, but they were disbanded by the Dusahn only days after the invasion. The population has no way of defending itself." After a pause, the commander added, "Your only choice is to *destroy* the Orswellan ships, and to do so as if they were *Dusahn.* That is the only hope my people have of avoiding genocide."

Nathan leaned back in his chair, letting out a long breath. "How many people aboard an Orswellan ship?"

"The ones currently in our home system? An average of seventy, I believe."

"So, I have to kill two hundred and eighty, in order to save..."

"Four million," the commander finished for him. "Mathematically, an easy decision."

Nathan looked at the commander. "The word is *obvious*, not *easy*."

* * *

"Got a minute?" Commander Verbeek asked from the doorway.

"Sure, Verbee," Commander Prechitt replied. "What's up?"

"I was wondering how the pilot training is going?"

"Faster than I would have thought," Commander Prechitt admitted. "None of these guys are even close to being true fighter jocks, but as long as all they have to defend against are a bunch of poorly equipped pirates, they should be able to hold their own someday."

Commander Verbeek walked into the room, closing the door behind him. "Any idea when *someday* might be?"

"A few weeks, a month maybe. Why?" Commander Prechitt wondered. "Your people getting homesick?"

Commander Verbeek handed his data pad to Commander Prechitt. "It's not me asking."

Commander Prechitt studied the data pad for a moment. "A surface attack?"

"Apparently," Commander Verbeek replied. "Against troops and, possibly, some shuttles."

"They want you to fly cover?"

"I'm assuming so," Commander Verbeek replied. "Eagles aren't much good for ground attacks. I expect he'd use the Reapers."

"Makes sense," Commander Prechitt agreed.

"So, can the Casbons defend themselves?"

"The ones with the AIs might be able to, assuming the Ahka don't attack in numbers greater than they have, thus far."

"They don't *have* numbers," Commander Verbeek

reminded him. "Our last recon shows they still only have four raiders and no more in the works...that we can *detect*."

Commander Prechitt took a deep breath, thinking for a moment. "It will take the Inman and the Gervais *three days* to get your Eagles back to the Aurora. Add two or three days for the mission cycle, itself, and that's nine to ten days that Casbon's defenses are minimal, at best, and that's *assuming* your Eagles come back."

"Oh, we'll come back," Commander Verbeek insisted.

"I wasn't talking about *surviving* the mission, Verbee," Commander Prechitt told him. "Scott may decide to keep you there, or there may be additional missions in the works. There's not enough in the message to tell."

"Good point," Commander Verbeek agreed.

"It only takes *eighteen hours* for a Nighthawk to reach the Rogen system."

"You want to send *Nighthawks* instead of my Eagles?" Commander Verbeek questioned. "You said they wouldn't be ready for at least a few weeks."

"I wasn't thinking about sending the *Casbon* pilots in those Nighthawks."

"You want to send *my* pilots?"

"Not all of them," Commander Prechitt assured him. "Maybe half. If the Ahka only have four operational raiders, your pilots could handle them with a *pair* of Eagles."

"True, but..."

"Using Nighthawks, your pilots would be back in four to five days at the most, and the Nighthawks *are* superior to our Eagles."

"In the right hands, yes," Commander Verbeek

agreed, "but the message wasn't *asking* for recommendations," the commander pointed out. "It was asking for *readiness.*"

"It included the reason for the request, which in *my* mind *invites* recommendations."

* * *

Loki sat in the hospital pediatric ward, staring at his baby girl as she slept. A million things ran through his head, at times making him feel as if he might throw up. For the third time in less than a year, his world had been turned upside down. Only, this time, it had been partially gutted, as well. Loki's thoughts were interrupted by the sound of footsteps behind him.

"I'm sorry," Nora Montrose said from the doorway. "I didn't realize you were here," she added, turning to depart.

"That's alright," Loki replied in hushed tones.

"I was visiting my mother, and I just wanted to check on Ailsa," Nora explained, keeping her voice down as she entered the room.

"How is she?" Loki asked.

"A punctured lung, a few broken ribs, multiple lacerations, but she'll be fine."

"That's good to hear," Loki said, looking back at his sleeping daughter. "I never did thank you and Dunner for saving Ailsa."

"You would have done the same for any of us," Nora replied. "I only wish..."

"I know."

Nora took a breath. "How are you doing?"

"Confused, scared, depressed," Loki admitted. "I ran out of tears, though, so that's good...I guess."

"Did they say when Ailsa will be released?"

"A few days."

"If you need someone to watch her while you are away, we'd be more than happy to help out."

Loki forced a smile. "Thank you, but I don't think that will be necessary."

"You're not returning to duty?" Nora wondered, surprised.

"How can I?"

"I don't understand."

"Ailsa has already lost her mother. How can I risk her losing her father, as well?"

"I can see your point," Nora admitted. "However, I'm not sure you're looking at things correctly."

"No offense, but how would you know?" Loki wondered.

"My father left us to go to war," she explained, "more than once, I might add."

"It's different," Loki insisted.

"At first, I resented him for it. I thought he was being selfish...putting us through all the worrying, the heartache."

"But you had your mother."

"Actually, we didn't," Nora corrected. "Not the first time, anyway. Our biological mother died when we were young. He left us with our grandparents. Terris is our step-mother. She came along a few years later."

"Did you ever ask your father *why* he left you behind to go to war?"

"No, my grandfather explained it to me," Nora replied. "He told me that had my father not gone, he would not be the man my mother had married. He explained that he fought to protect me and my brother, as well as everyone else. He told us that if our father had chosen to stay home, it would have been unfair to all the other men who were leaving *their* families behind, as well."

"Did you understand?"

"Not at the time, no," Nora admitted, "but later, I did."

"How much later?" Loki wondered.

"When I was a teenager, and he left to liberate Earth." Nora moved closer to Loki. "If you do not return to your post, Ailsa will feel as if she is to blame. She would always wonder if you regretted your decision."

"But..."

"Loki, I can't tell you what you *should* do. All I *can* tell you is that what you, my father, and all the others do is important...*very* important. People like you are all that stands between the Dusahn and the rest of us."

"Then, you would think less of me if I did not return to duty?"

"Of course not," Nora assured him, taking his hand. "I would think you are a man who loves his daughter and is afraid that she will feel abandoned, should he not return from war."

"You're not making this any easier," Loki said.

"There is nothing about any of this that is easy, Loki. Nothing at all."

* * *

Nathan stood staring at the image of Rakuen on the view screen in the command briefing room as it slowly rotated beneath the Aurora.

"You wanted to speak with me, Captain?" General Telles asked as he entered the room.

"It was a mistake not giving her windows," he declared as he continued staring at the beautiful, azure planet. "I know this view is exactly what it would be, were there a window to the outside here, probably even in better detail, but it's not the same. There's a disconnect. In your mind, you still know you're looking at a reproduction. You're not *really* there."

"In this case, you are," the general disagreed. "There is just an intermediate step, that of the camera, the processors, and the display."

"You could put any planet on that screen, though," Nathan replied. "*That* knowledge is what takes so much away from it." Nathan turned to look at the general. "The *Seiiki* had windows. What you saw was what was *really* out there. I miss that ship."

"You brought me here to reminisce about the Seiiki?"

"No, I need your help," Nathan replied. "I find myself facing a difficult decision."

"About whether or not to fight Lord Dusahn?"

"No, I've shelved that decision for the time being," Nathan said, taking a seat at the conference table. "According to Commander Andreola, at least two Dusahn battleships, perhaps even *heavy* battleships, are nearing completion at the Orswellan shipyards. We need to destroy that facility, hopefully taking those two warships out, as well. The problem is that the *existence* of that facility is possibly the only thing keeping the Orswellans alive. Destroy it, and the Dusahn have no reason to remain in the Orswellan system."

"You believe the Dusahn will glass the planet on their way out," General Telles surmised.

"If they were willing to booby-trap the Orswellan ships, so they could not be used against them, it stands to reason that they would do the same with the Orswellan shipyards and, by extension, their entire civilization. Why leave it behind to support their liberators or to be rebuilt and, someday, turned against them?"

"It is common for a mobile force to leave nothing behind of value to their enemy or potential enemies," General Telles agreed.

"Then, I'm not crazy," Nathan said.

"That is a different topic," the general replied.

"More Ghatazhak humor."

"There is only one logical solution to the problem," the general said. "Destroy the shipyards and as many warships as possible, *especially* the Orswellan ships, and then leave. The Dusahn will believe that you attacked Orswella in order to deny them the logistical support it provides."

"But what if they decide to *abandon* Orswella and *glass* it on their way out?"

"That is not your concern."

"You're talking about four million people, General," Nathan argued. "How can I turn my back on them?"

"Compared to the trillions of lives you will save by defeating the Dusahn, it seems an acceptable loss."

"*Four million innocent people,*" Nathan reiterated.

"The inability to accept the necessity of collateral damage has always been your greatest weakness."

"Some might say it's my greatest quality," Nathan argued.

"Now, you're going to ask me if there is a way to eliminate the Dusahn forces on the surface of Orswella, *without* harming the civilians."

"You know me too well, General."

"It may be possible; however, we have almost no intelligence on those forces—location, dispersion patterns, training, armaments, transportation, air cover... The only information we *do* have is that there are at *least* one hundred thousand troops on Orswella, possibly more. *Because* of this lack of intelligence, I cannot answer your question."

"Can you speculate?" Nathan asked.

"The only speculation I can offer is that if the Dusahn have *any* experience in surface-occupation tactics and logistics, and they *do* have a hundred thousand troops on the ground, then there is no way we can liberate Orswella without a *massive* loss of life. Not only that, but you would also then be responsible for the protection of Orswella, something that would be quite difficult given the distance." General Telles leaned forward, looking Nathan in the eyes. "Captain, your *only* play here is to take out those shipyards, as well as *all* the ships guarding them, and leave the Orswellans to their fate, whatever it may be."

"That's unacceptable," Nathan replied. "There has to be another way."

"I'm not saying there isn't," General Telles replied. "But without good intel, it *is* the only safe play."

"Then, we need better intelligence on Orswella," Nathan decided.

* * *

"Try it again," Vladimir instructed, sighing.

"Commander, you only changed the initiation feeds by point zero one four percent. That isn't enough to do anything."

"Wait, I almost forgot." Vladimir got up off his knees and kicked the side of the massive device before him. "*Chort bui tebya probral*!" He wiped his hands on his shirt, turning back to his assistant. "Try it now."

"But, sir..."

"*Davai*!" he yelled.

That word, the technician understood. He pressed a few buttons on the control station on the side of the massive starboard drive. After a few moments, a series of green lights appeared. "Oh, my God!" he exclaimed. "It worked!" He looked at Vladimir in disbelief.

"Sometimes all it needs is a good kick and a few bad words," Vladimir said.

"What did you say to it?" the technician wondered.

"Loosely translated, I told it to go to hell," Vladimir said as he tapped his comm-set. "Bridge, Cheng, main propulsion is fully restored."

"Commander, we still have to align the injectors and test the backup power feeds."

"Details," Vladimir replied. "First, I'm getting something to eat."

* * *

Josh walked down the corridor of the pediatric ward, peeking into each room as he went. Finally, he found the room he was looking for. "There you are," he said.

Loki turned and gestured for Josh to keep his voice down.

"Sorry," Josh apologized, reducing his volume. "How's she doing?" he asked, stepping up to Ailsa's crib and looking down at her.

"She's doing well," Loki told him.

"She's a real looker," Josh said as he admired baby Ailsa. "She's going to break some hearts when she gets older. I can't believe you made her."

"My part was rather small," Loki admitted. "It was mostly Lael."

Josh took a seat next to Loki, taking a deep breath and letting it out slowly. "This really sucks, man. I don't know what else to say."

Loki did not respond, he just continued staring at his sleeping child.

"If there is anything I can do to help, you know I'm here for you," Josh promised.

"I know," Loki replied.

"Have you decided what you're going to do?"

"Honestly, I don't see how I can leave her," Loki admitted. "I'm all she has left. I mean, I can't leave her with Lael's family, they're still on Corinair. Hell, I don't even know if they're still alive."

"Listen, I'm the last person to be giving advice about parenting," Josh said. "Hell, I was raised by Marcus, and we all know what a shining example of good parenting *he* is. But you have to consider what's best for your daughter, and as much as you love her, *you* might not be the best person to raise her, at least not by yourself."

Loki looked at Josh in disbelief. "What are you suggesting, Josh, that I put her up for adoption, or something?"

"No, nothing like that, man. Maybe a nanny, or something, or a family who could take care of her while you're at work. I mean, you still have to earn a living, right? So, you're going to be gone at work half the time. Whether you stay or go, you're still going to need help."

"I can get a job working from home," Loki told him. "Something that's just enough to pay the bills. We don't need much, just a tiny place."

"Dude, you're a pilot, a *really good* pilot. Probably the best pilot I've ever known...besides myself, of course. You'll be miserable if you're not flying, and you know it."

"Not a whole lot of flying jobs allow you to bring an infant along in the cockpit," Loki said.

"Have you thought of asking one of the other families if they can help?" Josh suggested.

"I don't think I can do that," Loki replied. "She's *my* daughter; *my* responsibility."

"This is an alliance, *remember*? We help each other."

"How do I justify risking the only parent she has left?" Loki asked him. "How can anyone be that selfish?"

"Jesus, Lok, half the people in the Alliance have families, and a lot of *them* are single parents, as well. The Mystic is full of kids who are being raised by a community while their parents are serving in the Alliance. What makes you any different?"

"I don't know, Josh," Loki replied. "I just don't know."

"Look, you do what you've got to do. If you want to come back, great. If not, that's fine too. You're my bud. I'll *miss* you, but I'll get by."

"I know you will," Loki said. "You always do."

"And so will you," Josh insisted, "and so will Ailsa." Josh patted his friend on the leg, then rose and headed for the door. "Maybe you should ask yourself what *you* would want *your* father to do if *he* was in *your* position."

"I can't believe you actually got that out correctly," Loki said, smiling for the first time in three days.

* * *

Nathan threw up his left hand, sweeping it to the outside to block his opponent's jab. Spotting an opening in the opposition's midsection, he dropped his right shoulder and drove his right hand forward, but it didn't work. Instead, he felt his right leg being swept out from under him. Before he had a chance to react, he was on his back, his opponent's foot on his throat.

Nathan quickly tapped the mat, and Jessica removed her foot from his neck. "You telegraphed your attack by dropping your right shoulder, first," she said, reaching out to help him up.

"I was trying to put some power behind it," Nathan said, climbing to his feet.

"As you should," Jessica agreed, "but you have to do it in one smooth motion, or your opponent will see it coming."

"Got it."

"By the way, I left my midsection open so you would go for it with your right hand, setting you up for a leg sweep." Jessica smiled as she took a drink from her water bottle. "And you fell for it like a newb."

"Glad I didn't disappoint you," Nathan replied, picking up his own water bottle. "Now that you've smacked me around a bit, you should be in a good mood, right?"

"Yup, I'm feeling pretty steely right now."

"I've got a mission for you," Nathan said, taking another drink.

"Orswella, right?"

"How did you know?"

"You went to see Andreola, then you talked to Telles. I put two and two together..."

Nathan looked skeptical.

"Okay, Telles told me."

"What do you think?"

"I don't think I can learn the Orswellan version of English fast enough for your timeline. I'm going to need a guide."

Nathan looked at her. "You're thinking about

taking Andreola, aren't you? Are you sure you can trust him?"

"No, but saving his world should provide the right motivation," Jessica replied.

"He could turn you in, once you get there, and win himself points with the Dusahn. He could even be part of a plot to lure us in."

Jessica laughed. "Now, you're thinking like me," she said, taking another drink. "He doesn't strike me as the devious type, though. Besides, I can't think of any reason he would have to betray his own people."

"Unless he's lying about not having a family," Nathan suggested.

"Possibly, but Siddens interrogated every member of the Amonday's crew, multiple times. They all said that Andreola had no family and hated the Dusahn more than anyone. He even turned down his own ship because he didn't want to kiss their ass directly."

"They could be well rehearsed," Nathan said.

"Siddens would've tripped them up," Jessica insisted. "He's *really* good."

"Then, you think taking the commander to Orswella as your guide is a good idea?"

"No, but it's the best one we've got."

"Then, you don't agree with the general's recommendation to take out their ships and leave them to their fate," Nathan surmised.

"Actually, I do," Jessica corrected. "It's by far the safest play, but that doesn't automatically make it the *right* play; not without sufficient intel, anyway."

"But just getting the intel is risky," Nathan reminded her.

"Pretty low risk, I'd say," Jessica insisted, setting her bottle back down.

"You call sneaking onto an enemy-held world, with a local who could be a double agent, low risk?"

"It's what I do," Jessica replied, shrugging her shoulders. "Now, are we going to fight, or what?"

CHAPTER SEVEN

"Are you watching this?" Cameron asked as she entered the captain's ready room.

Nathan extended his right hand toward the view screen on the wall.

"In a surprising gesture of interplanetary cooperation and goodwill, the Neramesean prime minister has offered to loan its missiles to Rakuen until such time as Rakuen's own planetary defenses can be resupplied. In addition, Minister Cornell has pledged all available Neramesean resources to the repair and rebuilding of Rakuen, after the recent Dusahn bombardment."

The image on the view screen changed from the news anchor to Prime Minister Cornell in the Neramesean pressroom. *"The people of Neramese stand with our allies on Rakuen. We make this gesture of goodwill so that all..."*

Nathan picked up the remote and muted the view screen. "It took him long enough."

"You orchestrated this?"

"I made a strong suggestion," Nathan admitted.

"You realize that the leaders of Rakuen will take this as an insult," Cameron pointed out.

"I'm expecting a call from them at any moment," Nathan replied.

"Do you really think that's a good idea?"

"No, but it does maintain the balance of power."

"You could have just given *our* missiles to Rakuen and left Neramese's missiles alone."

"And miss an opportunity to chip away at that stubborn, Rakuen-traditionalist pride?" Nathan replied. "Not a chance."

"Is it really necessary to meddle in their relations?" Cameron wondered.

"These two worlds are more linked than they'd like to admit," Nathan explained. "Economically, strategically, politically, even socially. The only thing separating them is Rakuen's stubbornness."

"Neramese *did* attack Rakuen first," Cameron pointed out.

"Decades ago," Nathan replied, "and they've been living up to the terms of surrender ever since. Neramese has moved on; Rakuen has not. In fact, they've been clinging to their defeat of Neramese as proof of superiority. They need to admit to Neramese, and to themselves, that they cannot survive without each other. Rakuen may have the water, but Neramese has the land. The war occurred because both worlds chose to ignore that balance."

"I don't disagree with you, Nathan," Cameron said. "I just wonder if we shouldn't allow them to restore that balance naturally."

"The Rogen system may not be of strategic value to the Dusahn, but it is to us. The sooner its worlds begin to truly work together, the sooner *this ship* will be able to take the battle *to* the Dusahn."

"*This ship* isn't *ready* to take the battle *anywhere*," Cameron reminded him.

"It will be."

"You're pushing your crew too hard, Nathan," Cameron insisted. "Vlad is taking shortcuts in order to get everything ready by *your* deadline, and that's dangerous."

"Vlad knows what he's doing," Nathan assured her.

"He's ignoring engineering protocols and safety

procedures," Cameron argued. "Procedures that were written to *protect* this ship."

"If this ship doesn't start moving soon, the Dusahn will come in force," Nathan replied. "We've been lucky so far, but that luck is not going to last. The Dusahn aren't stupid. With each attack, they've seen the Aurora's condition improve. They can do the math, Cam, and that math tells them they can't wait much longer, that they have to send everything they've got and finish us off, *now*. To be honest, I'm surprised they haven't already done so."

"Which makes one wonder *why* they haven't done so," Cameron said.

"You think I haven't wondered that, myself?" Nathan replied. "That's all I *can* think about."

"Maybe they're waiting for those battleships Commander Andreola told you about?" Cameron suggested. "Maybe they *want* you to bring the battle to them? Maybe..."

"There are a million maybes, Cam, trust me. You and I both know that, if they come for us in full force, we'll lose everything—the Aurora, Rakuen, Neramese...*everything*. This ship *must* leave this system. We *must* take the fight to the Dusahn, and we must do so *before* the next attack."

"Recon has shown no significant changes in the deployment and movement patterns of the Dusahn fleet," Cameron reminded him. "Perhaps they aren't on the 'attack a week' schedule you think they are."

"Look, Cam, I have no intention of running off half-cocked and attacking the Dusahn *before* this ship is ready."

"Yet, that is exactly what you are gearing up to do."

"Cam, Vlad has always taken shortcuts to keep

this ship in action," Nathan argued. "The only difference, now, is that he is *telling* us he's taking them. He *is* the chief engineer. He *knows* which shortcuts are safe to take and which are not."

"Are you sure about that?" Cameron wondered. "Because what I see is a man trying to help his friend, regardless of the risks."

"You mean, like you did?"

"It's not the same," Cameron argued.

"Actually, it is."

"*I* gave everyone a chance to decide for themselves if they wanted to take the risk. Vlad isn't."

"No, he's passing *that* decision to his captain, exactly as he should to do."

"He is supposed to run it past you, *first*, and let you decide," Cameron argued. "Instead, he's doing it and then telling you after the fact."

"Because I insisted he not waste time consulting with me on those decisions. We're in a war. We don't have the luxury of debating every little thing, and we shouldn't be second-guessing our chief engineer. The man is doing his *job*. After seven years with him as *your* chief engineer, I'd expect you to have more trust in him."

"I do trust him, Nathan," Cameron insisted. "I just worry that *you* trust him *too much.*"

"I always have you to keep him honest, don't I?"

"That's *my* job," Cameron reminded him.

Nathan sighed, leaning back in his chair. "Look, I promise to make Vlad correct all the shortcuts he has taken, but not until all our primary systems are fully operational again. However, if the Dusahn show *any* signs of gearing up for another attack, this ship *will* return to action, shortcuts or not."

"Understood."

"*Captain, Comms,*" Naralena called over the desk intercom.

"Go ahead," Nathan replied.

"*The Prime Minister of Rakuen is requesting a vid-link with you, sir.*"

Nathan sighed. "I hate being right."

"Lucky for you," Cameron said as she turned to exit, "it doesn't happen that often."

* * *

Lieutenant Rezhik pressed the call button beside the door and waited for a response. After a few moments, the door opened, revealing Gunwant Vout.

"Mister Vout," the lieutenant greeted in a calm, unemotional tone. "I am Torren Rezhik."

"The man who has been investigating me for the past week," Gunwy replied. "Please, come in, Lieutenant."

The lieutenant's left eyebrow raised slightly at the use of his rank.

"It is an honor to meet an actual Ghatazhak," Gunwy complimented as he stepped aside to allow the lieutenant to enter. "My people have only heard stories."

"You seem to know much about me," the lieutenant said as he entered the spacious suite.

"I think it is only prudent to learn as much as possible about someone who is trying to do the same about me."

"Indeed."

"To what do I owe the pleasure, Lieutenant?"

"It seems that you have considerable influence on this station. I have asked many questions and have received very little substantive information. Either you are new to this station, as you claim, or everyone is afraid to speak about you."

Gunwy laughed as he made his way to the kitchen. “I assure you, no one is afraid of me, Lieutenant. However, they *may* be concerned about my employer.”

“SilTek.”

“Yes. It is a large and powerful company. Many would liken it to a planetary government, albeit one whose primary concern is profit.”

“Which makes me wonder why the people of Sanctuary fear it.”

Gunwy returned from the kitchen with a multicolored bottle and two glasses. “SilTek provides the defensive system that protects this base from those who might do it harm.”

“Then, they should be praising your company, not fearing it,” the lieutenant pointed out.

“Join me in a drink, Lieutenant?”

“No, thank you.”

“Are you sure? It is the best vintage my world has to offer.”

“Alcohol dulls the senses,” Lieutenant Rezhik stated. “But I appreciate the gesture.”

“As you wish,” Gunwy replied, pouring himself a drink.

“Perhaps you could elaborate as to why the people of this station seem to avoid answering questions about you and your employer.”

“I’d be happy to,” Gunwy replied, sipping at his beverage. “You see, Sanctuary was once a very remote outpost, with only the occasional visit by faster-than-light ships from other systems. As word of the station’s hospitality grew, ships began to utilize it as a rest stop of sorts. Being so removed from any heavily populated worlds, the station became a hiding place for pirates, smugglers, and confidence artists. At its height, the station, although economically strong, was a dangerous place to be."

"I am aware of Sanctuary's troubled history, Mister Vout," the lieutenant assured him.

"The introduction of the jump drive only made matters worse," Gunwy continued. "That's where SilTek came into the picture. We quickly recognized the economic potential of this facility, as well as its markets, particularly its tech and weapons markets. In exchange for access to those markets, we upgraded their defenses, their internal security systems, their environmental systems, their fabricators..."

"And all SilTek wanted in return was access to the station and its markets," the lieutenant stated, in obvious disbelief.

Gunwy paused a moment, examining his guest. "Why are you here, Lieutenant?"

"I am attempting to determine whether or not it is safe for Mister Taggart to continue his association with you; more importantly, if the Karuzari Alliance should establish a relationship with SilTek."

"Is that not for Marcus to decide?" Gunwy wondered.

"Mister Taggart is a good man, but the security of our contingent on Sanctuary is my responsibility."

"Wouldn't that be the responsibility of the station's security forces?" Gunwy said.

"Would you be here if SilTek had not corrected this station's security problems?"

"I suppose not," Gunwy admitted.

"I am simply trying to determine if you and your employer should be considered an ally or an enemy."

"That's a rather simplistic view of things, don't you think?"

"It is a starting point," the lieutenant insisted.

"SilTek seeks mutually beneficial business arrangements. My job on Sanctuary is to monitor its markets for technologies that we feel are worthy of investment."

"For the purposes of profit," the lieutenant stated for clarity.

"Is that not the motivation of all successful business entities?" Gunwy asked.

"In my experience, mega-corporations often seek more than just wealth," the lieutenant replied. "They also seek power."

"Power over market share, perhaps, but nothing more," Gunwy assured him.

"Yet, SilTek owns an entire world *and* its population."

"SilTek does own the entire planet; however, its citizens are there by choice. They are free to leave at any time. SilTek even provides transportation to those seeking to emigrate elsewhere."

"Interesting arrangement."

"SilTek wants its employees to be happy. It improves productivity and, therefore, profit," Gunwy explained.

"So, *all* the people of your world are *employees* of SilTek?"

"That is correct." Gunwy thought for a moment. "Perhaps your leaders would like to *visit* SilTek?"

"You can arrange this?"

"I can contact the appropriate people, and *they* can make the arrangements," Gunwy explained. "I am just a technology scout."

"I will pass the invitation on to my superiors," Lieutenant Rezhik said, rising from his seat.

"I hope I have answered all of your questions," Gunwy said, also rising.

"For now," the lieutenant replied. "Although, I suspect I will have more in the future."

"I am always happy to help," Gunwy assured the lieutenant. "And, please, tell Marcus I look forward to resuming our lunches together."

* * *

Vladimir strolled into the captain's ready room, looking quite pleased with himself as he plopped down on the couch.

"Does anybody knock anymore?" Nathan wondered.

"On metal bulkheads?"

"Aren't you supposed to be fixing my ship?"

"I came to update you," Vladimir announced, "and to see if you wanted to get some lunch."

"It's twenty-two thirty."

"A late-night snack, then," Vladimir suggested.

"Out with it," Nathan instructed.

"This ship now has ten times the energy production capacity than it had with all four antimatter reactors," Vladimir bragged, "and in less than half the space, I might add."

"What about the jump drive?" Nathan asked.

"Did you hear what I just said?"

"I did," Nathan replied. "What about the jump drive?"

"There are eight more emitters to be installed, after the four that are being installed as we speak."

"When?" Nathan asked, growing impatient.

"Day after tomorrow, at the latest," Vladimir assured him, putting his feet up on the edge of Nathan's desk. "But we will need another day or two after that, to install the additional energy banks in the two empty reactor bays."

"That's a day late."

"Actually, you are getting a *working* jump drive four days *ahead* of the original schedule, which was impossible to begin with. You just won't be able to jump more than twenty light years until the additional energy banks are ready."

"Cameron will not be happy," Nathan pointed out.

"Cameron is never happy."

"She doesn't like the shortcuts you've been taking," Nathan warned. "I told her not to worry, that you knew what you were doing." Nathan looked at his chief engineer. "I'm right, aren't I?"

"No, I have been making it all up as I go," Vladimir declared indignantly. "Of course, I know what I'm doing, Nathan. I've been fixing this ship for nearly ten years. Cameron is spoiled by seven years of strict adherence to all her lovely little policies and procedures, most of which go *out* the airlock as soon as the shooting starts."

"Please, don't ever say that in front of her," Nathan advised.

"You think I'm an idiot?" Vladimir chuckled. "One of the first two things you learn in engineering is to never tell your captain how you manage to do all the miraculous things you do."

"What's the second?" Nathan wondered.

"Always tell your captain it will take you twice as long to fix than it truly will. That way, you always look good."

"So, you've been lying to me all these years?"

"It has not been necessary," Vladimir boasted. "I am that good."

"Just make sure none of your 'shortcuts' come back to bite us in the ass in the middle of battle or, worse, during a jump."

"If I thought they would, I would not have taken

them," Vladimir assured him as he rose from the couch. "Do you want to eat or not?"

* * *

"No, a *hanna* is a beautiful woman," Commander Andreola corrected as they sat in the jump seats of the Reaper, facing the jump sub aft of them. "Are you sure this thing is safe?"

"I've used it a number of times," Jessica assured him.

"I didn't ask how many times you've used it. I asked if it was safe."

"As safe as it can be," Jessica replied, "considering it's jumping more than a light year and has to hit a target that is miniature, by astronomical standards, *and* that it must do so at *exactly* the right speed and angle, or we'll both be killed instantly."

"So, *not* safe."

"I'm still here," Jessica pointed out.

"That is because you are a *kicka*," the commander told her. "Someone who is hard to control or hard to kill, depending on context."

"Fits. What else you got?"

"A *yakka* is someone who talks too much."

"Are you making an observation?" she wondered.

"Not at all," the commander assured her. "I'm assuming that you will *not* be speaking very much once we are on Orswella, so I wouldn't be surprised if someone were to say, 'She's not much of a yakka, is she?'"

"Your people have an unusual way of speaking."

"It seems perfectly normal to us," the commander insisted. "*Unusual* would be getting into *that* thing and jumping into a puddle of water."

"You volunteered," Jessica reminded him.

"Agreed would be more accurate," the commander corrected. "I was your only option."

"Which reminds me," Jessica said, "I never asked you *why* you agreed to go."

"Yes, you did," the commander corrected, "and my answer is still the same: because it is a chance for my people to be free of the Dusahn, once and for all."

"There's no guarantee that Captain Scott will agree to take out the Dusahn's ground forces on your world," Jessica reminded him. "In fact, it's highly unlikely at this point."

"I understand."

"Did I warn you that I'll kill you if I suspect you're playing us?"

"Three times, now," the commander replied.

"Just so we're clear."

"Is this how you build trust?"

"Nope," Jessica replied. "Fear. I find it works better than trust."

"Well, you're definitely a *binka*."

"Okay, I understood *hanna* and *yakka*, but what the hell's a *binka?*"

"In your vernacular—a scary-ass bitch."

"So, I'm a *hanna-binka*?" Jessica asked.

"Precisely," the commander confirmed.

Jessica smiled as she looked at the time display on the wall. "Keep them coming," she told him, "we've still got a few hours until we arrive."

"*Jarmers*," the commander replied. "That means wonderful."

* * *

Lieutenant Vulan sat down on the park bench next to General Hesson. After looking around, he spoke. "It is becoming difficult to evade the trackers.

Soon, the entire net will be complete, and I will no longer be able to meet with you."

"I have made arrangements with the houses handling the project," General Hesson assured the lieutenant. "You will have the ability to deactivate your tracking chip at will."

"Is that not just as risky?"

"When you deactivate your chip, the system will show it as still active. The trick will be to reactivate at the same location, so it appears that you had not moved."

"Then, the nobles are on our side," the lieutenant realized.

"Enough of them, yes," General Hesson replied. "Men of greed are easily manipulated. They care not under which flag they operate, as long as their profits continue to flow."

"Then, they have agreed to grant you nobility."

"Once I have assumed command over the caste, each house will gift me ten percent of their assets, and house Hesson will become the most powerful house on Takara, making *it* the ruling house. It will all be in strict accordance with both Takaran *and* Dusahn law."

"And what of the rest of us?" the lieutenant wondered.

"Those who wish to continue to serve will be allowed to do so, either as crew on our ships or as employees of one of House Hesson's new acquisitions. The Dusahn will finally have both an empire *and* peace. The only cost will be the removal of the Dusahn name from that empire."

"There are those who will be unable to accept the loss of their heritage, General."

"Those who do not adapt to change are left

behind," the general stated. He turned toward the lieutenant, measurably lowering his voice. "Takara has far more to offer than glory and conquest. These people once had a serum that extended the human life span for hundreds of years, one that works far better than our own genetic manipulations."

"Why have I not heard of this?" the wide-eyed lieutenant wondered.

"It was supposedly lost when the empire of Caius Ta'Akar fell, but I believe it is still on this world, waiting to be found."

"Have you told Lord Dusahn about this?"

"I have not," the general replied. "He would tear this world apart looking for it. He does not understand diplomacy and negotiation. He only knows war. Decades of studying only one side of the Chankarti has made him this way. There are other ways to build an empire, ones that do not require massive loss of life."

"An odd statement, coming from a man who has sent hundreds of thousands to their deaths in the name of the empire."

"As I said, times change, and we must change with them."

"Change is difficult for many of us," the lieutenant said, "especially our leader."

"His dream of being the one who finally returns our caste to greatness, and seizes control of Nor-Patri in the name of his family, has all but consumed him."

"He is planning a massive invasion of the Rogen system," the lieutenant said.

"What?"

"If he cannot destroy the Aurora, he will destroy

the worlds that support her. Those were his very words."

"How many ships?"

"I am uncertain," the lieutenant replied. "At least three battleships, *including* his flagship."

"Then, he will lead the attack himself?" the general asked.

"That was my understanding."

"When will this attack occur?"

"The battle group departed this morning."

"The man is a fool," the general said with disgust.

"You must act sooner than planned," the lieutenant urged.

"No, we will wait," the general insisted. "Even if Captain Scott survives, his forces and the Rogen worlds will be desperate. He will have little choice but to accept our offer."

"Then, you will *not* be warning him?" the lieutenant surmised.

"I will," the general replied. "If for no other reason than to maintain appearances."

"What are we to do now?" the lieutenant wondered.

"All is in place," the general replied, appearing quite satisfied. "Everything is going as planned."

* * *

Commander Andreola slid down into the jump sub, taking the seat directly behind Jessica. "This really does not seem like a good idea," he complained as he pulled the hatch above him closed.

"You can swim, right?"

"Yes, but..."

"Then, you've got nothing to worry about," Jessica assured him as she powered up the jump sub's systems. "There are a lot more difficult ways to be covertly inserted onto an enemy-held world. Trust me, Commander, I've used them all."

"Perhaps it is time you started calling me Stethan."

"Reaper Six, Jump Sub," Jessica called over comms. "Ready for release."

"*One minute to release point,*" Ensign Weston replied.

"I cannot believe I am returning to Orswella," Commander Andreola said, half to himself.

"How long has it been?" Jessica asked as she checked her systems.

"More than a year. They keep the Orswellan ships away for months at a time."

"If you've been away that long, how can you be sure the Dusahn don't have some sort of tracking system set up to keep tabs on the movement of all your people?" Jessica wondered.

"They have never installed such a system," the commander insisted. "Their focus was always on building and maintaining their ships. It is unlikely they would do so now."

"But you can't be certain."

"No, I cannot," the commander admitted.

"And there is no planet-wide identity database that the Dusahn can check at will?"

"There is not. Our world has avoided computer networks since the beginning, fearing the same thing that happened to Earth might happen to us. All technology on Orswella is very localized. My people are only required to carry an ID card."

"Isn't that easy to forge?"

"Yes, but the Dusahn have never seemed concerned with that fact. That may be due to the swiftness and severity of their punishment. Dusahn soldiers are known to execute criminals at the moment of apprehension."

"Sounds like a lovely place," Jessica replied.

"It was."

"*Five seconds to release,*" Ensign Weston reported. "*Good luck, sir.*"

"See you in a week," Jessica replied.

"*Three......two......one......release.*"

The jump sub shook slightly, the clunk of metal clamps letting go of its hard points. Commander Andreola felt his stomach churn as the jump sub fell away from its underside, leaving them in zero gravity.

"Ten seconds to jump," Jessica warned. "I'd suggest you brace yourself."

"What?" the commander replied, his eyes widening. "I thought you said it was easy."

"I lied," she said, smiling to herself. "Jumping in three..."

Commander Andreola grabbed his shoulder restraints, pulling them as taut as possible.

"Two..."

He braced himself by putting his hands on his armrests and grasping them tightly.

"One..." Jessica reported, grabbing her own armrests. "Jumping."

A split second later, there was a terrible thud, as if they had slammed headfirst into a solid wall, the sudden deceleration throwing both of them forward against their restraints.

Commander Andreola felt his restraints dig into his shoulders, his breath nearly blown from his lungs. He immediately felt the jump sub sway gently, accompanied by a sensation he had not felt in some time...the gravity of his homeworld.

* * *

"You called, Lieutenant Commander?" Nathan announced as he entered the Aurora's intelligence shack.

"Yes, sir," Lieutenant Commander Shinoda replied. "These scans from the Darvano system show that one of the Dusahn's battleships departed the system approximately three hours ago."

"For where?"

"The Haven system. They were there just long enough to recharge, then they jumped to the Volon system."

"Are they still there?" Nathan wondered.

"No, sir," the lieutenant commander replied. "Again, they stayed long enough to recharge, then jumped away. I had the Falcon locate the old light of their departure jump. They appeared to be headed for Ursoot, but they haven't shown up there yet."

"Then, we lost their track," Nathan surmised.

"Yes, sir. I have tasked the Falcon with locating them."

"Maybe they've changed course?" Nathan suggested. "Maybe they're trying to shake any tracks?"

"Possibly, but they haven't shown up in any of the outer systems."

"So, it could be headed here," Nathan surmised.

"We're still waiting for the latest recon data from the systems, but the Dusahn have *never* sent a battleship *outside* the cluster, except that one time they sent one here."

"Yeah, I won't forget *that* engagement for quite some time," Nathan commented.

"They could just be using the battleship as a show of force in the outer systems."

"If so, they would probably go to Haven, Volon, Ursoot, Paradar, and Palee, before returning to Darvano."

"That's what we thought, but they haven't shown up in any of those systems."

"And the estimated time for a battleship to travel here from the cluster is still three days, right?" Nathan asked.

"We have no data to suggest otherwise," the lieutenant commander agreed.

Nathan took a deep breath, letting it out slowly as he examined the map of the Pentaurus sector. "Keep an eye on *all* the Dusahn-controlled systems," Nathan instructed. "I want to know if any other ships go missing."

"Yes, sir."

Nathan continued to stare at the star map.

"Something troubling you, sir?" the lieutenant commander wondered.

"It's not like the Dusahn to send a single ship, even if it *is* a battleship. They're up to something."

"We'll figure it out, sir," the lieutenant commander promised.

* * *

"How are you doing back there?" Jessica asked as she guided the jump sub silently along the seafloor.

"I will survive," Stethan assured her. "I find it odd that such a violent transition is considered normal for your people."

"I wouldn't call it normal," Jessica admitted. "Additional room for cargo and passengers means we don't have enough room for inertial dampeners."

"Couldn't you just make the vessel larger?"

"We could, but then you're talking about a complete redesign, as well as retooling a larger ship to launch and retrieve it. *This* size works well with our Reapers. Besides, the bigger the ship, the bigger the splash."

"Of course," the commander replied. "How long until we arrive at our debarkation point?"

"Another ten minutes, but that's just a guess. We didn't have much data on your world, so we came in a pretty good distance from shore," Jessica explained.

"I should warn you that staying too close to the bottom of the sea might be hazardous."

"Why?"

"*Tantils.*"

"What's a *tantil*?" Jessica wondered.

"A very large sea creature, perhaps a few hundred meters in length," Stethan explained. "They are docile creatures, for the most part, but can become quite aggressive if they feel threatened, especially if they are nursing a pup. The fact that this ship is similar in size to their favorite food, a *jora seal*, adds an additional element of risk."

"I'm pretty sure my sensors will pick them up," Jessica replied.

"Doubtful," the commander warned. "A sleeping tantil is difficult to distinguish from the seafloor."

"Great," Jessica grumbled as she changed the sub's assigned cruising depth. "It would've been nice if you'd told me this *before* we jumped."

"My apologies," Stethan said. "It did not occur to me. However, tantils are generally found at deeper depths. If we are only ten minutes away from the shore, we are likely already in waters too shallow for them."

"Feel free to warn me ahead of time if you think of any other risks we might encounter," she said somewhat sarcastically.

"I shall."

"What did you say the name of the town was?" Jessica questioned as she leveled the sub off at its new depth.

"Pentarna. It is one of several suburbs of our main city, Ausley."

"Why Pentarna?"

"I spent my summers there as a boy, so I know the area fairly well."

"And Ausley is the largest city on Orswella?"

"Yes," the commander confirmed. "There are other cities close to Ausley's size, all of which are along the same coastline, as well as hundreds of smaller towns and villages. Orswella has very mild weather patterns and very little rainfall, so it was necessary to colonize coastal areas, to ensure adequate supplies of water. Even our agricultural lands are near the coast."

"What about the rest of your world?" Jessica wondered.

"There are a few settlements here and there," the commander explained, "mostly separatists who wanted nothing to do with the rest of Orswellan life, for either religious or political reasons."

"It seems odd that your world remains so sparsely populated after centuries."

"Orswella was hastily colonized," the commander reminded her. "The original settlers were poorly prepared and had insufficient numbers. It is a miracle our world survived at all. However, the real reason we have not grown to larger numbers is because we have chosen not to. The carrying capacity of our world, *without* the use of technologies that might improve that value, was calculated to be around one billion. Our people decided long ago not to exceed that number."

"But at four million, you're not even close."

"True, and we *are* growing, but we are doing so at a pace that is *manageable* and allows our infrastructure to be developed wisely. Or at least we *were*."

"So, you had some sort of reproductive restrictions?"

"Yes, each registered parenting couple was allowed to produce a single male and a single female child, thus replacing themselves. The ability to have additional children required an application, and the winners were chosen by a lottery system. Unfortunately, all of that changed when the Dusahn arrived. They altered the system, creating strict controls on reproduction, in order to reduce the impact on our natural resources, thus giving themselves *more* resources for their *own* uses."

"So, your world basically became a massive slave labor camp?"

"In a manner of speaking, yes," the commander agreed, "but only in the sense that we no longer have the free will to choose our own destinies. The Dusahn assign jobs to us, based on their own assessment testing. The illusion of freedom is all that is left of what was once a truly free society. You see, the Dusahn do not believe in freedom. They believe that all of society must work for the common good and not for the good of the individual."

"And I suppose the Dusahn decide what the common good is," Jessica surmised.

"There is a house of representatives," Stethan explained, "but they, too, are more for appearance's sake. They can make recommendations based on the concerns of their constituents but, in the end, it is still Lord Dusahn, himself, who decides our fate."

"Hell of a way to live," Jessica said.

"Since the arrival of the Dusahn, our society has slowly deteriorated. The Orswellan people are simply holding on, hoping for the day when the Dusahn will move on to more lucrative worlds."

Jessica thought for a moment. "Then, your people probably *want* the Dusahn to succeed in conquering the Pentaurus sector."

"In some ways, this is true," Stethan admitted. "However, no Orswellan would wish such a life on others. It is simply not in our belief structure. We are a people who believe in balance— with nature, with one another, and with other worlds."

"Yet, you were in a war *before* the Dusahn came."

"Yes, but that was not of our doing."

"That's what they all say," Jessica said as she slowed the jump sub and prepared to settle it on the seafloor.

"I suppose that is true."

"Break out your breather," she warned. "We're at the debarkation point."

Commander Andreola reached into the compartment on the side wall and pulled out the small device, examining it. "This device does not appear substantial enough for the task required."

"They're actually really simple devices," Jessica explained. "A rebreather supplemented by a small cartridge of highly compressed oxygen. With a little practice, it will give you an hour of time underwater."

"I have no intention of testing your assertions," the commander assured her.

Jessica shut down the jump sub, putting its primary control module in standby mode. "The water *is* warm here, right?" she asked as she reached for the flood valve.

"This time of year, the inland seas average about twenty-eight degrees," the commander replied.

"Perfect," she said, opening the flood valve. "Just like home."

Water immediately began to flood the floor of the jump sub's interior. Commander Andreola's first instinct was one of concern as the water level quickly rose above his ankles and crawled up his legs.

"Put on the goggles, as well," Jessica told him, "and don't forget your weight belt under your seat on the way out. Without it, you won't be able to stay along the bottom."

"This part seems like an even worse idea," the commander admitted as he put on his goggles. The water quickly reached his chest, and the commander placed the breather in his mouth, taking a few breaths to confirm it was working.

Seconds later, the water had reached the ceiling, and the jump sub's cabin was completely flooded. The commander fought to remain calm, anxious from the fact that he had not been in the water for longer than he could remember. He reached up and unlocked the overhead hatch, pushing it outward. He floated up off his seat, steadying himself as he turned around to lift it, gaining access to his weight belt.

With the hatch open, the commander was able to stand on his seat, his head out of the hatch, looking around as he donned his weight belt. Once properly fitted, he climbed up through the hatch, stepping over the edge of the jump sub, dropping himself to the seafloor below.

Jessica popped up through the hatch next,

closing it behind her as she exited. A moment later, she was down on the sandy sea bottom, next to the commander. She gestured to him, checking that he was all right, to which he responded with the OK sign she had instructed him to use.

As they made their way to shore, the commander was surprised to find it easier to walk along the seafloor than he'd expected, thanks largely to the additional counterweight he was wearing.

After a few minutes, they began to notice tall grasses swaying in the bottom currents, signaling they were close to shore. The commander stared up at the shimmering water above them. The amber hue of their surroundings told him the sun above them was rising, which was precisely what they had wanted, since curfews existed on Orswella that prohibited being outside when it was not daylight.

Another minute later, Jessica gestured for the commander to stop. She went a few more steps ahead of him, slowly peeking her head out of the water just enough to get a clear look at the shore.

Jessica peered in all directions, scanning for any signs of movement, but saw none. She submerged again, signaled the commander to follow her, and then walked up out of the water onto the shore.

Once out of the sea, the two of them moved quickly across the narrow strip of beach to a nearby clump of bushes and rocks. "We'll bury our stuff here," she told him.

"How will we find it?"

"The breathers have a locater in them. If I ping it with my comm-unit, it will respond with its position."

"Your comm-unit is quite different from anything we have on Orswella," the commander warned. "If we are searched by a Dusahn patrol..."

"Let's try to avoid that," Jessica said, not wanting to debate the issue.

After quickly burying their breathers and weight belts, Jessica broke one of the branches of a bush so that it was hanging down and then did the same to a nearby tree branch.

"What are you doing?"

"Markers," Jessica replied, "just in case. Where do we go now?"

"There is a recreational path over there. It is a little early, but it is not uncommon for a couple to be walking. The morning breeze should dry us out before we reach the center of Pentarna."

"Are you sure our clothing won't attract attention?" Jessica wondered.

"Pentarna is a very casual community," he assured her. "We should be fine. However, we will need to obtain more appropriate attire before we head into Ausley."

"Any ideas?"

Commander Andreola thought for a moment. "I may know someone in town, but it has been some time since I have seen her. It is quite possible that she no longer lives there."

"An old girlfriend?" Jessica wondered.

"More like the *daughter* of an old friend."

"Worth a shot, I guess," Jessica replied. "Lead the way."

* * *

"As you know, earlier today, the Dusahn battleship stationed in the Darvano system *left* that system." Lieutenant Commander Shinoda began. "We detected the battleship in Haven and then Volon, but lost track of it. Two hours later, we discovered that the number of Dusahn ships in the Takar system had decreased by four ships: two battleships and two missile frigates." The lieutenant commander paused a moment, looking at the officers gathered around the conference table in the command briefing room. "One of those battleships was the Dusahn flagship."

"The dreadnought?" Cameron asked for clarification.

"Yes, sir," the lieutenant commander confirmed. "We immediately retasked the Falcon to find their old departure light and determined that *all four ships* are on a course *out* of the Pentaurus sector."

"Are they headed here?" Cameron asked from her seat at the conference table in the Aurora's command briefing room.

"Their departure track would suggest that," the lieutenant commander replied. "However, their course could also indicate that they are headed to the Orswellan system."

"Why would they send *that many ships* back to the Orswellan system?" Nathan wondered.

"It is their only shipyard," General Telles pointed out. "If they discovered that we are aware of its existence, they could be moving to protect it."

"And leave their new empire unprotected?" Cameron argued.

"The Dusahn *still* have adequate forces to protect the cluster," Lieutenant Commander Shinoda insisted.

"Have you been able to locate the battleship that left the Darvano system?" Nathan asked.

"No, sir, but we *are* looking," the lieutenant commander assured him. "If all five ships *are* headed here, then we have just over two days before they are within striking range. Add in the time required to recharge their jump drives prior to the attack, and we have about seventy hours to prepare."

"Two battleships and a dreadnought," Cameron stated. "How are we going to defend against *that* kind of firepower?"

"What's our current missile inventory?" Nathan wondered.

"One hundred and forty," Cameron replied. "Production is currently at sixteen per day, so we'll have around one hundred and eighty to one hundred and ninety missiles by the time the Dusahn arrive."

"That's not too bad," Nathan said.

"If we were talking about *one* battleship, I would agree," Cameron remarked. "Even two, but two and a dreadnought?"

Nathan sighed. "Any chance we could increase production?"

"We're lucky to get sixteen out per day," Cameron replied. "We lost two plants in the last attack."

Nathan thought for a moment. "A few days ago, I sent a message to Commander Prechitt asking for a readiness report. More specifically, I wanted to know if he could spare some Eagles for a few days to be used as air support, *if* we decide to attack the troops on Orswella. He suggested we use Nighthawks instead, since they are better armed and can make the journey more quickly, leaving Casbon with reduced forces for a shorter period."

"You want to use Nighthawks against battleships?" Cameron wondered, a bit surprised.

"It worked before," Nathan reminded her.

"That was an accident, and the crew was nearly killed," Cameron argued.

"But it *did* work," Nathan insisted.

"Perhaps, if you only used the Nighthawks that

contained AIs," General Telles suggested. "Their reaction times would be far better. Once inside the enemy's shields, they could take out the emitters far more quickly and jump away."

"The problem wasn't with the crew's reaction times," Cameron explained. "Passing through the Dusahn's shields killed their reactor. It took nearly a minute to get it back up and have enough power for maneuvering and weapons. That's a *long damn time* when you're a mere thirty meters away from a battleship."

"Maybe Abby and Deliza could find a way to solve that problem," Nathan suggested.

"That would help," Cameron agreed, "but even if you sent for the Nighthawks, now, it's going to be at least a day before they arrive."

"They could use the Nighthawk we have on hand to experiment with, in the meantime," Nathan pointed out.

"That would still leave them with only a day and a half to get the ships ready," Cameron pointed out. "For this to work, you'd need at least two Nighthawks per battleship, with one as a backup. They would all have to attack at the same time, or the Dusahn will figure out what we're doing and find a way to defend against it."

"That's assuming they haven't already determined how we took down their last battleship," General Telles warned.

"There were no indications that the battleship was able to get a message off before they were destroyed," Lieutenant Commander Shinoda insisted, "and the other ships were not in a position to witness the event."

"What about old light?" Cameron wondered.

"Even if they managed to slip a few recon drones in, they would've had to be in just the right place to see anything," the lieutenant commander replied. "Even then, it would have been awfully difficult to determine exactly what was happening. A Nighthawk against the hull of a battleship is almost impossible to detect from that range. I'm betting the Dusahn still believe it was a lucky shot."

"Well, if those ships *are* headed this way, we're going to need a *lot* of those lucky shots," Cameron said.

"I want that battle group found and tracked," Nathan instructed Lieutenant Commander Shinoda. "And I want constant recons of all Dusahn-held systems."

"Yes, sir," the lieutenant commander acknowledged.

"What about the Orswella system?" Cameron wondered. "Maybe we should recon *that*, as well?"

"I don't want to take a chance of tipping off the Dusahn," Nathan insisted. "Besides, Jess will be back tomorrow. Hopefully, she'll bring us all the intel we need."

* * *

As the recreational path penetrated deeper into Pentarna, it became more populated, even in the morning hours. Although there were a few lingering stares by passersby, the commander was certain it was due to the age difference between himself and Jessica, and not their attempt to mimic Orswellan fashion using Rakuen clothing.

Once well inside the town, they left the path and took to the city streets and pathways. The city was obviously well planned, with meandering paths that reached every residence and business, and streets designed to provide delivery and logistical support to all buildings without creating a nuisance.

The people of Pentarna seemed quite content to walk or ride the readily available public transit buses.

"Do most of these people work in Ausley?" Jessica wondered.

"Most of those in the suburbs work in the factories and shipyards. Those who do not, work in shops that support the local population," Commander Andreola explained.

"How do they get to the factories?"

"There are buses that depart at scheduled times from various locations throughout the city. Those going to the shipyards are taken to a nearby spaceport, where they are shuttled to and from work."

"They don't live *at* the shipyards?" Jessica wondered.

"Originally, they did, but once the Dusahn got jump drives, they converted the living spaces on the shipyards into fabrication facilities, in order to increase production. I guess it was easier to move workers to and from the shipyards than have the parts fabricated on the surface."

"More likely, security had something to do with that decision," Jessica surmised.

"Perhaps." The commander stopped, staring at an apartment building to their left. "This is it."

"She lives in there?"

"The last time I spoke with her, yes."

"How long ago was that?" Jessica asked.

"Several years," the commander answered, sounding somewhat sad.

"I take it there's a reason," Jessica said, noticing the commander's expression.

"Yes. She may not be very happy to see me," he admitted. "In fact, she might not even recognize me."

"Well, as long as she doesn't scream and call for help, it's worth a try. Otherwise, we're going to have to resort to stealing stuff."

The commander took a deep breath and headed up the walkway. They entered the building and traveled down the corridor, which opened up onto a large courtyard at the other end. The commander made his way across the courtyard, directly to the door marked with the number seventeen. He paused, staring at the number.

"What is it?" Jessica wondered.

"Ironically, that may be the number of years since I last saw her."

Jessica cast a suspicious glance at the commander as she stepped up to the door and rang the bell.

"Maybe she has already left for work," the commander suggested, looking around to see if anyone had noticed them.

Jessica ignored him, ringing the bell again.

When no one answered, the commander reiterated his concerns. "Maybe we should go."

"Why are you so jumpy?" Jessica asked.

"If we keep ringing the bell, the neighbors may take notice."

"What, is there a customary number of rings on Orswella?"

"No, but..."

Jessica rang the bell one more time.

"*Just a minute!*" an annoyed female voice called from inside.

"There, see?" Jessica said. "You just have to be persistent."

Finally, the door opened, revealing a petite, young woman dressed in a robe, with wet hair. "Can I help..."

"Hello," Stethan said, his voice unsteady. "I'm sorry I didn't call first, but..."

"Uh..." The young lady seemed completely thrown off. "You should come inside," she suddenly decided, her expression changing from annoyance to nervousness.

Jessica was immediately suspicious but followed the commander inside, nevertheless.

"What the hell are you doing here?" the young woman demanded. "I thought you said it was too dangerous?"

"What the hell is going on here?" Jessica wondered. "Who are you?"

"He didn't tell you?" the young woman wondered. "Of course, not..."

"Someone needs to start explaining things," Jessica demanded, turning toward the commander, "and I'm pretty sure that someone is you."

"Marli, this is Jessica Nash," Stethan told the young woman. "Jessica, this is Marli Ayers...my daughter."

CHAPTER EIGHT

Nathan walked briskly across the Aurora's main hangar bay toward Abby's shuttle as it pulled to a stop. As he approached, the side hatch opened, the boarding steps extended, and Abby came out.

"What took you so long?" Nathan asked jokingly.

"We literally dropped everything and came as quickly as we could," Deliza assured him as she came through the hatch after Abby.

"He's kidding," Abby told her. "What's the emergency?" she asked Nathan.

"I need a way to protect the Nighthawk's systems from being disrupted when they pass through the Dusahn's shields. They need to be able to fire the moment they are inside their shield perimeter."

"You're talking about using their gravity drives to get inside their shields, right?" Deliza realized.

"That's correct," Nathan replied.

"I'm afraid to ask why," Abby added.

"We've got three battleships headed our way," Nathan told them. "Josh and Loki found a way in, by accident, last time. The problem is the full minute it took them to get their power restored and be able to attack. *That's* what nearly got them killed."

"How long do we have?"

"The attack will come in just under seventy hours," Nathan replied. "I'm actually embarrassed that we didn't pursue this idea earlier, but..."

"We've already looked into it," Abby said. "We determined that the repulsive force exerted by the Nighthawk's gravity lift systems disrupted the Dusahn shields in the area of contact."

"But they weren't *using* the gravity lift systems at the time," Nathan argued.

"No, but they *were* running," Deliza explained. "They are charged and idling at all times. If the reactor is charged, then so are the gravity lift plates. They're just not putting out much force."

"What happens if you increase the force?" Nathan wondered.

"Nothing," Abby replied. "It isn't the gravity, itself, that is disrupting their shields; it's the low-power field it is creating, combined with the slow speed at which the Nighthawk makes contact with the shield barrier. Any faster, and it wouldn't have worked. In fact, according to the computer analysis we did, the Nighthawks *should* be able to *jump* through the Dusahn's shields. They just need to do so at the correct closure rate."

"Or?"

"*Splat*," Deliza replied.

"Then, solve the systems disruption, and we have a way to bring down their shields," Nathan surmised.

"My team has been working on this for the purposes of creating missiles that can jump *inside* the Dusahn's shields and *then* detonate," Abby explained.

"Oh, my God," Nathan exclaimed, "that would be incredible! Is there any way you can retrofit our current missiles?"

"No," Abby replied. "They will need to be reengineered from the ground up. Our current missiles don't have the room for a gravity lift system, and we're still a long way from being able to produce a prototype."

"How much longer do you need?" Nathan wondered.

"A lot more than three days," she replied. "Even if we stopped working on everything else, which would be a mistake."

"What about the Nighthawks?" Nathan wondered.

"The Nighthawks have very robust energy banks for their jump drives," Deliza explained. "The quickest way to solve the problem is to simply link their weapons systems *to* those energy banks so they have the power to fire immediately."

"What about having the power to jump clear?" Nathan wondered.

"As long as they start with a full charge, and their attack jump is short-range, there should be plenty of power to do both," Abby assured him.

"How long will it take you to modify six Nighthawks?" Nathan asked.

"Do you *have* six Nighthawks?" Abby asked.

"We will by this time tomorrow," Nathan promised.

"So, a day and a half to modify all six fighters," Deliza said. "Not easy, but not impossible."

"It would help if we could use the one you have on board as a prototype," Abby suggested.

"Make a step-by-step guide," Deliza realized. "I like it."

"That's why I brought you here," Nathan instructed. "I've got a team waiting for you in the fighter maintenance hangar."

"We'll get right on it," Deliza promised.

"*Captain, Intel,*" Lieutenant Commander Shinoda called over Nathan's comm-set.

"Go ahead," Nathan replied.

"*We have a new message from our friend on Takara.*"

"I'll be there shortly," Nathan replied. "One more thing," Nathan said to Abby, "if things don't go well, you need to be ready to destroy your labs and all the research in them."

"We're always ready to do so," Deliza assured him. "We update our files to the Aurora several times a day, and all our facilities are rigged to self-destruct on command."

"We just need fifteen to twenty minutes of lead time to make sure everyone is evacuated beforehand," Abby added.

"I can't promise I can give you that," Nathan responded. "So, all your people need to be out, and all files need to be transferred to the Aurora *before* the attack comes. In fact, better start moving your families back to the Mystic now, just so we're not all running out at the last minute. It would scare the hell out of the Rakuens."

"Yes, sir," Abby replied.

* * *

"She's your what?" Jessica exclaimed.

"My daughter," the commander repeated.

"What's going on here?" Marli wondered.

"You've got about five seconds before I go all *hanna-binka* on your ass," Jessica threatened.

"I can explain," the commander assured her.

"You bet your ass you can."

"Who is this woman?" Marli demanded. "Why are you here, after all this time?"

"You said you had *no* family," Jessica said.

"A small untruth, I admit."

"Nice word."

"The Dusahn do not know about Marli," the commander assured Jessica.

"How the hell is that possible?" Jessica challenged. "Surely, they do background checks on all command personnel."

"They do, but Marli's mother and I were never married. Her mother's husband is her father of record. It's all very complicated."

"Someone had better tell me what's going on here, or I'll call the constables, myself."

"No, you won't," Jessica stated firmly. "Not if you want to live."

"I had no choice, Lieutenant Commander," Stethan insisted.

"Lieutenant Commander?" Marli said.

"You suck as a spy, you know that?" Jessica said.

"Then, you outrank her," Marli realized.

"Not exactly," the commander replied.

"I don't understand."

"*Technically*, I am her prisoner."

"That's it, I'm calling the constables," Marli decided, turning to pick up her comm-unit.

"Sit down and shut up," Jessica instructed her.

"I will do nothing of the sort," Marli argued.

"Marli, please," Stethan begged.

Jessica grabbed Marli's arm from behind and spun her around, striking her in the face with her open palm, and knocking her to the sofa. "The next one's going to hurt a lot more," Jessica warned. She spun around to face the commander, who was stepping toward her in his daughter's defense. "Don't!" Jessica warned, holding up her hand, "I'll drop your ass right here, in front of your little girl."

The commander froze in his tracks.

"She's crazy!" Marli exclaimed, holding her nose.

"No, I'm pissed," Jessica corrected, "which is worse." She turned back to the commander. "Sit your ass down next to her and start explaining, or I'll take you both out now and take my chances alone."

The commander glared at Jessica, his pulse racing.

"I promise you, I am far more deadly than I look," Jessica added.

The determination in her eyes convinced the commander to do as he was told. He slowly walked around Jessica and over to his daughter, sitting next to her on the sofa. "Are you all right?"

"Stay away from me!" she objected, pushing him away.

"I'm sorry," the commander told his daughter. "This wasn't supposed to go this way."

"What fucking way did you expect it to go?" Jessica wondered.

"I will do whatever you want," the commander promised. "I will take you wherever you want to go, help you with whatever you need to do...on *one* condition."

"Let me guess," Jessica snarled.

"She has to come back with us," Stethan finished.

"You are in no position to make any demands, you know."

"Perhaps not," the commander admitted, "but if you want my assistance, that is the price."

"What makes you think I won't agree to your terms and then kill you both after I get what I need?"

"I pride myself on being a good judge of character," Stethan told her. "I believe your captain to be an honorable man; although, I admit I am currently undecided about you."

"You should be," Jessica agreed. "Now start talking."

Commander Andreola took a deep breath before beginning. "I was very close to Marli's mother, right up until a few weeks before her wedding."

"I see," Jessica said. "So, you were shtupping the bride, huh?"

"It is not an indiscretion I am proud of, but it did give me my Marli."

"How is it that *she* knows, but the Dusahn do not?" Jessica inquired.

"Marli's mother and her father *of record* were killed when the Dusahn invaded," Stethan explained. "I was devastated at the time, believing she had perished, as well. Years later, I discovered that she had survived and had been adopted by an elderly couple. They passed when she was still in her teens. At that point, I had no choice but to risk contacting her. I set her up here, in this apartment, and made arrangements for her schooling and employment. However, I did not dare visit her, for fear of being discovered."

"Lots of officers serving the Dusahn have families," Jessica pointed out.

"And those families are under constant scrutiny," the commander replied. "It was difficult enough for me to turn a blind eye to our people's current plight. Giving Marli some semblance of normality was the best I could hope for."

"And you figured yanking her from this life and taking her to a faraway world, one where *you're* a prisoner, would be *normal*," Jessica commented.

"Family is very important to Orswellans," Commander Andreola explained. "Marli is the only family I have left, and I am the only family *she* has left."

"You haven't seen her in more than a decade, right?" Jessica said.

"Seventeen years," the commander confirmed.

"How did you even know she would agree to any of this?"

"It was a chance I had to take," the commander replied.

Marli slowly raised her hand. "May I ask a question?"

"Why not?" Jessica replied.

"Who *are* you?"

Jessica sighed, throwing her hands up. "Tell her."

Commander Andreola turned to his daughter. "She is a member of an alliance that is battling the Dusahn more than six hundred light years from here. If they succeed, *our* world may be freed, as well."

"I don't understand," Marli said. "How did you..."

"My ship was defeated by their forces, and I was taken prisoner. I have been cooperating with them by sharing everything I know about the Dusahn."

"The Dusahn will *kill* you," Marli said.

"If they learn of my actions, yes," Stethan admitted, "but I was the only one who *could* help them." He put his hands on her shoulders. "I did this *for* you, Marli; for *us*."

"Why are you here?"

"They need information on the Dusahn's ground forces," Stethan explained. "Where they are based, how many there are, their defenses, air power, deployment patterns."

"Why?" Marli's eyes suddenly widened. "They're going to attack, aren't they?"

"The Dusahn have taken control of the Pentaurus sector," Jessica explained, jumping in. "We've managed to destroy their shipyards there, but we need to destroy the shipyards *here,* as well; particularly, the two battleships that are almost completed. If we don't take those ships out *before* they become operational, the Dusahn will have enough firepower to destroy us, once and for all."

"If you are talking about the Jar-Oray and the Jar-Yella, they are already completed," Marli said. "They left yesterday."

"Damn," Jessica cursed. "Are you sure?"

"I saw it on the news last night," Marli assured her. "Three troop ships left with them."

"This just keeps getting better," Jessica muttered. She turned to Commander Andreola. "How many troops can those ships carry?"

"It depends on how they are configured. If equipped with drop pods, only ten thousand. If not, twice that number."

"This mission just got really short."

"I do not understand."

"We have to get this information back to the Aurora as soon as possible. There's only one reason they'd be sending that many troops. They're going to *invade* the Rogen system."

"How can you be certain of this?"

"They already have complete control over all the worlds in the Pentaurus cluster, and they don't really care about the outer worlds."

"Then, you are no longer planning to destroy our shipyards?"

"No, we're still going to destroy them," Jessica assured him, "but maybe not as soon as we thought."

"But there are still enough troops on the ground to kill hundreds of thousands of people!" Stethan exclaimed.

"I don't understand," Marli complained.

"If the Dusahn ships are destroyed, along with the shipyards, the Dusahn will, most likely, abandon Orswella since it will no longer be of strategic value.

The Guard was sworn to *protect* those shipyards. The punishment for our failure will likely be the annihilation of our entire civilization, just as they did to Toramund."

"But if you destroy their ships..." Marli began.

"Their goons on the ground will mow your people down on their way out," Jessica added. "Trust me, I've seen them in action; both them and their predecessors."

"But the rumor is that *more* Dusahn soldiers are preparing to depart," Marli said.

Jessica's curiosity was suddenly piqued. "How do you know this?"

"Everyone is talking about it," Marli explained. "In private, of course. I even have a friend who is married to one of the Dusahn security officers. They have children and will be going with them."

"The Dusahn security forces would be instructed *not* to tell *anyone* about their pending departure," Commander Andreola insisted.

"Are you sure about this?" Jessica asked Marli.

"I cannot be certain, but that is what Brianna told me. I have heard similar discussions from others. Many believe the day we have been hoping for has finally come; the day that the Dusahn will leave our world for good."

"There's no way the Dusahn are abandoning this world any time soon," Jessica insisted. "At the very least, they'll keep using your shipyards to crank out warships until they can build new facilities in the Pentaurus sector. Even if they ever *do* leave, there's no way they'll leave your world in any condition *close* to good."

"Why would they do that?" Marli wondered. "We are no threat to them."

"Never leave an enemy behind who might seek revenge later," Jessica stated. "A primary tenet of the Jung warrior castes." She looked at Commander Andreola. "I don't like the sound of any of this."

"Perhaps they will use the troops to secure the other worlds in the Pentaurus sector?" Commander Andreola suggested.

"Doubtful," Jessica replied. "They've got all the troops they need to control the cluster, and they don't really give a rat's ass about the rest of the worlds in the sector, at least not enough to pull troops from the only world that's producing any ships for them." After a moment, Jessica added, "No, they're *going* to invade the Rogen system."

"How can you be certain?" the commander wondered.

"I can't be," Jessica admitted. "But it's the only thing that makes sense. If they send *two* battleships and thirty thousand ground goons to the Rakuen system, we won't be able to stop them. We *might* be able to take out *two* battleships, but if the Dusahn send any additional ships from the Pentaurus sector to join in the attack, those forces will be on the ground before we can do anything about it. Even if we won the battle in space, we don't have the troops to take back the surface, not without killing hundreds of thousands of civilians in the process."

"What are you going to do?" Commander Andreola asked.

Jessica glanced at her watch. "We have about twenty-two hours until the first scheduled recovery window."

"I thought you told them you would see them in a week?" the commander replied.

"That was for your benefit," Jessica said with a smirk. "You think I tell you everything?"

"I guess not."

"Our primary goal is to get this intel *back* to the Aurora, as *soon* as possible. In the meantime, I'll set up a Sig-Int unit on the roof to see if we can pick up any comm-traffic to verify what *Marli,* here, has told us."

"Then, you agree to take her back with us?" the commander asked.

"I'm not *agreeing* to anything," Jessica stated firmly. "However, I don't see any reason not to, assuming *both* of you are telling the truth."

"I assure you, Lieutenant Commander, I have no other secrets."

"We *all* have secrets, Commander," Jessica insisted. "And for the record, I might've had *more* faith in your motivation to come on this mission, had you told me the truth to begin with."

"Or you might have suspected that I would turn you over the moment we arrived, so as to protect my daughter," the commander pointed out. "I could not take that risk."

Jessica smiled. "Maybe I was wrong about you."

"How so?" the commander wondered.

"You might make a good spy after all."

"I'll take that as a compliment," the commander replied, nodding.

"I said *might,*" Jessica added.

* * *

"What does the general have to say this time?" Nathan asked as he entered the Aurora's intel shack. "Let me guess, there's a battle group headed our way?"

"How did you know?" Lieutenant Commander

Shinoda said, going along with the joke. "The general reports that a battleship, a dreadnought, two missile frigates, and twelve gunships all left the Takar system approximately thirty-five hours ago."

"How did you miss the gunships?" Nathan asked.

"The Dusahn have gotten better at detecting our recon drones," the lieutenant commander explained. "We've been forced to do the majority of our recon passes from further and further out. We can only send a drone deep enough into the system, to detect ships as small as gunships, about once every other day or so, and even then, for only a minute or two. Any longer and they're toast, and we've only got so many drones left."

"Good answer," Nathan agreed. "Did he say anything about the battleship from the Darvano system?"

"Negative, sir, but he did suggest that you give his proposal more consideration."

"I'll bet."

"Should we send a response this time?"

"Negative," Nathan replied, smiling. "I don't want the good general to feel like we're in cahoots with him."

"Yes, sir," the lieutenant commander replied.

"We still need to find that battle group."

"We're working on it."

"And the battleship that got lost on the way to Ursoot," Nathan added, turning to depart.

"Yes, sir."

Nathan's comm-set squawked as he stepped into the corridor.

"*Captain, Cheng,*" Vladimir called.

"Tell me something good, Vlad," Nathan replied.

"*The jump array is installed,*" Vladimir announced proudly, "*a day early, I might add.*"

"That *is* good news," Nathan congratulated as he turned the corner and headed toward the bridge.

"*Just don't attempt to jump further than twenty light years until I get the additional energy banks installed,*" Vladimir added.

"Or what?"

"*I am not certain. Just do not do it.*"

"I'll do my best," Nathan promised, tapping his comm-set as he entered the bridge. "XO, a moment?" Nathan called to Cameron as he turned toward his ready room.

"Commander Yosef, you have the conn," Cameron instructed, rising from the command chair and heading aft.

"Aye, sir," Kaylah acknowledged.

Cameron followed Nathan into the ready room, closing the hatch behind her. "I sent the message to Commander Prechitt as ordered," she reported as she took a seat.

"Thank you," Nathan said as sat down behind his desk.

"What did Hesson have to say?"

"That we're going to be attacked in a couple days." Nathan threw up his hands. "Who knew?"

"Anything else?"

"Just that they're bringing extra guests," Nathan replied. "Twelve gunships."

"Well, it's not a party without gunships."

Nathan leaned back in his chair, surprised. "Cam, why didn't you tell me you had a sense of humor?"

"I've got Ensign Penchev running diagnostics on the jump drive, now that it's back online."

"That was going to be my next announcement."

"It's hard not to notice when the status light on the helm, that's been red for weeks, suddenly turns green," Cameron said.

"Vlad felt it necessary to remind me to avoid jumping any further than twenty light years until he gets the additional energy banks ready, or else."

"Or else what?"

"Don't ask," Nathan said. "I have no intention of jumping until he's done but, if we have to, let's be sure to stay *well* under that."

"Agreed," Cameron replied. "What did Abby and Deliza have to say?"

"They're confident they can rig a solution in time. In fact, they've already analyzed the interaction between the Nighthawk's gravity lift system and the Dusahn's shields. They're hoping to develop an enhanced jump missile that can penetrate enemy shields."

"Wouldn't *that* be nice," Cameron said.

"Why don't you take a break," Nathan suggested.

"I wouldn't mind," Cameron said, standing again. "By the way, I got a call from Commander Kaplan on the Mystic. She said Loki inquired about working there."

"And?"

"She offered him a job as a helmsman."

"What about Ailsa?" Nathan wondered.

"Doran's family is going to help him. His wife and daughter became very close to Lael and Ailsa over the past few months. They're all moving back to the Mystic."

Nathan sighed. "Then, he's taking the position."

"I'm afraid so."

"Good for him. He can do what he loves and be with his daughter every day. I'm happy for him."

"You sure about that?" Cameron wondered, noticing the disappointed expression on his face.

"I'll miss him, but I am happy for him. He deserves to be happy, especially after all that's happened."

"We all do, Nathan."

Nathan looked oddly at Cameron.

"What?" she asked, noticing his change in expression.

"I'm just wondering what *your* happiness is."

"What's yours?"

"Don't evade the question," Nathan said.

"I'll be happy when I'm in command of my own ship again," Cameron replied.

"Now, you're making me feel guilty," Nathan confessed.

"Not of the Aurora," Cameron assured him. "She belongs to you. She always has, since the day you first assumed command."

"She was yours a lot longer than she's been mine," Nathan insisted.

"No, she was Galiardi's. I was just sitting in the chair; and only because your father wouldn't have it any other way. Both times you've been in command, you were able to call your own shots, without anyone to answer to. That allows a completely different style of leadership. I'm talking about the Celestia. *That's* the only time I was truly in command."

"But you had to answer to me back then."

"You pretty much let me do what I wanted," Cameron reminded him.

"Yeah, I was a good boss, wasn't I?"

"So, Nathan, what is your happiness?" Cameron asked again.

Nathan took a deep breath and sighed. "You know, as much as I love this ship, life on the Seiiki wasn't bad. I got to take whatever job I wanted, for the most part. I visited a lot of different worlds and experienced different cultures. A lot of it was repetitive, but for the most part, it was pretty good."

"I never would have pegged you for an explorer," Cameron admitted.

"I've always liked to travel," Nathan told her. "I took trips all over the world when I was in college. Every break, I was heading somewhere different. I really miss that."

"It must have been nice to be able to afford all that travel."

"When I was Connor, we used to dream about earning enough to just head out into the galaxy, discovering all the lost colonies of Earth."

"How did you expect to survive?" Cameron wondered.

"We were going to travel beyond the jump veil and sell the specs to civilizations that did not yet have jump tech."

"The 'jump veil'," Cameron repeated. "I've never heard that expression."

"When you look at all the good the jump drive has brought to the worlds *within* the veil, you realize how much better humanity would be if *everyone* had it."

"That thinking is what brought us the Dusahn," Cameron reminded him.

"Yeah, there's that."

"So, your happiness would be to take the Aurora out to explore the galaxy, finding all the lost colonies of humanity," Cameron surmised.

"Yes, I suppose that would make me happy," Nathan admitted, "but that's never going to happen."

Cameron rose from her seat again. "Never give up

on your dreams, Nathan, for if you do, they never come true."

* * *

"Are you sure Marli won't call the *constables* while we're gone?" Jessica asked as she and Stethan stepped onto the roof of Marli's apartment building.

"She will not," Stethan assured her.

"Wow," Jessica exclaimed as she took in the view. "Nice view. It kind of reminds me of pictures of Earth from a few hundred years ago."

"We have tried to keep technology out of our civilization as much as possible," Stethan said.

"Why?"

"A light switch that senses who has entered the room and sets the lights to that person's recorded preferences is nice, but it is also expensive and requires a special technician to repair when it fails. A simple mechanical switch may not be as convenient, but it works just fine."

Jessica looked at him funny. "But not as well as the one that sets the lights just the way you like, without you having to do anything."

"We believe that technology, although useful in many applications, can make life *too* easy. When that happens, the struggle that *is* life is gone."

"I don't know about you, but I've had enough *struggle* to last me a lifetime," Jessica insisted as she opened up the small black package in her hand. "*This* tech is *good* tech, trust me."

"That little device will collect all the transmissions in the area?" Stethan wondered, looking unconvinced.

"This *little device* will collect transmissions from the whole planet, from space, from everywhere, assuming you people use satellite communications," Jessica insisted.

"We do."

"But they're expensive and difficult to repair," she joked.

"The curvature of the planet requires them..."

"I was joking," Jessica clarified as she activated the device. A small antenna rose from the box. After reaching a meter in length, a collector dish opened up to form a circle and then twisted itself into a sphere.

"That's impressive," Stethan admitted.

"Picked it up on Sanctuary," Jessica told him.

"Sanctuary?"

"Long story." Jessica adjusted the device, checked its display, and then activated it. "That should do it."

"I hope the Dusahn do not detect it."

"It's completely passive and uses so little power that you'd have to be standing right next to it for a scanner to detect it. So, unless the Dusahn regularly patrol your rooftops, we should be good."

* * *

Commander Prechitt entered the training offices on Casbon, data pad in hand.

"Good afternoon, Commander," Talisha greeted from her desk. "Want some mellani root salad?" she offered. "There's a huge batch of it in the fridge. One of the trainee's wives dropped it off. It seems she is worried that we instructors are not eating well enough."

"Then, she's been to our mess hall," the commander quipped. "Got a minute?"

"Sure, what's up?" she asked, putting her bowl down.

"You mentioned that *all* the Nighthawks have AIs, right? That they just hadn't been activated?"

"All of the single-seat ships, yes, but not the two-seat trainers. Why do you ask?"

"Any chance we could activate the AIs on *all* of them?"

"Sure, but you would have to pay the license fee for each AI. They're owned by SilTek."

"SilTek?"

"The company that built the Nighthawks for the Sugali."

"Are they expensive?"

Talisha laughed. "Almost as much as the damned fighters, themselves," she replied. "That's why the Casbons only purchased temporary licenses for sixteen ships, to be used for training. The licenses expire in one Casbon year."

"Then what happens?"

"The AIs switch off," she replied. "Why are you asking?"

"We need to borrow at least six ships," the commander said, "*with* AIs."

"What for?"

"It seems the gravity lift systems emit some type of field that disrupts Dusahn shields just enough to allow the fighters to *penetrate* them. This is how two of our pilots disabled the shields on a Dusahn battleship and saved the Aurora."

"Really. How the hell did they figure that trick out?"

"It was by accident."

"I see." Talisha's expression suddenly changed. "You're going to attack some *battleships*, aren't you?"

"Actually, they're coming to attack *us*," the commander corrected. "I mean, the Aurora; the entire Rogen system, actually. The Nighthawks may be the only way we can stop them."

"Why not just integrate the tech into a weapon of some sort, like a missile, or something?"

"I'm sure we will, eventually," the commander agreed, "but there's no time. The attack is in *two days*."

"How many battleships?"

"At least three," the commander replied. "One of them is a dreadnought."

"I'm not familiar with that term," Talisha admitted.

"A *really* big battleship with *really* big guns."

"Then, you're definitely going to need *more* than six ships," Talisha insisted, "not to mention pilots." After a moment, she added, "When do we leave?"

"I need you here, Talisha, to train the Casbon pilots," Commander Prechitt insisted.

"Your Corinari pilots are doing all the training," Talisha pointed out. "I'm just a consultant. The Casbon pilots aren't even *ready* for the type of flying *I* can teach them."

"It's dangerous."

"So?"

"I mean, *really* dangerous," the commander said. "Not like flying against the Ahka."

"Are you going?"

"Yes, I have to. Not that many of us have flown the Nighthawks."

"All the more reason I should go," Talisha insisted.

Commander Prechitt sighed. "I'm not going to talk you out of this, am I?"

"Nope," Talisha replied, rising from her desk. "I'll get ten ships prepped for departure."

"Can we spare that many?"

"How long will we be gone?"

"Four or five days, at the most," the commander replied, "assuming we all survive."

"The first group of pilots is just starting their dual-instruction rotations. The second group is still in the simulators. Those ships are just going to be sitting there, doing nothing, for at least another two weeks."

"Very well," Commander Prechitt agreed. "I'll round up eight of our pilots with Nighthawk experience, and we'll meet you on the flight line in a couple hours."

"Outstanding!" Talisha exclaimed with excitement.

"You really shouldn't be happy about this, Talisha," the commander said.

"Sorry. I won't let it happen again," she promised as she fought back a smile.

* * *

Jessica came out of the bathroom and looked around the living room of Marli's apartment. "Where's your father?"

"*Stethan* is taking a nap in the spare bedroom," Marli replied.

"You have a spare bedroom?"

"My roommate moved out last month," Marli replied. "I'm still looking for a new one."

"You don't have to go to work?" Jessica wondered.

"I work evenings as a medical tech in a clinic down the street."

"I see."

"What do you do?" Marli wondered. "Are you some kind of spy?"

"You know, I'm not sure what I am," Jessica admitted. "First I was spec ops, then a Ghatazhak, now I'm a tactical officer, sort of."

"I don't know what any of those are."

"Let's just go with 'covert operative'."

"Have you known Stethan long?"

"You people call your parents by their first names?" Jessica wondered.

"No, not usually," Marli admitted, taking a seat on the chair across from Jessica. "It's just not an easy thing to do, suddenly. I met him seventeen years ago, and even then, I only spent a few days with him. Then, he was gone again."

"Yeah, I guess it would be hard to just suddenly start calling him 'pop'."

"Pop?"

"Another word for father," Jessica explained.

"Your people call their fathers 'pop'?"

"Pop, papa, dad, daddy...all kinds of things, really. Depends on what part of the planet you're from and what language you speak," Jessica explained.

"You have more than one language?"

"Oh, God, we have hundreds of them, probably thousands."

"You must have a very big population."

"We do, now," Jessica said.

"Where are you from?"

Jessica thought for a moment. "I don't suppose it would hurt anything to tell you," she decided. "I'm from Earth, although I left there more than seven years ago."

"You're from Earth?" Marli exclaimed in disbelief. "I thought everyone on Earth and all the core worlds were killed by a plague."

"We nearly were," Jessica admitted. "But we rebuilt. *All* the core worlds did."

"Incredible," Marli said. "I had no idea."

"Most worlds aren't aware of our recovery," Jessica explained. "We only got back out into space recently."

"You have jump drives, as well?"

"Indeed, we do," Jessica replied. "We invented them, actually."

"Then, the Dusahn did *not* invent them?"

"Are you kidding?" Jessica laughed. "The Dusahn are leeches, just like the Jung. They conquer worlds and steal their technology."

"Have you seen many worlds?" Marli asked.

"I lost count a long time ago."

"It must be amazing."

"Not always," Jessica admitted. "Some worlds are so bad you wonder why anyone ever settled there."

Marli thought for a moment. "Where are you taking *us*?"

"I haven't *agreed* to take you *anywhere,* yet," Jessica reminded her, "but if I do, you will most likely be going to Neramese, at least until your father can be released."

"Then, he *is* a prisoner?"

"Yes."

"But he's *helping* you, *right*?"

"Yes, he is."

"I don't understand."

"I'm sure we can work something out," Jessica promised.

Marli thought again, afraid to speak.

"Something bothering you," Jessica wondered, "besides the obvious?"

"Would the Dusahn *really* kill everyone?"

Jessica sighed. "I've seen them glass entire worlds, two of them while I was still on them."

"But you survived," Marli said, looking for some thread of hope to cling to.

"Only because I had a way to get *off* those worlds before it was too late."

"Then, you think I should leave Orswella?" Marli asked.

"Look, Marli, I don't know what's going to happen to your world. I don't even know if you'll be better off leaving it. I *do* know that my people are going to destroy your shipyards, that Dusahn battleship guarding it, and any other ships that get in our way."

"But why?" Marli pleaded. "We've never done anything to your people. Why would you put us at risk like that?"

"You're already at risk," Jessica insisted. "The Dusahn are never going to leave your world in peace. When they go, the last warship will destroy your civilization from orbit with the press of a button. Your people's best bet is to arm yourselves and try to kill the troops on the surface *before* they kill you."

"That's impossible," Marli argued.

"Not if most of them leave," Jessica insisted. "In fact, this may be the *perfect* time to rise up. When the Alliance takes out that Dusahn battleship, the troops on the ground will have no support. We could even supply your people with weapons..."

"Orswellans are non-violent."

"You won a *war*," Jessica reminded her.

"From space," Marli argued. "I wasn't even alive, of course, but from what I understand, there was no face-to-face, armed conflict. My people wouldn't even know how to *use* a weapon."

"You'd be surprised what people can do when they have to," Jessica said.

"There has to be a better way."

"If we knew exactly where all the troops were stationed, we *might* be able to take them out," Jessica told her, "but I can't *promise* anything."

"I can tell you where they are stationed," Marli

promised. "Every station, checkpoint, base, airfield... all of them."

"How do you know where all these places are?" Jessica wondered, looking suspicious.

"Are you kidding? All young women on my world know where they are. We avoid them at all costs."

"Got a map?"

"Are you going to take me with you?"

Jessica smiled. "You're more like your father than you know."

* * *

"*You can speak to her from anywhere,*" Vladimir replied over the intercom on the ready room desk.

"I can?"

"*Da. Through the intercom or your comm-set.*"

"She's in the ship's computers?"

"*That would be impossible,*" Vladimir replied, forcing back a giggle. "*Our computers are not compatible. It would be like connecting a light panel to a hydraulic line. Her program is still running on her own native system in the Nighthawk fighter. She is just connected to the ship through a complex software interface, which allows her to communicate with the Aurora's systems.*"

"Who wrote *that* program?" Nathan wondered.

"*She did,*" Vladimir replied.

"That's incredible," Nathan exclaimed.

"*I told you she was amazing,*" Vladimir boasted. "*She is available to you anytime; just call her the same way you would call me. You can even make it a secure link, if you like.*"

"And it won't interfere with what Abby and Deliza are doing?" Nathan asked.

"*She can conduct multiple simultaneous conversations,*" Vladimir assured him.

"Good to know," Nathan replied. "Thanks."

Nathan clicked off the intercom, then leaned back in his chair, thinking. After a few moments, he donned his comm-set and tapped the side of it. "Aurora, Captain," he called, feeling a bit strange making the hail.

"*How may I help you, Captain?*" the AI asked in the familiar, female voice.

"Is this Leta or Aurora?"

"*I am the same construct that you know as Leta. I have simply been renamed Aurora by Commander Kamenetskiy.*"

"Weird," Nathan said, more to himself.

"*I can use a different voice when responding as Aurora, if you'd prefer.*"

"I think that would help," Nathan agreed.

"*Would you prefer a male or female voice?*"

"Female," Nathan replied. "Definitely. Aurora is not exactly a masculine name."

"*Any particular type?*"

"Pick something," Nathan instructed.

"*How is this?*" Aurora asked, her voice taking on a husky tone.

"A little too deep."

"*How about this?*" she asked, her voice changing again.

"That's better," Nathan decided.

"*Are there any accents, regional dialects, or types of syntax you prefer? I have studied your language files and can speak all of the Earth languages, as well as thousands of languages you have likely not yet encountered.*"

"Interesting," Nathan commented. "Can you do a British accent?"

"Of course," she replied in the requested accent. *"I can be as British as you like."*

"That might be a little *too* British."

"You'd prefer something less obvious, then, like Captain Taylor's accent."

"I guess that would work," Nathan agreed. "Just, don't sound *too* much like Captain Taylor. That would be weird."

"Of course, sir," Aurora agreed. *"Is this better?"*

"Let's give that a try." A thought suddenly occurred to him. "Are you currently speaking with Doctor Sorenson and Deliza Ta'Akar?"

"Not at the moment, but they are nearby," Aurora replied. *"My last conversation with them was thirteen minutes ago. However, they have been addressing me as Leta."*

"And you answer them in your original voice?"

"That is correct," Aurora replied, using her Leta voice to reassure him.

"Good. From now on, when addressed *as* Aurora, use this new voice."

"With everyone, or just with you, Captain?"

"Everyone, to avoid confusion."

"As you wish, Captain," Aurora acknowledged, using her new voice with an accent similar to Cameron's. *"Was there anything else, sir?"*

"Yes. Are you aware of the current tactical situation?"

"There is a Dusahn battle group composed of two battleships, one dreadnought, two missile frigates, and twelve gunships on their way to the Rogen system. It is expected that they will launch an attack in approximately sixty-five hours, give or take a few hours. This is, of course, after they have staged

somewhere outside the target system in order to fully recharge their jump drives."

"And you are aware of the Rogen system's defenses, as well as those of the Karuzari fleet?"

"*I am,*" Aurora replied. "*Would you like me to list them for you?*"

"That won't be necessary," Nathan assured her. After a sigh, he said, "Are you able to calculate our chances of success?"

"*Yes, but first I will require a proper definition of success,*" Aurora answered.

"Fair enough," Nathan replied. "Success would be that the Dusahn forces are either defeated or forced to retreat, and neither of the Rogen worlds, nor our forces, has suffered too much damage or loss of life."

"*That still leaves a lot of room for error; however, I will attempt to answer your question.*" The AI paused, giving the impression that it was giving the matter some thought. "*Without the ability to penetrate the Dusahn shields, your odds of success are less than thirty percent. However, there will be considerable losses of both life and assets.*"

"And the Aurora?"

"*The Aurora has a twenty percent probability of survival.*"

"What about Rakuen and Neramese?"

"*They will survive, but the number of deaths will be in the millions,*" Aurora replied with no undue emotion in her otherwise natural tone. "*Would you like me to list the probable asset losses for you?*"

"That won't be necessary," Nathan replied. "What about *with* the Nighthawk fighters?"

"*If the Nighthawk fighters are able to penetrate the shields and disable them, the Aurora's survival probability improves greatly, and the loss of life on*

Rakuen and Neramese will be in the tens of thousands, possibly even fewer. How many assets will be lost depends largely on which battle plan you select."

"Which battle plan?" Nathan wondered.

"Correct. There are several."

"You can make battle plans?"

"I have been discussing the matter with Captain Taylor for several hours, now."

Nathan was shocked. "Really?"

"How do you think I was able to emulate her accent so well?" Aurora stated.

Nathan smiled as he rose from his seat. "That will be all, thank you."

"If you are looking for Captain Taylor, she is currently in her quarters."

"Amazing," Nathan said with a laugh as he headed toward the exit.

"Thank you, Captain."

* * *

Stethan came out of the spare bedroom rubbing his eyes, still groggy after his nap. In the past two months, he had traveled further from his home system than nearly every Orswellan in history. He had been captured, interrogated, nearly killed while trying to retrieve files from his own ship, interrogated some more, and then imprisoned. Finally, he had ridden a frighteningly small jump sub into the bay on his homeworld and found himself in the apartment of the daughter he had not seen in seventeen years. Needless to say, he had plenty of reasons to be exhausted.

After all he had been through, the sight that greeted him as he entered the living room should not have been such a surprise—his estranged daughter reviewing maps with the trained killer-spy of the very forces who were trying to destroy his conquerors.

"What's going on here?" he asked.

"Your daughter is giving us some great intel," Jessica announced. "That's what's going on."

"What kind of intel?" Stethan wondered.

"The kind that may save your people, after all," Jessica replied.

Stethan glanced down the hallway toward the spare bedroom and then back to Jessica and Marli. "How long was I asleep?"

* * *

"*The agreed-upon documents and funds are in a trust, the control of which will be given to the new leader of the Dusahn caste, only upon the death of its current leader,*" Lord Mahtize reported over the secure vid-link.

"Thank you for your cooperation, Lord Mahtize," General Hesson replied. "I look forward to working with the noble houses of Takara to *restore* this world to its former greatness."

"*Just be sure to hold up your end of the arrangement, General,*" Lord Mahtize stated, abruptly ending the link.

"It seems our dear Lord Mahtize is feeling a bit emboldened these days," the general decided, one eyebrow raised.

"It matters not," Lieutenant Vulan reminded the general. "Now that the trust is in place."

"Indeed," the general agreed. "However, I believe that House Mahtize should be the first to be done away with, once we seize power."

There was a loud noise from outside the room—yelling and the clunk of boots on the stone floors. Before the general could react, the door flew open, and four heavily armed Zen-Anor rushed in, their weapons sweeping from side to side.

"*Room is clear,*" one of the soldiers called from behind his helmet visor.

"What is the meaning of this?" General Hesson demanded.

The sound of boots walking toward them echoed from the corridor, becoming louder with each step. When they stopped, Lord Dusahn was standing in the doorway. The Dusahn leader removed his gloves, tucking them into his belt without a word. He looked at the lieutenant. "You are dismissed, Lieutenant, with the thanks of your lord."

Lieutenant Vulan rose from his seat, glared at the general indignantly as he straightened his jacket, then turned and walked away.

General Hesson looked down at his desk, realizing his situation. "How long?" he asked, not looking up.

"Since the moment I allowed you to retire," Lord Dusahn responded. "A pity you did not take advantage of my generosity." Lord Dusahn walked up to the chair where the lieutenant had been sitting, taking a seat himself. "What am I to do with you, old man?"

"Perhaps you should thank me," General Hesson suggested. "After all, I have prepared the ultimate victory for you."

"Yes, you have," Lord Dusahn agreed. "I have to admit, you are quite clever. I win, and you are honored as the mastermind who lured Captain Scott into the Chankarti arena. If I lose, you become leader of the Dusahn Empire, have your champion executed, and become the most powerful house on Takara. Either way, your retirement is secured, quite lavishly, I might add."

"I was only protecting the empire *you* have created for our caste, my lord."

"Your words are hollow, old friend," Lord Dusahn stated. "You played the game too long and missed your chance for a safe exit." Lord Dusahn rose from his chair and headed for the exit.

"If you kill me, you will be forfeiting the millions in credits and assets in the trust account," General Hesson reminded his leader.

"On the contrary," Lord Dusahn stated as he walked toward the door. "That trust is the evidence I need to convict *all* the nobles of treason." Lord Dusahn stopped and turned to face the general again. "Your trust will become null and void as having been created in conjunction with that crime. All the nobles will be sentenced to death, and *all* the wealth of Takara will fall to the state, which of course is controlled by me." Lord Dusahn smiled. "Goodbye, old friend," he said, turning and continuing out the door.

General Hesson stood proudly behind his desk as the senior Zen-Anor officer stepped forward, pulled his sidearm, and shot the general in the head.

CHAPTER NINE

Stethan and Marli followed Jessica past the bushes and onto the beach.

"What about the breathers?" Stethan asked, glancing back at the bushes.

"We don't need them," Jessica replied, taking the same small device she had used to collect transmissions out of her pocket.

"You're going to collect more transmissions?" Stethan wondered.

"This thing does more than just collect Sig-Int," Jessica replied.

"I don't understand," Stethan said. "How are we going to reach the jump sub without breathers?"

"Remote," Jessica stated, pushing a button on the device. "The jump sub will pull onto the beach, in front of us, in a few minutes."

Stethan looked around, spotting nobody on the beach in the early morning hours. "What if somebody sees it?"

"It's a chance we'll have to take," Jessica pronounced. "Besides, even if they do, by the time the Dusahn get here, we'll be long gone or, at the very least, deep underwater."

"It would be safer to use the breathers," Stethan insisted.

"Three people, two breathers," Jessica reminded him. "Another reason you should have told me about Marli, up front."

"I don't understand," Marli said. "Are we going by *boat*?"

"*Sub*, actually," Jessica replied.

"What's a *sub*?"

"A *boat* that goes underwater."

Marli looked at Stethan. "She's kidding, right?" She looked to Jessica, then back to Stethan. "I can't swim."

"You won't need to," Jessica promised.

Stethan continued to look nervously up and down the beach, fearful that someone would spot them.

"You came here this way?" Marli asked Stethan. "In this *sub* thing?"

"Yes," Stethan replied, "and it was not a pleasant experience."

Jessica noticed the fear on Marli's face. "Relax; it's a lot easier on the way *out* than on the way *in*."

"It would almost have to be," Stethan commented.

A tiny beep emitted from Jessica's device. She scanned the water, looking for the sub, but had difficulty finding the black body against the water in the early light of dawn. "There," she finally declared, spotting the sub as it grounded itself in the lapping waves. She checked up and down the beach, herself, just to be sure. "It's now or never," she announced, heading out quickly across the open beach.

"We must go," Stethan told his daughter.

"Are you sure about this?" Marli asked, unwilling to move.

"Yes, yes! Quickly, Marli!" Stethan begged, grabbing his daughter's arm and pulling her toward the water.

Marli followed her father, hesitant at first but, within a few steps, broke into a run along with him. They reached the water as Jessica was climbing up onto the sub and opening its topside hatch.

Jessica glanced around again, making sure no one was watching them, before dropping down inside and sliding into the pilot's seat.

Marli stepped carefully into the knee-deep waves, her eyes wide with fear.

"Quickly, we need to get inside," Stethan urged, pushing her upward.

"It looks too small," Marli argued as she reluctantly climbed up the side of the slender, black vessel.

"There is plenty of room," Stethan insisted. "Just climb in and move over."

Marli did as instructed, stepping up over the edge of the hatch, getting both legs inside, and then lowering herself down into the sub. Once inside, she could see Jessica in the single seat in front of her.

"Slide to your right," Jessica instructed as she prepared the sub for departure.

Marli immediately moved over as her father's legs came down through the overhead hatch. Stethan quickly dropped down into the left seat, reaching up to pull the hatch closed. "The hatch is secure," he reported as he reached over to strap his daughter in.

"Hang on," Jessica warned as she increased the sub's buoyancy and activated its reverse water jets. The sub bounced a bit in the waves, and there was a grinding sound coming from under its nose as it dragged along the coarse, sandy bottom, pushed backward by its reverse water jets.

After a moment, the sub's nose broke free, allowing it to sway and roll with the waves.

"I don't do well on boats," Marli admitted, her hands grabbing for anything she could find to steady herself.

"It will get better once we're out of the shallows," Jessica promised.

The sub continued to slide backward, being pushed away from the shore by its water jets.

"Come on," Jessica complained, watching the displays.

"What's wrong?" Stethan wondered.

"Nothing's *wrong*," Jessica insisted. "It's just slow going. The incoming tide is pretty strong, and this thing isn't exactly a speedboat, especially in reverse."

"Can you turn it around?"

"Not until we reach deeper water."

"The water is very shallow here," Marli told her. "You can walk out for at least fifty meters and still be only knee-deep, during low tide."

"When is that?" Jessica asked.

"Usually in the early morning."

"I guess I should've considered that," Jessica admitted as she continued to monitor the sub's displays.

"I don't feel well," Marli said as the sub continued rocking in the waves.

"Barf bags are in the seat backs," Jessica told her.

"I'll be okay," Marli assured her.

"We've almost got enough water under us to submerge," Jessica told her. "I'm going to take her down a bit, now." Jessica pressed a button, allowing water to enter the sub's four ballast tanks. After a few seconds, the sub began to slowly sink, and the rocking subsided, becoming less pronounced with each passing second as the sub became completely submerged.

Jessica adjusted the rate at which the sub was taking on ballast water, keeping them a meter above the sea bottom as it gradually sloped toward deeper waters.

"Coming about," Jessica finally reported, twisting

her control stick to bring the sub's nose around one hundred and eighty degrees, while also killing the reverse water jets and engaging the sub's main propulsion jets as their nose came around. The force of the jets gently pushed them back in their seats, and the rocking motion was all but gone.

Marli looked relieved, easing her grip on the wall and Jessica's seat back. "Are we underwater?" she asked her father.

"I believe so," Stethan replied.

"We've got two meters of water above us," Jessica reported.

"How deep are we to go?" Marli wondered.

"About a kilometer," Jessica replied.

"Oh, my God," Marli exclaimed.

"We need to go deep enough to have room to pick up speed and get on our departure course."

"This does not seem like a good idea," Marli said.

Jessica laughed. "Like father, like daughter."

* * *

Loki stood in the doorway to the quarters that he and Josh shared while aboard the Aurora. Although he had spent most nights with his family in their apartment on Rakuen over the last few weeks, there had been times when their rotation schedule required him to sleep here, in the company of his oldest friend. Next to packing up all of his late wife's belongings, this was the task he was dreading the most.

Summoning up his courage, he pushed the door open, and stepped inside. As expected, the compartment was less than tidy. Josh's dirty clothing was heaped in a pile in the corner, and the remains of his last two or three meals were still sitting on the table. It was easy to tell which bed was Loki's. It was the one that didn't look like a hurricane had hit it.

Many a night had been spent in this room, talking about women, debating issues, arguing about trivia, and more talking about women. They had been completely unproductive moments, but ones he wouldn't have traded for anything in the world.

Well, almost anything.

Loki approached the locker next to his bed. Inside was his spare uniform, a picture of his wife and daughter, and his data pad. If it hadn't been for the picture, he doubted it would have been worth coming back.

"I heard you'd come aboard," Josh said from the doorway.

Loki said nothing, just continued staring at his open locker.

"I take it you're not coming back to work," Josh surmised.

"I am," Loki replied quietly. "Just not here."

"The *Mystic*?" Josh surmised. "You do know how *boring* that's going to be, right?"

"I know."

"You're going to miss all of this," Josh pointed out. "The bad food, the long shifts, the lack of sleep, and *me*. You're going to miss *me*."

"The dirty dishes, half-eaten food, piles of dirty clothes, the farts in the middle of the night?" Loki replied. "Yes, it will be difficult."

"You sure about this, Lok?" Josh asked, becoming serious.

Loki sighed, finally turning to face his friend. "No, but I don't have a choice. Ailsa needs me."

"She's a *baby*, Loki. She doesn't even know who you are."

"She knows."

"Fine, she knows, but it's not like she's going to miss you any more if you're working *here* than if you're working on the *Mystic.*"

"Except that I'm far less likely to make her an orphan if I'm working on the Mystic," Loki told him. "I have to do what's best for my daughter. I hope you can understand that."

"This isn't about your daughter, Loki," Josh argued. "You're leaving for the same reason you didn't stay on the Seiiki with us the first time."

"What are you talking about?"

"That need for a *normal* life. That sense of *responsibility* that makes you feel obligated to do what society expects, instead of doing what makes you *happy.*"

"You mean, like you."

"Hell yes, like me!" Josh exclaimed.

"I'll be *happy* knowing that my daughter will have a father," Loki insisted. "As my friend, I was hoping you would understand that."

"I *do* understand, Loki," Josh assured him, "but did you ever consider what *Ailsa would* want you to do?"

"Ailsa's a baby, Josh, you said so yourself."

"How is she going to feel when she's older, knowing that her father left his true calling when he was needed most, all for her?"

"I don't know...*loved*?"

"She's going to feel guilty, Lok," Josh insisted. "Guilty that you gave up what you loved, for her. Guilty that you stopped making a difference for *everyone* just to change her diapers. Think about it, did *Lael* ever ask you to quit and take a safer job? No, she didn't, and you know why? Because she *knew* how it made you feel. She *knew* that her husband made a difference."

Loki continued staring down at the floor. "Ailsa needs me."

"She needs more than just a warm body," Josh argued. "She needs her *father*, her *real* father, a man she can look up to and respect. If you do this, you won't respect *yourself.* I *know* you. Every day you step onto the Mystic's bridge to sit and stare at her flight displays for hours on end, you'll be reminded of what your life *could* have been; what it *should* have been; what you *wanted* it to be. You'll resent your own daughter, and she'll *feel* it."

"Josh," Loki begged.

"Look, you do what you have to do, Lok," Josh insisted, "and I'll support your decision, no matter how *dumb* it is. That's what best friends do."

"Thanks," Loki replied, finally looking up at Josh. He turned back around, taking his data pad and picture from the locker. "I'll leave the uniform for the quartermaster to pick up."

"I'm going to hide it and say you took it with you," Josh insisted. "That way, I'll have a spare."

"You'll have to get it tailored," Loki joked, "you being so short, and all."

"I'm not short," Josh insisted, "you're just freakishly tall."

Loki turned back around to face his friend, extending his hand. "Until the next adventure?"

"Until the next adventure," Josh agreed, shaking Loki's hand and pulling his friend in for a hug. "Take care of yourself, buddy, and protect that baby of yours."

"We'll be fine," Loki said, ending the embrace.

"We've got the galaxy's greatest pilot flying the ship that protects us all."

"I'm only the greatest when I've got *you* backin' me up," Josh admitted.

Loki patted his friend on the shoulder, then headed for the exit.

Josh watched with a heavy heart as his friend walked out the door and out of his life for the second time.

* * *

"Explain to me, again, why we're just sitting here?" Marli asked.

"We either sit *here* or in space," Jessica replied. "Here, we can turn around and go back if we need to. Once we jump out, there's no way for us to return."

"But someone will pick us up, right?"

"That's the way it works, yes," Jessica agreed, "but there's no use in jumping out before the recovery window. Besides, the Dusahn aren't scanning your seas. They *are* scanning your *space*."

"You're not claustrophobic, are you?" Stethan asked Marli.

"I don't *think* so," she replied. "It's never come up until now. Maybe it's just knowing we're a kilometer underwater, and that if this thing breaks, we'll die."

"You're not going to do well in space, then," Jessica warned.

"Your ships are bigger than this, right?"

"Much bigger," Stethan assured her. "So big that you wouldn't even know you were *in* a spaceship."

"And you've *lived* aboard one for the last seventeen *years*?"

"Twenty, actually, but I went back to the surface on occasion. You get used to it."

"I can't imagine going so long without seeing the sky."

"The other things you see, things that most people will *never* see, more than make up for it," Stethan assured her. "At least, for me it always has."

"But what will I *do* there?"

"You said you're a med-tech, right?" Jessica said. "We *always* need more medical personnel."

"I just take vitals and give injections, and stuff," Marli insisted.

"I'm sure they'll find you a job," Stethan promised.

"We're coming up on the recovery window," Jessica announced, adjusting herself in her seat. "I'm activating the auto-jump sequencer." Jessica activated the jump navigation computer and turned the sub's piloting controls over to the computer. The ship began to accelerate sharply and then pitched upward. At the same time, its ballast tanks began filling with air, increasing the sub's buoyancy and adding to its acceleration toward the sky.

Marli, again, grabbed both the wall and the back of Jessica's seat, bracing herself as the sub pitched up and accelerated. "Is this normal?" she asked her father.

"I don't know," Stethan admitted. "It's my first time."

"It's normal!" Jessica insisted.

"Are we going to come out of the water before we jump? Can this thing fly?"

"Hang on," Jessica warned as the surface came rushing toward them. "Three seconds to jump... two......one......jumping."

There was a blue-white flash of light, and everything became still. Marli felt her stomach turn as the gravity disappeared. "Oh, my God," she exclaimed. "Are we in space?"

"We are," her father replied.

Marli noticed Jessica's hair floating upward. "Your hair!" She leaned to one side to peer around Jessica's seat, looking out the front windows of the sub at the starry blackness outside. "Oh, my God!" she exclaimed again.

"Incredible, isn't it," Stethan said.

There was a small flash of light in the distance.

"What was that?" she wondered, pointing forward.

"*That* is our *ride*," Jessica replied, "and they're right on time."

* * *

Nathan mimicked General Telles's movements, flowing smoothly from one position to the next. "What is this supposed to teach me, again?" he wondered.

"For one to master *anything* that involves movement, one must strive to have the body immediately do what the mind wills it," General Telles explained. "To do so, the body must know *how* to do what the mind wills, without the mind having to send movement instructions."

"You're talking about muscle memory," Nathan realized as he followed the general into the next movement.

"It is more than that," General Telles insisted. "It is precision, it is deliberate and intentional movement without thought. In essence, it is *instinct.*" The general ceased his movements, standing normally.

"Are we done already?" Nathan wondered.

"Hardly," the general replied, one eyebrow raised. "Show me the solo tree branch."

"Right or left hand?" Nathan wondered.

"Left."

Nathan repositioned his feet, then raised his left arm in a sweeping motion over the top.

"Why did you position your feet first?" the general asked.

"I was trying to be in the correct balance position," Nathan replied. "Was that wrong?"

"It was not wrong," the general replied. "However, it was also not necessary."

"But you taught me that position with my feet evenly spaced, facing forward."

"All things must have a starting point."

"Okay."

"The solo tree branch can be done from any position," the general said. "Attempt to punch me in the face, repeatedly."

Nathan prepared himself and then let loose a flurry of punches—left, right, left, right—all toward the general's face. As expected, every punch was swept away. What he didn't expect to see was the general doing so with only his left arm, and in a normal stance.

"Again," the general instructed, turning forty-five degrees.

As expected, each blow was easily redirected by the general, using only a single arm.

"Try harder," the general insisted.

Once more, Nathan let loose a flurry of punches, this time changing it up a bit. Left, right, right, left, right, left, left... He even threw in some uppercuts and crosses. Again, not a single punch found its mark, each of them being easily redirected by the general's left and right arms, as well as several changes of body position that allowed Nathan's punches to find nothing but air. In the end, Nathan was panting and sweating profusely, while the general appeared to be completely unaffected, as if he had been standing still the entire time.

"You're not exactly......doing much for......my confidence," Nathan said in between pants. "How the hell do you move so quickly?"

"There are multiple components involved. My mind, my body, your mind, and your body."

"What?"

"My mind watches your body. When your left hand is attacking, the next attack has a greater chance of coming from your right hand. If you *do* use your left hand two or more times in succession, each following attack will be weaker than the one that came before it and will require less effort to counter. My mind watches your patterns, looks for repetition, predictability, anything that would allow me to anticipate your next move before your mind wills it. My mind also knows what patterns of combat you know, either by analyzing your performance or your previous training sessions."

"Okay, that covers minds," Nathan said. "What about bodies?"

"The more practiced the motion, the less fatiguing it will be when executed. The muscles have formed specifically to perform that movement. Those who train for size and geometry are no more suited for combat than they are athletics."

"Are you trying to tell me that I've been training wrong?"

"You have been training toward the wrong goal," the general corrected. "Muscle and strength do not win wars. They are won with the brain first, the body second."

Nathan sighed. "How long did all this take you?"

"I have been training for thirty years, and I still have much to learn," the general confessed.

"Great," Nathan said. "I'm lucky if I've got thirty *days*."

"Fighting Lord Dusahn would be a mistake," General Telles insisted.

"You don't think I can beat him, not even if I train like an animal?" Nathan wondered.

General Telles's eyebrow shot up at the expression. "I am certain of it."

"Could you?"

"It would be an interesting contest," the general admitted, "but I am confident that I would prevail."

"Maybe we should just tell Hesson to choose *you* as his proxy," Nathan suggested.

"I suspect that General Hesson's interpretation of Dusahn law is somewhat dubious," General Telles insisted. "Were Lord Dusahn to honor the general's challenge, it would be because *you,* his archrival, were the proxy. There is no honor in defeating an old man, even one with similar training. However, defeating you in the Chankarti arena would solidify his position as leader and would obliterate any hope from those he has already conquered, as well as those worlds he has yet to invade."

"Then, why are we even here?" Nathan wondered.

"Just in case I am wrong," the general said.

"You, wrong?" Nathan teased, returning to his stance.

"Hard to believe, I know," the general agreed. "Shall we continue?"

The wall intercom beeped.

"*Captain, Comms,*" Naralena called.

Nathan walked over and pressed the intercom button. "Go ahead."

"Commander Prechitt and the Nighthawks have arrived."

"Great, I'll meet them in the main hangar."

"Aye, sir."

"Saved by the bell," Nathan said to the general, smiling. "You coming?"

* * *

Commander Prechitt climbed down from his Nighthawk, dropping to the deck from the bottom rung of the boarding ladder.

"Welcome home, Commander," Nathan greeted as he approached. "It's good to see you."

"It's good to be back, Captain," the commander replied, shaking Nathan's hand.

"How many ships did you bring?"

"Ten in total. These four, and six more are still cycling in."

"I didn't know you had that many pilots with Nighthawk experience."

"We lost a few Eagles in the first few days, so I moved those pilots into Nighthawks. Over time, they trained others to fly the Nighthawks, in case we had Eagles down for maintenance."

"The Casbons didn't have an issue with you borrowing ten of their ships?"

"The Ahka haven't attacked in over a month, now; not since *we* attacked *them*. It seems they don't have any interest in attacking people who fight back."

"They understand there's a possibility that some, or even *all*, of these ships might not make it back, right?" Nathan wondered.

"They do, sir. It's going to be months before they have pilots to fly these ships. Besides, I promised that if we broke them, we'd buy them."

Nathan turned, noticing Talisha Sane walking

toward them from the other three Nighthawks. "Miss Sane," he greeted. "I wasn't expecting to see you again."

"It took a bit of convincing, but I talked the commander into letting me join the party," Talisha replied.

"Only nine of us had Nighthawk experience," the commander added, "and ten seemed like a nice round number."

"The commander told me about your plans," Talisha added. "I brought along a dozen spare gravity lift emitters for your people to experiment on."

"I'm sure they'll appreciate that," Nathan replied. "Get your people fed and rested, Commander."

"How long until we see action?" the commander wondered.

"Just under two days," Nathan replied.

"How's the Aurora?"

Nathan smiled. "Better than ever."

* * *

Lord Dusahn walked confidently down the boarding ramp from his shuttle, onto the hangar deck of his flagship, the Kor-Dusahn.

"My lord," the ship's captain greeted.

"Captain," Lord Dusahn replied, not breaking his stride. "I trust all is in order."

"We will be at full charge in twenty-seven minutes," the captain replied.

"How long until we reach the staging point?"

"Approximately twenty hours, my lord."

"Any word from the Jar-Oray and the Jar-Yella?"

"There was a communications drone waiting for us when we arrived at this recharge point, my lord. It contained a message from the Jar-Oray, confirming that both ships are en route and will arrive at the final staging point on schedule."

"Excellent," Lord Dusahn replied as he continued across the hangar deck. "We will attack them during their morning. They will begin the new day as either *subjects* of the Dusahn Empire or as casualties."

* * *

"I thought you were a party of two," Nathan mused as he joined his officers in the Aurora's command briefing room. "I didn't realize you were on a recruitment mission."

"Neither did I," Jessica retorted.

"Glad you made it back safely," Nathan added as he took his seat at the head of the table.

"This is Marli Ayers," Jessica said, gesturing toward Marli. "She has provided us with critical intel."

"How is it that you made contact with Miss Ayers?" General Telles wondered.

"She is my biological daughter," Commander Andreola revealed.

"Indeed," the general responded, one eyebrow raised.

"What did you learn?" Nathan asked.

"Kind of a good news-bad news sort of thing," Jessica began. "The good news is we shouldn't have any problem taking out the ground forces on Orswella. The bad news is *why*."

"I'm not liking the sound of this," Nathan commented.

"The two battleships that were *supposed* to still be under construction have already *left* Orswella," Jessica reported.

"Oh, my God," Cameron exclaimed.

"When?" Lieutenant Commander Shinoda asked.

"About sixty hours ago," Jessica replied.

"I thought you said they were several months away from completion," Nathan questioned Commander Andreola.

"As far as I knew, that was the case," Commander Andreola defended.

Marli began to meekly raise her hand.

"That makes *five*," Cameron said to Nathan. "We can't defend against *five* battleships."

"Whoa, what?" Jessica exclaimed, leaning forward in her chair.

"Miss Ayers," Nathan said, "do you wish to say something?"

"Yes, sir," Marli replied, somewhat shyly. "The Dusahn stopped all other ship production in order to speed up completion of the Jar-Oray and the Jar-Yella."

"How long ago?" Nathan asked.

"Two months ago, I think."

"Then, shouldn't you have known about this?" Nathan asked Commander Andreola.

"Two *Orswellan* months," the commander clarified.

"That would be about forty of *our* days," Lieutenant Commander Shinoda explained.

"Then, the Dusahn increased their efforts just after we destroyed their battleship over Rakuen," General Telles surmised.

"I guess they didn't like that very much," Nathan commented.

"Let's get back to those *five* battleships," Jessica insisted.

"The Dusahn have a battle group en route here," Nathan explained.

"Let me guess," Jessica said, "it has three battleships in it."

"Twelve gunships, two missile frigates, two battleships, and a dreadnought," Lieutenant Commander Shinoda clarified.

"Shit," Jessica cursed, falling back in her chair.

"You mentioned Miss Ayers provided you with intelligence," Lieutenant Commander Shinoda asked.

"She was able to identify the locations of all the Dusahn ground assets."

"How is it she was aware of these locations?" General Telles wondered.

"Apparently, all young women know of, and *avoid,* these locations," Jessica explained. She turned to Nathan. "Then, we *aren't* going to attack Orswella?"

"No, we still are," Nathan replied calmly.

"What?" Cameron replied, shocked.

"That shipyard is still a threat," Nathan insisted.

"Maybe we should be concentrating on the five battleships headed our way," Jessica suggested.

"I'll handle that," Nathan replied.

"How the hell are *you* going to handle that?" Jessica wondered. Then, it dawned on her. "*Bad* idea, Nathan."

"That's *Captain,*" Nathan reminded her.

"It's *still* a bad idea," Jessica reiterated.

"My understanding is that if I lose, nothing changes. The Karuzari are still free to fight the Dusahn," Nathan explained. "If I agree to General Hesson's plan, it might delay the attack long enough to build up more missiles and get all ten of those Nighthawks ready."

"What Nighthawks?" Jessica wondered, becoming more flustered.

"Prechitt brought back ten ships," Cameron

explained. "Abby and Deliza are preparing them to be used to take down the Dusahn's shields from inside their perimeter, the same way that Josh and Loki did."

"What the hell," Jessica exclaimed, "did everyone go crazy while I was gone? Josh and Loki got shot down, remember?"

"Which is why we're trying to figure out a way to increase their odds of success," Nathan replied.

"Did anyone ever consider that it may be time to cut and run?" Jessica insisted.

"Commander Andreola," Nathan interrupted, "I'm sure you and your daughter are tired after your adventure." Nathan signaled to the guard at the door. "If you will follow this man, he will take you to the appropriate accommodations."

"What?" Jessica exclaimed.

"Lieutenant Commander," Nathan continued, speaking to Jessica, "please see to their needs."

"Captain," Jessica began to object.

"We will speak later," Nathan stated in no uncertain terms.

Jessica glared at him for a moment, then replied, "Yes, sir," before rising to depart.

Those remaining waited patiently until Jessica and the guard had escorted Commander Andreola and his daughter out of the command briefing room.

General Telles was the first to speak. "It is worth considering, Captain."

"I know," Nathan replied. "I'm just not there, yet."

"Yet, you *are* ready to sacrifice yourself to save Rakuen," Cameron stated.

"I don't know that I'm *there*, either," Nathan admitted. "Both are options."

"Well, you've got about a day and a half to decide," Cameron said.

"So, no pressure," Nathan joked.

* * *

General Telles appeared at the entrance to the captain's ready room on the Aurora. "You were a little short with Lieutenant Commander Nash, earlier."

"I've found that it's not wise to give her too much rope."

"I'm not familiar with that expression," the general admitted, closing the hatch behind him.

"Enough rope to hang herself?"

"I see," the general replied, taking a seat across the desk from Nathan. "Quite applicable, in her case."

"Mostly, I just didn't think it was appropriate to have the argument in front of the commander and his daughter," Nathan explained. "Did you review the intel she brought back?"

"Indeed, I did," the general replied. "Quite interesting. The Dusahn have spread themselves dangerously thin on Orswella, giving us an opportunity that is difficult to ignore. However, Captain Taylor's concerns are valid. The defense of the Rogen system *is* a higher priority."

"I know."

The general studied Nathan for a moment. "That is not what is bothering you, is it."

"No, it's not."

"You are considering General Hesson's idea."

"It *does* give the Aurora *and* the Rogen system the greatest chance of survival."

"Perhaps, but it also will result in your death."

"I'm already supposed to be dead," Nathan pointed out. "Maybe *this* is why I was saved."

"When you sacrificed yourself to save the Sol sector, all you did was buy us time. Eventually, the problem returned. Sacrificing yourself, yet again, would only do the same."

"I could have Doctor Sato scan me again; clone me again," Nathan suggested.

"That is an option, yes," the general agreed. "But, again, that is not a guarantee of resurrection. Many things could go wrong, and your long-term strategy cannot be to continue getting yourself killed with the assumption that you will be revived."

"But we are talking about millions of lives," Nathan reminded the general.

"We are always talking about millions of lives, Nathan."

Nathan leaned back, sighing. "*Five* battleships."

"*Captain, Intel,*" Lieutenant Commander Shinoda called over the intercom.

Nathan's eyes rolled back. "Nothing good ever comes over that thing. Go ahead."

"*We just received an urgent message from one of our operatives on Takara. General Hesson is dead.*"

"What?" Nathan exclaimed. "How?"

"*Executed in his home...by Lord Dusahn.*"

Nathan sighed again. "Understood," he replied, turning off the intercom.

"It appears your decision has been made for you," General Telles said.

Nathan looked at the General. "Do you think Jess was right?"

"About abandoning the Rogen system?" General Telles thought for a moment. "*Right* is not the word I would use. However, it is true that it may become necessary."

"How can we do that?" Nathan asked. "How can

we expect any worlds to join us if they know that we cut and run when the odds are bad?"

"If we are defeated in the defense of the Rogen system, the Dusahn will rapidly become the greatest force in all the galaxy. If we *cut and run*, as you put it, the Rogen system *may* be doomed, but we will still be alive to continue the fight. *How* we will do that, I do not know."

"He who fights and runs away, lives to fight another day," Nathan said, remembering the idiom.

"An age-old strategy," the general said, "and for good reason."

"This is not going the way I'd hoped," Nathan admitted. "I was planning on *liberating* the Orswellans with the shipyards intact, giving us *another* valuable ally. With our new long-range jump system, we could defend *both* systems, and we'd finally have the ability to grow our own fleet."

"The result would be an arms race," General Telles pointed out. "One that we would lose. The Pentaurus cluster has far greater resources and infrastructure."

"But they don't have a working shipyard," Nathan argued.

"If we gained a shipyard, the Dusahn would be forced to increase their efforts at building their *own* shipyard in the Takar system. Our advantage would diminish quickly."

"We could harass them, slow them down, and keep them from completing it."

"As could they."

"But *we* have the jump range advantage," Nathan argued.

"They can still send swarms of smaller ships back to the Orswellan system in less than a day," the general pointed out. "Escalation is not always the answer. If they fear they are about to lose what they have, they will only fight harder."

"What are we supposed to do, then?" Nathan wondered. "Continue to hide out in the Rogen system, and wait for them to attack again?"

"You speak of battles, Captain. I speak of *wars.* You must *force* the Dusahn to do what *you* want them to do," the general explained. "*That* is how *wars* are won."

* * *

"We're getting awfully close to home," Ensign Lassen warned from the Super Falcon's copilot's seat.

"If they changed track..." Sergeant Nama started.

"They didn't change track," Lieutenant Teison interrupted.

"If they didn't, then we should've found them by now," Sergeant Nama insisted.

"We've still got one search zone left," the lieutenant said. "If we don't find them, we'll switch tracks, as well."

"Which way, is the question," Ensign Lassen said.

"I'll make that decision when the time comes," Lieutenant Teison replied.

"End of grid coming up in ten seconds," Ensign Lassen warned.

"Give it an extra minute," the lieutenant instructed. "They've got to be in one of these last few grids."

"Jas, that isn't..."

"Humor me, Tomi."

"Whatever you want, Lieutenant," the ensign replied.

"Nothing behind us, Riko?" the lieutenant wondered.

"Negative," the sergeant replied from the back station. "This would be a lot easier if we went active, though."

"You know the drill, Sarge," the lieutenant said.

"Sometimes this stealth stuff sucks," Ensign Lassen complained. "I'm replotting the jump for a minute later."

"Thank you," the lieutenant said.

Sergeant Nama's eyes squinted as a trace appeared on his sensor display, then immediately disappeared. "That's weird."

"What's weird?" Lieutenant Teison wondered.

"I thought I had something, but then it was gone."

"An echo?" Ensign Lassen suggested.

"Could have been an area of dust or a rogue body of some sort," the sergeant admitted. The trace appeared again, disappearing a moment later. "There it is, again."

"Coming up on the jump point," Ensign Lassen warned.

"Lieutenant," the sergeant called, "can you turn twenty to starboard and come up twenty?"

"We'll have to replot," Ensign Lassen warned.

"Sarge?" the lieutenant asked.

"It could be nothing, then again..."

"Scrub the jump," the lieutenant instructed.

"Lieutenant," the ensign complained.

"It only takes a degree of course change for them to end up on the far edge of our sensor range," the lieutenant defended as he changed course.

"My dessert says its nothing," Ensign Lassen challenged.

"I'll take that bet," Sergeant Nama agreed.

"You want us to jump ahead?" the lieutenant asked the sergeant behind him.

"We're already going faster than they should be," the sergeant replied. "Just give it a minute or two."

"You got it," the lieutenant replied. "What is the dessert tonight, anyway?"

"Boca cake, baby," Ensign Lassen replied enthusiastically.

"Oh, shit!" Sergeant Nama exclaimed. "Go cold! Go cold!" he added as he quickly began shutting down all of his systems.

"Emergency shutdown!" the lieutenant ordered as he, too, started shutting off the Super Falcon's systems. Within seconds, the ship was completely dark.

"Talk to me, Riko," the lieutenant ordered.

"Two octos jumped in about four hundred clicks to port," the sergeant said, his voice low.

"They can't hear us," Ensign Lassen teased.

"I can't help it," the sergeant said, still whispering.

"Did they see us?" the lieutenant asked.

"I don't think so," the sergeant replied. "They were traveling away from us."

"If that trace was a battleship on a recharge layover..." Ensign Lassen began.

"Then, those octos are flying a BARCAP, and we're *inside* it," the lieutenant finished.

"We need to get the hell out of here," Ensign Lassen urged.

"We can't," the lieutenant reminded his copilot. "We're under strict orders to *avoid* detection, *at all costs*."

"How the hell are we even going to know if they spot us?" Ensign Lassen argued.

"Oh, we'll know, trust me," the lieutenant replied.

"Not funny, Jasser," Ensign Lassen said.

"I've got the low-power passive pointed in their

direction," Sergeant Nama told them. "If they sweep us, I'll know."

"If they paint us, I'll tie the jump drive energy banks into the shields, to buy us a minute of use while we spin the reactor back up," Lieutenant Teison explained.

"What do I do?" Ensign Lassen wondered.

"You get that damned reactor up as fast as you can," the lieutenant replied. "And Riko, you throw every countermeasure we've got at them. We'll have to move fast. If we're not gone in a minute, we'll be dead, and that battle group will move, and command will never know."

"I really hate this part," Ensign Lassen stated as he nervously waited. "If they're flying a standard BARCAP, then they jumped right under us. If we hadn't changed course, they would've slammed right into us."

"That's why *he* wears the bars," Sergeant Nama said.

"Damn, Jasser," Ensign Lassen exclaimed. "If we get out of this alive, *you* get *all* our desserts."

"I'll take them," the lieutenant replied as he sat staring at his dark console.

"You see anything, Riko?" Ensign Lassen asked the sergeant.

"Nope."

"Are they still heading away from us?"

"I don't know," the sergeant replied. "This thing will only tell me if we're being painted."

"How are we even going to know if they're gone?" Ensign Lassen wondered.

"You know the drill, Tomi," the lieutenant reminded him. "We go dark, and if there is no contact in five minutes, we bring up the passive suite and take a peek."

"*Five fucking minutes*," the ensign complained.

"Three and a half, now," Lieutenant Teison pointed out.

"This is not your first time, Tomi," Sergeant Nama chuckled.

"And I didn't like any of the other times, either," the ensign assured him.

"You could always apply for work on one of the shuttles."

"No way," the ensign protested. "At least *we* have *weapons*, although we rarely get to use them."

"I much prefer to *not* need them," Lieutenant Teison said. "When you do, there's usually someone shooting back."

"At least we'd *know* what they're doing, instead of sitting on our hands, blind," the ensign complained.

"You're getting to be as bad as Torwell," Sergeant Nama laughed.

Lieutenant Teison checked the clock. "Time's up, spin up the passive."

"Spinning up passive," Sergeant Nama acknowledged.

"Well?" Ensign Lassen asked after a few moments.

"Nothing," the sergeant replied, "at least not where the octos were."

"What about that trace?" the lieutenant asked.

"It isn't a trace anymore," the sergeant replied. "It's a contact, and a big one. Holy shit, Lieutenant! One, two, three...*five* battleships, two frigates, and a dozen or so smaller ships that we're too far out to identify."

"How's our jump line?" the lieutenant asked.

"It's clear."

"Let's get the hell out of here while we can, Jasser," Ensign Lassen urged.

"Lock down their course and speed, Riko," the lieutenant ordered. "Tomi, plot a jump to a point ten light minutes behind them. We need to figure out how long they've been there."

"Christ, Jasser, they're only *five light years* from Rogen; they don't even need a full charge to attack."

"I know, Tomi," the lieutenant replied. "I know."

* * *

The morning air was crisp and frigid, Nathan's exhalations sending clouds of steam that swirled about briefly, before being swept away by the breeze that always blew across the lake.

Most of his friends were already on the ice, skating about, trying to take pucks away from each other and generally assaulting the poor kid unlucky enough to have put on the pads and guard the net.

During the winter, Nathan looked forward to Saturday mornings all week long. A whole day of pond hockey with his friends. Most Saturdays, they played non-stop, from sunup to sundown, stopping only to munch on whatever sandwiches their parents had prepared for them to get them through the day.

"*Hurry up, Nathan!*" his friend Jacob called from the ice.

Nathan was usually the first one out, but he had been forced to attend one of those boring political rallies with his family, smiling for an endless stream of pictures. Nathan so wanted to make an inappropriate face at every camera pointed in his direction, but he knew that his day of fun would be canceled if he had done so.

Nathan finished lacing up his skates, grabbed his

gloves and stick, and hit the ice, skating out toward the area they usually considered to be center ice.

"Finally," Jacob complained as Nathan came to a stop beside him. "Let's show these shitheads how the game is played!"

"Dream on," Landon, the leader of the opposing group of kids, jeered.

Nathan took his spot at center ice, preparing to take the face-off. He looked around at the five boys on the opposing team, suddenly realizing that each of them was at least twice his size. "What the hell?" he wondered.

"What?" Landon asked.

"Who are all these goons?"

"What are you talking about?"

"What the hell happened to you, Landon?" Nathan wondered. "You have a growth spurt overnight?"

"Stop stalling, Nathan," Landon insisted, taking position for the face-off.

"You guys are all, like, twice our size," Nathan complained. "What did you do, go down to Pewton and recruit their junior team?"

"What, are you scared?" Landon accused. "You can always forfeit if you're afraid of getting hurt."

Nathan looked up at Landon, whom he had never remembered being so much taller than him. "I'm not scared of anything," he replied with a sneer.

"We'll see how you feel after the face-off, kid," Landon challenged as he bent over.

Nathan also bent over, placing his stick on the ice, with his blade on the opposite side of the puck from his opponents. Landon started the count, one... two...three...with them tapping their sticks above the puck on each count. On three, Nathan went for the puck, but Landon didn't. Nathan felt the shaft of Landon's stick as it struck him in the face, just below his nose, knocking him backward.

There was a loud beeping sound, and Nathan's eyes snapped open.

"*Captain, Comms,*" the B-shift communications officer called over the intercom.

Nathan blinked several times, regaining his senses.

"*Captain, Comms,*" the comms officer called again. "*Flash traffic.*"

Nathan rolled over and pressed the intercom button on the nightstand. "Go ahead."

"*Flash traffic from the Falcon, sir. They've located the Dusahn battle group five light years outside of the Rogen system, thirty minutes into their recharge cycle.*"

"What's the Falcon's status?" Nathan asked.

"*They're playing peek-a-boo with the battle group, keeping tabs on them, waiting for orders.*"

"Understood," Nathan replied. "Alert the fleet and Rogen Defense Command, wake the senior staff, and have everyone meet me in the command briefing room in ten minutes."

"*Aye, sir.*"

Nathan sat up on the edge of his bed. "It's going to be a long night."

CHAPTER TEN

Nathan left his quarters five minutes later, heading straight for the bridge, a mere thirty steps away. "Comms, contact Commander Kaguchi on the Gunyoki platform," Nathan instructed as he stepped onto the bridge. "Tell him I need two squadrons with full combat loads, ready to move to our flight deck within the hour."

"Yes, sir," the comms officer responded. "The XO asked me to add Doctor Sorenson to the briefing roster."

"Good idea," Nathan replied, turning to exit, tapping his comm-set on his way. "Cheng, Captain."

"*I'm on my way, Nathan,*" Vladimir promised.

"How long until those additional energy banks are ready?" Nathan asked as he headed down the corridor.

"*Seven, maybe eight hours.*"

"Skip the meeting and get them done in six."

"*That's impossible!*"

"Not for you, it's not," Nathan replied, turning the corner toward the command briefing room. "Make it happen."

"*Chort,*" Vladimir cursed, ending the call.

Nathan reached the end of the starboard corridor leading into the command briefing room.

"Captain on deck!" the guard called from the doorway.

"As you were," Nathan ordered before anyone could stand.

"Sorry, I'm late," Abby apologized, entering from the doorway on the opposite side of the room.

"Close it up," Nathan instructed the guards as he took his seat at the head of the table.

The guards at both doors stepped outside of the room, closing the doors behind them.

"Lieutenant Commander Shinoda," Nathan began, "if you'll please update the room."

"Aye, sir," the lieutenant commander replied as he switched on the holographic map display floating over the center of the conference table. "Fifteen minutes ago, the Falcon located a Dusahn battle group here, approximately five light years outside the Rogen system."

A flashing red icon appeared in the hovering, three-dimensional star chart.

"The group is as we expected: two battleships, a dreadnought, two frigates, and twelve gunships from the Pentaurus sector, along with the two battleships from the Orswellan system."

"Is the Falcon still in sensor contact with the target?" Cameron asked.

"After avoiding detection by the Dusahn BARCAP, the Falcon moved to a position trailing the battle group and located just enough old light to establish their arrival time, course, and speed, before disengaging long enough to dispatch a comm-drone. They are currently conducting a trailing PAB op to monitor the target."

"Pardon my ignorance," Abby said, "but what's a PAB op?"

"Peek-a-boo," Jessica told her. "They stealth-jump in at the edge of sensor range, conduct a quick scan, then jump back out."

"And you seriously call it a 'peek-a-boo'?"

"It fits," Jessica said, shrugging her shoulder.

"What's the Dusahn battle group's current status?" Cameron asked.

"They are on course for a direct attack against the Rogen system; however, due to the current positions of Rakuen and Neramese, it is impossible to tell which planet they'll target first."

"Aren't they about twelve hours early?" General Telles wondered.

"Yes, they are," the lieutenant commander confirmed. "Based on their current speed, we believe that they've accelerated to maximum jump speed in order to get here faster than usual."

"They knew that Hesson warned us," Nathan realized. "They were *counting* on it, so we'd think we'd have more time to prepare and get caught off guard. *That's* why they killed him...to prevent him from warning us, once he became aware of their faster rate of travel."

"General Hesson is dead?" Cameron asked. "When did this happen?"

"We learned about it a few hours ago," Nathan replied. "I didn't think it was worth waking anyone."

"Can't say that I'm going to miss the bastard," Jessica commented.

"If they're traveling that fast, then they'll have to decelerate before they can attack," Cameron realized.

"Otherwise, they'd zip right past us, barely able to get off a shot," Nathan added.

"If the Dusahn ships accelerated, then they have probably spent considerable propellant to do so," General Telles said, "and they'll spend even more to *decelerate*. This could work to our advantage."

"Maybe they'll have to stick to minimal maneuvering," Jessica said.

"Unlikely," Nathan insisted. "No ship's captain

would go into battle without a fully charged jump drive and more than enough propellant."

"They might have done a gravity-assist maneuver along the way, to accelerate," Cameron pointed out.

"Well, they won't be able to use one to slow down," Jessica said.

"The fact that they'll have to slow down helps us," Nathan said. "It gives us warning and a way to calculate *when* they can attack. It gives us a *safe window.*"

"A safe window?" Cameron wondered.

"As long as they're going too fast to attack, we know they *won't* attack," Nathan explained.

"Unless, of course, they attack with a batch of jump missiles targeted at Rakuen and Neramese," Jessica said.

"They won't," Nathan insisted.

"Why not?" Abby wondered.

"They don't want the Rogen system," Nathan reminded them. "They want the Aurora and *me.* If they destroy Rakuen and Neramese, we'll cut and run, and they'll have to try to locate us, again. That's why they haven't already glassed it. That's why they've been sending just a few ships at a time to attack us."

"Well, they're not sending just a few ships, now," Jessica stated.

"No, they've probably decided they couldn't wait any longer, for fear that we'd be back at full strength," Nathan said.

"At least, we know all those Gunyoki anti-recon patrols weren't a waste of time," Cameron commented.

"Indeed, they were not," the general agreed. "Had the Dusahn been able to monitor the Aurora's progress, they *may* have attacked in force long ago."

"How long do we have?" Nathan asked.

"We know their battleships take eight hours to recharge a fully drained jump drive," Lieutenant Commander Shinoda explained. "Assuming they began recharging the moment they came out of the jump, and assuming they were making max-range jumps, then we have about seven hours. As the captain said, once they begin decelerating, we'll be able to make a pretty good guess at how long we have before they can attack."

"That's a lot of assumptions," Cameron commented.

"Yes, but we believe they are reasonable ones," the lieutenant commander defended.

"How do we know what speed they're looking for?" Jessica wondered.

"We're using the maximum speed we've seen them use during an initial attack, the accuracy and maximum tracking rate of the turret weapons, and some basic physics, to come up with a best guess. However, Captain Taylor is right; it is based on a lot of assumptions."

"Abby," Nathan began, "how long until the Nighthawks are ready?"

"With Leta's help, we've come up with a pretty straight-forward way to protect the Nighthawks from the disruptive effects of the Dusahn shields," Abby explained. "It's really a combination of three things: tying the Nighthawk's reserve jump energy banks into the weapons, taking its reactor down to idle *before* passing through their shields, and wrapping its reactor with a simple physical shield using gravity plating from our own decks."

"How many have you modified?" Nathan asked.

"Just the one, so far," Abby replied. "However,

the first one is the hardest. Now that we've got the process documented, we can have multiple teams working simultaneously."

"Can you have all eleven of them modified in time?"

"*Ten* of them, yes," Abby replied. "The one we used as a prototype had to be taken apart in order to figure everything out. It's going to be a while before we get *that* one back together."

"But you can get the other ten ready in time," Nathan confirmed.

"Yes. It won't be easy, but I feel confident that seven hours is sufficient."

"More like five or six," Nathan corrected. "Once the Dusahn start slowing down, we'll have to attack right away, or they'll jump into the Rogen system and begin bombing both planets just to put us on the defensive."

"*That*, I'm *not* so sure about," Abby admitted, "but we'll do our best."

"I thought he said seven hours," Cameron stated. "Why five or six?"

"Because I intend to attack Orswella *before* we attack the Dusahn battle group," Nathan replied.

"Captain," Cameron began to object.

"The matter is not open for debate, Captain," Nathan interrupted. "The moment that battle group starts decelerating, we're jumping to Orswella."

"Assuming our long-range jump drive is working by then," Cameron said, a little testy after having been cut off.

"Captain," General Telles said, "while I do not oppose your plan to take out the Orswellan shipyards, I see no reason why it could not wait until *after* the Dusahn have been dealt with."

"*After* dealing with that battle group, we may not be *able* to attack Orswella," Nathan replied. "Besides, I don't intend on just destroying those shipyards," Nathan added, "I plan to *liberate* the Orswellans." Nathan immediately raised his hand to stop the many objections and questions that his staff would undoubtedly have. "This, too, is not up for debate. I have thought this through, and I have my reasons for this decision. This *is* the best course of action. Now, there is a lot to do, and little time to do it in, so I suggest we get started." Nathan paused again, waiting to make sure everyone in the briefing room was on board. "Commander Prechitt, since Commander Verbeek is still on Casbon, you're acting CAG. I need you to come up with an attack plan to take out the Dusahn ground forces on Orswella using precision weapons launched from Reapers. Lieutenant Commander Nash has the enemy positions."

"What about air cover?"

"You don't have any," Nathan replied, "but we're bringing two squadrons of Gunyoki with us to keep any fighters launched by the Jar-Razza from getting down to the surface. Hopefully, that will be enough."

"Fifty Gunyoki?" Commander Prechitt said. "It's going to be standing room only on the flight deck."

"Park them on the aprons if you have to," Nathan said. "We don't have time for them to fly there on their own. They'll have to piggy-back with us."

"I'll make it work, sir," Commander Prechitt promised.

"Cam, while we go to Orswella, you're staying here with a Reaper carrying a tac-com pod."

"Shouldn't I be with the ship?" Cameron insisted.

"I need you, here, to supervise the defense of

the Rogen system, should something happen to the Aurora."

"You mean, if you don't make it back," Cameron surmised.

"I don't think I need to tell you how many things could go wrong with this," Nathan said.

"Not going to be much of a fight without the Aurora."

"Do what you can but cut and run before it's too late. You never know, we might still be alive, and if we are, we'll meet up at the fleet rendezvous point."

"Then, the defense of the Rogen system is *not* a fight to the death," Jessica surmised.

"No, it is not," Nathan confirmed. "If everything goes south, we *will* cut and run. I'm not going to risk losing everything to win a battle, when there's still a war to fight."

"What about the Orochi?" Cameron said.

"I'm taking half of them with me when we attack the Dusahn battle group," Nathan explained. "You can figure out how best to use them to defend the Rogen system, if it comes to that. *That's* why I need you in the tac-com pod." Nathan looked around at the faces in the room. "Rock," he said, putting his left fist on the table. "Hard place," he added, putting his right fist down. "Us," he finished, pointing to the center with his left hand. "It's not the first time we've been in this position, and it probably won't be the last. Let's get to work, people."

Everyone in the room rose from their chairs and headed out, except for Cameron who waited until they were all out of earshot before speaking. "Are you *sure* about this, Nathan?"

"Hell, no," Nathan admitted, "but, like I said: rock, hard place, us."

* * *

Vladimir threw his hands up in frustration as he looked up at the stack of energy cells, in what was once the compartment for an antimatter reactor. "What are you doing?" he yelled at the technicians busily connecting the cells together. "One connection per cell! One connection!"

"What about a backup?" one of the technicians questioned.

"We don't have time for a backup!" Vladimir argued.

"But, if the draw is too high for a single line, the breakers will blow!"

"That is why we are using breakers with higher loads! What do you not understand?"

"But the lines might overheat!"

"They won't overheat unless we do several long jumps in a row," Vladimir explained. "We do one jump there and one jump back, and then we're done with it. Single connections! We can add backups later when we have time. Now, do as I say!"

"Aye, sir!" the technician replied.

"*Gospadee*!" Vladimir exclaimed, storming away.

"Damn, he's pissed," one of the technicians commented.

"He's crazy if he thinks these things are going to hold," the other technician insisted as he continued connecting cells. "They are going to fry, and we're going to be stranded in the middle of nowhere."

"What was he talking about? Jumping to *where* and back?"

"I don't know," the other technician said. "They don't tell us anything."

* * *

"There are twelve bases spread all around

the main city of Ausley, each of them designed to house around six thousand troops," Commander Prechitt explained. "In addition, there are numerous substations all over the suburbs surrounding the city. These stations usually support, maybe, one hundred troops each, all of whom live in private residences."

"If they don't live in the stations, how are we going to target them?" Nathan wondered.

"Based on my discussions with Commander Andreola's daughter, I believe the men assigned to the suburb stations were the first to be moved out. We'll take as many of the stations out as we can, just in case, but our focus needs to be on those twelve bases, since that is where most of their remaining ground forces will be concentrated."

"Agreed," Nathan said.

"What about other infrastructure?" Cameron wondered.

"There are multiple spaceports all over the city," Lieutenant Commander Shinoda said. "They're like bus stops, shuttling people to and from the shipyards. Those might be worth taking out."

"If we take out the shipyards, there's no need to take out the spaceports," Nathan argued. "Besides, I'd prefer to leave their infrastructure intact."

"Even if we take out every base and every station, there will still be armed troops on the ground," General Telles warned. "The Orswellans are not prepared to deal with them."

"What do you suggest?" Nathan asked the general.

General Telles took a deep breath. "We will need boots on the ground," he said reluctantly.

"You've only got one hundred men, General," Cameron stated.

"And nearly *five* hundred Corinari, itching for revenge," the general added.

"Will that be enough?" Nathan asked.

"If you leave the Reapers and Gunyoki behind for our use, and send the Glendanon as support, it will be. I can use the Reapers to move my teams around, as needed, and act as close air support."

"It will take the Glendanon twenty hours to get there," Cameron warned. "That means you'll be on your own for nearly a day."

"Then, I suggest you get them en route as soon as possible," General Telles urged.

"Boxcars can get you there in just a few hours," Jessica suggested. "Three of them should be enough."

"We'll add a fourth one with fuel and ordnance for the Reapers and Gunyoki," Nathan added. "Worst-case scenario, you retreat to the boxcars and wait for help to arrive."

"This is all assuming you are successful in taking out the Jar-Razza *and* those Orswellan cruisers."

Nathan nodded agreement. "I'm kind of hoping that once we take out the Jar-Razza, the cruisers will lose their desire to fight."

"And if they don't?" Jessica asked.

"Then, we attempt to disable them," Nathan replied. "*Destroying* them will only be done as a last resort."

"There is one more thing," Lieutenant Commander Shinoda said. "The Gunyoki have taken out two Dusahn recon drones over the last two hours."

"How close?" Nathan wondered.

"The closest one was two light hours out from Rakuen."

"We can't let them get a recon drone inside that

distance," Cameron insisted, "or they'll see that the Aurora is gone."

"She's right," Nathan agreed. "Once we jump away, not a *single* recon drone can get within that two-light-year perimeter."

"That's not going to be easy," Lieutenant Commander Shinoda warned. "That's a lot of space to cover, and those drones only jump in for a few minutes at a time."

"How many drones have they averaged over the past few weeks?" Nathan wondered.

"One every few days, or so," the lieutenant commander replied.

"Maybe discovering that the Aurora is *not* here would be a good thing?" Cameron suggested. "Maybe they won't attack."

"No way they'd pass up an opportunity to crush our industrial support while it's undefended," Nathan insisted.

"The Dusahn would not *assume* the Aurora was gone based on a *single* recon scan revealing its absence. It would take several scans from various angles to confirm."

"They'll attack no matter what," Nathan reiterated. "The question is *what* they'll attack." Nathan took a deep breath and sighed. "Send the Glendanon to the Orswellan system, best possible jump speed, but instruct them *not* to enter the system until they receive orders to do so."

"They'll need time to load supplies, fuel, and ordnance," Cameron pointed out.

"We can use boxcars for that. Tell Captain Gullen to send us a list, and we'll have boxcars deliver what he needs at one of his recharge layover points."

"I'll take care of it," Cameron replied.

* * *

"These two are ready to go," Abby announced.

"Shouldn't they be tested?" Talisha asked.

"Yes, but I've got all your pilots helping out with the mods on the other ships," Abby replied.

"We need to move them to the surface, right?"

"Correct," Abby replied. "We were going to move them all at once, though."

"I'll take one down to the surface, putting it through its paces on the way, then use that flight profile for the rest of the ships, so their AIs can fly them down."

"You can do that?"

"Yes," Talisha assured her. "The AIs can do anything a human can do, and do it better. They just can't depart or fire without human authorization. The AIs are programmed to recognize myself, Commander Prechitt, and Commander Verbeek as command authorization for the entire wing."

"What about their pilots?" Abby wondered.

"You need them here. They can be shuttled down to the surface, once all the ships are complete."

"Great," Abby agreed. "I'll leave all that to you, then."

"My pleasure," Talisha replied, climbing up the boarding ladder to the first modified Nighthawk.

* * *

"They're not all going to fit, sir," the deck boss insisted.

Commander Prechitt stood in the middle of the Aurora's flight operations center, looking at the view screens showing the Aurora's various flight aprons, decks, hangars, and transfer airlocks. "Park as many as you can on the aprons for now. Once the

Nighthawks are out of the main bay, we'll have more room."

"It still won't be enough," the deck boss argued.

Commander Prechitt glanced at the clock. "We still have at least an hour before the Dusahn start decelerating. I need every Gunyoki within our jump envelope when the time comes. I don't care if they're *hovering* in *layers* in the recovery bays, as long as every one of them is *inside* by the time we jump."

"Those pilots are going to be spending a lot of time in the cockpit," the controller commented.

"With the patrol schedules they've been keeping, they're used to it," the commander insisted. "Besides, when the Glendanon gets to Orswella, they'll all fit inside her with ease. Just make sure you don't block the exit path for those Nighthawks."

"They're all cycling out the top pad," the deck boss replied. "They've been departing in pairs."

"How many are left?"

"Four, and they should be done within the hour."

"Then, I guess I'd better suit up," the commander said. "Good luck, Lieutenant."

"You too, sir."

* * *

Vladimir stepped through the service hatch at the bottom of the energy bank containment compartment. Behind him, two more technicians, both of them just as dirty and sweaty as their boss, walked through the hatch after him. Vladimir tapped his comm-set. "Engage the power trunk to the starboard stack at ten percent."

"*Give me a moment,*" the technician replied over his comm-set.

Vladimir looked at the other technicians. "You connected the last two banks, right?"

"I thought you did," one of the technicians said.

"*Oh, bozhe,*" Vladimir exclaimed.

"I'm kidding, Commander," the technician admitted.

"Not funny," Vladimir scolded.

"*Starboard stack is engaged and charging at ten percent, max,*" Vladimir's comm-set squawked.

Vladimir leaned inside the hatch, peering up at the tall stack of energy cells filling the space. "Take it to twenty and check for wave variance."

"*Twenty, stand by.*"

"It's good, sir," one of the technicians insisted.

"*No variance at twenty,*" the technician on his comm-set reported.

"Take it to fifty and check," Vladimir instructed.

"*Taking it up to fifty.*"

"We connected it the same way we connected the port stack, and it's been charging at one hundred and twenty percent of max load for over an hour," the first technician said.

"*Looks good at fifty.*"

Vladimir took a deep breath and sighed. "Take it up to one-twenty."

"*One-twenty it is.*"

"And keep a close eye on it," Vladimir added.

"Better close the hatch and crank up the fans," the second technician said. "It's going to get hot in there."

"*One-twenty and still no variances.*"

Vladimir looked over at his two technicians, smiling. "We did it."

"Hell, yes, we did!"

Vladimir tapped his comm-set, again. "Captain, Cheng. Energy stacks are online and charging. You should have long-range jump capability within an hour."

"*Good work, Commander,*" Nathan congratulated. "*I knew you could do it.*"

Vladimir deactivated his comm-set, taking it off his head. "Honestly, I wasn't so sure."

* * *

"I hate this peek-and-boo shit," Sergeant Nama complained from his sensor console in the Falcon. "Where did that stupid name come from, anyway?"

"A children's game from Earth," Lieutenant Teison said. "And it's 'peek-*a*-boo'."

"Still, a stupid name."

"What would you call it?" Ensign Lassen wondered.

"I don't know. Quick-scan and repeat? Momentary contact scans? Peek and retreat? Anything but peek-a-boo."

"At least you only have to do thirty seconds of work, once every fifteen minutes," Ensign Lassen defended. "We have to constantly recalculate jumps back and forth, up and down, in and out. It's a pain."

"It's better than getting spotted," Lieutenant Teison pointed out.

"We're in the pipe," Ensign Lassen reported.

"What is this, like the twentieth *peek*?" Sergeant Nama wondered.

"Twenty-fourth," Ensign Lassen corrected.

"Time," the lieutenant said.

"*Peek* jump in three......two......one......"

"Jumping," Lieutenant Teison announced as he pressed the jump button on his flight control stick.

"Starting the *peek*," Sergeant Nama said as he activated his passive scans, directing the ship's array toward the position he expected the Dusahn battle group to be. "Whoa, wait a minute."

"What's wrong?" the lieutenant asked.

"They're not where they're *supposed* to be."

"They're gone?"

"No, they're there... I mean, here, but... They're slowing down, Jasser," the sergeant realized.

"Are you sure?" the lieutenant asked.

"Time, Lieutenant," Ensign Lassen warned.

"I'm sure..." the sergeant confirmed.

"Jumping," Lieutenant Teison announced as he altered course slightly to starboard and jumped.

"I've checked it three times, Lieutenant," Sergeant Nama said. "The entire group is decelerating, and at a constant rate."

"Plot us a jump back to the Rogen system," Lieutenant Teison ordered. "Get us close enough to communicate directly with the Aurora."

"You got it," Ensign Lassen acknowledged.

Sergeant Nama looked up from his console. "So, does this mean that peek-a-boo time is over?"

* * *

Loki stepped onto the bridge of the Mystic Empress, pausing to look around. It was quite different from the Aurora's, and the first thing to hit him was the row of actual windows lining the forward bulkhead.

There were some similarities, of course, most notably a command chair on a raised pedestal at the center of the compartment.

"Mister Sheehan," Commander Kaplan greeted from his right.

Loki turned to greet the commander. "Good morning, sir."

"You're a bit early, aren't you? Your shift doesn't start for more than an hour."

"I thought I would get an early start," Loki replied.

"Familiarize myself with everything before I actually have to fly this thing, myself."

"You got the procedures manual, right?"

"Yes, sir," Loki replied. "I've studied it from front to back."

"Then, you shouldn't have a problem," the commander assured him. "Besides, the Mystic is pretty easy to fly."

"You have *actual* windows," Loki commented, pointing to them.

"My understanding is that the original designers were going for the look of a traditional-style, luxury, ocean-going, cruise ship," the commander explained.

"I guess I'm just used to the Aurora's view screens," Loki said. "You were her XO, right?"

"Yes, I was."

"Do you mind if I ask you something?"

"Go right ahead."

"Do you miss her?"

"Every day," the commander admitted. "Especially the people, but the Mystic has a pretty good crew, as well, and the accommodations are excellent, as is the food."

"Yeah, I've noticed."

"I understand you have a baby girl."

"Yes, sir," Loki replied. "Ailsa. She's about six months old."

"I was sorry to hear about your wife."

"Thank you, sir."

"How about I introduce you to your counterpart?"

"That would be great," Loki agreed.

Loki followed the commander forward to the single-seat helm station, located along the forward bulkhead, tucked in against the row of windows.

"Cain, this is Loki Sheehan, your new relief

helmsman," Commander Kaplan said. "Loki, this is Cain Delgad, the best helmsman on the Mystic."

"The *only* helmsman on the Mystic, until now," Cain said. "Nice to meet you, Loki. I've heard a lot about you."

"Pleasure to meet you," Loki replied, shaking Cain's hand.

"My condolences on your loss," Cain said.

"Thanks. Quite a view you have, here," Loki said, peering out the windows down at the clear dome covering the center promenade on the main passenger deck.

"Yeah," Cain agreed, quickly glancing over his shoulder to make sure the commander was no longer in earshot. "If you're ever on duty during one of the dances they hold down there, bring a scope. You can zoom in on a lot of cleavage."

"I'll try to remember that," Loki replied uncomfortably.

"How was it flying the Aurora?" Cain asked. "Must have been incredible."

"It was pretty nice."

"Is Captain Scott really as amazing as everyone says?"

"He's a pretty good guy, yes."

"It must have been difficult to give up *that* assignment."

"So, this is the helm?" Loki asked, attempting to change the subject.

"Sure is," Cain confirmed. "Pretty straightforward, really. After the Aurora, this ship will be a breeze. Just know that she's pretty slow to maneuver. She's basically a smooth-cruiser. You spent some time on the sim?"

"A couple of hours, yesterday," Loki replied.

"Then, you shouldn't have a problem. If you do, the captain and the XO are both pretty easygoing and can help you out, until you get the hang of things. Most of your time will be spent just monitoring systems. Everything is highly automated. Just tell it where you want to go, and it will go there. You don't even have to worry about station-keeping. It's all automated. We're basically just backup for the flight computers."

"Good to know," Loki replied.

"Incoming flash traffic from the Aurora, Commander," the communications officer announced.

"What's the message?" Commander Kaplan asked.

Loki and Cain both turned to listen.

"We've been ordered to prepare to jump to safe rally point Alpha Seven. Jump is in thirty minutes."

"Did they say why?" the commander wondered.

"The Aurora is leaving," the communications officer replied.

Commander Kaplan looked at Loki. "You hear anything before you left the Aurora, Loki?"

"No, sir," Loki replied, also curious.

"There's been a lot of traffic inbound to the Aurora in the last hour," the sensor officer reported. "Including about forty or fifty Gunyoki."

"They're going into action," Commander Kaplan realized.

"The Glendanon departed nearly four hours ago," the communications officer added, "and they've been running boxcars out to her at her first recharge layover point."

"How do you know that?" Commander Kaplan wondered.

"I monitor all frequencies and channels, sir," the

comms officer explained. "It gets pretty boring up here at night."

Loki felt something come over him. A pull, a sense of responsibility, a sense of duty. His ship was going into harm's way. His *friends...*

Josh's words echoed in Loki's head. *What your life could have been......should have been.*

Commander Kaplan glimpsed the look on Loki's face. "Mister Sheehan? Is something wrong?"

Loki's eyes moved from the floor to the commander. "I'm not sure, Commander, but I think I've made a terrible mistake."

Commander Kaplan smiled. "At least twenty of the Aurora's crew are probably on their way to the shuttle bay, right now. If you hurry, you can join them."

Loki looked at Cain. "I'm supposed to be your relief."

"You think I'm giving up this seat just when there's some actual *piloting* to do?" Cain replied, also smiling. "Go already!"

Loki turned and headed for the door, pausing just long enough, while passing the commander, to say, "Thank you."

Commander Kaplan watched Loki exit her bridge, then turned to her comms officer. "Patch me through to Captain Taylor aboard the Aurora."

* * *

The Aurora's main hangar bay was bustling with activity. Reapers were being loaded with precision weapons pods, Nighthawks were preparing to move to the surface, and Gunyoki fighters were being squeezed into anyplace they could fit.

Cameron made her way across the crowded bay toward her Reaper at the far end. "How's it going?" she asked Abby as she passed by the last four Nighthawks still aboard. "Did you get them all finished?"

"All except these four," Abby replied. "They still need shielding installed around their reactors, but they'll finish that on the surface."

"They?" Cameron asked, stopping in her tracks.

"I'm staying," Abby explained.

"Are you sure you want to do that?"

"Not really," Abby admitted, "but if something goes wrong with the long-range jump system, I'm the best person to troubleshoot the problem."

"What about your family?" Cameron asked.

"They're already on board the Mystic, like everyone else's," she replied.

"And they're okay with this?"

"No, but they understand. Besides, it will work," she insisted, "assuming Vladimir didn't screw anything up by taking shortcuts."

Cameron rolled her eyes. "Good luck," she said, continuing toward her Reaper.

"You too, Cameron," Abby replied, turning back to her team preparing the Nighthawks for departure.

"There's no room in the shuttle for the tools *and* the shield components," her assistant said.

"Just put the components in the Nighthawk's cargo bays and close up their maintenance panels so we can get them out of here," Abby explained as she noticed a familiar face among the line of Aurora crew members who had just arrived from the Mystic. "Loki?"

"Hi, Doctor Sorenson," Loki replied, stopping.

"Are you okay?"

"I'm not sure," he admitted. After a moment, he cocked his head and looked at Abby. "I feel guilty for being here, but I felt guilty for *not* being here, as well."

"You and me, both," Abby replied, putting her hand on his shoulder, "but you should never feel guilty for doing what you believe is right."

"But, if something should happen to me..."

"Your daughter would be without *both* parents, I know. You can't look at things that way, Loki. It will paralyze you, and you'll never be the father she needs you to be. Your wife was a victim of a brutal attack. If you should die, you will do so fighting to *prevent* that very thing from happening to others. Your daughter will know that her father was selfless and fought to defend others. She will be proud of you. She'll mourn your loss, but she *will* understand."

Loki nodded agreement. "I should get to the bridge."

"I'll go with you," Abby said.

"But, shouldn't you..."

"I'm staying, as well," she told him, smiling.

* * *

"Flight ops reports that all the Nighthawks are away, and the last of the Gunyoki will be on deck within five minutes," Naralena reported.

"Very well," Nathan replied from the Aurora's command chair. "Mister Canlis, how long until we have a full charge in the auxiliary energy banks?"

"Approximately forty minutes," the navigator replied. "However, we already have enough power to make the jump to Orswella *and* back."

"Thank you," Nathan replied. "Any update from the Falcon?"

"Last report was twenty minutes ago," Jessica replied from the tactical station. "The Dusahn battle group is maintaining the rate of deceleration. They should reach maximum orbital velocity in just over an hour."

"Very well," Nathan replied. "Set the ship to readiness condition one."

"Condition one, aye," Naralena replied.

The trim lighting around the Aurora's bridge changed from blue to orange.

"Attention, all hands, set condition one," Naralena announced over the ship's all-call.

"Helm?" Nathan queried.

"Propulsion and maneuvering are green," Josh replied. "Jump drive shows ready."

Nathan glanced at the clock.

"Excuse me, Captain," Abby called from the entrance.

Nathan turned in his chair, spotting Abby and Loki standing at the entrance.

"Request permission to assume our stations?" she asked.

Nathan smiled. "Permission granted." He watched as Loki made his way down to the navigator's station. "Nice to see you back, Mister Sheehan," Nathan added as Loki passed.

"I hope you don't mind, Jerry," Loki said to Mister Canlis.

"Not at all, Loki. Glad to have you back where you belong," the navigator said as he vacated his seat.

Josh watched Loki sit, beaming from ear to ear.

"What?" Loki asked.

"I knew you'd be back," Josh replied as he monitored his displays.

"Oh, did you?"

"Abby?" Nathan queried as she took a seat at the starboard auxiliary station.

"I was sitting right here the first time the Aurora

jumped," she explained, "just in case something went wrong."

"Yeah, and look what happened," Jessica joked.

"Actually, that was the second jump," Abby corrected. "And imagine how things might have gone had I *not* been there?"

"Good to have you," Nathan agreed.

"Captain, all decks report condition one," Naralena announced. "Flight ops reports that all departing vessels are away, and all Gunyoki are on deck."

"Flight deck is red," Jessica confirmed.

"Mister Sheehan," Nathan called. "Plot a course to the Orswellan system and prepare to jump."

"Aye, sir," Loki replied. "The entire distance in one jump?"

"Doctor Sorenson?" Nathan queried.

"I'm sure the system is good up to at least that far," Abby assured him. "However, it wouldn't hurt to conduct a few incrementally longer jumps along the way, just to be sure," she added. "After all, we don't want to accidentally end up a thousand light years away, now, do we?"

"We most certainly do not," Nathan agreed. "Mister Sheehan, let's try one hundred light years to start, shall we?"

"One hundred light years it is," Loki acknowledged. "Course plotted."

"Take us out of orbit, Mister Hayes," Nathan instructed.

"Breaking orbit and heading for Orswella," Josh confirmed.

"Jump plot loaded and ready," Loki reported.

Nathan turned to look over his shoulder at Abby again.

"Everything looks good, Captain," Abby replied.

"On course and speed for Orswella," Josh reported.

"Mister Sheehan, execute our first jump," Nathan ordered.

"Jumping one hundred light years," Loki acknowledged, "in three......two......one......"

CHAPTER ELEVEN

"Jump three, complete," Loki announced as the Aurora completed its longest jump, yet.

"Threat board is clear," Jessica reported.

"Conducting long-range scans," Kaylah added from the sensor station.

"Any variance that time?" Nathan asked Abby.

"Negative, sir," she replied. "The adjustments Commander Kamenetskiy made seem to have done the trick."

"Then, we can safely return to the Rogen system in a single jump?"

"If necessary, yes," she agreed. "However..."

"I know, better to keep them shorter for now," Nathan finished for her. "How long until we're fully recharged?"

"Approximately one hour and forty-seven minutes," Loki responded.

"How long until we can single-jump back?" Nathan wondered. "If needed," he added for Abby's benefit.

"We only used about twenty percent of an eighty percent charge," Loki replied, "so, technically, we have enough to jump back now."

"So, on a full charge, we could jump nine hundred light years?" Nathan wondered in disbelief.

"Theoretically, yes," Abby answered proudly.

"Well done, Doctor."

"Thank you."

"Long-range sensors detect no ships within five light minutes," Kaylah reported.

"Launch the recon drone," Nathan ordered.

"Recon drone away," Jessica replied.

"Flight Ops, Captain, green deck," he added over his comm-set.

"*Green deck, aye.*"

* * *

One by one, Gunyoki fighters began to lift off the Aurora's midship hull, thrusting safely away before engaging their main propulsion.

Once those sitting on the hull were clear, the rest began filing out of all four openings onto the Aurora's port and starboard flight decks, headed for their own rally points a few kilometers away.

* * *

"GHATAZHAK!" General Telles barked. "MOVE OUT!"

In two lines, all one hundred Ghatazhak soldiers, fully outfitted in level-three combat armor, filed out of the cargo bay they had been waiting in for the last hour. They jogged across the corridor, into the storage hangar located directly below the Aurora's main hangar bay, across the bay, and into the two waiting cargo shuttles.

After the last man had exited the cargo bay, General Telles and his second-in-command, Commander Kellen, nodded at one another, followed their men across the corridor and, eventually, up the ramps into their waiting shuttles.

The aft boarding ramp of General Telles's shuttle began to rise as he reached the top. The back of the shuttle was packed, with twenty-five armed Ghatazhak lining each side of its cargo bay. The general walked through the center of the group of men as they fastened their restraints, exchanging confident nods with each man as he passed. Once at the front of the cargo bay, the general turned to face his soldiers. After tapping the comms controller on the side of his helmet to broadcast to all his men on both shuttles, the general spoke. “Once again, we are called to defend those who know not of us, but are deserving of our protection, nonetheless. We fight for freedom; we fight for honor; we *fight* for the *Alliance*. Most importantly, we fight of our own free will for that which we believe: no human shall be forced to serve an unwanted ruler. Being willing to fight, *and die*, for such a cause is what *honor* is all about, and it is *my honor* to lead you all. LONG LIVE THE GHATAZHAK!”

“LONG LIVE THE GHATAZHAK!” his men proudly echoed.

“Long live the Ghatazhak,” the general seconded, taking his seat.

* * *

The large port transfer airlock doors slid open, revealing a pair of Reapers, which immediately began rolling onto the Aurora’s port flight deck.

Lieutenant Commander Manes steered his Reaper onto the port flight deck and turned right, toward the gaping, forward opening as his copilot completed their pre-launch checks.

“All systems are green,” Ensign Sell reported. “Flight, Reaper One, ready for departure.”

“*Reaper One, Flight, cleared for departure, port forward.*”

“*Flight, Reaper Two, ready for departure.*”

“*Reaper Two, Flight, cleared for departure, port forward.*”

“How you feelin’, Buzz?” the lieutenant commander

asked as he pushed their throttles forward ever so slightly, causing them to rise up off the deck.

"*Feeling good, baby,*" Lieutenant Karimi replied from Reaper Two. "*Got my best duds on and some rockets in my pockets.*"

"Let's go have some fun, shall we?" the lieutenant commander added as he accelerated his Reaper out of the front of the port flight deck. As soon as they cleared the opening, he angled his Reaper slightly to port, steering away from the Aurora as its bow slipped past them.

"Reaper One, away," Ensign Sell announced over comms.

"God, I love this job!" the lieutenant commander exclaimed as he pushed his throttles to their stops.

* * *

"Jump flash," Kaylah announced. "Recon drone has returned."

Nathan stopped pacing and stepped over to stand beside Jessica and Commander Andreola at the tactical console. "What are we looking at?"

The images from the recon drone began popping up on the transparent display glass lining the front of the tactical console.

"The Jar-Razza is here," Jessica said, pointing to the icon representing the old, Dusahn battleship. "High orbit over Orswella. Agosti One Four Seven is here, about one hundred million kilometers from Orswella. All four Orswellan cruisers are in orbit above the Agosti shipyard ring."

"How big a threat are these ships?" Nathan wondered.

"None of *our* ships are a threat to you, Captain," Commander Andreola assured him. "Our shields are not powerful enough, and our rail guns and plasma weapons are no match for your shields. These three ships are the oldest ships left. Just like the Jar-Razza, they were never fitted with jump drives, as they were deemed unworthy. In fact, the Dusahn planned to retire them just as soon as they built replacements. The only reason they fitted *any* of our cruisers with jump drives was that they needed a few more ships to fill out their own fleet, in order to invade the Pentaurus cluster. However, they kept these in reserve."

"So, the Jar-Razza doesn't have a jump drive, either," Nathan confirmed.

"No, it does not. In fact, I'm not even sure how well it's linear FTL system is working. It has been in the same orbit above Orswella since their arrival."

"How do you know its weapons still work?" Jessica wondered.

"A few times per year, the Jar-Razza demonstrates their power by targeting unpopulated areas on Orswella."

"If that ship hasn't left orbit in twenty years..." Jessica began.

"They may not even be able to," Nathan said, finishing her sentence.

"That rumor has been going around the Guard for years but has never been confirmed," Commander Andreola said. "The Dusahn do not let *any* Orswellans aboard the Jar-Razza."

"Well, she still has full power," Kaylah told them. "Scans show three active antimatter reactors *and* active shields."

"Their shields are up?" Nathan wondered, suddenly concerned.

"The Jar-Razza's shields have been up since the Dusahn left to invade the Pentaurus cluster,"

Commander Andreola assured him. "They only bring down small sections at a time, to allow for incoming traffic."

"What kind of traffic?" Jessica asked.

"Shuttles, fighters, that kind of thing."

"No octos?" Nathan asked.

"I am not familiar with this term," the commander replied.

Jessica called up the specs on a Dusahn octo fighter on one of her screens.

"Ah, a Teronbah fighter. I can see why you call them octos. No, the Jar-Razza's flight decks are not designed to accommodate Teronbah fighters. As I said, she is quite old."

"But still powerful enough to keep all four of your cruisers from even *thinking* about turning against them," Jessica pointed out.

"*Again*, it is not the Jar-Razza that my people fear."

"Flight ops reports all Reapers are away, Captain," Naralena reported.

"Very well," Nathan replied, turning back to Jessica and Commander Andreola. "If most of their soldiers are gone, then your people may have even less to fear than before," Nathan commented.

"I hope that is true," Commander Andreola stated. "What happens if your people land and discover that the number of Dusahn troops on the surface is greater than they anticipated?"

"Worst-case scenario, they withdraw, and we attack them from the air," Nathan explained.

"Will that not cause many civilian casualties?" the commander wondered.

"Yes," Nathan admitted, "which is why it will be our last resort."

* * *

Vol Kaguchi checked his flight displays as his Gunyoki fighter came out of the jump.

"Jump complete," Isa announced from the back seat. "We are at our rally point."

Vol said nothing, watching the tactical display as the other twenty-three ships in his squadron jumped in around him, still in proper formation. "Tekka Squadron, Tekka Leader," he called, once his entire squadron had arrived. "Our target is the orbital shipyard ring around an asteroid called Agosti One Four Seven, located one hundred million kilometers from the system's only inhabited planet, Orswella. According to the latest recon, there are four Orswellan cruisers guarding the ring. Their offensive capabilities are limited, but they do have shields and point-defenses so, make no mistake, they can kill us. Be swift, and do not remain within their engagement area for more than ten seconds."

"*What are the rules of engagement?*" Dosne asked from Tekka Two.

"With the cruisers, defend only. Do not destroy them. Their crews are only serving to protect their families against retaliation by the Dusahn soldiers on the surface. Our target is that ring."

"*That's going to make it interesting,*" Damus commented from Tekka Three.

"Indeed," Vol agreed. "Even more interesting is that, although not shielded, the ring does have its own point-defenses. However, they face outward, so attacking from the asteroid side is your safest bet."

"*How much distance between the surface and the ring?*" Rodai asked from Tekka Four.

"Only ten kilometers," Vol replied.

"Are you kidding?" Jenna wondered from Tekka Five.

"The ring is situated around the asteroid's equator. We will be jumping in just above its poles and skimming the surface around to the ring. The asteroid is only sixty-two kilometers in diameter, on average, so it will take less than a minute to reach our attack point. Once the ring is destroyed, we turn our attention to *disabling* the cruisers."

"What is Dota Squadron doing?" Sten asked from Tekka Six.

"They will be flying cover for the surface attack, in case the Dusahn battleship, in orbit over Orswella, launches fighters."

"I'd rather be skimming an asteroid than dealing with octos," Kiori commented from Tekka Seven.

"Apparently, there are no octos in this system, only the older fighters."

"Are they jump equipped?" Andrik asked from Tekka Eight.

"Nothing currently defending this system has jump drives," Vol replied.

"Can I request a transfer to Dota?" Dosne joked.

Vol smiled. "One minute to attack jump."

* * *

"We're at the jump point," Lieutenant Latfee reported from the cargo jump shuttle's cockpit.

"Understood," General Telles replied as he examined the latest intelligence from the Aurora's recon drone on the inside of his tactical visor.

"Did you notice the pattern of checkpoints in relation to stations?" Lieutenant Brons asked the general. "Each is positioned to easily reinforce four others within minutes. Very efficient."

"No doubt necessitated by a lack of manpower,"

the general commented. “According to Commander Andreola’s daughter, those checkpoints are not always manned.”

“If she’s wrong, we may have a problem on our hands,” the lieutenant warned.

“I am aware of the possibility,” the general replied. “That is why we are targeting selected checkpoints first, since they are the most likely to be manned.”

“According to the daughter of an officer who serves the Dusahn,” the lieutenant commented.

“It is an imperfect world, Lieutenant.”

“Yes, sir,” the lieutenant agreed.

“*One minute,*” Lieutenant Latfee warned.

“Regardless of what we find down there, it is good to have you back in action, sir,” the lieutenant stated.

“It is where *all* Ghatazhak belong,” the general replied.

* * *

“Second recon drone confirms original orbital track of the Jar-Razza,” Kaylah reported from the Aurora’s sensor station.

“Thirty seconds to attack jump point,” Loki announced.

“All weapons are fully charged and pre-aimed,” Jessica reported.

“All decks report general quarters,” Naralena added.

“Divert all available power to forward and ventral shield sections,” Nathan ordered.

“Already done,” Jessica assured him.

“Don’t forget to hold your fire until you have a lock, Josh,” Nathan said. “There’s a planet on the other side of that battleship.”

“I got it, Cap’n,” Josh assured him.

"Ten seconds," Loki warned.

Nathan pressed the all-call button on the intercom panel, located on the right armrest of his command chair. "All hands, prepare for action."

"Attack jump in three......"

"Pitching down ten degrees," Josh announced as he pushed his flight control stick slightly forward.

"Two......"

"Full-power triplets loaded in all forward tubes," Jessica added.

"One......"

"Weapons free," Nathan ordered.

"Jumping."

"Helm, trigger is hot," Jessica replied as the Aurora's bridge flashed with blue-white light.

When the flash cleared, a split second later, the Jar-Razza filled the main portion of the Aurora's massive, semi-spherical view screen, with the planet Orswella directly behind it.

"Target acquired," Jessica reported calmly. "Five kilometers and closing fast."

"Good lock!" Josh reported. "Firing!"

The Aurora opened fire, sending waves of red-orange plasma torpedoes streaking from the openings under her bow into the old Dusahn battleship below and ahead of her. As the initial impacts slammed into the enemy ship's shields, the battleship's point-defenses immediately responded. Dozens of turrets, located all over the old battleship, popped up out of the hull and spun around to face the Aurora. The turrets opened fire, sending streams of rail gun slugs toward the Aurora, lighting up her own shields.

The battleship's main cannons also came to life, albeit much more slowly. They struggled to keep pace with the Aurora as she passed over the top of the battleship; the attacker adjusting her angle in relation to her flight path, to keep her nose on the target and continue pounding the Dusahn ship. By the time the main cannons could get a target lock, the attacker disappeared in a flash of blue-white light.

Reaper Six rocked violently as it came out of the jump in the lower atmosphere of Orswella.

"Damn, this is some thick air," Ensign Weston exclaimed as he quickly selected targets on his weapons display.

"I'm picking up targeting beams from the surface," Lieutenant Haddix reported. "They've got some sort of defenses down there."

"*Six, Five, are you being painted?*"

"Affirmative," the lieutenant replied.

"*Where the hell is it coming from?*"

"The surface!"

"*I'm picking up anti-aircraft emplacements powering up!*" another Reaper pilot reported.

"Take 'em out, Wes," the lieutenant urged.

"The AAs or the bases?" Ensign Weston asked.

"Fuck," the lieutenant cursed, glancing at the clock. They had been in the attack zone for less than thirty seconds, and they already had problems. "Someone needs to target those AAs!"

"*Two, Four, Six, target AAs!*" Lieutenant Commander Manes ordered from Reaper One. "*Everyone else, keep your original target packages!*"

"*Two copies!*"

"*Four copies!*"

"Six copies," the lieutenant replied.

"Targeting anti-aircraft emplacements," Ensign Weston announced.

"*What about those other bases?*" Ensign LaValla asked.

"*Evens will switch to their original targets on their second pass. Odds will handle the stations,*" the lieutenant commander instructed.

"Incoming fire!" Ensign Weston reported as the sky around them lit up with explosions, rocking their Reaper.

"*What about the checkpoints?*" Lieutenant Taren wondered. "*We're not going to have enough ordnance.*"

"*We'll have to attack with guns,*" Lieutenant Commander Manes insisted. "*Otherwise, the Ghatazhak are going to be screwed!*"

"Weapons away," Ensign Weston reported.

Lieutenant Haddix rolled the ship onto its right side, pulling the nose up hard as he pushed his throttles to their stops. "Give me a new vector," he instructed. "We're winging it from now on."

"Two two five, angels one five," Ensign Weston replied, "then come hard to port, back to one four three, so I can get new target locks."

"Two two five, angels one five," the lieutenant acknowledged. "Jumping."

"Whoa," Vol exclaimed as they came out of the jump, his eyes suddenly widening as he pulled back slightly on his flight control stick to keep from slamming into the surface of the asteroid. "That's close."

"That's why I never look outside when you jump," Isa said.

"Probably wise," Vol agreed as he checked his threat board. "Uh..."

"I see them," Isa replied. "Better go lower."

"Tekka Leader to Squadron, they've got point-defenses on the surface. Take it down to the deck. Use the canyons as much as possible. If you have to pop up over a ridge, be ready to evade fire, and get back down quickly."

"*Just like the Convay Challenge!*"

"*Except they're shooting real slugs!*"

"Their targeting systems are lighting up!" Isa warned. "They know we're here!"

"*Someone's intel sucks!*"

"Focus, boys and girls," Vol urged as he guided his Gunyoki fighter down into the deep canyons. "Focus."

"*Yes, Shenzai.*"

"Can you map these canyons, Isa?" Vol asked as he snaked their ship through the narrow valley.

"The surface is full of heavy metals, including radiologicals," Isa replied. "The best I can do is to give a few seconds' warning before you hit a dead end... *LIKE NOW*!"

Vol pulled up sharply, barely clearing the vertical wall that appeared at the last second after coming around a bend. The moment he cleared the ridge, rail gun slugs began to pound his shields from all sides, causing them to flash brilliantly with each impact. "Old school isn't going to work," he decided. "Micro-jumps!" he added, quickly adjusting his jump-range dial. "Random range, keep them short, and don't overshoot the target, or we're going to have to do this again!"

Vol pressed his jump button, causing his ship to jump forward a single kilometer. The move gained him five seconds of rest while the surface defenses recalculated and adjusted their aim. Again, his shields flashed and, again, he pressed his jump button; this time, jumping only half a kilometer.

Vol continued the process, staying a few meters above the surface, jumping ahead short, random distances, and pitching down slightly between each jump to maintain his altitude above the relatively rounded surface of the asteroid.

"Target coming up," Isa announced. "Suggest a two-kilometer jump to firing point."

Vol didn't hesitate to follow his partner's recommendation. He quickly dialed up a single two-kilometer jump and pressed the button. The ring suddenly appeared before them, and he pressed and held his firing trigger.

The main plasma cannons on the front of his port and starboard engine nacelles flashed repeatedly, sending streaks of red-orange plasma toward the unshielded ring. Explosions erupted as the bursts of energy struck the ring's hull, tearing sections of it open.

A split second later, his wingman joined in the attack, adding his own plasma cannons to his leader's. Seconds after that, more fighters joined, and by the time Vol was forced to break off and jump away, every fighter in his squadron was pounding away at the massive shipyard ring.

The fighter came out of the jump, and Vol immediately pitched tail over nose, so he was flying backward. A few kilometers behind him, the massive ring encircling Agosti One Four Seven began breaking apart at the point of bombardment. Secondary explosions spread quickly, expanding outward around the ring, itself. Large sections of the shipyard began breaking away from its connections to the asteroid, drifting outward and spinning wildly from the explosions.

Cheers were heard across comms as, one by one, other fighters jumped forward to join Vol, each of them also pitching back over to witness the results of their efforts.

"We've got two cruisers coming towards us," Isa warned. "Ten kilometers, one five two, closing fast."

"Thirteen through twenty-four, engage the cruisers. Everyone else, return to finish off the rest of that ring," Vol instructed.

"*Isn't it damaged enough?*" Damus asked from Tekka Three.

"Our mission is complete when the *entire facility* is destroyed," Vol insisted, flipping his ship back over and initiating a turn.

"Reapers report surface air defenses," Naralena reported from the Aurora's comm-station.

"Relay that to the Ghatazhak," Nathan ordered. "Target damage report!"

"Target's port midship shields are down by sixty percent," Kaylah reported.

"Turn complete," Josh reported.

"Ready to jump back," Loki added.

"Negative," Nathan replied. "Attack jump to the port side, passing under."

"There's not a whole lot of room between the target and the atmosphere," Loki warned.

"Which means they won't suspect it," Nathan replied. "I'm betting he thinks we're going to keep pounding the same shield."

"Dota Squadron is attacking the target's starboard side," Kaylah reported. "Target is rolling over to protect his weaker side."

"See?" Nathan said.

"Ready to thread the needle," Loki replied.

Nathan smiled. "It's good to have you back, Loki. Do it."

"Jumping in three......"

"Adjusting pitch," Josh stated, pulling the Aurora's nose upward.

"Two......"

"Target has rolled one hundred and eighty degrees," Kaylah reported.

"One......"

"Target is slowing," she added.

"Jumping."

Gunyoki fighters repeatedly appeared off one side of the Dusahn battleship, opposite the planet, opening up with their nacelle-mounted plasma cannons the moment they appeared. The battleship's shields flashed reddish-yellow with each impact of the enemy plasma weapons as it flew upside down, slowing down to fall into a closer orbit.

Each Gunyoki fighter slid across the top of the old Dusahn warship, pitching continually downward as they passed, to keep their guns on the target until each ship jumped away, alternating forward and aft with each departing fighter.

A blue-white flash of light suddenly appeared above the Dusahn battleship and at least two kilometers closer to the planet, revealing the Aurora, sliding sideways between the target and Orswella. The Aurora's forward torpedo tubes immediately began spitting out triple shots of brilliant red-orange plasma energy, pounding the battleship's beleaguered shields into submission. After only ten seconds, shield emitters all over the side of the ship's hull began to explode in bursts of sparks, and her shields failed.

The Aurora continued to pitch up as she passed downward, sending the next wave of plasma torpedoes directly into the battleship's unprotected hull. Sections of the ship's black and crimson hull came off, torn open by the massive amounts of plasma energy being dumped into her.

"Picking up secondary explosions," Kaylah reported.

"Losing the angle," Josh added.

"Jumping clear," Loki announced as the blue-white flash filled the Aurora's bridge.

"Bring us about and prepare to jump in directly astern of the target," Nathan ordered.

"*The Aurora reports our Reapers are encountering anti-aircraft defenses!*" Lieutenant Latfee reported over comms as the cargo jump shuttle rocked violently with each nearby explosion of anti-aircraft fire.

"*No shit!*" Sergeant Torwell exclaimed while holding onto the overhead rail near the open end of the shuttle as the next squad of Ghatazhak jumped out the door. "*Clear!*"

"*Jumping to next deployment point,*" Commander Kainan announced.

The back of the cargo shuttle filled with blue-white light as General Telles and his squad stepped up to the back door, preparing for deployment.

As soon as the jump flash dissipated, the ship began to rock from the nearby explosions, once more.

"*Have fun down there, General,*" Sergeant Torwell joked.

"Don't get your ass blown out of the sky, Sergeant," General Telles commented as he followed his men out the door.

"*You heard him, Commander. Orders are orders.*"

General Telles stepped off the ramp of the cargo shuttle, twisting around as he fell the fifty meters to the surface. He immediately spotted a group of four Dusahn soldiers, running down the street toward their landing point, and opened fire on them as he fell.

As he continued to fire, he raised his feet slightly and bent his knees, angling the soles of his boots forward. At ten meters, the thrusters attached to the sides of his armored boots fired, slowing his rate of descent at the last second.

Two enemy soldiers immediately fell to the rain of energy weapons fire from above, with the rest of them diving for cover.

The general's thrusters shut down the moment he landed. As he assumed an immediate crouch, the thrusters disconnected from his boots and fell to the sides.

General Telles charged ahead, changing his tack every few steps while he continued firing on the enemy positions. Within seconds, he overcame the enemy, jumping up and over them as he pulled a grenade from his belt, activated it, and dropped it into the middle of the group of men.

The general tucked and rolled as he landed, the grenade detonating as he came back to his feet, and continued on his way, confident that he had eliminated the most immediate threat.

"*Contact!*" Corporal DaPra reported over the general's helmet comms. "*One Red Alpha One! One block east of checkpoint one five! Twenty-plus hostiles in tactical vehicles!*"

"*One Red Alpha One! Reaper Four! Heads down! Coming in hot!*" Ensign Paszek warned.

General Telles glanced up as Reaper Four streaked low over his head, its side cannons blazing. Explosions erupted in the distance as the Reaper pounded the enemy position.

"*Say bye-bye to the tacticals,*" Ensign Paszek declared as his Reaper broke off its attack and disappeared in a blue-white flash of light.

General Telles paused momentarily, checking the myriad of red icons displayed on the tactical map on the inside of his helmet visor. "Tac One, on me," he ordered. "Checkpoint Two Seven, three blocks southwest."

The door of a nearby shop opened suddenly, an old man looking out at him in shock.

"Stay inside and take cover!" the general barked at the old man, hoping he understood.

The old man's eyes bulged, and he immediately turned around and hurried back inside.

"*Tac One Leader, Reaper One,*" Commander Manes called over the general's helmet comms. "*Primary targets destroyed, working on secondaries, now. We had a bit of a distraction with the AA cannons, but we took care of them. Give us a few more minutes, and we'll have things softened up for you.*"

"Good work, Commander," General Telles replied as his men joined up with him. "Let's move out, gentlemen."

Vol steered his Gunyoki fighter beneath the Orswellan cruiser, hugging its shield as he passed underneath, accelerating at full power so the cruiser's nearest point-defense cannons could not keep up with him.

As they passed, Isa channeled the majority of their available energy from their dorsal shields to those protecting their stern, just in time to protect them against the point-defenses further out on the cruiser's bulky hull.

"Pods," Vol ordered.

"Missile pods are hot," Isa replied. "Targets acquired."

Vol pressed the firing trigger on his flight control stick, sending a flurry of self-guided, close-range snub missiles from the large missile pods on either side of their fuselage.

The missiles spread out as they raced toward the, yet, undamaged portion of the shipyard ring still surrounding at least a portion of the Agosti asteroid.

Dozens of explosions appeared all along the

massive ring as Vol's missiles reached their targets, causing it to break apart even further.

"That's it, baby," he said as he pitched up and pressed his jump button again, "you're goin' *down.*"

"Where?" Lieutenant Haddix yelled over comms. "Two Gold Charlie One! Where do you want the fire?"

"*Reaper Six! Two Gold Charlie One!*" Corporal Mullins finally replied. "*Four hundred meters south of my marker! A whole fucking platoon of unfriendlies in the tan, three-story building.*"

"Any civilians in there?" the lieutenant asked.

"*Unknown!*" the corporal admitted. "*If there are, they're probably already dead, just like we're going to be in a few minutes!*"

"Fuck!" Lieutenant Haddix cursed. "You got their marker?" he asked his copilot.

"Grid one five by two seven," Ensign Weston replied. "About twenty degrees right of our current heading."

"Two Gold Charlie One! Heads down!" the lieutenant called as he rolled his Reaper into a turn to starboard. "Coming in hot! Ten seconds!"

"*Two Gold Charlie One! Heads down, roger!*" the corporal replied.

"Fuck!" Lieutenant Haddix cursed again as he dove toward the target and unleashed his Reaper's vengeance on the building in question, blowing the front of it wide open and sending Dusahn body parts flying in all directions, along with the building's debris.

"*Two Leader! Two Blue Leader!*" Sergeant Morano called over comms as Reaper Six ceased fire and pitched up to clear the building. "*Twenty goons just charged into the hospital in sector four! They're shooting up the place!*"

"*Two Blue Leader! Two Leader!*" Lieutenant Zelle replied. "*Pursue and eliminate! Watch your friendlies! No grenades!*"

"*Roger that!*" Sergeant Morano replied.

"*Two Blue Alpha and Bravo! Two Blue Leader! Pursue unfriendlies into the hospital and eliminate with precision; no grenades!*"

"Jesus," Ensign Weston exclaimed as the lieutenant circled around. "Those fuckers are brutal!"

"*Reaper Six! Tac One Leader!*" General Telles called over comms. "*Request immediate pickup at intersection five one, cold, for redeploy!*"

"Tac One Leader, Reaper Six," Lieutenant Haddix replied as he rolled his ship in the opposite direction toward the general's location. "Thirty seconds!"

"*Roger that!*" the general replied.

Ghatazhak soldiers pursued the enemy into the hospital, firing with precision as each target presented itself. Unfortunately, the mayhem, caused by the indiscriminate slaughter of innocent Orswellans inside, created massive chaos, which slowed their advance.

Corporal Venezia ducked in behind a vertical support beam, avoiding the incoming fire that struck civilians behind him, who were standing out in the open. A glance at his tactical visor showed the targets had entered the stairwell and were heading for the next floor up. "Bandits heading up the south stairwell! Two Blue Alpha pursuing!"

"*Two Blue Alpha, Tac One Leader!*" General Telles called over comms. "*Drive them toward the roof! We'll be on top in one minute and come down toward them to cut them off!*"

"Roger that, Tac One!" the corporal replied as he headed for the stairwell, jumping over bodies, his squad hot on his heels.

"*Half that ring is gone!*"

Jenna Hayashi pulled her Gunyoki fighter up sharply, settling in behind one of the Orswellan cruisers desperately trying to defend what was left of the Agosti shipyards. As soon as she was in position, she opened up with her main plasma cannons. Her first shot brought down the cruiser's already-weakened aft shields, and her next few shots slammed into its main engines, blowing them apart. "Woo-hoo!" she exclaimed, rolling into a spiraling dive to the right to avoid hitting the now-disabled cruiser. "That guy's not going anywhere!"

"Maybe not, but he's still shooting at us!" her weapons officer reminded her from the back.

"Details," Jenna scoffed, pressing her jump button to escape the drifting cruiser's attempt at retaliation. "Tekka One, Tekka Five! Target three is disabled and adrift. His stern shields are gone, but he's still got main power and guns. Shall we continue our attack?"

"*Negative,*" Vol replied. "*The section of the ring that target three can defend is gone, so ignore him. Do you have any missiles left?*"

"All of them," Jenna replied.

"*Good,*" Vol replied. "*Feel free to take out another piece of that ring!*"

"You got it, boss!" Jenna replied happily, pulling her Gunyoki fighter into a tight left turn toward the surviving section of the ring.

General Telles and his squad braced themselves against Reaper Six's rocket wash as it swooped in and touched down in the middle of the intersection. All four Ghatazhak immediately ran out and jumped on board, the ship's engines rising in pitch again as it lifted back up off the ground.

"*Where to, gentlemen?*" Lieutenant Haddix asked from the cockpit.

"The hospital in sector four," General Telles replied as he sat in the opening of what was originally the Reaper's weapons bay. "Put us on the roof."

"You got it," the lieutenant replied.

General Telles surveyed the area below as they streaked overhead. He could see pockets of resistance still battling his troops on the ground. Another Reaper jumped in from his right and opened fire on a group of Dusahn troops giving one of his Ghatazhak squads trouble. Radio chatter from the ground battle filled his helmet comms, but his subordinates were handling their teams just as he, himself, would.

"*How's it going on the ground, guys?*" Ensign Weston asked the Ghatazhak.

"Not bad!" Specialist Knaff boasted from the back. "The Dusahn can't shoot worth a damn!"

"*Then, what the hell do you need us for?*" the ensign joked.

"Unfortunately, they have really good fucking body armor!" Corporal Smida replied.

"*Thirty seconds,*" the lieutenant warned.

General Telles peered at the hospital while their Reaper circled around to the facility's rooftop landing pad. "Four floors, and they're already on two," he told his men. "We'll have to move fast."

"We're a tac team!" Corporal Smida barked proudly. "Fast is what we do!"

General Telles smiled as the Reaper swooped down into a hover over the landing pad. "Let's get this done," General Telles announced as he jumped from the Reaper to the rooftop landing pad five meters below.

"The battleship is still intact," Kaylah reported from the Aurora's sensor station. "She's lost all starboard shields and most of her ventral shields, but she's still got power and weapons."

"How did you know what they were going to do?" Josh wondered.

"If they haven't left orbit in twenty years, there's a reason," Nathan said.

"You think they *can't*?" Josh asked.

"They have never even left for maneuvers," Commander Andreola stated.

"They should have left orbit to get maneuvering room for battle," Nathan explained. "The fact that they moved *closer* to the surface and rolled their weak shields *toward* the planet confirmed it for me."

"Like putting your back against the wall," Jessica surmised.

"They left the Jar-Razza here because she *isn't*

space-worthy," Nathan said. "She's just got power, guns, and shields."

"And maneuvering," Kaylah added, "and she's still moving toward the surface."

"Her captain doesn't give up easily, I'll give him that," Jessica said.

"Target is launching fighters," Kaylah reported. "Gunyoki are vectoring to intercept." She turned to the captain. "They're launching escape pods, as well, and increasing their rate of descent."

"With antimatter reactors," Nathan realized. "Josh..."

"Turning toward the battleship, now," Josh replied, anticipating Nathan's orders.

Vol pressed his jump button, sending his Gunyoki fighter jumping ahead to resume his attack. The Agosti asteroid appeared before him and, once again, he pulled up sharply, skimming the surface as the few remaining surface defense turrets opened fire on him, yet again.

"*I'm hit!*" Dugan called from Tekka One Four.

"*You're trailing smoke from your starboard side!*" Bran warned from Tekka One Seven. "*Vent your starboard tanks!*"

"*Venting!*"

Vol's fighter crested the last ridge, and the surviving portion of the ring came into sight. "Good lock," he reported. "Firing."

"*Firing,*" his wingman, Dosne added.

Red-orange bolts of plasma streaked away from both ships, slamming into the ring, breaking it open. A massive explosion from deep within the structure lit up its interior, and the ring began to crack open, section by section, spreading around the last quarter of the asteroid.

"*Holy shit!*" Dosne exclaimed. "*It's coming apart! We did it!*"

Vol ceased fire, pulling back on his flight control stick, causing his fighter to climb. "Tekka Squadron, disengage and jump to rally point Delta Two," he ordered.

"*What about the other three cruisers?*" Jenna asked.

"They've got nothing left to defend," Vol explained, "and by the time they make it to Orswella, the battle will be over."

"*But they're such easy targets,*" Suli joked.

"They're victims, just like us," Vol reminded them. "We've just struck a serious blow against the Dusahn. We've done our job," he added as he pushed his jump button.

The Aurora rocked as all the battleship's guns pounded her forward shields.

"Message from Tekka One," Naralena announced. "The shipyard ring around Agosti One Four Seven has been destroyed, and one cruiser has been disabled."

"Man, what I wouldn't give for a few jump missiles right now," Nathan said to himself as the ship continued to rock with each rail gun slug impact against their forward shields. "How long will our shields hold?"

"Not more than a minute," Jessica warned.

"I've got a lock, Captain," Josh urged.

"Comms, send a message to that ship, all channels

and all frequencies: stand down, now, and your crew will be spared. You have ten seconds."

"Aye, sir," Naralena replied as the ship continued to shake.

"Forward shields are down to sixty percent," Jessica warned.

"How are the target's shields?" Nathan asked Kaylah.

"Their starboard shields are at forty percent," Kaylah replied. "Dorsal, stern, and port shields are all gone."

"No response from the Dusahn battleship," Naralena reported.

"Forward shields down to fifty percent," Jessica warned.

"Forward torpedo tubes, full power, one round of triplets on all tubes," Nathan instructed. "Fire when ready."

"Oh, I'm ready," Josh assured him.

"Then fire."

"Firing," Josh replied, eagerly pressing his firing trigger.

A single wave of four triple-shots of plasma torpedoes streaked out from under the Aurora's nose, slamming into the battleship's starboard shield, causing its emitters to overload and erupt in showers of sparks.

"Target's starboard shields are gone," Jessica reported. "She's a sitting duck."

"Kaylah," Nathan called, "what's under that ship right now?"

"On the surface? Mostly water," Kaylah replied, "but the main inhabited portion of the planet will be coming around in about ten minutes."

"What happens if we take them out, now?"

"At this altitude, there will be some interaction with the planet's atmosphere."

"How much?"

"Forward shields down to forty percent," Jessica warned.

Kaylah took a deep breath, letting it out slowly. "I cannot be certain."

"I need a best guess," Nathan urged.

"All I can tell you is that if we don't take them out, at their current rate of descent, and assuming their reactors don't lose containment until impact, the results are going to be a *lot* worse."

Nathan rotated his command chair to confer with Commander Andreola as the Aurora continued to shake from the incoming rail gun rounds coming from the doomed battleship's main guns.

"Forward shields are now down to *thirty* percent," Jessica pushed, her tone becoming more concerned.

"I don't see that you have a choice, Captain," the commander stated, anticipating Nathan's thoughts.

Nathan looked at Jessica. "Prepare all forward tubes. Full power. Triple shots. All forward plasma cannons. We keep firing until they lose containment."

"Got it," Jessica replied. "By the way, forward shields are down to *twenty* percent, now," Jessica reiterated.

"Helm, begin increasing our distance from the target, but keep all tubes on them."

"Increasing distance from target," Josh acknowledged.

"Loki, be ready on that escape jump."

"Understood," Loki assured him.

"Comms, tell Dota Squadron to jump to their rally point and stand by," Nathan added.

"Aye, sir."

"How much time do we have to safely take them down?" Nathan asked Kaylah.

"Five minutes, tops."

"Our shields aren't going to hold that long," Jessica stated.

"If their reactors lose containment, we don't have enough distance to be safe," Abby warned, "not with our shields down to twenty percent."

"Make that fifteen percent," Jessica corrected.

"That's why we're going to jump *before* they lose containment," Nathan replied.

"I wouldn't cut it *too* close," Abby insisted. "Don't forget what happened last time."

Nathan turned to Abby. "Good point. Jess, be prepared to channel all our energy to our forward and ventral shields as we jump, just in case."

"Understood."

"Captain, the closer to the atmosphere they get, the worse it will be for the planet," Kaylah warned.

Nathan watched the image of the battleship as it continued to send streams of rail gun slugs into the Aurora's forward shields.

"Shields at ten percent," Jessica warned, feeling as if her warnings were falling on deaf ears.

Nathan studied the image of the doomed battleship once more, expecting to feel a sense of sadness, but did not. "Fire."

General Telles and his team burst onto the fourth floor of the hospital and were immediately fired upon by Dusahn troops heading down the corridor toward them. The general ducked down low, firing as he ran across the corridor to the nurses' station, striking one of the enemy soldiers in the armor plating at the man's knees. The impact did not injure the man, but it did knock his feet out from under him, putting his face in line with the general's next two shots.

Another glance down the corridor revealed multiple casualties, both medical staff and patients. The general signaled to his three men on the other side of the hallway, and Sergeant Spira immediately returned fire, dropping two of the six Dusahn soldiers at the far end.

As the sergeant fired, Corporal Smida and Specialist Knaff charged across the hallway to join the general at his position.

General Telles tapped Specialist Knaff on the shoulder as Corporal Smida joined the sergeant in sending suppression fire down the corridor.

General Telles crossed the nurses' station, gesturing for the medical staff, huddled within, to stay put. He peeked out the other side, observing that the corridor was clear. He then proceeded quickly, but quietly, down the corridor on the opposite side of the floor, pausing at each doorway to his left, to ensure that the room didn't open up to the corridor on the side containing the Dusahn soldiers.

Sergeant Spira spotted a section of ductwork above the enemy combatants and got an idea. "I can force them to your side if you're ready, sir."

"*Ten seconds,*" the general replied cover comms.

"Be ready, Smida," the sergeant warned as he took aim at the ductwork and fired, sending it crashing down upon the four Dusahn soldiers.

The sergeant and the corporal both stepped

out from behind their cover, walking in a crouch toward the enemy as they continued to pour energy weapons fire down the corridor while the Dusahn soldiers tried to free themselves from the rubble of the collapse. The first soldier up took several blasts to his chest armor and, finally, a blast to his exposed upper neck and chin, melting them away.

The second guard took multiple hits to his chest and torso but managed to survive. As he attempted to scramble to safety, he stumbled over some ductwork and took a blast to the side of the face, killing him instantly.

The remaining two Dusahn soldiers managed to escape through a door on their left, charging through a patient's room and into the corridor on the other side, where they were met with more energy weapons fire coming from General Telles and Specialist Knaff, dropping the first soldier through the door.

General Telles charged forward, his weapon remaining ready at his shoulder and aimed forward, immediately rounding the door.

The general stopped dead in his tracks. Inside the room, the remaining Dusahn soldier had a small boy in his left arm, holding him in front of his chest like a shield, shouting angry warnings in his own language, his sidearm held at the child's head. General Telles stood firm, his weapon trained on the small portion of the soldier's face that was not covered by the child's head.

"*What's going on?*" Sergeant Spira asked over comms.

"One goon, using a child as a shield," General Telles replied quietly over comms.

"*Take the shot, sir,*" the sergeant urged. "*He's got*

a belt full of grenades he can still use to rip this place wide open."

The Dusahn soldier repeated his angry demands, shaking the crying boy as he yelled at the top of his lungs.

"Stand fast, Sergeant," the general ordered quietly over comms. "If he comes out your side, you can take the shot."

"*Understood.*"

The soldier yelled some more, first pointing his weapon at the general, then at the floor, and then back at the child he held before him.

General Telles held up his left hand, spreading his fingers slowly, and then began lowering his weapon toward the floor without saying a word, his eyes locked on those of his enemy.

"*What are you doing, sir?*" Specialist Knaff wondered from the corridor.

"Be ready, Knaff," the general said in a low, confident tone.

"*Oh, shit,*" the specialist replied over comms.

General Telles took a step forward as he slowly lowered his weapon, entering the room. The Dusahn soldier yelled at him incoherently, again gesturing for the general to lower his weapon. The general glanced left and right, spotting at least six more children in the room—some in their beds, unable to move, their faces twisted in fear.

"*General?*" Sergeant Spira asked, getting nervous.

"I've got this, Sergeant," the general assured him as he took another step forward, continuing to lower his weapon closer to the floor.

The Dusahn soldier yelled again, becoming increasingly nervous as his world came apart before his eyes.

The general said nothing, taking one last step forward as he stretched out his right arm and placed his weapon on the floor.

The guard moved the child slightly to his left, his eyes on the general's gun.

General Telles pulled his right hand back slowly, then suddenly, in one fluid motion, reached back to grab his combat knife from its quick-draw sheath on his right hip and sent it flying in an underhanded throw at the Dusahn soldier's face.

The knife landed in the middle of the soldier's right eye, causing him to release the child and grab for his eye while screaming in agony. General Telles charged forward as the soldier pulled the knife from his eye and raised his weapon to fire.

The general went straight for the little boy, scooping him up and crouching down on the floor, his back to the enemy as the half-blinded soldier opened fire.

Three blasts struck him in the back, bouncing off his body armor. He could feel the heat from the blasts build, as well as the force of their impacts, but he held firm, shielding the child from harm.

Another shot ran out from the doorway, and the Dusahn soldier fell, after which Specialist Knaff charged into the room to make sure the enemy combatant was dead.

"Clear!" Specialist Knaff yelled.

General Telles eased his grip on the child, dropping to one knee and looking him over. "Are you unharmed?" he asked the little boy.

The little boy stared into the general's face, wide-eyed and unafraid as he reached out to touch the general's visor, in awe of all the tactical symbols glistening on its inside surface.

General Telles picked the child up and carried him over to a nearby bed, setting him down as Sergeant Spira and Corporal Smida charged into the room from the opposite door.

"*First three floors are clear,*" Sergeant Morano reported over comms.

"Fourth floor is clear," Sergeant Spira replied.

"*Blue Alpha, I want a sweep of the entire facility,*" Sergeant Morano ordered over comms. "*Blue Bravo, secure the external perimeter until Alpha finishes the sweep.*"

General Telles turned and headed for the exit, passing Sergeant Spira on the way.

"Why didn't you take the shot, General?" the sergeant asked. "It would have been far more efficient."

General Telles stopped, looking at the sergeant. "Sometimes, the most *efficient* way is not the *best* way," he replied, before continuing out the door.

Red-orange balls of plasma energy streaked out from under the Aurora's bow, traveling the few kilometers between the Aurora and the doomed battleship within seconds. Each plasma torpedo ripped the old battleship's hull open a bit more than the previous one, igniting secondary explosions deep within her. Red-orange bolts of plasma energy from the Aurora's forward turrets carved into the enemy hull's already-open wounds, breaking the ship up even further.

The aft section was the first to give up the fight, exploding into multiple pieces. The midship section collapsed, and the forward section broke off, tipping downward, as more explosions ignited within.

The Aurora suddenly ceased fire and began to glow a light blue. A split second later, that light blue covered the entire ship, turned to a brilliant, white flash, and then disappeared along with the Aurora. A split second after that, the battleship's reactors lost their containment, resulting in a blinding, white explosion, which spread outward for tens of kilometers in all directions, dissipating almost as quickly as it had come.

"Jump complete," Loki reported with a sigh of relief.

"Three operational Orswellan cruisers, dead ahead," Jessica warned. "They're locking weapons on us."

"What the hell are they doing?" Josh wondered. "There's nothing left to defend!"

"They may not know it, yet," Nathan pointed out.

"Our forward shields are still only at nine percent," Jessica reminded him. "Shall I target them?"

"Target, but do not fire without orders," Nathan instructed.

"Aye, sir," Jessica replied.

Nathan turned to Kaylah. "Status of Orswella?"

"The antimatter event has caused no significant damage to the planet," Kaylah replied. "We took them out just in time."

Nathan continued turning to face aft. "Comms, all channels and frequencies."

"All channels and frequencies," Naralena replied, nodding at him.

"Orswellan Guard ships, this is Captain Scott of the Karuzari Alliance ship, Aurora. The Jar-Razza has been destroyed, and the Dusahn troops on your planet's surface are being dealt with by our ground forces. Stand down, and your crews will be spared."

Nathan waited patiently for a response but received none. "Are they still targeting us?" he asked Jessica.

"Yes, and they're still closing."

"Orswellan Guard ships, I assure you that you cannot defeat us. Your deaths will serve no purpose."

Again, there was no response.

"No change," Jessica added.

"The fact that they haven't fired means they're thinking about it," Nathan insisted.

"Perhaps I should speak to them?" Commander Andreola suggested.

"Give him a comm-set," Nathan said.

"Commander," Naralena offered, handing a comm-set over her console to the commander.

Commander Andreola donned the comm-set. "Orswellan Guard cruisers, this is Commander Andreola of the Amonday. Authorization code One Five Seven Five, Strike Four, Alpha Seven Zulu. Confirm."

A moment later, a voice replied. "*Stethan? This is Captain Yofferst of the Twellaby. You are on the enemy vessel?*"

"Affirmative," the commander replied.

"*Then, you are a prisoner?*"

"No, Marlon, I am not," the commander insisted, "and the Karuzari Alliance is *not* our enemy. They, too, fight the Dusahn, and they have *liberated* our world."

"*The Dusahn will return,*" Captain Yofferst replied.

"And the Karuzari Alliance *will* defend you," Nathan promised.

"I'm sorry, Captain, we did not wish to fire upon you, but we have no choice," Captain Yofferst said. *"Our families..."*

"Are free once again," Nathan interrupted. "Stand down and vacate your ships using your escape pods. Once clear of their blast zones, we will recover them and rescue your crew."

"That will not be necessary," Captain Yofferst assured him. *"Our escape pods are programmed to return us to Orswella."*

"Then, we shall stand by to assist if needed," Nathan replied, "but we cannot remain for long. There is a Dusahn battle group on its way to another allied system, and we must defend them, as well. However, one of our support ships will be arriving in a few hours. In the meantime, our forces on the surface will provide assistance, as well, and our heavy fighters will remain to protect your world until we return."

"The lead ship is powering down its weapons," Jessica reported.

"I will contact the other ships," Captain Yofferst promised. *"I am certain they will comply."*

"Thank you, Captain," Nathan replied. "I look forward to meeting you, once things have calmed down a bit."

"As well, I," Captain Yofferst replied.

Nathan looked to Commander Andreola. "You believe him?"

"I have known Marlon Yofferst for most of my adult life," the commander replied. "He is a man of his word."

"The rest of the cruisers are also powering down

their weapons," Jessica reported. "All Orswellan ships are lowering shields, as well."

"Very well," Nathan said. "Helm, take us to a safe blast distance and hold station. Comms, contact General Telles and see how they're doing." Nathan glanced at the clock. "We've got about an hour before that battle group finishes decelerating and attacks the Rogen system. I'd like to get back *before* that happens."

CHAPTER TWELVE

Ten Sugali Nighthawk fighters were parked in two lines on either side of the Ranni flight operations pad on Rakuen. Portable lighting was clustered around the last two ships on the line as technicians and pilots, alike, worked together to complete their modifications.

"How's it going?" Cameron inquired of Commander Prechitt upon approaching the flight line.

"We had a few problems with the shielding on Lieutenant Cristos's ship, but Deliza came up with a workaround."

"Then, all ten ships will be ready?"

"Looks like it," the commander replied. "Have you heard anything?"

"Not a peep."

"It must be difficult for you to be on the ground while your ship is in battle."

"*Agonizing* would be a better word," Cameron countered. "Make sure your pilots get a chance to rest a bit and grab something to eat. We have no idea what's ahead of us."

"Doubtful it's anything easy," the commander agreed.

"You need to take a break, as well," Cameron added, continuing on her way. "We've got less than an hour, now."

Cameron traveled down the line toward the hangar, entering the office in the corner.

"Captain," Talisha greeted.

"Miss Sane," Cameron replied. "How is your project going?"

"I'm pretty sure Leta has things figured out. She's

in the process of writing mission-specific algorithms right now, based on the Dusahn ship intelligence you've provided. When she's finished, she should be able to recommend the most efficient way for us to bring down the enemy's shields without getting blown to bits."

"That *would be* preferable," Cameron agreed.

"Captain," a man called from the doorway to the communications room. "Incoming call from Aurora Actual."

"Finally," Cameron exclaimed, heading to the communications room. She donned the comm-set handed to her and tapped the side of it. "Actual, Taylor, welcome back. How did it go?"

"*The shipyards are gone, and the Jar-Razza is destroyed,*" Nathan replied. "*Telles is cleaning up on the surface but doesn't expect any problems.*"

"What about the Orswellan cruisers?"

"*We disabled one, and the others surrendered and abandoned their ships, once the Jar-Razza went down and they learned the Dusahn troops on the ground were no longer a threat.*"

"How's the ship?" Cameron wondered.

"*Not a scratch,*" Nathan bragged. "*How are things going down there?*"

"The Dusahn battle group is still maintaining their rate of deceleration, and the last two Nighthawks should be ready shortly."

"*We need them ready, now, Cam,*" Nathan insisted.

"The Dusahn won't be down to maximum attack speed for another fifty-four minutes."

"*We need to deal with them while they are still going too fast to jump in and attack the Rogen system. The last thing we want is to be forced into playing defense.*"

"Give us fifteen minutes," Cameron told him.

"*No more,*" Nathan insisted. "*And get back up here as soon as possible. I need my XO.*"

"On my way," Cameron replied. "Taylor out." Cameron turned to the communications officer. "Alert everyone, the Nighthawks depart in fifteen minutes."

"Yes, sir."

* * *

"This is dumb," Nathan commented as he studied the latest images from the Falcon. "Why would they bunch everyone up like this?"

"Strength in numbers?" Jessica suggested. "It does reduce the amount of exposed area of nearly every ship in the formation."

"Yeah, but it makes it really easy to attack multiple targets at the same time," Nathan insisted.

"Assuming you're crazy enough to jump *in between* them."

Nathan smiled.

"Not a good idea, Nathan," Jessica objected.

"Aurora?" Nathan called.

"*Yes, Captain?*" the Aurora's voice answered.

"What is the probability of successfully jumping in between any two of the ships in the Dusahn battle group?"

"*For the purpose of attack?*"

"Yes."

"*The best course would be between the number three and four battleships, here,*" Aurora explained as a course plot appeared on the tactical display. "*If you jump in ten seconds prior to passing between them, it will provide adequate time to adjust course to avoid a collision, should such maneuvering be required.*

Assuming this course of action, the probability of success is seventy-four percent."

"Can you do that jump, Loki?" Nathan asked.

"If Aurora backs me up, yes."

"You're only going to have a few hundred meters of clearance on either side," Jessica pointed out.

"I didn't say it wouldn't be close," Nathan retorted.

"Plenty of room," Josh boasted.

"Why not play it safe and just attack from *outside* the formation?" Jessica wondered.

"The *first* attack is the *best* opportunity to inflict *maximum* damage," Nathan insisted. "After that, every gun will be up and ready, and every captain will be trying to anticipate our next move...and some of them *will*." Nathan sighed. "We're threading the needle."

"I just have one question," Jessica said. "Why does the Aurora sound like Cam?"

"It doesn't *sound* like Cam," Nathan insisted. "It just has a similar accent."

"I think she's right," Josh said. "It does sound like Cameron."

"Nobody asked you," Nathan snapped.

* * *

"Max?" Commander Prechitt called over his remote as he walked out of the pilot's lounge in full flight gear.

"*Yes, Commander?*" his ship's AI replied.

"Power up and prepare for immediate takeoff."

"*Powering up and preparing all systems for takeoff,*" Max acknowledged.

"Have all the attack algorithms been shared with the other AIs?" the commander asked Talisha.

"Yes, sir," she replied, "and we've received the order

of attack from the Aurora. All AIs are programmed and ready to go."

"Good work," the commander congratulated. "Shall we?"

"We shall," Talisha agreed, picking up her helmet and following him to the door. "Leta," she called over her remote. "Power up for departure."

"*Powering up for departure*," Leta responded.

Commander Prechitt exited the hangar offices and strode out across the flight deck. All ten Nighthawks were already powered up, their navigation and ground safety lights flashing and blinking in the early morning darkness. With the work lights gone, the effect was somewhat surreal as Jonas and Talisha walked to their respective ships.

"Good luck, Commander," Talisha said, stopping at the access ladder to her fighter.

"To you, as well," the commander replied as he continued walking.

A few moments later, Commander Prechitt reached his own ship, ducking under the port section of the split nose, and turned to face the gaping open-front cockpit that awaited him. It was the weirdest cockpit access design he had ever seen, but there was something simple and elegant about its concept.

The commander climbed up the few rungs, stepping onto the small ledge in front of the pilot's seat, turning around to sit. He donned his helmet, plugged its umbilical into the side of the cockpit, and then fastened his restraints. "Close her up, Max," he instructed. Max didn't reply, but simply activated the cockpit's canopy motors, causing the clamshell-like top and bottom canopy sections to close, trapping the commander inside.

Once closed, the walls of the cockpit came to life

as the Nighthawk's sophisticated external cameras and sensors created the illusion of being surrounded by a clear bubble. The commander could see the split nose of his ship, as well as its fuselage and wings, just as if it really were a transparent bubble. Green icons indicating friendly ships appeared to his left, and directly ahead and left, each icon centered on one of the other Nighthawk fighters on the flight line.

"How are we looking, Max?" the commander asked.

"*All systems are functioning normally,*" Max replied. "*The ship is fully armed, fully fueled, and ready for departure, as are all other ships in the squadron.*"

"Very well," the commander replied. "Squadron comms, please."

"*You are connected.*"

"Razor One to Razor Flight. Depart by the numbers," the commander ordered.

"*Would you like me to take us up?*" Max asked.

"No thanks, Max," the commander insisted, easing his lift throttle forward. "I'm saving you for the actual battle."

"*Of course.*"

Commander Prechitt smiled as his ship rose from the ground. "You with me, Nikki?"

"*Always,*" she replied.

The commander twisted his flight control stick slightly to the right, causing his ship to yaw ninety degrees to starboard. At the same time, he increased his lift throttle slightly, then eased his main drive throttle forward, increasing his rate of acceleration with each millimeter of movement. Finally, he rammed the main drive throttle to its stops, and after a few seconds, pressed the jump button.

* * *

"XO on the bridge!" the Ghatazhak guard at the door announced with a smirk on his face.

Cameron exchanged glances with the man as she passed. "I'm having a hard time figuring out Ghatazhak humor," she confessed as she approached the tactical console.

"It takes a while," Jessica assured her. "Wait until you see Nathan's plan to deal with the battle group."

"I heard that," Nathan said from his command chair as he studied the step-by-step replay of the battle plan on the main view screen.

"Is that it?" Cameron wondered, looking at the screen. "That first jump is cutting it a bit close, isn't it?"

"The insertion jump will only be a few light minutes, so it shouldn't be a problem," Nathan insisted.

"What does Aurora say?" Cameron asked.

"*The probability of successfully completing the initial insertion jump is seventy-four percent,*" Aurora reported.

"Why does she sound like me?" Cameron wondered.

"Nathan says it makes her sound smart," Jessica told her.

"Sounds like something he'd say," Cameron replied.

"You're okay with it?" Jessica asked.

"The jump, or the AI sounding like me?"

"It doesn't sound like you," Nathan insisted. "It just has a similar accent."

"The jump," Jessica replied, laughing to herself over Nathan's defensive reaction.

"If the Nighthawks can take out the port and

starboard shields of those two ships, then we have a pretty good chance of crippling them on the first pass; and with that many battleships around, the first pass is the *only* one we're going to be able to linger on for more than a few seconds."

"I could use you on tactical, again," Jessica told her.

"Same as last time?" Cameron asked. "I'll take port, you take starboard?"

"Sounds good."

"Captain, all Nighthawks have jumped away," Kaylah reported from the sensor station.

"Very well," Nathan replied. "Josh, take us out of orbit, and put us on course for the rally point."

"Aye, sir," Josh replied. "Taking us out of orbit."

"Jump us to the rally point when ready, Loki."

"Yes, sir."

"Just out of curiosity," Cameron said, "how many jumps did it take you to get back?"

"One," Jessica said with a smile. "Pretty cool, huh?"

* * *

"Multiple contacts astern," Sergeant Nama reported from his station at the back of the Falcon's cockpit. "Ten Nighthawks."

"*Falcon, Razor One,*" Commander Prechitt called over comms. "*Anyone see a Dusahn battle group around here?*"

"We've been trying to play peek-a-boo with them for the last four hours, but they don't seem interested," Lieutenant Teison replied.

"*How rude. Any change?*"

"None," the lieutenant replied. "They're pretty boring. They do have BARCAPs, though. They maintain a one-light-hour spherical perimeter, but their patrol patterns and timings are fairly regular. Either they are confident no one is watching, or they feel so damned superior that they don't care."

"I'm guessing the latter," Commander Prechitt replied. *"Thanks."*

"No problem," the lieutenant replied. "Tell them we said 'hi'."

"Will do," the commander promised. *"Okay, Razors, move to your attack jump positions and stand by."*

* * *

"Jump complete," Loki reported as the jump flash subsided.

"Multiple contacts," Kaylah stated calmly. "Falcon and ten Nighthawks. The Nighthawks are spreading out into their jump positions. No other contacts."

"Threat board is clear," Jessica confirmed. "We're receiving the latest recon intel from the Falcon, now."

Nathan stood next to the comm-station, watching the main view screen as the images from the Falcon's last recon scan came in.

"No apparent change in formation," Jessica reported.

"Are you ready?" Nathan asked Naralena quietly.

"Just finished," she answered, glancing up at him.

"Nighthawks are in position and are beginning their deceleration," Kaylah reported.

"Two minutes to attack jump," Loki announced.

Nathan took a deep breath. "Set general quarters," he instructed Naralena before turning and heading for his command chair.

Cameron watched him walk by without a word and then exchanged a concerned glance with Jessica.

"This should be interesting," Jessica muttered under her breath.

"Everything ready on tactical?" Nathan asked as he took his seat.

"Forward torpedo tubes are fully charged and ready," Jessica reported. "Plasma cannons and rail guns are online and pre-aimed, and our broadside plasma cannons are also ready."

"Aurora has control of all turrets and broadsides, and is aware of the target order," Cameron reported. "Since she will see Josh's flight inputs as they happen, she should be able to compensate for changes in the ship's attitude, in relation to the targets, much faster than we could."

"Which means it's all up to you, Josh," Nathan said.

"There's something seriously wrong with that phrase," Josh admitted.

"*Please* don't do anything too crazy," Cameron begged.

"I make no promises," Josh replied, holding up one hand.

"One minute," Loki warned.

"All decks report general quarters," Naralena announced. "Lieutenant Anders is in combat, and the chief of the boat is in damage control."

"Very well."

"One minute," Loki warned.

"Nighthawks should jump in thirty seconds," Cameron added.

Nathan turned his command chair slowly around, stopping once he faced aft, noticing the concerned looks on the faces of Cameron and Jessica. "This *will* work," he assured them.

"We didn't say anything," Cameron replied.

"You didn't have to."

* * *

"A flat V," Commander Prechitt noted as he studied the intel transmitted from the Falcon. "About the least effective fleet combat formation possible."

"*Is that a problem?*" Talisha asked over comms.

"Just an observation," the commander replied. "Its only real value is that it allows all ships to fire forward without hitting one another, but you could accomplish the same thing with a five-ship box formation and provide better protection for one another."

"*Then, why are they using it?*" Talisha wondered. "*Surely, they are aware of its limitations.*"

"*Orbital bombardment,*" Ensign Topetti suggested from Razor Two. "*They're planning to jump straight into orbit, spread out a bit, and bombard Rakuen.*"

"That's a pretty good guess, Nikki," Commander Prechitt agreed. "Scary, but good."

"*Then, it will be our pleasure to stop them,*" Ensign Tellor said from Razor Four.

"*We are now at the proper speed to pass through the target's shields,*" the Nighthawk's AI announced. "*Assuming they are the same type of shields used by the battleship that Mister Hayes and Mister Sheehan helped defeat.*"

Commander Prechitt glanced at his mission clock. "Such a positive attitude," the commander chuckled. "Are you ready, Max?"

"*I assume that is a rhetorical question,*" Max responded.

Commander Prechitt grinned. "You're starting to grow on me, buddy." He glanced back over his left shoulder, spotting his wingman. "Stay tight, Nikki.

And remember, just fly the ship and let your AI handle the guns."

"*Got it,*" Nikki replied.

"Max, you have firing authorization for the designated targets."

"*Acknowledged,*" Max replied.

"Here we go," the commander said, pressing his jump button as the mission clock reached zero.

The solid canopy and bulkheads of his Nighthawk grayed out momentarily as the ship jumped forward. There was a slight bump, as if they had hit something small, then the canopy and bulkhead came back to life.

"*Firing all turrets,*" Max reported as the exterior images returned. Short, staccato bolts of red-orange cannon fire streaked over the commander's head as the starboard side of the number three Dusahn battleship passed over his head, a mere twenty-eight meters away. His cannon fire slammed into shield emitters all over the battleship's starboard side, destroying them with each impact. It was a marvel to behold as Max guided the two turrets with speed and precision, firing a single shot into each emitter as they slowly traversed the side of the enemy warship.

Commander Prechitt paid careful attention to his flight displays, having chosen to fly the ship manually in case the transition through the battleship's shields caused any problems with its auto-flight systems.

As Max continued to fire, the commander glanced forward just in time to see one of the ship's point-defense cannons spinning around toward him. "We gotta go, Max!"

"*Five seconds,*" Max replied.

The commander watched as the point-defense

turret came quickly around and took aim at him. "Oh, shit," he exclaimed as it opened fire.

"Four..."

His entire canopy flashed yellow-orange as incoming fire slammed into his forward shields.

"Three..."

The commander glanced at his shield status display. His forward shields were already down to fifty percent and dropping fast.

"Two..."

Their shields were now down to twenty percent.

"One......"

The commander slid his finger to the jump button on his flight control stick as his shield strength indicator neared zero.

"Target's starboard shields are down," Max reported calmly.

Commander Prechitt had already pressed the jump button by the time his AI had said *shields.*

"Holy crap!" Talisha exclaimed as she skimmed the port side of battleship number five, while inverted, from a distance of only twenty-five meters. Red-orange bolts, coming from the two topside turrets on the aft section of her Nighthawk, lit up her cockpit as they passed overhead from left to right and along her right side. Sparks flew as emitters along the battleship's hull exploded, sending small bits of debris flying out in all directions.

Leta systematically took out every emitter within range of the Nighthawk as they skimmed along the enemy warship's port side for nearly a full ten seconds.

The interior of the ship flashed a bright yellow-orange as nearby point-defense cannons opened fire on them.

On the opposite side of the warship, Razor Four was firing away in the same manner, taking out as many sets of shield emitters as possible before their own shields were overwhelmed by incoming energy weapons fire.

"*Target's port shields are down,*" Leta reported.

Talisha did not hesitate to push the jump button. "That was *insane*!" she exclaimed once they were safe again.

"*Can you believe that shit!*" Ensign Tellor hollered over comms.

"Are you okay, Kish?" Talisha asked, checking over her own systems.

"*My port and forward shields are down to about three percent, but other than that, I'm good,*" Kishor replied. "*Hell of a rush, though!*"

"You can say that again," Talisha agreed. "Let's just hope we don't have to do it twice."

"Nighthawks have jumped," Kaylah reported from the Aurora's sensor station.

"Ten seconds to attack jump point," Loki announced.

"*Captain?*" the Aurora's AI called, "*I will require your authorization to fire the weapons assigned to me.*"

"You are authorized, Aurora," Nathan replied.

"*Firing authorization acknowledged.*"

A million thoughts ran through Nathan's head at that moment. Seven warships, each of them able to destroy them—five of them with ease—and he had just handed control of three-quarters of his ship's weapons to an untested AI. One that, his chief of security argued, *could* be a digital covert operative for the very enemy he was about to face.

"Three..." Loki began counting down.

"All shields at full power," Nathan ordered.

"Two..."

"Shields at full power," Jessica replied.

"One..."

Nathan slid open the tiny panel on his command chair's left armrest and flipped the hidden rocker switch, then hovered his forefinger over the flashing red button next to it.

"Jumping."

Nathan closed his eyes temporarily as the jump flash washed over the bridge.

"Holy crap," Josh exclaimed, his eyes wide.

On the Aurora's semi-spherical main view screen, the aft end of two Dusahn battleships appeared only a few hundred meters away, closing fast. To make matters worse, the space between them, through which the Aurora intended to pass, seemed awfully narrow. There was debris floating about from the damage the Nighthawks had just inflicted, and the gunships that had escorted the battle group were quickly turning away from the fleet in order to make room to defend them.

Nathan glanced upward as they came out of the jump, just as the Aurora's AI opened fire, with the ship's midship rail gun and plasma cannons, on the missile frigate sliding past them overhead. At the same time, their forward topside plasma turrets also opened fire, targeting the aft-most sections of the two battleships ahead and to either side of their course of travel.

Josh immediately twisted his flight control stick slightly right, causing the ship to yaw to starboard, adding a touch of downward pitch to bring their torpedo tubes onto the main engines of the battleship to their right. As programmed, a red targeting reticle on the main view screen indicated where the torpedoes would land, if fired. The reticle quickly moved to the battleship's port engine and changed to green. Josh pressed the firing trigger, sending four groups of triple shots of plasma torpedoes streaking toward the target.

"Aurora is firing on the assigned targets," Jessica reported, sounding almost surprised.

Nathan watched in silent fascination as his ship unleashed a hailstorm of firepower on the unprotected warships. Before the first round of plasma torpedoes could reach their target, his helmsman was already swinging their nose onto the battleship to port, while unleashing additional rounds of torpedoes as the Aurora yawed back to port.

Nathan watched in awe as his ship's plasma torpedoes slammed into the starboard battleship's port engine and then walked up the port side of its hull, tearing it open with each impact. The firing paused for a moment and then continued again, this time walking down the starboard side of the port battleship, tearing it apart, as well, finally landing on the second ship's starboard engine.

"Multiple shields are down on every battleship!" Kaylah exclaimed. "The first frigate is coming apart."

"*Retargeting midship guns to second frigate,*" Aurora announced.

"Battleships three and five have both lost one of their main engines," Kaylah added.

"Jesus, she's jumping from target to target so quickly, I can hardly keep track of it," Cameron exclaimed in disbelief.

"I didn't know our guns could move that fast," Jessica added in amazement.

"Watch this," Josh said to Loki with a wink.

Secondary explosions rocked the aft ends of the two battleships, on the starboard side of the Dusahn battle group, as the Aurora translated downward. With its nose still pointed forty-five degrees to port, as soon as the ship descended below the bottom of the battleship to port, it gained a clear line of fire on the dreadnought and opened fire with its plasma torpedoes on it, as well.

The Aurora's AI adjusted its guns to compensate for the Aurora's change in position in relation to the enemy warship's, making certain that every shot fired found their intended targets.

"Single main engines down on targets three, five, *and one*!" Kaylah announced with surprise.

"Nice," Loki congratulated.

Ten seconds after they had jumped in, the Aurora's forward shields lit up as incoming fire from five different battleships, as well as half a dozen gunships, impacted every shield around the forward half of the ship.

"Jesus," Nathan exclaimed as the Aurora's bridge

flashed repeatedly, and the ship shook from each impact.

"Shields are falling fast!" Cameron warned.

Josh quickly translated back up as he brought the Aurora's nose back onto its course.

His finger no longer hovering over the flashing red button, Nathan held onto the arms of his command chair with both hands as the Aurora's nose passed the aft end of the battleship to starboard.

"Multiple hull breaches on targets three and five!" Kaylah continued, not missing a beat.

"Thirty seconds to jump point," Loki announced.

"Shields down to fifty percent!" Cameron added.

"Target three has lost one of their reactors," Kaylah added. "They're jettisoning its core!"

"Track that core!" Nathan ordered.

"Our shields aren't going to last!" Cameron warned.

"We're past the halfway point!" Nathan replied. "Hold your course and jump as planned!"

"Broadside cannons coming onto target five!" Jessica announced, her finger on the firing button for all four of their starboard mark three plasma cannons.

"Christ," Nathan exclaimed, "they're not going down without a fight, that's for sure!"

"Firing starboard broadsides!" Jessica announced.

As the Aurora overtook the target, all four starboard broadside plasma cannons opened fire on the stern port side of the Dusahn battleship. At less than one hundred meters away, each shot found its target a split second after leaving its barrel. One by one, the massive bursts of plasma energy slammed into the already-damaged hull of the warship, three times the size of the Aurora, tearing it open from stern to bow. Massive pieces of the doomed vessel broke off, spinning wildly, propelled by secondary explosions from under the hull. Debris slammed into the aft end of the Aurora's starboard shields, bouncing off harmlessly.

"Target five is coming apart!" Kaylah announced.

"*Retargeting all starboard guns to target three,*" Aurora announced.

"Shields at thirty percent!" Cameron warned.

"Incoming from starboard has ceased!" Jessica announced. "Channeling all power from starboard shields to port shields!"

Nathan's eyes were locked on the starboard battleship they were about to overtake as the incoming fire from the port battleship continued.

"Dreadnought is translating upward," Kaylah warned.

"Josh!" Nathan called. "Translate down to keep us out of that dreadnought's line of fire and roll to maintain firing angle with the port broadside cannons!"

"Translating down, and rolling to starboard, aye!" Josh responded as the Aurora continued to rock.

"Dreadnought has stopped her deceleration," Kaylah continued. "She's veering to starboard, as well!"

"They're trying to block our jump path!" Jessica warned.

"Port broadsides coming in range," Cameron announce. "Give me four more degrees of roll, Josh!"

"You got it!"

"Don't let them box us in," Nathan urged.

"Not gonna happen, Cap'n!" Josh insisted.

"Firing port broadsides!" Cameron reported.

"Aft port cameras," Nathan ordered.

The main view screen suddenly changed its view from facing forward to facing the port side, from the aft end of the Aurora, looking slightly upward at the massive warship. Flashes of red-orange lit up the screen as the Aurora's broadside cannons walked a line of destruction up the starboard ventral aspect of the Dusahn battleship to port.

"Target one will have us blocked in fifteen seconds!" Kaylah warned.

"Jump point in *eighteen*!" Loki warned.

"Josh!"

"*Recommend immediate two degrees of yaw,*" the Aurora's AI suggested.

"DO IT!" Nathan ordered.

Josh twisted his flight control stick a touch, released it, waited a second, and then twisted it back in the opposite direction to stop the yaw.

"*Adjusting port broadside angles to same intersect point and range,*" Aurora announced.

"What?" Cameron exclaimed. "I didn't authorize that!"

"KEEP FIRING!" Nathan demanded.

Cameron pressed the firing button, opening up with the port broadside cannons again.

"Direct hit on their reactor bay!" Kaylah yelled. "They're losing containment!"

"JUMP!" Nathan ordered.

A split second after the Aurora disappeared in a blue-white flash of light, the dreadnought did, as well. A moment later, the second battleship's antimatter reactor lost containment, and the entire ship became a brilliant flash of blinding, white light. When the light cleared, the ship was gone, and the battleship three kilometers to port was at an odd angle to its course of travel with large portions of its starboard side were missing.

"Damn, that was close!" Kaylah exclaimed.

"What the hell happened?" Jessica wondered.

"Aurora's suggestion of two degrees yaw and aiming all four cannons on the same point and range, is what happened," Nathan declared. "Hard to port, Mister Hayes. Bring us around for a fore-aft pass between targets two and four."

"What?" Jessica wondered.

"The yaw brought our cannons in line with the target's reactor bay," Kaylah explained.

"And aiming the broadsides on the same point and range punched through their hull, straight through to their reactors," Nathan added.

"She wasn't supposed to have control over the broadsides," Jessica objected.

"She didn't," Cameron realized, "at least not enough control to fire them, otherwise she would have."

"No, she wouldn't have," Nathan insisted. "I didn't authorize her to do so. Only the plasma turrets and rail guns."

"Then, how did she re-aim them?" Jessica wondered.

"She had access to their aiming motors for evaluation and testing during their repairs," Cameron realized. "I guess we forgot to disconnect her from them."

"Good thing," Nathan said.

"Captain, I'm getting readings on the battle group, now," Kaylah reported. "Targets three and five are *gone*."

"You mean, they're *destroyed?*" Nathan asked.

"No, I mean *gone*. Not a trace. Target three's containment breach caused an antimatter event that not only erased what was left of *both* ships, but it *severely* damaged target two, as well."

"How severely?" Nathan wondered.

"Massive sections of their starboard side are gone, like they were carved away with a knife. She's venting atmosphere, and all her reactors have jettisoned their cores, as well. They're on battery power, and life support is failing all over the ship."

"Are you saying we just took out *three battleships* in *one minute*?" Cameron asked in disbelief.

"Don't forget about the two frigates," Jessica added.

"Let's not get too excited," Nathan insisted. "There's still a dreadnought out there, somewhere."

"I'm searching for it, now," Kaylah assured him.

"Turn will be complete in twenty seconds," Josh reported.

"Reduce to one KPH," Nathan ordered. "We'll be passing that last battleship in the opposite direction, and I don't want to pass by her so fast that we don't have time to get a shot off."

"Did you say *one* KPH?"

"One KPH," Nathan repeated.

"One KPH it is," Josh acknowledged, "although I'm pretty sure that's going to be the *slowest* speed I've ever flown."

"I've got the dreadnought," Kaylah reported. "She only jumped out ten kilometers. She's decelerating even harder now, to fall back to the last battleship."

"What condition are the dreadnought's shields in?" Nathan asked.

"Her forward shields are gone, as are her stern shields, and all of her port shields. Most of her other shields are intact and at one hundred percent power."

"And the last battleship?"

"Port and starboard shields are down, from stern to about two thirds up the ship, after which they are fully operational."

"So, don't bother taking a shot at her bow," Nathan surmised.

"We could jump past, come about again, and come up from behind," Jessica suggested. "It worked the first time."

"It would take too long," Nathan insisted. "We need to attack before that dreadnought gets close enough to defend it."

"They can defend it from where they are," Cameron pointed out.

"Not as well as if they were alongside her, serving as protection for one of her unshielded sides," Nathan insisted. "Kaylah, how long until the dreadnought can get alongside target four?"

"Based on their distance and current rate of deceleration, two minutes and thirty-eight seconds," Kaylah replied.

"Wouldn't it be faster for them to turn around and go back?" Jessica wondered.

"It takes time for a ship that size to come about," Cameron explained. "Falling back *is* faster."

"Aurora, are you able to fire the port broadside cannons?" Nathan asked.

"*Able, yes, but I do not have authorization to do so,*" Aurora replied.

"You do now," Nathan told her. "Add them to your list of authorized weapons to fire for this engagement."

"*Understood.*"

"Josh, change course to pass on target four's port side, same relative altitude," Nathan ordered. "Loki, plot your jump to come out with our port broadsides even with her bow."

"That's not going to give us much time to shoot," Loki warned.

"Aurora, how many rounds can you get off *before* we lose our firing angle on the port broadsides?"

"*Based on your intended rate of closure and planned jump arrival point, you will be limited to one round of triplets,*" Aurora replied.

"Can you do that same trick a second time?" Nathan asked. "Punch them in the reactor bay?"

"*Affirmative,*" Aurora replied, "*and with a forty-seven percent probability of success.*"

"Is there any way to increase those odds?"

"*Not without getting the enemy ship to slow down,*" Aurora replied.

"Great, an AI with a sense of sarcasm," Jessica commented.

"*Sarcasm was not my intention,*" Aurora stated. "*I was simply pointing out that the speed of the other vessel is the biggest factor in the equation.*"

"I was kidding," Jessica explained.

"I'll take those odds," Nathan decided.

"On course to pass on the port side of target four," Josh reported. "Crawling along at *one* KPH."

"Attack jump plotted and ready," Loki added.

"Are you ready, Aurora?" Nathan asked.

"*Of course.*"

"See, was I wrong?" Jessica asked Cameron.

"I should point out that most of our shields are still well below fifty percent," Cameron warned Nathan.

"Unless *both* ships hit us with everything they've got, and in the *same* shield section, we should be fine," Nathan replied. "Jump us in, Loki."

"Aye, sir. Jumping in three......two......one......"

One lone Dusahn battleship remained, escorted by the dreadnought still six kilometers ahead and four kilometers to the battleship's starboard side. Gunships that had scattered, in order to maneuver and combat the attacking vessel, were just now heading back to rejoin what was left of their battle group.

The Aurora appeared from behind a flash of blue-white light, alongside the forward half of the Dusahn battleship, not more than five hundred meters off its port side. She opened fire a split second after coming out of the jump, releasing a single blast of four triple shots of plasma, all focused on the same point of the battleship's port midship section. The balls of plasma slammed into the enemy warship's hull, the first group of shots opening it up, and the following shots burrowing deep into the doomed vessel's hull.

No sooner had the single round of triple shots left the Aurora's broadside cannons, the Aurora, once again, disappeared behind a blue-white flash of light.

Seconds later, the remaining Dusahn battleship also disappeared, but in a brilliant, white ball of light, erased from existence by the very technology that powered it, taking what was left of target two along with it.

"Jump complete," Loki reported as the Aurora's jump flash subsided.

"Where's that dreadnought?" Nathan asked.

"Checking," Kaylah replied. "They're holding course and speed, sir."

"Are they still headed for the Rogen system?"

"Yes, sir."

"Helm, come about hard to starboard, and accelerate to match the Dusahn battle group's last known speed," Nathan ordered.

"Coming about hard to starboard and accelerating," Josh replied as he increased power and began his starboard turn.

"What are you doing?" Cameron wondered. "The rally point is in the other direction."

"We're not done," Nathan replied. "There's still one more ship out there."

"Yeah, the *big* one," Jessica pointed out.

"Maybe we shouldn't push our luck," Cameron suggested.

"I agree," Jessica said. "We've yet to get a clean look at that dreadnought. If it's more heavily armored than their battleships, we may be biting off more than we can chew, even *with* half its shields down."

"It's still a direct threat to our allies," Nathan pointed out. "All *three* of them."

"There's no way they're going to press an attack against the Rogen system with *one* ship, even if it *is* a dreadnought. Not after losing *six* ships in *four* minutes," Cameron insisted, "but they *will* stand and fight if you force them to."

"That dreadnought is their *flagship*," Nathan pointed out, "and I'm betting that Lord Dusahn, *himself*, is on it."

"So what?"

"This is an opportunity to send him a clear message," Nathan insisted, "one we may not get again. Worst-case scenario is we duke it out and end up retreating."

"Or he jumps to the Rogen system and makes a bombardment pass over Rakuen or Neramese," Jessica countered.

"In which case, he faces about a hundred jump missiles with only *half* his shields to defend him," Nathan argued. "Trust me, I know what I'm doing."

Cameron swallowed hard and replied, "I don't have to *trust* you, Nathan. You're the captain, and I'm your XO. And for the record, I *do* trust you."

Nathan looked at Jessica.

"You know damn well *I* trust you," she told him.

"Turn complete," Josh announced. "We are on the same course as the dreadnought, same speed, two hundred meters above it."

"Very well," Nathan replied. "Loki, plot a jump that puts us ahead of that dreadnought, with one kilometer of space between us."

"Aye, sir," Loki replied, exchanging glances with Josh.

"Spin us around one-eighty and be ready on all

forward tubes," Nathan added, "full power triplets. Do not fire unless ordered, and if so ordered, don't stop until that ship is obliterated."

Josh turned slightly, glancing over his shoulder at Nathan, unsure of the sanity of his orders.

"It's all right, Josh," Nathan assured him, winking.

"Yawing one-eighty," Josh acknowledged, starting the maneuver. "Standing by to blast the shit out of them with all forward tubes."

"Close enough," Nathan said. "How are our forward shields looking?" Nathan wondered.

"About eighty percent right now," Jessica replied. "I can steal power from our other shields to boost them if you'd like."

"Better keep them as they are," Nathan decided. "The last thing we need is for a few gunboats to sneak in and sucker punch us while our guard is down."

"Aye, aye, Captain," Jessica said with a sigh. "I can't believe we're going to do this," she whispered to Cameron.

"After all the shit he's pulled, *this* surprises you?" Cameron replied.

"Good point."

Nathan rose from his command chair, turning around to look aft. "Everyone ready?"

"If I said no, would that stop you?" Jessica joked.

"Let's finish this," Nathan said, turning around to face forward again. "As soon as we jump in, translate down as quickly as you can, Josh. I don't want them jumping before they hear me out."

"Assuming they don't blast the shit out of us, first," Josh muttered.

"Execute your jump, Mister Sheehan."

"Jumping in three..."

"*Pre-aiming all gun turrets forward,*" Aurora announced.

"Two..."

"Good idea," Nathan agreed.

"One..."

"Here goes nothing," Nathan stated, mostly to himself.

"Jumping," Loki said as the Aurora's jump flash lit up the bridge.

Josh immediately sent the Aurora translating downward. "Oh......my......God," he exclaimed as the massive dreadnought slid up in front of them, filling the entire view screen. "That thing is *huge.*"

"We're being targeted!" Kaylah warned.

"Hail them on all channels and frequencies," Nathan ordered.

"Hailing on all channels and frequencies," Naralena answered.

"Be ready with an escape jump if needed," Nathan told Loki.

"Are you kidding?" Loki replied.

Nathan glanced at the helm, noticing that Loki's finger was already hovering over the jump button.

"Their guns are coming around to take aim at us," Cameron warned.

"They're scanning us," Kaylah reported. "Jamming..."

"Negative," Nathan ordered, "don't jam them. Let them see what they're facing."

"I'm not so sure *that's* a good idea," Jessica said. "Those guns will take down our shields with a *single* shot."

"Any response?" Nathan asked, looking back at Naralena and ignoring Jessica.

"Nothing yet."

"Well, they're not firing, so they must know we're hailing them," Nathan surmised.

"I'm getting detailed scans on that ship," Kaylah said. "They're not bothering to jam *us* either."

"Anything interesting?" Nathan wondered.

"So far, only that Captain Taylor was right, their hull is *extremely* well armored."

"Are you telling me we *can't* blast our way through their hull?" Nathan asked.

"No, we can, but it's going to be a lot more difficult than those battleships. They were completely dependent on their shields. It's almost like they skimped on the hull skin when they built them."

"I'm getting a response to our hails, Captain," Naralena announced. "They're attempting a vid-link."

"Put them up," Nathan instructed, turning forward again.

"*You are either a fool, or...*" Lord Dusahn began.

"I did not call you to exchange insults, sir," Nathan interrupted. "Stand down now, and withdraw your forces from the Rogen sector, and we will allow you to depart without further damage."

Lord Dusahn laughed. "*You have but a single warship and are* grossly *outgunned.*"

"Yet, this single warship just took out *four* of your battleships, and *two* frigates, all without a single scratch on our hull...at least, not a *new* one," Nathan said. He suddenly held up his right hand and said, "Wait, I miscounted, we took out *five* of your battleships, not to mention *four* cruisers."

"*What are you talking about?*" Lord Dusahn demanded.

"Have you *heard* from the Jar-Razza lately?" Nathan asked.

Lord Dusahn looked concerned, turning to whisper something to a subordinate off-camera.

"Transmit the video to our friends," Nathan instructed to his comms officer.

"Transmitting video," Naralena acknowledged.

"Take your time, my lord," Nathan told Lord Dusahn, his voice dripping with sarcasm.

"What video?" Jessica asked in a soft tone. "What did you send him?"

Nathan tapped his comm-set to mute it. "The destruction of the Jar-Razza *and* the shipyards."

Jessica smiled. "Oh, he's going to be pissed."

"That's an understatement," Nathan replied, tapping his comm-set again and turning back around to face his adversary on the main view screen.

"*You do realize you have doomed the people of Orswella,*" Lord Dusahn warned, barely able to control his seething anger. "*My troops on the ground will slaughter the people of that...*"

"No, they won't," Nathan insisted, cutting him off. "You see, we took ninety percent of your ground forces out in the first few seconds of the engagement and then cleaned the rest up with our own ground forces."

Lord Dusahn paused for a moment, his anger threatening to get the best of him. "*You cannot protect both Orswella* and *the Rogen system,*" he declared. "*They are too far apart.*"

"Wrong again," Nathan said. "That seems to be a recurring theme for you today. You see, I *can*, and I *will*, protect *both* systems. Not only *can* I protect them both, but I can *also* reach out and fuck with *your* little empire any time I wish, *without* leaving *any* of our allies unprotected. All with one little warship...and a few hundred pissed off Gunyoki, a dozen or so missile gunboats, and of course those lovely, little fighters that can magically slip through your shields." Nathan stood there for a moment, smiling, letting Lord Dusahn's new reality sink in before continuing. "Listen, it seems your day isn't going *quite* the way you had hoped. I know how that is, having your plans fall apart, and all." Nathan suddenly turned serious. "Withdraw your forces from the Rogen system, *right now*, and stay the hell *out* of both the Rogen *and* the Orswellan systems...... *or else*."

"*Or else what?*" Lord Dusahn sneered.

Nathan smiled. "I think you're smart enough to figure that out for yourself. After all, you *are* a lord." Nathan suddenly stopped smiling, and his face became deadly serious again. "You have thirty seconds." Nathan held up his hand, and Lord Dusahn disappeared from his view screen, replaced by the image of the massive dreadnought standing nose to nose with them, less than a kilometer away.

"Contact terminated," Naralena reported.

"I assume all weapons are locked on that dreadnought," Nathan inquired.

"Since the moment we jumped in," Cameron assured him.

Josh spun around to face his captain. "That was the coolest bluff I have ever seen!"

Nathan stood there, still looking steely-eyed as he stared at the dreadnought on the view screen. "I wasn't bluffing."

Josh turned back around to face his console, exchanging a glance with Loki in the process.

"Dreadnought is changing course," Kaylah announced. "They're turning to a clear jump line."

"Should I move to block?" Josh wondered.

"Negative," Nathan said.

"Incoming vid-link from the dreadnought," Naralena reported.

"On screen," Nathan instructed.

Again, Lord Dusahn appeared on the main view screen, only this time he appeared quite unhappy. "*Do not think for a moment that this is over, Captain. We will return, and when we do, all worlds allied with you will pay the price for their actions.*"

"I look forward to it," Nathan replied confidently.

Again, Lord Dusahn disappeared from the main view screen, replaced by the image of the dreadnought as it turned away from the Aurora, disappearing moments later in a blue-white flash of light.

"All Dusahn ships are jumping away," Kaylah reported in disbelief. She turned to Nathan. "I can't believe that worked."

"Neither can I," Nathan admitted. "Naralena, contact the Falcon and have them search the Dusahn battle group's jump line. I want to be *certain* they've left the Rogen system and are headed *back* to Takara."

"Aye, sir."

"What do we do now?" Jessica wondered.

Nathan turned around to face her. "We get ready," he replied. "*He* wasn't bluffing either."

CHAPTER THIRTEEN

Doctor Symyri entered the intensive care ward of his medical facility on Sanctuary, ready to begin his morning rounds. As usual, his facility was full of patients, meaning his accounts were full, as well. To him, there was no better feeling than knowing he could afford to do what he loved without any fear of restrictions, both financial and political, which made practicing medicine on industrialized worlds so difficult.

"How are you doing this morning, Eta?" he asked the nurse at the monitoring desk.

"Ready to head home," Eta responded.

"Difficult night?"

"Not at all," she replied, "which makes it all the more tiring. Everyone slept through the night with no worrisome readings."

"That's a first," Doctor Symyri joked.

"I much prefer to have, at least, a *few* things to do," Eta insisted.

"Well, if it makes you feel any better, we are going to fast-grow a new arm for Mister Nettenney today, using Doctor Chen's new system. I'm sure *that* will give you *plenty* to do on your next shift."

"We're doing *that* today?" Doctor Imber asked as she approached. "I thought it wasn't ready, yet."

"Doctor Chen works very fast," Doctor Symyri replied.

The conversation was suddenly cut short by an alarm at the monitoring station behind Eta. Before she could turn around, a woman screamed in panic from one of the rooms.

Both Doctor Symyri and Doctor Imber responded immediately, both of them running toward the screams, followed by Eta. A med-tech also came running from the other end of the ward, arriving at the room from where the woman's screams were coming, at the same time as the others.

Doctor Symyri was the first to enter, stopping dead in his tracks when he saw Miri sitting bolt-upright in the stasis pod that she had just forced open. Her arms were cut and covered with blood, and her intravenous tubes had become disconnected. She was completely disoriented, screaming in abject fear at the top of her lungs as if she had just witnessed something horrible.

Doctor Imber pushed past the stunned Doctor Symyri, followed by the med-tech, and finally Doctor Symyri and nurse Eta.

"Quickly!" Doctor Symyri instructed. "We must sedate her!"

"It is all right, Miri," Doctor Imber murmured patiently, trying to calm her down.

"WHO ARE YOU?" Miri yelled in a nearly unintelligible fashion. "WHERE AM I? WHAT ARE YOU DOING TO ME?"

Eta handed Doctor Symyri an injector, which he quickly placed against the side of Miri's neck and pressed the button, sending the sedative into her carotid artery.

Miri immediately relaxed, falling into the arms of her caregivers, who lowered her gently back down into the stasis pod.

"We'll have to move her out of this pod to a monitoring bed," Doctor Symyri said.

"Who are..." Miri mumbled, now barely conscious. "Where are my..."

The last thing she said as they put the oxygen mask over her mouth was, "*Nathan.*"

Thank you for reading this story.
(*A review would be greatly appreciated!*)

COMING SOON

Episode 12
of
The Frontiers Saga:
Rogue Castes

Visit us online at
frontierssaga.com
or on Facebook

Want to be notified when
new episodes are published?
Want access to additional scenes and more?
Join our mailing list!

frontierssaga.com/mailinglist/

Made in the USA
Las Vegas, NV
11 August 2022

53090444R10229